~~SOUVENIR BOOK~~

ANTHOLOGY

Edited by Linda D. Addison

Edited by Linda D. Addison
Cover design by Lisa Morton
Cover artwork by M. Wayne Miller
Interior design by Kate Jonez

Published by the Horror Writers Association www.horror.org

IN MEMORIAM

Dallas Mayr / pseudonym **Jack Ketchum** (11/10/1946–1/24/2018) was a former actor, singer, teacher, literary agent, lumber salesman, and soda jerk. His short story "The Box" won a 1994 HWA Bram Stoker Award®, his story "Gone" won again in 2000—and in 2003 he won Bram Stoker Awards® for Superior Achievement in a Collection for *Peaceable Kingdom* and Superior Achievement in Long Fiction for *Closing Time.* He wrote over twenty novels and novellas, the latest were *The Woman* and *I'm Not Sam*, both written with director Lucky McKee. Five of his books were filmed—*The Girl Next Door, The Lost, Red, Offspring* and *The Woman*, the last won him and McKee the Best Screenplay Award at the Sitges Film Festival. His novella *The Crossings* was cited by in Stephen King's speech at the 2003 National Book Awards. In 2011 Dallas was elected Grand Master by the World Horror Convention. See jackketchum.net for a full bibliography.

"There's no replacing somebody you love. You love them forever. But there is room for another soul to come into your environment, into your sphere." (from *A Conversation with Jack Ketchum*, published 1/31/18 with Mike Noble, Cemetery Dance Publ.)

Poet and teacher, **Dr. Tiffany Austin** (4/26/1975–6/26/2018) received her B.A. in English from Spelman College, MFA in creative writing from Chicago State University, J.D. from Northeastern University School of Law, and Ph.D. in English from Saint Louis University. She taught at Florida Memorial University, Mississippi Valley State University and University of the Bahamas. She published poetry in the journals *Obsidian, Callaloo, pluck!* and *Warpland.* Her poetry chapbook, *Étude*, explored the blues aesthetic within femininity. Two of her poems were published in the Bram Stoker short-listed anthology, *Sycorax's Daughters.* The First Annual Tiffany Austin Poetry Competition was announced this year in her honor.

From *Sycorax's Daughters.*

Gotraskhalana ("stumbling upon the name"): A Blues*

There is a South in sound. Pear shaped sounds.
Inside—skinned rose flesh. Hard mattresses.
  Gussing up to a yard
full of opened graves. Familiar dust. Moored to bud
—all in the body. Only scar that remains
is leaning. Coltrane's sheets. Otis
rubybreasted. Burlap thighs sitting on water.

Harlan Ellison (5/27/1934–6/28/2018) wrote or edited seventy-five books; more than 1700 stories, essays, articles, and newspaper columns; two dozen teleplays, for which he received the Writers Guild of America award four times. He won the Mystery Writers of America's Edgar Award twice, the HWA Bram Stoker Award® six times, the 1996 HWA Lifetime Achievement Award, the Nebula Award three times, the Hugo Award 8½ times, and the Silver Pen for Journalism from P.E.N.; as well as the World Fantasy Award, the British Fantasy Award, the American Mystery Award, two Audie Awards, and the Ray Bradbury Award. He edited two influential anthologies of speculative fiction, *Dangerous Visions* and *Again, Dangerous Visions.* Several of his stories, including "Repent, Harlequin!," "Said the Ticktockman," "I Have No Mouth, and I Must Scream" and "The Beast That Shouted Love at the Heart of the World," are recognized as classics. One of his most renowned works the novella, *A Boy and His Dog*, was made into a film in 1975.

See his site (harlanellison.com) for a complete bibliography and biography. *A Briefer Biography of Harlan Ellison* by Harlan Ellison, from the *Afterword to The Essential Ellison:* "For a brief time I was here; and for a brief time I mattered."

The comic book writer, editor and, publisher **Stan Lee** (12/28/1922–11/12/2018) revolutionized the industry in the 1960s when he created the mythic figures Spider-Man, the X-Men, the Fantastic Four, most of the Avengers (Hulk, Iron Man, Thor), Daredevil and Doctor Strange. Lee was Marvel Comics editor-in-chief from 1941 and publisher from 1972 until 1996. Lee's own numerous on-screen credits began with a jury foreman in *The Trial of the Incredible Hulk* (1989). He played himself in Kevin Smith's *Mallrats, The Simpsons* and *The Big Bang Theory*, and virtually every 2018 Marvel movie, including *Black Panther* contained a cameo from him. Lee was inducted into the comic book industry's Will Eisner Award Hall of Fame in 1994 and the Jack Kirby Hall of Fame in 1995. He received the NEA's National Medal of Arts in 2008.

Lee once said: "Our goal is that someday an intelligent adult would not be embarrassed to walk down the street with a comic magazine. I don't know whether we can ever bring this off, but it's something to shoot for."

William Goldman (8/12/1931–11/16/2018) was the Oscar-winning screenwriter who penned classics like *Butch Cassidy and the Sundance Kid, All the President's Men*, and *The Princess Bride.* Goldman wrote sixteen novels, three memoirs, magazine columns, twenty-three produced screenplays, a fan-driven sports book, two plays, and a children's book. He was just as prolific as a script doctor—a writer who was whisked into a project to tune up or overhaul an existing screenplay. Goldman's final screenplay credit came in 2015 when he adapted his novel *Heat* (made into a 1986 film starring Burt Reynolds) into a remake titled *Wild Card.*

William Goldman: "I've been writing a very long time. Probably I started before most of you were born. And I believe this: Everything is about story. If any of you want to be writers, please try and believe me about story. If you have the story right for you, you have a chance. If you mess up the story, no matter how dazzling your style, you'll be in trouble." (from CNN com, Chat Books transcripts©2001)

Paul Dale Anderson (9/11/1944–12/13/2018) was the author of *Claw Hammer, Daddy's Home, Winds, Abandoned, Darkness, Light*, and more than twenty other novels and hundreds of short stories, mostly in the horror, fantasy, science fiction, and suspense-thriller genres. Paul also wrote contemporary romances, mysteries and westerns. He was a Active Member of SFWA and HWA, and he was elected a Vice President and Trustee of the Horror Writers Association in 1987. He was also a member of International Thriller Writers, the Authors Guild, and MWA. Paul taught creative writing for the University of Illinois and Writers Digest Schools and was an editor at *2AM Publications, Morningstar*, and for several medical publishers. He was a book reviewer for *Fantasy Review*, and his articles appeared in *Mystery Scene* and other genre publications.

"My stories are cautionary tales that, like your own parents should have done, warn you not to cross the street without first looking both ways, not to stick a screwdriver into a live electrical socket, not to put your hand into the flame. And, if all hell does break loose, my stories teach you how best to act and react in order to survive." (From his site www.pauldaleanderson.net)

Billie Sue Mosiman (6/5/1947–12/26/2018) wrote over 100 books in horror, suspense, thriller, memoir, mystery and more than 150 short stories. She was co-editor of six anthologies, a columnist, writing instructor (Writer's Digest School), and editor. Two of her books were nominated for an Edgar Award for best novel and a HWA Bram Stoker Award® for Superior Achievement in a Novel. In 2014 *The Grey Matter* received a nomination for the Kindle Book Award. In 2016, she edited the anthology, *Fright Mare—Women Write Horror*, which was nominated for a HWA Bram Stoker Award®. She was a featured author on CNN Interactive Online in the "Ask the Author" book section.

"…the greatest reason that I write stories and novels at all—to discover the story, to have it told to me, or dictated or taken from the movie screen I see flickering in my head. I want to know. I am interested. I want to read the book, this book no one else has written and only I can write. It's my book, but I don't know it until I write it. So I began again, page one, chapter one." (from Mosiman's site: billiesuemosiman.weebly.com)

Artist **gak/ Glenn Denny** (July 1961–1/13/2019) Gak's work appeared in many horror zines like *Phantasm, Cabal Asylum, Scavenger's Newsletter,* and *Weird Times.* He created book covers for authors Gerard Houarner (*Dead Cat Bounce, Dead Cat: Bigger Than Jesus* (which contains a story by gak)), Brian Keene (*4X4, A Darker Dawning* series, *Sympathy For the Devil, Leader of the Banned*), Edward Lee (*Incubi*), Gene O'Neill (Thunderstorm covers for *The Cal Wild Chronicles, Doc Good's Traveling Show*, etc.), Michael Laimo (*Return to Darkness*). He edited and illustrated the anthologies *Infernally Yours* (based on Edward Lee's *Vision of Hell*) and the Dead Cat series (*Dead Cats Bouncing*, etc.) with Gerard Houarner. A long list of short stories in anthologies (ex. *Fear of the Unknown*) and magazines (*Cemetery Dance*, etc.) were illustrated by gak.

gak's art speaks for him. Look up the book trailer for the *Library of the Dead* anthology, which received a HWA Bram Stoker award® in 2015, to see his illustrations.

Ursula K. Le Guin (10/21/1929–1/22/2018) was the author of more than twenty novels (excluding over a dozen books for children and young adults), a dozen books of poetry, several short story collections and seven books of essays. *The Earthsea* books, have sold in the millions worldwide. Saga published a collection of her novellas, *The Found and the Lost*, alongside a short story collection, *The Unreal and the Real.* Her recent nonfiction included *Ursula K. Le Guin: Conversations on Writing* and *No Time to Spare: Thinking About What Matters.* Her themes include Taoism, feminism, anarchy, psychology and sociology.

"All of us have to learn how to invent our lives, make them up, imagine them. We need to be taught these skills; we need guides to show us how. If we don't, our lives get made up for us by other people."—Ursula K. Le Guin, *The Wave in the Mind: Talks and Essays on the Writer, the Reader, and the Imagination.*

7 SINS · 7 AUTHORS · 7 STORIES
1 BOOK YOU DON'T WANT TO MISS
LUST
SLOTH
PRIDE
AVARICE
WRATH
GLUTTONY
ENVY
THE SEVEN DEADLIEST
EDITED BY PATRICK BELTRAN
AND D. ALEXANDER WARD
Cutting Block Books
www.cuttingblockbooks.com

Contents

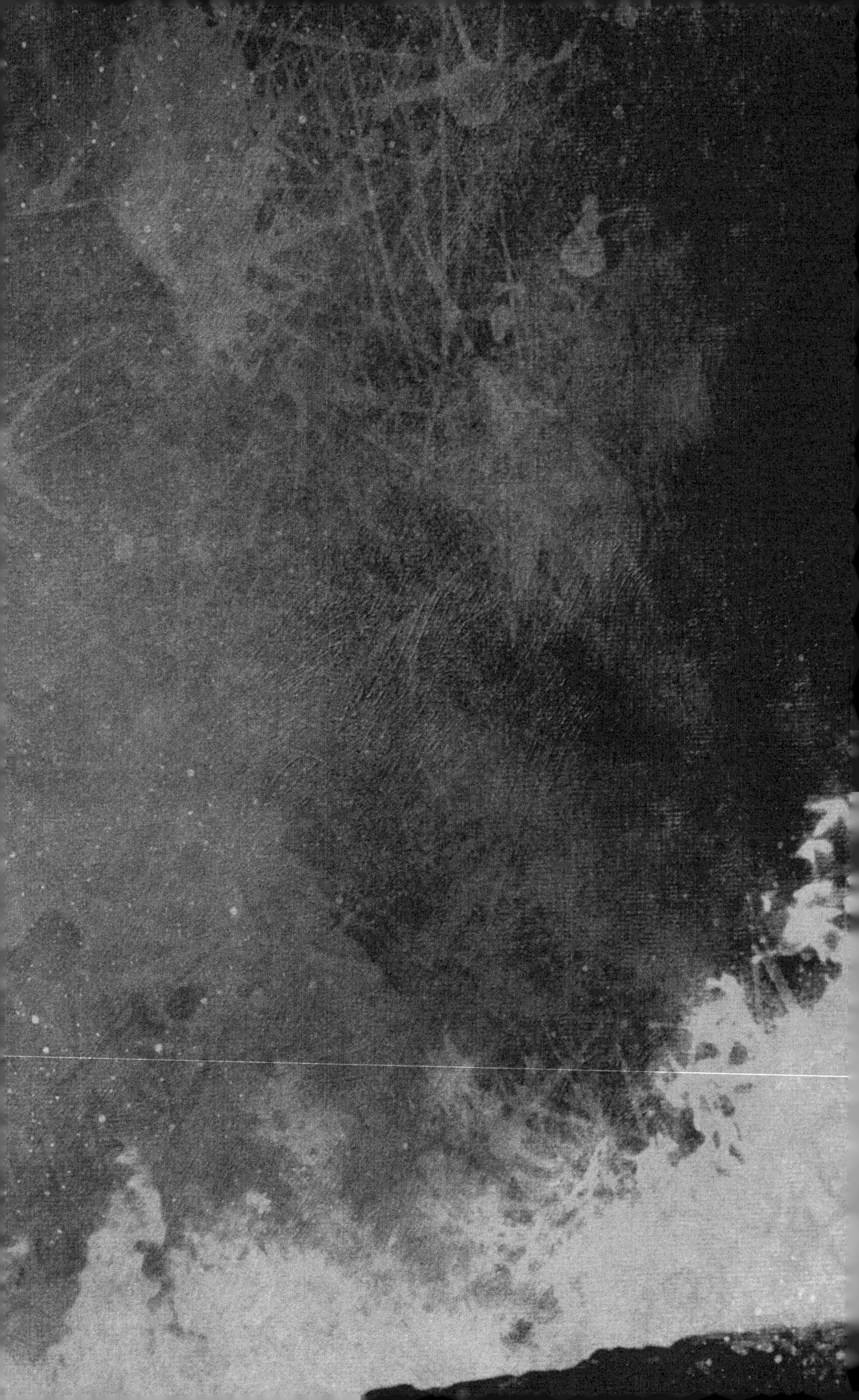

Jill
2011

A Note From the Editor

By Linda D. Addison

The convention books I have from the past generally consisted of interviews and contributions from the guests (my first one is from 1995 I-Con XIV on Stony Brook LI) where I collected signatures from my heroes like Octavia Butler, Frederik Pohl, etc. Then Michael Bailey started this thing—this convention anthology thing with the 2018 HWA StokerCon™ Souvenir Book by adding essays written by creators in the horror field (ex. *Novels: The Challenge* by Josh Malerman, *Readings* by Tom Monteleone, Jack Ketchum, etc.), poetry and artwork.

Opening the 2018 book was a journey through the GOH inspiring work, interviews and a treasure trove of informative and entertaining articles from others in the fields. I loved it and kept it out where I could grab it to read!

So when I agreed to edit the 2019 HWA StokerCon™ book I went down the same road (or rabbit hole, depending on your point of view). Naturally I began with the center stone of the book: the GOH interviews and contributions, as well as write-ups about others being honored with awards for their contributions to HWA and the horror field.

The Guests of Honor span different areas of the horror genre (fiction, poetry, film) and travel here from as far away as Australia. I was lucky to be the first to read the stories, scripts, storyboards and poetry they sent for the book—you're going to love each piece (and want more)!

Adding a poetry section and art was enjoyable, since poetry is a main thing for me and I love art. There were two kinds of essays to gather: write-ups on the many motivating events happening at StokerCon™ and the free range ones from different people about creating work.

A great guide to the many offerings this weekend is the excellent essay on events available *While at StokerCon™* by our hard-working 2019 chair, Brian W. Matthews. This gives a concise high level summary of the fantastic goings-on. Then you can dig into the individual pieces for each event to see what you can schedule in your day.

The free-range essays share valuable experiences of creators (known and new) in this business. Some pieces are about areas like short fiction, films, first novels, interview tips. I added a new idea from essays titled *A Writer's Life* telling how *life* (you know that thing we're doing when not writing?) takes us on unexpected journeys. Why *A Writer's Life?* Because everything we experience flavors our work and I'm always curious about how others incorporate being creative in daily life.

Earlier in my career I did interviews with authors I admired and I'm fascinated with process. I'm always looking to add something to my toolbox. Every piece was enlightening in some way, either affirming my own experience or giving a new slant.

I hope you will find essays that speak to you, there are many here on my list to re-read. Let's get started…

Anti-Harassment Policy

Horror Writers Association

StokerCon™ is dedicated to providing a harassment-free convention experience for everyone, regardless of gender, gender identity and expression, sexual orientation, disability, physical appearance, body size, race, age or religion. We do not tolerate harassment of convention attendees in any form. Attendees violating these rules may be sanctioned or expelled from the convention without a refund at the discretion of the chairs.

Reporting Harassment

As evidenced by our anti-harassment policy, we at StokerCon™ take any type of harassment at conventions seriously. To that end we would like to announce the process for reporting harassment.

All of the StokerCon™ staff and volunteers will be identifiable by their specially-marked badges. Each volunteer will be briefed before the con begins on StokerCon's anti-harassment policy and on how to handle reporting. If anyone sees or experiences an instance of harassment, they can bring their complaint to a volunteer or event staff.

Additionally, we have created an email address specifically for this issue. That address is complaint@stokercon.com. Anyone who sees or experiences harassment can, if they aren't comfortable speaking to someone in person, file their complaint through that email address.

All complaints will be immediately brought to the Convention Chairs. They will then follow-up with any needed communication or investigation. If they determine that a formal investigation is called for, they will follow the procedure outlined below.

As said, we take this topic very seriously and want to ensure that everyone who attends StokerCon™ has a great time free from any type of harassment.

Bram Stoker Awards®

Passing the Bloody Baton

By Jeff Strand

In 2018, I emceed the Bram Stoker Awards® for the tenth and final time. I decided that I'd hogged the prestige, wealth, groupies, and discounts on sporting goods for long enough. It was time for somebody else to come up with bits like stabbing a sock puppet to death at a dignified awards banquet.

There was much talk of who would replace me. Stephen King? Rob Schneider? John Schneider? Lisa Morton against her will? Somebody in a creepy mask who just stood up on the stage and stared at the audience without speaking a word? Somebody in a Jeff Strand mask, prancing around going "*Dur,* I'm Jeff Strand, you couldn't get rid of me, haw haw haw, *derp!*" Vincent Price? Jonathan Maberry? Meryl Streep?

In the end, they chose Meryl Streep, who canceled at the last minute when she was told that some members of the audience might be kind of weird. And so they went with the backup plan: a young up-and-coming writer yet to be crushed by the brutal realities of the business, Jonathan Maberry.

I've been asked to share some advice for Mr. Maberry as he embarks on this exciting new adventure. The truth is, the Powers That Be are worried that he's going to walk up there and say something like, "Hey, everybody, awards are just a big dumb popularity contest! Go home!" Dude's known to be a loose cannon. There will be professionals with tranquilizer darts stationed on each side of the stage, just in case, but the optics are bad when you have to drag your unconscious Master of Ceremonies away in the middle of the event, so the hope is that Mr. Maberry will read these words and learn from them.

1. *If you bring the ashes of the late Richard Laymon up on stage, R.L. Stine will be all like "WTF is wrong with these people?"* Yes, one year, as part of the introduction to the Richard Laymon President's Award, Kelly Laymon and I had the actual (unopened) container of Richard Laymon's ashes up at the podium. It was meant to be a joke about how I had abandoned all pretense of good taste, but the audience gave thunderous applause, so I figured, hey, I'm not going to turn down thunderous applause. However, I'm told that R.L. Stine was not a fan of this bit. This is not a criticism of Mr. Stine—one could argue that the person who didn't appreciate a dead author's ashes being incorporated into an awards banquet was on the correct side of the debate—but if you

choose to recycle this bit, just know that he won't be heaping lavish praise upon you.

2. *Control your envy.* You'll be standing there while lots of people receive Stokers. These people will not be you. It's going to be rough. You're going to gaze at their beaming faces and think, "Why not me? *Why not me?*" but it's important to not let this effect your work. You must remain calm and professional despite your blinding jealous rage. Just remember that not all of the winners are present, and a little thievery is expected if not encouraged.

(Note: I have zero Stokers, and you have, I dunno, seventeen or eighteen of them, so the envy may be easier for you to cope with. The thievery part is still applicable.)

3. *Do not say "Seriously?" when the winner is announced.* Over the course of ten years and about a hundred and fifty winners announced, I am proud to say that not even *once* did I say "Seriously?" when the presenter read the name of the winner. Not once. The eyes of the world are upon you, and it's crucial that you do not express disgust and disbelief. Similarly inappropriate comments include: "For real?" "You've got be frickin' kidding me!" "No, no, no, no, no, that can't be how the voting worked out—we're gonna audit those records right now before we hand out another [expletive deleted] award." It's okay to roll your eyes or pretend to stick your finger down your throat, but only when you're safely out of view of the webcam.

4. *Have fun.* Smile! For God's sake, Maberry, you're not presiding over a funeral. Everybody is there to enjoy themselves! Enough with the gloom and misery. When you walk up there with dark circles under your eyes moving as if the weight of the world is upon you, you lessen everybody else's good time. Lighten the hell up.

5. *I want to come back! Please! I never should have retired, I don't know what I was thinking, I've cried myself to sleep every night since that shortsighted decision! The Stokers are the only thing I have and you've taken it from me and please, please, please can't I at least stand beside you I won't get in the way I need this oh how I need this it's just not fair don't make me beg okay I'm begging I just want to emcee again does that make me a bad person please Jonathan you can't take this away from me nooooooo!!!* Self-explanatory.

6. *"Pull my finger," while amusing, is not an appropriate opening joke for the Bram Stoker Awards® banquet.* It sets the wrong tone right off the bat. If you must use that gag, save it for later in the program, perhaps right before the Lifetime Achievement Award winner is announced.

7. *Don't let your assistant steal your thunder.* Emceeing the awards *and* handing the trophies to the presenters is too much work for one person. I did it one year. It was pure chaos. So you will have an assistant,

often referred to as a "Vanna," a clever nod to Ms. Vanna White from the television program *Wheel of Fortune*, in which contestants spin a very large horizontal wheel and then guess letters in a puzzle (consonants only, unless they choose to use their earnings to purchase a vowel). It's kind of like Hangman, except nobody is drawing a stick figure getting hanged, which is 90% of the fun of Hangman. Anyway, your assistant will try to upstage you, often by being attractive. You must not allow this to happen. *You* are the star. *You* are the one people are there to see. Who the hell does your assistant think he or she is? Your assistant wants to steal your job. Your assistant wants to turn everybody against you. There's only one answer—a vial of acid in the face. Your disfigured assistant isn't so attractive now, huh? You're the star again. That's right, you're the star again.

8. *Don't listen to advice provided in StokerCon™ souvenir books.* It's often written on a tight deadline for no pay and the advice-giver isn't fully invested in the project.

9. *Full disclosure: I actually had plenty of time to work on this.* Which makes the low quality of the advice I've provided thus far even more perplexing.

10. *All of the best lists contain exactly ten items.* It's why we have the metric system.

11. *No musical numbers.* This is true—every year after the first one I considered having a funny song be part of the proceedings, and every single year I decided against it. This was absolutely the correct decision, and I encourage you to continue this fine trend.

12. *Carefully walk the line.* My goal was always to find the sweet spot between being irreverent and poking fun at the awards and horror genre while still celebrating it. Many jokes were thrown out that were really really funny (I swear!) but on the wrong side of the line. You may not be going for this tone, relying instead on your natural charm and the fact that everybody loves you, in which case this advice, like the eleven items preceding it, is not useful. I did not have the luxury of charm and universal adoration, so I had to make jokes.

And that's it. Good luck to you, sir! You'll do fine. And if not, the tranquilizer darts only hurt for a second, unless they get you in the eye, in which case they hurt for quite a bit longer than that. Maybe invest in some goggles.

("Maybe invest in some goggles" is not a great joke to end on, but as a retired emcee, I no longer have the responsibility of finding a perfect ending joke. It's all on you now, dude! Enjoy the stress, you poor bastard! Hahahahahaha!!!)

Bram Stoker Awards® Emcee

Jonathan Maberry

StokerCon™ 2019 is Jonathan Maberry's first time as Master of Ceremonies for the Bram Stoker Awards® banquet.

Jonathan Maberry is a NY Times bestselling suspense novelist, five-time Bram Stoker Award® winner, and comic book writer. His vampire apocalypse book series, *V-Wars*, will be a Netflix original series, starring Ian Somerhalder (Lost, Vampire Diaries) and will debut in summer 2019. There is also a *V-Wars* board game, shared-world anthologies, and comics. His Joe Ledger thriller novels are in development for cable TV by Sony; and his YA zombie series, *Rot & Ruin* is being produced as a Webtoon and have been optioned for film. *Rot & Ruin* was included in the Ten Best Horror Novels for Young Adults. His first novel, *Ghost Road Blues* was named one of the 25 Best Horror Novels of the New Millennium. His other novels include *Glimpse, The Wolfman, Ghostwalkers, Mars One*, and many others. He is the editor of many anthologies including the *X-Files, Aliens: Bug Hunt, Nights of the Living Dead* (co-edited with Stoker lifetime achievement winner George A. Romero). His comics include *Captain America*, the Bram Stoker Award-winning *Bad Blood, Black Panther, Punisher, Marvel Zombies Return, Road of the Dead, Pandemica*, and more. He is the president of the International Association of Media Tie-in Writers and is on the board of the Horror Writers Association. He was a featured expert on the History Channel's *Zombies: A Living History and True Monsters.* He is one third of the popular and mildly weird Three Guys With Beards podcast. Jonathan lives in Del Mar, California with his wife, Sara Jo.

Jonathan Maberry www.jonathanmaberry.com

Calling Death

A Short Story by Jonathan Maberry

–1–

"It weren't the wind," said Granny Adkins, rocking back and forth. "Weren't the wind at all."

The young man perched on the edge of the other rocker, head tilted to lift one ear like a startled bird, listening to the sound. He was stick thin and beaky nosed, and Grinny thought he looked like a heron—the way they looked when they were ready to take sudden flight. "Are you sure?"

"Sure as maybe," said Granny, nodding out to the darkness. "The wind fair howls when it comes 'cross the top of Balder Rise. Howls like the Devil himself."

"Sounds like a howl to me," agreed the young man. "I mean, what else *could* you call it?"

Granny sucked in a lungful of smoke from her Pall Mall, held it inside for a five count, and then stuck out her lower lip to exhale in a vertical line up past her face. She didn't like to blow smoke on guests and there was a breeze blowing toward the house. A chime made from old bent forks and chicken bones stirred and tinkled.

She squinted with her one good eye—the blue one, not the one that had gone milky white when a wasp stung her there forty years back—and considered how she wanted to answer the young man.

Before she spoke, the sound came again. Low, distant, plaintive. She left her initial response unspoken for a moment as they sat in the dark and listened.

"There," she said softly, "You hear it?"

"Yes, but it still sounds like a—"

"No, son. That ain't what I meant. Can you *hear* the sound? The moan?"

He licked his lips and leaned into the wind, tilting one ear directly into its path. "Yes…"

"Now," said Granny, "can you hear the wind, too?"

"I…" he began, but let his voice trail off. Granny waited, watching his face by starlight, looking for the moment when he *did* hear it. His head lifted like a bird dog's. "Yes…I hear it."

They listened to the moan. It was there, but the wind was dying off again and the sound grew fainter, thinner.

"That, um, 'moan'," the young man said tentatively, "it's *not* the wind. You're right."

She nodded, satisfied.

"It's a separate sound," continued the young man. "I—I think it's being carried *on* the wind." He looked to her for approval.

She gave him another nod. "That's another thing about living up here in the hills," she said, tying this to their previous conversation. "When you live simple and close to the land, you don't get as blunt as folks in the cities do. You hear things, see things the way they are, not the way you s'pose them to be. You notice that there are more things around you, and that they're there all the time."

The young man nodded, but he was half distracted by the moans, so Granny let him listen for a spell.

His name was Joshua Tharp. A good name. Biblical first name, solid last name. A practical name, which Granny always appreciated because she thought that a name said a lot about a person. She would never have come out onto the porch if he'd had a foreign-sounding name, or a two first-name name, like Simon Thomas. Everyone Granny knew with two Christian names was a scoundrel, and half in the Devil's bag already. However, this boy had a good name. There had been Tharps in this country going back more generations than Granny could count, and she knew family lines four decades past the War of Northern Aggression. Her own people had been here since before America was America.

So, Joshua Tharp was a decent name, and well worth a little bit of civility. He was a college boy from Pittsburgh who was willing to pay attention and treat older folks with respect. Wasn't pushy, neither, and that went a long way down the road with Granny. When he'd shown up on her doorstep, he took off his hat and said 'ma'am', and told her that he was writing a book about the coal miners in Pennsylvania and North Carolina, and was using his own family as the thread that sewed the two states together.

Now they were deep into their third porch sitting, and the conversation wandered a crooked mile through late afternoon and on into the full dark of night. Talking about Granny and her kin, and about the Tharps here and the Tharps that had gone on. Joshua was a Whiskey Holler Tharp, though, but there was no one left around here closer than a third cousin with a couple of removes, so everyone told him to go see Granny Adkins.

"Hell, son," said Mr. Sputters at the post office, "Granny's so old, she remembers when God bought these mountains from the Devil, and I do believe the Good Lord might have been shortchanged on the deal. You want to know about your forebears—and about what happened when the mine caved in—well you go call on ol' Granny. But mind you bring your full set of manners with you, 'cause she won't have no truck with anyone who gives her half a spoonful of sass."

Granny knew that Sputters said that because the old coot phoned and told her. Wrigley Sputters was a fool, but not a damn fool.

Come calling is exactly what young Joshua did. He came asking about his kin. That was the first day, and even now they'd only put a light coat of paint on that subject. Granny was old and she was never one to be in a hurry to get to the end of anything, least of all a conversation.

Joshua's people, the true Whiskey Holler Tharps, were a hard working bunch. Worked all their lives in the mines, boy to old man. Honest folk who didn't mind coming home tired and dirty, and weren't too proud to get down on their knees to thank the good Lord for all His blessings.

Shame so many of them died in that cave-in. Lost a lot of good and decent folks that day. Forty-two grown men and seven boys. The Devil was in a rare mood that day, and no mistake. Guess he didn't like them digging so deep.

Granny cut a look at the young man as he sat there studying on the sounds the night brought to him. He was making a real effort to do it right, and that was another good sign. He came from good stock, and it's nice to know that living in a big city hadn't bred the country out of him.

"I can't figure that sound out," said Joshua, shaking his head. "What is it?"

Granny crushed out her cigarette and lit another one, closing her eyes to keep the flare of the match from stealing away her night vision. She lit the cigarette by touch and habit, shook the match out, and dropped it into an empty coffee tin that had an inch of rain water in it.

She said, "What's it sound like?"

That was a test. If the boy still had too much city in him, then there would be impatience on his face or in his voice. But not in Joshua's. He nodded at the question and once more tilted his head to listen.

Granny liked that. And she liked this boy. But after a few moments, Joshua shook his head. "I don't know. It's almost like there are two sounds. The, um, *moan*, and something else. Like a faint clinking sound."

"Do tell?" she said dryly, but with just enough lift to make it a question.

"Like…maybe the wind is blowing through something. A metal fence, or…I don't know. I hear the clink and the moan, but I can't hear either of them really well." He gave a nervous half laugh. "I've never heard anything like it."

"Never?"

"Well, I—don't spend a lot of time out of doors," he confessed. "I guess I haven't learned how to listen yet. Not properly, anyhow. I know Granddad used to talk about that. About shaking off the city so you could hear properly, but until now I don't think I ever really understood what he was saying."

Another soft moan floated over the trees. Strange and sad it was, and Granny sighed. She watched Joshua staring at the darkness, his face screwed up in concentration.

Granny gestured with her cigarette. "What do *you* think it *might* be?"

"Is it…some kind of animal?"

"What kind of animal would make a sound like that, do you suppose?"

They sat for almost two minutes, waiting between silences for the wind to blow. Joshua shook his head.

"Some kind of cat?"

That surprised Granny and now she listened, trying to hear it through his ears. "It do sound a might like a cat," she conceded, then chuckled. "But not a healthy one. Was a broke-leg bobcat got caught in a bear trap once and hollered for a day and a night."

"So—is that what it is? A wounded bobcat? Is that clinking sound a bear trap?"

Granny exhaled more smoke before she answered. "No, son, that ain't what it is."

"Then…?"

She chuckled. "It'll keep. You interrupted your ownself, son. You was asking me a question before we heard yonder call."

He nodded, but it was clear that he was reluctant to leave the other topic unfinished. Granny felt how false her smile was. The mysteries out in the dark would keep. Might have to keep without the other shoe ever dropping.

"I…" Joshua began, fishing for the thread of where they'd been. "Right…we were talking about the day Granddad left for Pittsburgh. He said it was because there was no work, but he never really talked about that. And when he moved to Pittsburgh, he always worked in a foundry. He never wanted to go back to the mines."

"No…I daresay old Hack Tharp would never set foot in a mine again. 'Specially not in these hills, and probably nowhere. Lot of folks around here with the same thought. Those that stayed here gave up mining. I know men who wouldn't lift a pickaxe to go ten feet into a gold mine, not after what happened. Hack was one of 'em."

"Tell me about him. He died when I was ten, so I never had a grown-up conversation with him. Never got to really know him. What was he like?"

Granny smiled, and this time the smile was real. "Hack was a bull of a man, with shoulders from here to there, and hands like iron. A good man to know and a handsome man to look at. Hack worked himself up to foreman down in the Hangood Mine. Swung a pickaxe for twenty long years down in the dark before he was promoted, and still sucked coal gas for twenty more as the foreman. The men liked him, no one crossed him, and his word was good on anything he put it to. Can't say as much about a lot of people, and can't say half as much about most."

Joshua nodded encouragement.

"But Hack up and moved," sighed Granny. "He was the first, and over the years more'n sixty families have left the holler. Ain't no more than a hundred people left on this whole mountain, and I know of four families that are fixin' to leave before long. Might be that I'll be the last one here come next year, if *I'm* even here a'tall."

"People started leaving because the mine closed?"

"They started leaving *after* the mine closed. This place went bad on us that day, and it ain't ever gone to get better."

The moaning wind and the soft metallic clank drifted past the end of her statements almost as if it were a statement itself.

Joshua cleared his throat. "Do you remember when Granddad left? I got the impression it was pretty soon after the disaster."

"It were on the third Sunday after the cave-in. Hack packed up only what would fit into that old rattle-rust Ford pickup of his and drove off. Never came back, never called, never wrote. But… before he left, though, he came to say goodbye to ol' Granny." She sighed. "'Course I wasn't Granny back then. Just a young, unmarried gal who thought the sun rose in the morning 'cause it wanted to see Hack Tharp."

"Pardon me if this is rude, but...were you and Granddad sweethearts?"

Granny blew out some smoke, thought for a moment, and gave a small shrug. "There was no official understanding between us, as you might say. Every girl in five counties wanted to catch Hack's eye, but for a while there I had me some hopes. Maybe Hack did, too, 'cause I was the only one he lingered long enough to say farewell to. And—I blush to say it to a young feller like you—but I was something back then. You wouldn't know it now, lookin' at this big pile o' wrinkles, but I could turn a few heads of my own. Thought for a while that Hack might have been charmed enough to stay 'cause I asked him, but the cave-in plumb took all those thoughts out of his mind. He was set on leaving and he knew that I never would."

"Even if he'd asked?"

She sighed again. "There are some things more important than love, strange as it sounds. At least I thought so back then. You see...I had a talent for the old ways. With a talent for dowsing and a collection of aunts who were teaching me the way things worked in the world. Herbs and healing and luck charms and suchlike. Some folks call us witches. Even seen it in books. Mr. Sputters at the post office showed me a book onest called *Appalachian Granny Magic*. And I guess it's fair enough. Witch comes from some older word that means 'wise', and that's all it is. Women who know such and such about things. My Aunt Tess was a fire witch. She could conjure a spark out of green wood with no matches and only a word. My own mammy was the most famous healer in the holler. People'd come from all over with a sickness, or send a car for her to deliver a baby."

"I heard about that. Granddad told me a little. He said you could find water when no one else could."

She nodded. "I been known to do that now and again. Mostly I make charms to ward off badness and evil. Half the rabbits in these hills walk with a limp since I started selling they's feet to ward off ill luck. And you can walk for two days and not find a soul who ain't wearing one of my snakeskin bags on their belts. Real toad's eyes in 'em, too, because fake charms don't stop nuthin.'" She smiled. "Does that scare you, young Joshua? All this talk about witches?"

"Not as much as that sound does," he said, nodding to the night. "It's really creeping me out."

Granny puffed her cigarette and only smile.

Joshua cleared his throat. "You were telling me about how Granddad came to say goodbye."

"So I was. Well…Hack Tharp stood foursquare in my yard, not two paces from where I sit right now. 'Mary Ruth,' he said, 'I'm gone. I can't live here no more, not with all the dead hauntin' me. My brothers, they never had a chance. They was so obsessed with earning that bonus that they went crazy, picking and digging like the Devil was whipping them, and then that whole mountain just up and *fell.* And it went down fast, too. Killed 'em before they could git right with God. I was right outside taking a smoke when the mouth of Hell opened up and swallowed those boys. I haven't had a night's sleep since it happened. And I won't ever sleep a night if I stay here.'"

"'Weren't your fault,' I told him. But Hack shook his head. 'I ain't saying it is. And I ain't losing sleep 'cause I feel guilty about being on this side of the grave when all my family was taken by death. No—the bosses killed all those men—killed my own brothers, two of my cousins. Killed 'em sure as if they blew the mountain down with dynamite. Killed 'em by digging too deep in a played-out mine. Killed 'em by greed, and that's an evil thing. Greed's one of the bad sins, Mary Ruth, one of them seven deadly sins, and it made my brothers sell their souls to old Scratch himself.'"

"I didn't know Granddad was so religious. He never went to church when I was a kid. Not even on Easter and Christmas."

"I suppose," said Granny, "that he lost the knack. Seen a lot of it after the collapse, just like I seen a lot of folks suddenly hear the preacher's call before the dust even settled. Since then, though… well ain't no one in this holler don't believe in the Devil anymore, so the unbelievers have started believing in God by default."

"Was there an investigation?" asked Joshua. "Did the authorities ever determine that the mining company was at fault?"

"Investigation?" Granny laughed. "You got a city boy's sense of humor, son. No, there weren't no investigation. And even if someone wanted to investigate, there weren't no way to do it."

"Why not? I've read a lot about mining, and a structural engineer could do a walk-through look at the shoring systems, the drill angles, the geologist's assessment of the load bearing walls of the mountain, and—"

"No one's ever going to do any of that."

"Why not?"

"'Cause they'd have to cut through a million tons of rock to take that look."

"They could just examine the areas dug out when the bodies were removed."

Granny studied him for a moment. "Your granddad didn't tell you?

"Tell me what?"

She sighed. "Those dead men are still there, son. The company never dug them out. *Nobody* ever dug them out. That whole mountain's a tomb for all those good men."

Joshua stood up and stared at the darkness again, looking toward Balder Rise. The wind blew from that direction, carrying with it the soft moan. "God," he said softly.

"Oh, God didn't have nuthin' to do with what happened that day," said Granny. "Your granddad spoke true when he said that it were the evil greed of the mining company that brought the ceiling down. They dug too deep."

"That's something Granddad said a couple of times, and now you've said it twice. What's that mean, exactly?"

"The mining company was fair desperate to stay in business even though most of the coal had already been took from old Balder. They kept pushing and pushing to find another vein. Pushed and pushed the men, too, tempting 'em with promises of bonuses if they found that vein. Understand, boy, miners are always poor. It's really no kind of life. Working down there in the dark, bad air and coal dust, it's like you're digging your own grave."

The moan on the wind came again, louder, more insistent. The black trees seemed to bend under the weight of it.

"The company kept the pressure on. Everybody needed that vein, too, because the company *owned* everything. They owned the bank, which means they held the mortgage on ever'body's house and that's the same like holding the mortgage on ever'body's souls." She shook her head. "No, a lot of folks thought the Devil himself was whispering in the ear of ever'body, from the executives all the way down to the teenage boys pushing the lunch trolleys. Infecting them good-hearted and God fearing men with their own greed. Spreading sin like a plague. Makin' 'em dig too hard and too deep, with too much greed and hunger."

"Digging too deep, though—you keep saying that. Do you mean that they over-mined the walls, or—?"

"No, son," she said, "that ain't what Hack meant, and it ain't what I mean."

"Then what—?"

The moan came again, even louder. So loud that Joshua stood up and placed his palms on the rail so he could lean head and shoulders out into the night. Granny saw him shiver.

"You cold?" she asked, though it was a warm night,

"No," he said, without turning. "That sound…"

Granny waited.

"…it sounds almost like a person," Joshua continued. "It sounds like someone's hurt out there."

"Hurt? Is that really what it sounds like to you?"

"Well, it's something like that. I can *hear* the pain." He shot her a quick look. "Does that sound silly? Am I being a stupid city boy here, or—?"

"You don't sound stupid at all, son. That's one of the smartest things you've said. You know what's happening?" she asked. "The city's falling clean off you."

He studied her.

"It's true," she said. "Your daddy might have been born in the city and you might have been born and raised there, too, but you still got the country in you. You still got some of the hills in you. You get that from ol' Hack, and I bet he was always country no matter how many years he lived in the city—am I right or am I right?"

"You're right, Granny," said Joshua. "No one would ever have mistaken Granddad for anything except what he was. He…loved these mountains. He talked about how beautiful they were. How they smelled on a spring morning. How the birds would have conversations in the trees. How folks were simple—less complicated—but they weren't stupid. Always said how he wished he could have stayed."

Granny closed her eyes for a moment, remembering Hack. Remembering pain. Remembering the horror of that collapse, and all the things that died that day. Those men, her love, this town.

"Is something wrong?" asked Joshua.

She opened her eyes and rocked back so she could look up at him. "Wrong?"

The moan cut through the air again. Louder still.

"I suppose you could say that nuthin's been *right* since that mine collapsed," she said, and Granny could hear the pain in her own voice. Almost as dreadful as the pain in that moan. "Close your eyes again and listen to that sound. Don't tell me what it ain't. Listen until you can tell me what it is."

Joshua closed his eyes and leaned once more on the rail, his head raised to lift his ears into the wind.

After a full minute, he said, "It sounds like a person…and that clinking sound…that's definitely something metal."

She waited.

Joshua laughed. "If it was Christmas, I'd say it was Old Marley and his chain."

When Granny did not laugh, Joshua opened his eyes and turned to her.

"That's from the—"

"I know what it's from, son. And it ain't all that far from the mark." She sucked in some smoke. "Not a chain, though. Listen and tell me I'm wrong."

He listened.

"No, you're right. It's, um…sharper than that. But the echoes are making it hard to figure it out. Almost sounds like a bunch of little clinks, almost at once. That's why I thought it was a chain; you know, the links clinking as it blew in the wind."

"But it ain't a chain," she said, "and it ain't blowing in the wind. Ain't echoes, either."

There was a stronger gust of wind and the moan was much louder now.

Joshua pushed off the rail and walked down into the yard. He stood with his hands cupped around his ears to catch every nuance of the sound. Granny dropped her cigarette butt into the empty coffee tin and lit another.

The moaning was so loud now that anyone could hear it. So loud that anyone could understand it, and Granny watched for the moment when Joshua understood. She'd seen it so many times. With friends, with her own daughter—who screamed and then ran inside the house to begin packing up her clothes and her babies. She hadn't come back.

Granny had seen a parade of people come through, stopping as Hack had stopped, wanting to say goodbye. Only one of them ever came back. Norm McPhee wandered back to the mountains after spending the last fourteen years in a bottle somewhere in Georgia. He came back to the holler, back to Balder, back to Granny's yard, and he stood there for an hour, his eyes filled with ghosts. Then Norm had walked into the woods, found himself a quiet log to sit on, drank the rest of his bottle of who-hit-John, took the pistol from his pocket, and blew his brains all over the new blossoms on a dogwood tree.

Granny smoked her cigarette and wondered what Hack Tharp's grandson would do, because she could see the set of his body changing. He was slowly standing straighter. His hands fell slowly from behind his ears. His eyes were wide, and his mouth formed soundless words as he sought to speak the thoughts that his senses were planting in his head.

Joshua turned to her. Sharp and quick, but his mouth wasn't ready to put voice to the thought that Granny could now *see* in the young man's eyes.

"I can hear them," he said at last.

Them.

"Yes," she said.

"It's not just one sound, and it's not an animal. There are a lot of them."

"Yes," Granny said again.

Something glistened on Joshua's face. Was it sweat?

"Granddad said that forty-nine people died that day. Mostly men, a few kids."

"Yes," she said once more.

"All of them digging down in the earth," said Joshua, and his voice sounded different. Distant, like he was talking to himself. Distant, like the wind. "All of them, digging like crazy." His eyes glistened. "What did Granddad say? You just told me... That those men were so obsessed with earning that bonus that they went crazy, picking and digging like the Devil was whipping them."

"And then that whole mountain just up and fell," agreed Granny softly.

"It killed them fast. Killed them before they could get right with God."

She nodded.

"Like the mouth of Hell opened up and swallowed those boys," Joshua said, his voice thick, his eyes filled with bad, bad pictures. "God."

"I already said it," whispered Granny, "God didn't have nuthin' to do with what happened."

The moans were constant now. The voices clear and terrible. The metallic clinks distinct.

Joshua laughed. Too quick and too loud. "Oh...come *on*! This is ridiculous. Granny, I don't mean any disrespect, but...come on. You can't expect me to believe any of this."

"I never asked you to."

That wiped the smile off his face.

"Granddad left because of this sound, didn't he?"

Granny didn't bother to answer that.

The moans answered it. The clank of metal on rock answered it.

"No," said Joshua. "You want me to believe that they're still there, still down there in the dark, still…digging?"

Granny smoked her cigarette.

"That's insane," he said, anger in his voice now. "They're dead! They've been dead for years. Come on, Granny, it's insane. It's stupid."

"Son," she said, "I ain't told you none of that. I ain't told you nuthin' but to listen to the wind and tell me what you think that is."

The voices on the wind were filled with such anger, such pain.

Such hunger.

The incessant clanks of pickaxes against rock were like punches, and Joshua actually yielded a step backward with each ripple of strikes. As if those pickaxes were hitting him. More wetness glistened on his face.

"Granny," he said in a hollow voice, "Come on…"

Granny rocked in her rocker and smoked her cigarette.

"All these years?" asked Joshua, and she could hear how fragile his voice was. It had taken three weeks of the sound before Hack had up and left. A lot of folks played their TV or radio loud and late to try and hide the sound.

One by one, people left the mountain. Took some only months; took others years.

Joshua Tharp stood in the yard and winced each time the wind blew.

He won't last the night, she thought. *He'll be in his car and heading back to the city before moonrise.*

"All these years…digging…"

His eyes were suddenly wild.

"Has…has…the sound been getting *louder* all these years?"

Granny nodded. "Every night," she said. "Every single darn night."

"'Every night,'" echoed Joshua. He stood his ground, not knocked back by the ring of the pickaxes this time. Granny thought that either he had found his nerve or he had lost it entirely.

"I 'spect one of these days they'll dig they'sselves out of that hole." She paused. "Out of Hell."

The picks rang in the night. Again and again. Over and over and over again.

Then there was a cracking sound. Rock breaking off. Or breaking open.

Joshua and Granny listened.

There no more sounds of pickaxes.

There were just the moans.

Louder now. Clearer.

So much clearer.

"God…" whispered Joshua.

"God had nuthin' to do with the collapse," said Granny. "And I expect he's got nuthin' to do with this."

The moans rode the night breeze.

So loud and so clear.

Emcee Interview

By Angela Yuriko Smith

Jonathan Maberry is well known in the horror writing community and the writing community at large. I first met Maberry during his "Act Like a Writer" workshop at World Horror Con in 2015. I walked into his class expecting some dry, writerly advice that may or may not pertain to me. Instead, Maberry changed the way I thought about the business of writing. I attribute that class, along with becoming a member of HWA the same year, as being two of the most important things I've ever done to lay out my own success as an author.

Maberry is many things—a prolific writer, multi-award winner, anthology editor, martial artist, playwright, content creator and writing teacher/lecturer—but in the HWA community he is known best for being a solid advocate for authors, both wise and generous with his knowledge, and a vital part of our community.

AYS: You are a prolific writer across many genres. What first attracted you to writing and how did you get started?

JM: I was born wanting to tell stories. No joke. Even before I could read or write, I was telling stories with toys. So, it's always been who I am. Of course, like most writers, I had to work other jobs along the way. I was a bodyguard, a bouncer in a strip club, a college teacher at Temple University, an expert witness for the Philadelphia District Attorney's Office (for murder cases involving martial arts), a graphic artist, and a very, very bad actor in regional musical theater.

I studied journalism, with a goal of becoming the intrepid investigative journalist who breaks the big case that tears down a crooked politician or a greedy corporation. But…I never actually worked as a reporter. I started writing magazine features while still in college—mostly on martial arts and self-defense. Then, while teaching at Temple U., I began writing textbooks for my classes and those taught by friends. Actually, I tried a lot of different writing gigs along the way. I sold greeting cards to Shoebox; wrote truly appalling and pretentious lyrics for a very bad heavy metal band; had two small plays produced; did copywriting for gardening products (which is hilarious since I can't even keep silk flowers alive); how-to manuals; and a slew of other things. I also wrote some mass-market nonfiction books on martial arts, folklore, the supernatural, and other topics.

Then in 2002 I had an itch to try fiction. Just to see if I'd enjoy it, and to see if I could be any good at it. I spent a few years writing my first novel, *Ghost Road Blues,* and when it was done I liked it enough to try and find an agent. I did—landing Sara Crowe, then of Trident Media—and suddenly I was off and running. That book won the Bram Stoker Award® for Best First Novel. As validation goes, you can't beat it. So I kept with fiction and now that's virtually all I do. And I love it.

AYS: If you had to pick a single genre at the exclusion of all others, what would it be and why?

JM: Almost everything I write is built on the model of a thriller. There's a race against time to stop something big and bad from happening. The thriller model works very well with horror, but it works equally well with mystery, science fiction, fantasy, and so on.

AYS: You have too many awards to list. What do you consider your greatest accomplishment?

JM: In terms of awards, winning the Best First Novel Stoker Award is a damn hard one to top. I never expected to be nominated, and sure as hell never expected to win. And it opened the doors to the larger horror community for me, and that has been the most welcoming extended family imaginable. Virtually all of my closest friends write in some aspect of the horror field.

AYS: In addition to writing, you are involved in film projects, including the upcoming Netflix *V-Wars* series, adapted from your books. What are some of the biggest challenges with having your work adapted for the screen?

JM: Here's the thing about adaptations…writers are often very defensive, possessive and argumentative when it comes to adaptations of their works. Enough so that Hollywood has become very wary of letting the show-runners, actors and production crew have exposure to the writers. There are plenty of horror stories. However, there is no actual way to adapt a novel into a film or TV series without changes. Books are not a visual medium. Movies and TV can't do what a novel—with its tens of thousands of words, interior POV, large casts, massive set pieces, etc—can do. Budgets alone require changes, as do many other aspects of visual storytelling. And, if the adaption is 100% faithful to the source material, then where is the mystery, tension and surprise in seeing that story on the screen? Especially in these days of social media, where spoiler-heavy posts are everywhere.

I had conversations about this with Ray Bradbury and Richard Matheson when I was a kid. Adaptations of their works were often different, but that wasn't always necessarily a bad thing. And the scripts they wrote seldom matched the final edited versions of films or TV episodes.

The more even-tempered friends of mine who have had their works adapted to the screen gave me a lot of good advice. *True Blood* varied in many ways from Charlaine Harris' *Sookie Stackhouse* novels; the *Dexter* television adaptation veered sharply way from Jeff Lindsey's books; and George R.R. Martin's *A Song of Ice and Fire* series could never possibly have been adapted unchanged into *Game of Thrones* Ditto for Robert Kirkman's *The Walking Dead.*

All that said, the show-runners for *V-Wars* Bill Laurin and Glenn Davis, have done an amazing job of preserving the heart and soul of my story while modifying the scope of it to the small screen. There is simply too much story to adapt faithfully, even with ten one-hour episodes per season.

Also, they are superb writers in their own rights, and they brought serious game to the process. The scripts they crafted make several substantial changes, but they are changes I approve of and wholeheartedly support.

Also, the actors—Ian Somerhalder (*Lost, Vampire Diaries*), Adrian Holmes (*Arrow*), Jacky Lai (*The Flash*), and Peter Outerbridge (*The Expanse, Orphan Black*) have all picked my brain on how to bring their characters to life in ways that fit my vision. So, I've been included in the creative process. My wife, Sara Jo, and I were on set for the first three days of shooting and were absolutely dazzled. And the director, Brad Turner (24, *Homeland Stargate*) brings a gravitas and emotional maturity to the TV version that I find very satisfying.

AYS: You will be taking the stage at StokerCon™ 2019 as emcee. What are you looking forward to the most with that experience?

JM: Not having the audience throw rotting fruit at me because I'm nowhere near as funny as Jeff Strand would be a win. Seriously, Jeff's one of my favorite people and I would have to be certifiable to try and out-funny him. So, my take will be a bit more wistful, touching on what I believe is the heartbeat and deep merits of our genre, and our HWA family.

That said, it's going to be a lot of fun. The Stoker banquet always is.

AYS: Do you have any rituals or habits that you engage in before sitting down to write? What is your process like?

JM: I am the least temperamental writer you'll ever meet. I can write anywhere up to and including a burning building. So, when I start my writing day I dive right in. I typically write in two four hour shifts per day. Exceptions are on days when I have to handle a bunch of business emails, calls or other related matters. Since moving to the West Coast five years ago I've had to adjust to the reality that New York publishing is on a different time schedule. So there's always emails to deal with, but that's budgeted into my writing time.

I like the feeling of 'going to work' at the start of each writing day, so several times each week I go to a restaurant or café to begin writing. And I usually write from home in the Afternoon.

I am a structure guy. I plot out my novels and bullet-point my short stories. I often write the opening of each and then jump forward to write the ending. Then I back up and write the rest. And, though I do plot it all out, I allow for organic changes along the way. I do like to have music playing, if possible. And my one writing superstition is that I generally buy a 'good luck charm' at the start of each major project. Usually something tied to some element of the project. For example, I bought action figures of Mulder and Scully before I edited the X-Files anthologies; I got a stuffed plushy Cthulhu (with Hawaiian shirt and sunglasses) before writing *Extinction Machine*; and a Steampunk pistol before writing *Ghostwalkers: A Deadlands Novel.* Like that.

AYS: You are well known for passing on your knowledge, experience and expertise to other writers, especially those that are up and coming. Why do you believe it is important to support each other?

JM: Nobody in the writing world ever reached a milestone of success without someone helping them along the way. Whether that's a word of advice, sharing a query letter draft, being a sounding board, or whatever. Despite the bad press we sometimes get, writers are generally good-hearted and generous people. And generosity is infectious. Earlier I mentioned that I knew Ray Bradbury and Richard Matheson when I was a young teen. I'd met them through my middle school librarian, who served as secretary for an authors' club to which they belonged. They had no reason, no visible profit or career boost in taking time to advise me, talk with me, or treat me like a real writer. I was twelve. But they believed I was serious about wanting to be a good writer and they encouraged me. They were generous, kind, supportive, and never condescending. How selfish would I be if I didn't continue to follow their example? And…how much fun would I miss by not wanting to share my toys on the playground with the other kids? Here's the thing…there is so damn much negativity floating around out there. It's not the biggest defining characteristic of the publishing world, but like many annoying sounds it's the thing we hear because it's shouted at us. Ditto for fear. People think that they are doing one another a service by warning them of the troubles and frustrations ahead in publishing. They aren't. All that does is perpetuate negativity, which is completely useless. I go at it from another angle: give advice, be a cheerleader for my fellow writers, offer tips and advice and solutions, celebrate everyone's victories (however big or small) rather than keep shouting about my own stuff, and invite as many more kids into the playground as I can. If we help each other then more good works will be written, more good works will be published, which will attract more readers, and then ALL of publishing—conventional or independent—will flourish. It's a repeatable and provable model.

AYS: What do you consider your best advice for other writers?

JM: Matheson and Bradbury told me that it was not enough to simply be a good writer. They urged me to understand the craft of writing, and to never stop learning; but at the same time they told me that I needed to learn and understand the business of publishing. They also said that I needed to move with the changes rather than resist, and to ride the wave of literary evolution. That advice was given in 1971, I think. And it is as vital now as it was then.

AYS: What projects are you working on now, and what can we expect from you in the near future?

JM: Jeez…every year I say that "I'm in the middle of the busiest year of my career", and each new year ups the game. (It's possible I need to learn to say 'no', even to fun new projects). At this writing I'm working on *Ink* my 34th novel. It's a standalone horror-suspense for St. Martin's. And I'm writing a horror comic for IDW. Then I have another novel due by the end of the year. I already wrote two—*Deep Silence* (tenth in my Joe Ledger weird science thriller series) and *Still of Night* (fourth in my *Dead of Night* series). I've also got a few short stories in various genres due…weird west, ghost story, cosmic horror, thriller and a mystery. Next year looks to be equally insane, and will likely include at least one original graphic novel, three-four novels, possibly an ongoing comic book, and a TV script. So…basically me juggling chainsaws.

But, you know…idle hands are the devil's tools.

Angela Yuriko Smith's work has been published in several print and online publications, including the *Horror Writers Association's Poetry Showcase* vols. 2-4, *Christmas Lites* vols. 1-6 and the *Where the Stars Rise: Asian Science Fiction and Fantasy* anthology. She has nearly 20 books of speculative fiction and poetry for adults, YA and children. Her first collection of poetry, *In Favor of Pain*, was nominated for an 2017 Elgin Award. Her novella, *Bitter Suites,* is a 2018 Bram Stoker Award® finalist.

Find her online at AngelaYSmith.com.

StokerCon™ 2019

Guests of Honor

The Horror Writers Association would like to welcome the following Guests of Honor at StokerCon™ 2019. The pages that follow include biographies, interviews, excerpts from forthcoming projects, fiction submitted specifically for this anthology, and samples of previously published work.

Josh Boone

Kathe Koja

Josh Malerman

Robert McCammon

Kaaron Warren

Stephanie M. Wytovich

Josh Boone

Guest of Honor

One of the biggest surprise hits of 2014 was the cinematic adaptation of John Green's young adult novel *The Fault in Our Stars.* With a budget of just twelve million dollars, the film went on to earn over three-hundred million worldwide, and gave its director Josh Boone carte blanche in Hollywood. But what Hollywood didn't know was that Boone was a lifelong horror fan who was more interested in adapting Stephen King than additional teen romances. With production partners Knate Lee and Jill Killington, Boone used his newfound success to pursue dream projects like cinematic adaptations of Stephen King's *The Stand* and the X-Men spinoff film *New Mutants.* He was recently tapped to write the screen adaptation of the Stephen King/Peter Straub novel *The Talisman*, and he continues to be a voracious horror reader, although he admits that these days his schedule keeps him confined mainly to short story collections since he spends his work days immersed in the novels he's adapting.

Jamie Meets Jacobs

A selection of storyboards from Josh Boone's adaptation of Stephen King's *Revival.* The illustrations are by Boone's longtime storyboard artist, Ashley R. Guillory.

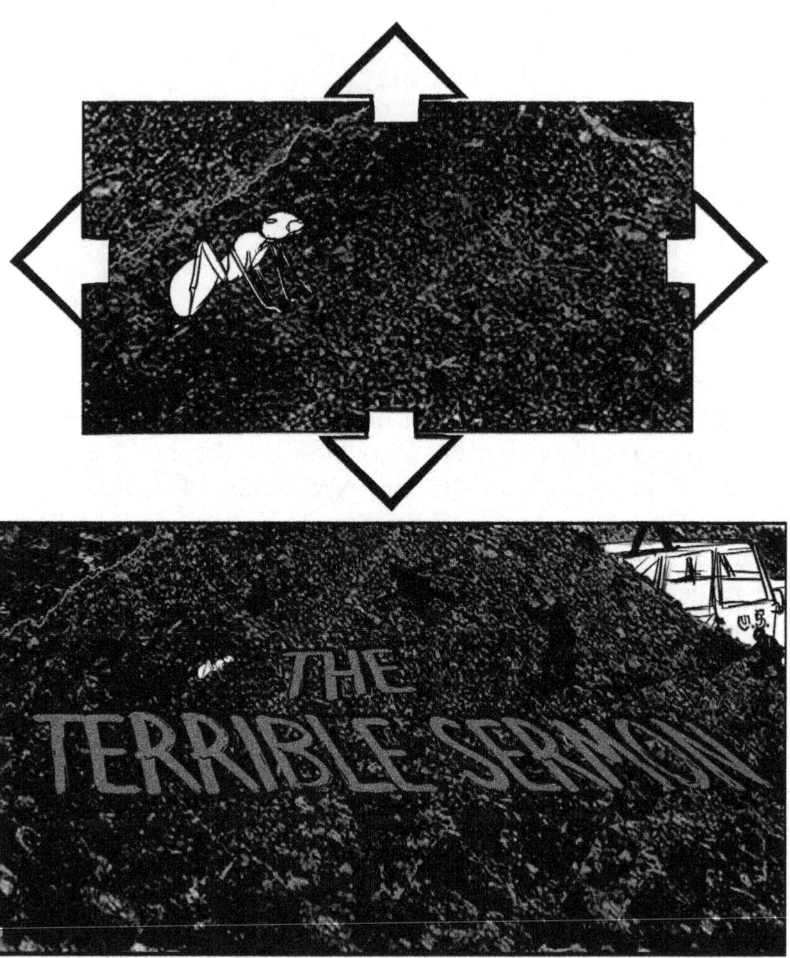

RATATATATATA
PEW
PEW
PEW!
RATATAT

U.S.

PROPERTY OF U.S. ARMY
PEW
PEW

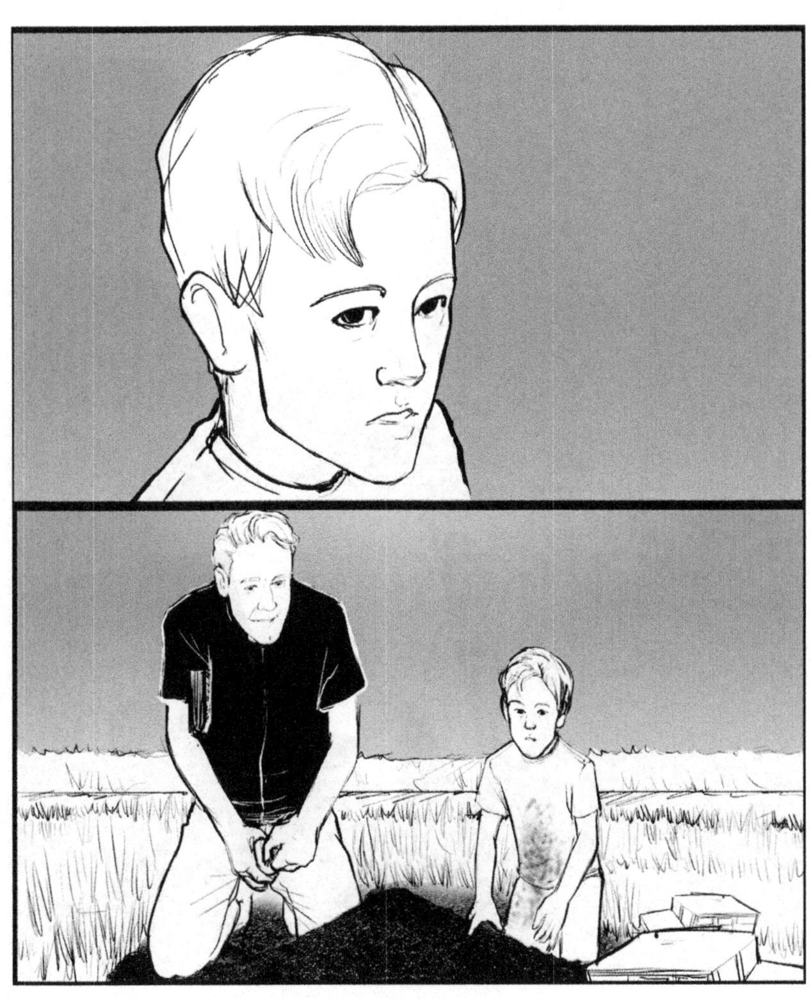

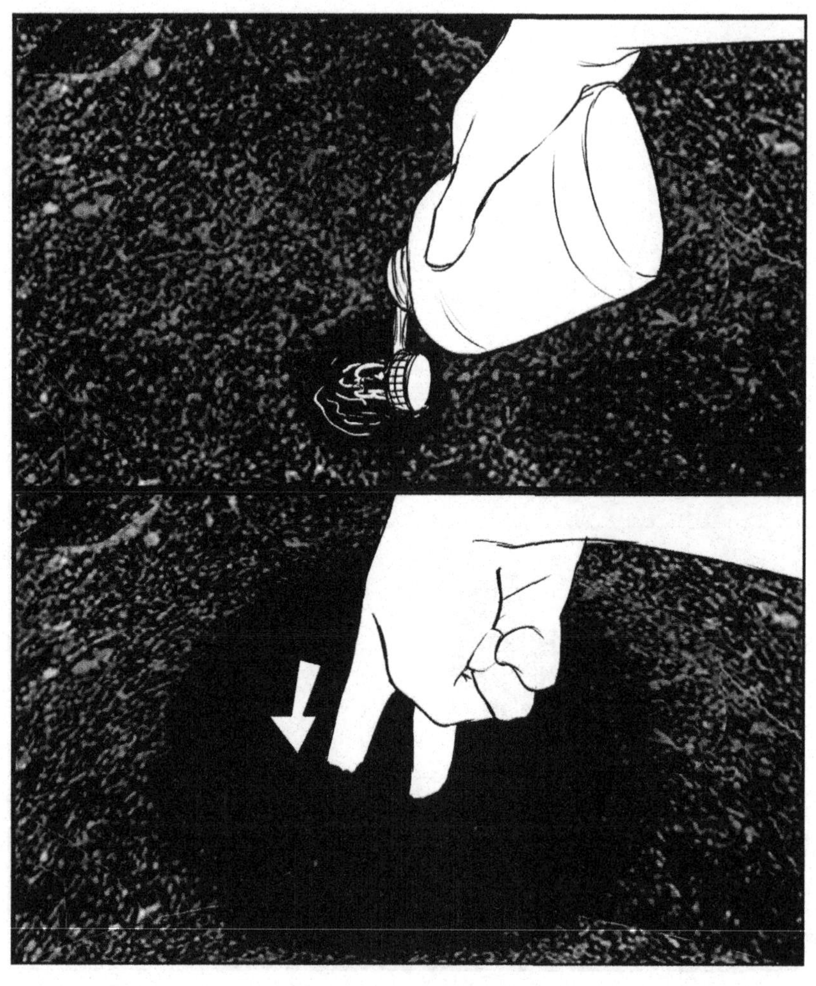

Battle on, General Morton!

Guest of Honor Interview

By Marc L. Abbott

MLA: Many directors tout a movie that inspired them to become directors? Was there any one particular film that inspired you to pursue filmmaking? Was it a horror film?

JB: That's a tough question. As a kid, I watched everything. Devoured it. Oliver Stone was one of my favorite directors. I saw everything he did. But when it comes to horror I have to admit I'm not a big fan of horror films. At least I am not a fan of ones that rely on gore or torture porn to tell a story. That's why I've never been a fan of slasher films. For me, I love performance driven films with strong characters. So when we talk about horror movies, I like films like *The Exorcist, Jacobs Ladder* and even Francis Ford Coppola's *Dracula.* The performances and well written characters drove those films.

MLA: The translation of literature to film isn't always easy. I think of Stephen King and how much of his work cinematically gets muddled. What do you feel is important in keeping the translation clean?

JB: As a director, I've done quite a few adaptations and what's important to me is preserving the voice of the writer. Stephen King is one of my favorite writers. Characters are very important and he knows how to write them.

But I do believe the writing has to be strong. You cannot get into the head of a character on a bad script. Take *The Stand.* It's one of Stephen King's best works and is so important right now. We're doing this as a ten-hour limited series with CBS ALL ACCESS, an idea we had already started working on before *IT.* Originally, we developed it as a two-part feature film and when it became clear we wouldn't be able to really make the book the way we wanted, we shifted to television. I wanted to do the book justice.

MLA: How did you apply that ideology and horror to Marvel's New Mutants?

JB: With the New Mutants, I always loved the Demon Bear story. It's the most well-known story in that universe and that's what I brought to them (Fox). It already had elements of horror in it but it is also a very character driven story. Those mutants were already dealing with the fact that nobody wanted to deal with them. They're not like the ones that live at school. They've been kicked out the house and on their own. I decided I wanted to do a more metaphysical film. Think *One Flew Over The Cuckoo's Nest* meets *The Shining.*

MLA: Any desire to write a horror or any genre novel one day?

JB: Books have always been a big part of my life. I read a lot but I'm more of an admirer of novels. I write all of these scripts for films I make and that's enough writing for me. (Laughs)

Marc L. Abbott is the author of the YA novel *The Hooky Party* and the children's book *Etienne and the Stardust Express.* His short stories "Welcome to Brooklyn, Gabe" and "A Marked Man" are featured in the 2018 Bram Stoker Award® nominated horror anthology *New York State of Fright* and *Hell's Heart* anthology. He is the co-author of the horror collection, *Hell at the Way Station.* He is the director of the horror short *SNAP.* A two-time nominated best actor for his role in *Impervia*, a 2015 Moth StorySlam and GrandSlam winner. He is the host of the monthly storytelling show *Maaan, You've got to hear this!* in Bushwick, Brooklyn and a member of the HWA New York Chapter. Find out more about him at www.whoismarclabbott.com

©2016

Kathe Koja

Guest of Honor

Kathe Koja is the Bram Stoker and Locus Award-winning author of *The Cipher, Bad Brains, Skin, Strange Angels*, the *Under the Poppy* trilogy, and *Christopher Wild*. She creates and produces immersive performance events, including *Dracula* and *Night School*.

Check out Kathe Koja's upcoming events on her website kathekoja.com, purchase her books at amazon.com, and follow her on Twitter @KatheKoja.

Baby

A Short Story by Kathe Koja

It's hot in here, and the air smells sweet, all sweet and burned, like incense. I love incense, but I can never have any; my allergies, right? Allergic to incense, to cigarette smoke, to weed smoke, to smoke in general, the smoke from the grill at Rob's Ribs, too, so goodbye to that, and no loss either, I hate this job. The butcher's aprons are like circus tents, like 3X, and those pointy paper hats we have to wear—"Smokin' Specialist," god. They look like big white dunce caps, even Rico looks stupid wearing one and Rico is *hot.* I've never seen anyone as hot as he is.

The only good thing about working here—besides Rico—is hanging out after shift, up on the rooftop while Rob and whoever swabs out the patio, and everyone jokes and flirts, and, if Rob isn't paying too much attention, me and Rico shotgun a couple of cans of Tecate or something. Then I lean as far over the railing as I can, my hands gripping tight, the metal pressing cold through my shirt; sometimes I let my feet leave the patio, just a few inches, just balancing there on the railing, in thin air… Andy always flips when I do it, he's all like *Oh Jani don't do that Jani you could really hurt yourself! You could fall!*

Oh Andy, I always say; Andy's like a mom or something. *Calm down, it's only gravity,* only six floors up but still, if you fell, you'd be a plate of Rob's Tuesday night special, all bones and red sauce; *smush,* gross, right? But I love doing it. You can feel the wind rush up between the buildings like invisible water, stealing your breath, filling you right up to the top. It's so weird, and so choice… Like the feeling I always got from you, Baby.

It's kind of funny that I never called you anything else, just Baby, funny that I even found you, up there in Grammy's storage space, or crawl space, or whatever it's called when it's not really an attic but it's just big enough to stand up in. Boxes were piled up everywhere, but mostly all I'd found were old china cup-and-saucer sets, and a bunch of games with missing pieces—Stratego, and Monopoly, and Clue; I already had Clue at home, I used to totally love Clue, even though I cheated when I played, sometimes. Well, all the time. I wanted to win.—There were boxes and boxes of Grampy's old books, doctor books, one was called *Surgical Procedures and Facial Deformities* and believe me, you did *not* want to look at *that.* I flipped it open on one picture where this guy's mouth was all grown sideways, and his eyes—his eye—Anyway. After that I stayed away from the boxes of books.

And then I found you, Baby, stuffed down in a big box of clothes, chiffon scarves and unraveling lace, the cut-down skirts of fancy dresses, and old shirts like Army uniforms, with steel buttons and appliqués. At the bottom of the box were all kinds of shoes, spike heels, and a couple of satin evening bags with broken clasps. At first I thought you were a kind of purse, too, or a bag, all small and yellow and leathery. But then I turned you over, and I saw that you had a face.

Right away I liked touching you, your slick wrinkled skin, weird old-timey doll with bulgy glass eyes—they looked like glass—and a little red mouth, and fingers that could open and close; the first time you did that, fastened on me like that, it kind of flipped me out, but then I saw I could make you do it if I wanted to. And then I wanted to.

I played with you for a long time that first day, finding out what you could do, until Mommy came and bitched me out for being "missing." How big was Grammy's house? Not very, Mommy was just mad that she had to be there at all, even once a year was too much. Mommy and Grammy never really got along. *Speak English*, Mommy used to yell at her. *This is Ohio!*

So when she yelled at me, I wasn't surprised: *What are you doing up here?* with the door open and the afternoon light behind her, like a witch peering into a playhouse; I was surprised at how dark it was in there, I could see *your* face perfectly fine. I knew to hide you, Baby, even though I didn't know why, I stuck you in the folds of one of the evening skirts and *I'm just playing dress-up, I said, but Mommy got mad at that, too: Stay out of that stuff, all her Nazi dancehall stuff, it's all moth-eaten and disgusting. And anyway come on, we're leaving now.*

Can I take these? I said, pointing to the board games, I threw the games away when I got you home. You slept with me that first night, didn't you? You got under the blanket, and fastened on… It was the first time I really had it, that feeling, like when you spin yourself around to get dizzy, or when you're just about to be drunk, but a hundred times sweeter, like riding an invisible wave. I could see into things, when you did that, see into the sky, into myself, watch my own heart beat. It was so *choice.*

It's funny, too, because I never liked baby dolls, or dolls of any kind. Grammy bought me like a million Barbies but I don't think

I ever played with any of them, or the Madame Maurice dolls that anyway aren't meant to be played with, Mommy ended up selling those on eBay. But you were different. It wasn't like we were playing, I wasn't the mommy and you weren't the baby, I didn't have to dress you up, or make you walk and talk. You were pretty much real on your own… If I'd been a little older, I might have wondered more about that; I mean, even then I knew you weren't actually a toy. Or a "real" baby, either. You never cried, for one thing. And what you ate never made you grow.

But I knew you loved me since I got you out of that clothes box, and so you did things for me, things that I wanted you to do. Like when Alisha Parrish wrecked my Lovely Locket, and wouldn't say sorry, and you puked—or whatever that was—all over her sleeping bag! That was choice. Or when I threw Mommy's car keys down the wishing well in the park, and she told me I couldn't come home until I found them. She was surprised, wasn't she, Baby?

I let you do things, too, that you wanted, like when we found that dead raccoon out by the storage shed, remember? Or the time I was so sick with the flu that the fever made me see things, and I let you fly all around the room; you were smiling, Baby, and swimming through the air. I wondered, later, how much the fever had to do with it, and for a long time after I kept watching, to see if you would smile again, or fly… It was kind of like having a pet, a pet who was also a friend.

And a secret, because I knew without even thinking about it that I could never show you to anyone, not sleepover friends or school friends or anyone, that you were only meant for me. You knew it, too. And you were happy, you didn't need anyone but me anyway.

For sure Mommy's never seen you—Mommy doesn't even go into my room—but Roger knew about you, or knew *something*; remember Roger? With the bald head and mustache? He used to look at me weird, like he was sad or something, and once or twice he asked me if I was OK: *You doing all right, Jani? You feeling all right?*

I'm fine.

Anything you want to talk about? If you're not—feeling good, or anything, you can always talk to your mom about it. Roger didn't know Mommy very well. And he didn't last very long.

Definitely Flaco knew about you, I don't know how but he did. He finally caught us in the hallway, in the Pensacola house, when Mommy was at the gym, he popped out of the bathroom like he'd been standing there waiting and *So there's your Santeria toy*, he said. *Come on, Jani, let's see it.*

He smelled like aftershave, and skunky weed; he was smiling. In the dusty hallway light, you looked yellower than normal; I could feel the heat coming off you, like it does when you're hungry. I tried to hide you under my arm.

It's just a doll, I said.

Ah, that ain't no dolly, girl, come on. That's a bat-boy! A familiar. My Uncle Felix had one, he called it Little Felix. We used to say it was the Devil's little brother. Flaco was still smiling; the skunk-weed smell was burning my throat. *He bites when you tell him to, don't he? Does anything you tell him to.*

I didn't know what to say. I didn't know how he knew. "Familiar"? With what? *The Devil's little brother.* Family. You were squirming under my arm, I couldn't tell if you were angry or afraid.

They can do some crazy shit, familiars. Come on, I won't tell your mama. Let me see—and he tried to make a grab for you, he put his hand on you and *Stop it!* I said.

Let me see, girl!

You stop it, or I'll tell Mommy you tried to touch me, I'll say you tried to touch me under my shirt.

I wouldn't never—That's a sick kind of lie, Jani! but we both knew that Mommy would believe me, Flaco was pretty much a straight-up man-whore from Day One. He let us go then, didn't he, Baby? and he never said anything about you again, to me or to Mommy, even though I let you do things to him, once or twice—OK, more than that, but whatever, he was passed-out high when you did it, and anyway he deserved it, right? And even though he knew—he had to know—how it happened, those bites, he never said a word.

Flaco moved out that Christmas Eve, and took all the presents with him, his *and* ours: *A real class act,* Mommy said, and then she threw a big Christmas party to celebrate, and get more presents. Mommy said she was tired of Flaco's drama anyway, and really tired of Pensacola, and so was I.

So I hid you in my backpack and we moved back to Ohio, Bay Ridge Ohio and I hated it, hated middle school, hated the girls who made fun of my jeans, and called me a trashburger and a slut; I was like eleven years old, how much of a slut could I have been? Even in Bay Ridge? In Ohio you wrinkled up like a raisin, and you barely moved at all—I think it was too cold for you there, I don't think you can, like, process the cold. In Pensacola you always smelled a little bit funky, like an old sneaker left in a closet, or a dog's chew-toy, but at least you could get around. Once or twice, in Bay Ridge, you were so stiff and so still in my backpack that I thought you were, you know, dead, and I cried, Baby. I really, really cried.

When we moved again, down to Clearwater, things got better; you liked it better here, too, at least at first, right? It was warm again, for one thing. And I started high school, which is a *lot* more fun than middle school, and our house is a lot nicer, too: there are two bathrooms, and the solarium with the hot tub, even if it leaks, and the home office where Mommy works, she's an online "consultant" now—

What kind of a consultant?

I'm a relationship counselor.

What kind of relationships?

—but the more I asked the madder she got, all pinched up around the mouth until she looked like Grammy; and really I don't care, right? At least we have money now, at least there are no more boyfriends wandering all over the house in their tighty-whities. Not hers, anyway… The first time I did it, with a boy, you knew somehow, didn't you, Baby? When I got back from the Freshman Spring Fling, you smelled all over my hands and face, and then you went all stiff at the side of the bed, and you didn't want to fasten on, you wouldn't until I made you.

And when I woke up the next morning you weren't there, even though I looked all over, and Mommy yelled at me for being late to school, I'm not going to call in for you again, Jani, I mean it! All day I thought, Oh god, what if Mommy finds Baby? I couldn't imagine what she would do to you, or to me. Kick me out, or—Who knows what Mommy would do.

I was pretty scared, and pretty mad, when I got home. Mommy was sleeping, so I tore apart the house again, and when finally I found you, curled up behind the washer—where Mommy could have seen you in a second, if she ever bothered to look, if she ever bothered to do a load of clothes—*Where were you?* I said. I think I shook you a little, or a lot. *Where the hell were you?*

You just rolled your glass eyes at me and didn't make a sound. All sad and cold and stiff, like—like beef jerky or something, you were *nasty*. So I stuffed you into the old backpack, I threw you into the back of the closet, and I almost didn't let you out. Almost. Except I finally did, and I let you fasten on, too. And you were happy, Baby, I could tell, that night it was like both of us were flying. After that, no matter what I did or who I hooked up with, or even if I didn't come home all night, you never ran away again. I knew you needed me, then, more than I needed you. And I realized that I didn't really need you much at all.

But that was going to happen anyway, right? because really, the older I get, the more I can do for myself, and the less I need the things that you can do—and the things I can't get you can't either, I mean I'm not going to send you into the liquor store, right? *Crawl up into the cold case, get me a six-pack of Tecate, Baby!* And even the fastening-on—even though we still do it, and I still like it, I can get to that place without you, now. Driving really fast, smoking up and then drinking—it's mostly the same feeling, not as pure or as, as good as with you, but I can be with other people when I get it. People like Bobby, or Justin, or Colin. Or Rico. Especially Rico.

I told Rico about you, Baby. I didn't plan to beforehand, but I did. We were in the storage room—Rob said to go unpack the napkins, there must have been like fifty boxes—but instead we were joking around, and flirting, and I was trying to think of ways to keep him talking; I wanted to stay that way, the two of us alone together, for as long as I could. I wanted to show him that I'm—different, from Carmen, and Kayla, and those other girls, those pervy night shift girls, I wanted him to know something about me. To be—familiar with me. So I told him about you.

At first it seemed like he was impressed: *Whoa, that's some crazy shit. How'd your grandma get something like that?*

She was like in a war, or something. "Her Nazi dancehall stuff"—that's creepy to think of, actually, because I'd never really thought about where you came from, or how Grampy got you. Or who might have—made you, or whatever. You weren't born like normal, that's for sure.

You saying the doll's, like, alive, Jani? For real?

Not alive-alive. But he moves around and everything. You should see him when he eats!

Rico was smiling—*That's so crazy*—but I couldn't tell if he thought it was cool-crazy or weird-crazy; I couldn't tell if I'd just made a big mistake. And then Rob came looking for the napkins, and bitched us both out for taking so long: *What were you guys doing in there anyway?* Everyone laughed, Rico too. Later on, I asked Rico if he wanted to come over and use the hot tub, but he said he was busy, and maybe we could just hang out at work instead. So I guess you can't help me with Rico, Baby, after all.

And even if I wanted to ask Grammy about you, or give you back, I can't: because she's gone, right, she finally died in that hospice in Ohio. Mommy said she found out too late to be able to go to the funeral, but she sure got there fast enough for the will, she must have taken half the furniture from that house. I wonder what happened to all of that other stuff, those old clothes, and the medical books… Maybe I should have asked Flaco about you, back when I had the chance.

The thing is, Rico finally said yes, Baby, when we were up on the roof last night, I was leaning over the railing and he was standing next to me, and I told him that Friday was my last night at Rob's Ribs, that I was quitting to go back to school; it's online school, but still. Mommy said I could quit working if I take at least one class, and anyway I didn't tell him that part. *I'd like to, like, be with you,* I said to Rico. *Before I go.*

And he smiled so you could see all his dimples, god he is so hot. And then he said, *OK, wild child, how about I come over tomorrow? I have to drive up to Northfield, but I can be over by midnight.* Mommy might be home, but Mommy doesn't bother me, she doesn't care what I do. So I said *Absolutely*, I said *Come over whenever you want.*

But the thing is, you can't be there, Baby, I don't want you to be there, I don't want Rico to ask Hey where's that crazy doll? And if he does I want to be able to say Oh that? Oh, I don't have that any more.

But I don't want to—to bury you alive in some old clothes box. You didn't like it the first time, right, when Grammy or Grampy stuck you in there? I know you didn't. Just like you don't like living in my old backpack with the April-May-Magic stickers and the black plaid bows, stuffed way down in the very back of my closet, behind the Princess Jasmine bedspread. When I take you out to feed you, now, you just—look at me. I hate the way you looking at me feels… I'm just too old to play with dolls.

It really does smell like incense in here, like hot sweet wood, burning. No one's supposed to mess with the smokers—Rob does that himself, all the cleaning—but Andy helps the cooks load, and he says it's not that hard; he's going to help me, too. He doesn't know what's in the backpack, when he asked I just said *Memories*, and he nodded. Andy will do what I want him to do; like you, Baby. They keep the smokers at, like, 250 degrees, but it can go a lot higher, a lot hotter, I bet it won't even hurt. Not like falling off the roof, right? No Tuesday night special, just ash, and gone… I'm going to throw in that stupid "Smokin' Specialist" hat, too.

I wonder if you knew that's why I let you fasten on, last night, for one last time? You seemed so happy to get out of the closet, and the backpack, to be close to me again… I'd take you out again to say goodbye, right here behind the shelves, but if I look at you, your sad glass eyes, then I won't do it, maybe. Maybe. But I can't keep you forever anyway, and Rico will be over tonight.

The smoke smell is everywhere in here, digging a barbed-wire itch in my throat, in my chest, it makes me cough… Afterward, when Andy's done, I'm going to go up onto the roof and lean over the railing, let my feet dangle and feel like I'm flying. Flying and crying, for you and for me: because I *am* crying, Baby, just a little, because I'm going to miss you a lot.

Guest of Honor Interview

Kathe Koja Writes Stabby Fiction

By K. Ceres Wright

Kathe Koja writes horror and weird fiction that claws the reader's sensibilities and lays bare the hypocrisies of society. Her characters embody traits and personalities that run the gamut of human experience. They are brain damaged, obsessed, angry, ambitious, debauched, secretive, honest, and deep. They come storming off the page, just like their creator came storming into the publishing world. For her first novel, *The Cipher,* Koja won the Locus Award for Best First Novel, the Bram Stoker Award® for Best First Horror Novel, and was nominated for the Philip K. Dick Award. She is still racking up publication credits, translated works, and film options. I was honored to get the chance to interview her by email. Her revealing answers follow:

KCW: Please tell us why you write horror and weird fiction.

KK: I believe that the subject chooses the writer. And all the books I love to read have in common a certain strain of ferocity, whether it's subtle (*Harriet the Spy*) or overt (*Wuthering Heights*) or anywhere in-between; I'm just not interested in fiction where the knives never come out, where nothing substantive is at risk.

And I believe, with J.B.S. Haldane, that everything, the universe and all its occupants, is really and truly weirder than we can imagine. So at that intersection, my novels took root.

KCW: Your book, *Under the Poppy,* is set in the Victorian era. How did you perform your research to make sure you 'get it right'?

KK: The books of the Poppy trilogy—*Under the Poppy, The Mercury Waltz,* and *The Bastards' Paradise*—take place in the place where the "modern" world, the 20th century, starts to clamber over and crush everything that's come before, and so my task was to take the main characters, Istvan and Rupert, and their colleagues and enemies, from the interior to the exterior, while their ongoing material circumstances of puppetry, sex, and violence stayed constant. All the rest was the fun of the details, the buttonhooks and laudanum, the radium silks, the locomotive soot, what Anthony Lane memorably called "feathering the nest." I read a *lot* of books about puppetry, I read what I needed to weed out all or any (I hope!) anachronisms, and I made up the rest.

KCW: Across your range of books, you have varied your writing style among first and third person, as well as past and present tense. What is your reasoning for each style?

KK: Every book for me begins with a character, and that character has a particular voice that drives the story; the tense is part of that voice.

I don't do a lot of pre-planning beforehand on any of my books, beyond the necessary research: once I have the viewpoint character, all the rest follows. And I never know how anything ends when I sit down to write it. That's been true not only of my horror novels, and YA, and historical, but of my performance work, too. I don't ever want to impose my own plans on what the story or novel or show wants to become.

KCW: In *Buddha Boy,* you incorporate Buddhism, bullying, and friendship. Do you draw on your own experiences to write your YA?

KK: Never directly, not with any of my work.

KCW: What resources do you use to help make your characters diverse?

KK: Humanity is so vast and yet it's so particular: making each character true to their own nature and experience is what I try to do every time, every character, in everything I write.

KCW: Which book was the hardest to write, and why?

KK: The ones I couldn't finish. Because no matter how much I wanted to write them—and I wanted that a lot—either I lacked the skill, or the story itself was beyond me, and all I had was the desire, and desire's not enough. Necessary heartbreaks, every one.

KCW: You host interactive productions for your own and other books. What made you decide to begin doing that?

KK: When I finished the first *Poppy* book, I thought that there should be a book trailer, so I collaborated with a filmmaker, a puppet artist, a musician, and some performers to make that happen. And then I found I loved the process, I loved the reimagining of the text into live action, the lessons and surprises of this very different way to tell a story, so I gathered a collaborative ensemble of artists and made a live immersive *Poppy* production. And then I just kept doing shows, twenty productions and counting, including *Dracula, The Heights, ALI<E*, and *Glitter King*, which took Christopher Marlowe's *Edward II* and put him in a 1980s punk bar in Berlin (for that event I got to collaborate with a scent artist, who designed bespoke perfumes for our characters and for the set itself). And I'm working on touring a performance called *River St.*, based on my novel *Christopher Wild*, that will be me and a musician local to the venues I visit.

Love is its own reason, and it's a good one.

KCW: What was your best interactive production and why?

KK: That's pretty much impossible to answer, like picking a favorite of my own novels. Each of them has something that the others don't, each was huge fun for differing reasons, each had its own frustrations and craziness, and with each I got to work with people whose creativity was a thrill to be around.

KCW: What's the best lesson you've learned from another writer?

KK: Shirley Jackson, the queen of us all, taught me in her sublime "Notes for a Young Writer" that readers don't have to be led by the hand through your stories or novels, they can figure out that people get from place to place and from moment to moment without the writer moving them around like counters on a game board. That one piece of sterling advice made me a much more fleet and economical writer.

KCW: What is your opinion on the trajectory of the publishing world?

KK: I know good writers will always exist. And I believe the best and most necessary writing works to find its way to its readers, through whatever process publishing is or might become. I'm an optimist.

K. Ceres Wright received an M.A. in Writing Popular Fiction from Seton Hill University and her published cyberpunk novel, *Cog*, was her thesis for the program. Her short stories, poems, and articles have appeared in *Luminescent Threads: Connections to Octavia Butler* (Locus Award winner; Hugo Award nominee); *Sycorax's Daughters* (Bram Stoker Award® nominee); *Many Genres, One Craft* (Best Non-Fiction London Book Festival); *The Museum of All Things Awesome and That Go Boom;* among others. Ms. Wright is the founder and president of Diverse Writers and Artists of Speculative Fiction; and the Director of Science Fiction Programming for MultiverseCon.

BIRD BOX

Josh Malerman

Guest of Honor

Josh Malerman is the author of the books *Bird Box, A House at the Bottom of a Lake, Black Mad Wheel, Goblin*, and *Unbury Carol.* He's also the singer/songwriter of the High Strung, whose song "The Luck You Got" can be heard as the theme song to the hit Showtime show "Shameless." He lives in Michigan with Allison Laakko.

Alarms of Eden

A Horror Play Script by Josh Malerman

Curtains part to reveal JOHN (early thirties, short hair, smart), a handy looking man in stagehand clothes, sliding a couch across a living room set. It's clear he doesn't fit into the scene he's adjusting as the couch and rug are lavish.

He slides the couch farther from a desk against the left wall. He moves a chair in front of the couch, checks the tape mark on the floor, and moves it more. A false door is to the right. A staircase to the far right. Pictures hang on the wallpapered walls. All the details of a lived in home.

John steps to the front of the stage, his back to the crowd, eyes the set-up.

JOHN

Tracy!

There is no answer, but John seems to be more concerned with the set design anyway.

JOHN

(to himself)

One day we'll work on a show where the marks are perfect and it'll be the most de-lightful thing we've ever—

The door opens and TRACY (early thirties, bright) enters. She wears a large fancy hat and a feather boa over her work clothes. Her work clothes match John's.

TRACY

(in a fancy accent)

Loooook at meeeee. I'm Susie from Alllaaaarrrmmmssss of Eden!

She flips the end of the boa over her shoulder, places a hand on her hip, smiles at John.

John shakes his head.

JOHN
Tracy, get that back to wardrobe. And help me. We gotta get this right by daylight.

Tracy ignores him. She struts across the room, exaggerating all her gestures, until she reaches the couch. There she plops onto it, sensually, her hand on her hip.

TRACY
It's such a yawn, being Susie from Alarms of Eden. How much leisure can one woman possibly take?

John pulls out a tape measure. He's measuring the space between the chair and the rug. He checks a sheet of paper on the desk.

JOHN
Faulty marks.

Tracy exaggerates sitting up.

TRACY
You know Faulty Marks? I thought only I knew Faulty Marks. Shame that Faulty is such a society whore. Lessens the meaning of our friendship.

On his knees, measuring, John points to the left side of the empty theater seats.

JOHN
See? If you're sitting anywhere over here, your view is obstructed by this chair.

He checks the sheet of paper.

There's a creaking sound from above them. Tracy looks up. Either John didn't hear it or he doesn't care.

JOHN
They just don't know what they're doing.

TRACY
(her own voice)
It's a Duggan play after all.

JOHN
He has no idea how much grief he's caused us.

Tracy gets up.

TRACY
I'm surprised he doesn't bark orders from a throne.

(pauses)

And we're the ones who'll have to position the throne just right so the people in the back can see it.

They both look to the back of the theater.

Tracy shields her eyes the way people do when looking far across a desert, blocking the sun.

TRACY
(with a second silly ac-
cent)
Do ya' see it, John?

She puts her arm around John.

JOHN

See what?

TRACY

Do ya' see the coming of tha' storm?

John smiles but looks.

JOHN

I see the coming of a family drama.

TRACY

Ah. In the form of blacks clouds, no doubt.

(pauses)

There it is, John. Don't take your eye off it. The minute you stop looking, it moves twice as fast. It's… it's…it's our deadline!

The sound of a dish crashing off-stage brings both to recoil.

JOHN

Shit.

TRACY

I'll check on it.

Tracy exits stage-left. John steps to the desk, adjusts it against the set wall, hears a creaking from above, and looks up.

Tracy enters stage-left. She's no longer wearing the boa or hat. She carries pictures to hang on the set walls.

TRACY

No idea.

JOHN
Something must have tipped over.

TRACY
Well, if it did, I didn't find it.

A beat. John's expression softens.

JOHN
Hey. It's nice to hear you joking again.

Tracy looks at him curiously, gets what he means, and shakes her head no.

TRACY
Well, that's not going to do us any good.

JOHN
What?

TRACY
Pointing out when we're okay.

JOHN
I felt like I had to. It's been a minute since you've gone into full stand-up mode.

TRACY
I'm just saying I'd rather you didn't point it out. Now it's gone. See? Sad all over again.

John crosses the room, makes to hug her, but Tracy backs up.

TRACY
Hey, I love you. But let's just get this done. I don't need to be thinking of him tonight.

She steps past him, pictures in hand.

JOHN
Holland.

Tracy stops just short of the wall. She turns to face him.

TRACY
Really? You're gonna do this right now?

JOHN
His name is Holland.

TRACY
Was. His name was Holland. And we named him after a character in a book. A character that turned out to be dead the whole time. Good thinking on our parts.

JOHN
He's not dead, Tracy.

TRACY
Well, he sure as shit can't be having a good time if he's still alive. Which would you rather have, John? Our kid was killed or our kid's been a slave in someone's basement for six years, huh?

John smacks the pictures out of her hands. They crash to the stage floor.

TRACY
Jesus, man. You broke one.

John clearly feels guilty.

JOHN

I can fix them.

TRACY

No, no. It's okay. I can do it.

(pauses)

Ugh. Sorry, John. That was ugly.

John nods.

JOHN

I'm sorry, too. Let's just do this. I'll get the tools. I broke those, I'll fix them.

John exits stage-left.

Tracy is on her knees, checking the picture frames.

She hears the creaking above again. She looks up. It's definitive. Sounds like someone walking across a wood floor.

She stands up, looks to the rafters, and hears the almost inaudible, far distant cry of a little boy.

Mommy!

Tracy brings a hand to her chest.

TRACY

Holland?

John enters stage-left with a hammer and some nails. He looks to Tracy, sees she's looking up, looks up, too.

JOHN

What's going on?

But Tracy looks too moved to respond. She still has one hand to her chest. She's still looking to the rafters.

JOHN

Tracy?

When she looks at him, her eyes are wide. Like she's seen a ghost.

TRACY

I just heard him.

John breathes deep.

JOHN

Hey, I didn't mean to bring this up.

TRACY

I just heard him.

John crosses the room and sets the tools on the couch. He stands beside her, looks to the rafters.

The creaking again.

TRACY

Did you hear that? Did you?

John nods.

JOHN

Yeah. It's gotta be the rafters.

Tracy shakes her head no.

TRACY

It's like…right…

She raises her hand as high as she can, jumps a little.

TRACY

…Here.

John tilts his head to listen. The creaking continues.

Tracy makes to leave the living room set.

JOHN

Where you going?

TRACY

Getting the ladder.

JOHN

What for?

Tracy exits stage-right and enters again, carrying a tall ladder. John meets her half-way to help her with it.

They bring it to the center of the stage and open it.

TRACY

Whatever it is, we can't rightly let it creak throughout the show tomorrow, now can we?

John climbs the ladder as Tracy holds the bottom. When he's halfway up, they hear the creaking.

TRACY

Tell me you heard that.

JOHN

I did.

He's looking about two feet above Tracy's head. A foot below where he stands on the ladder.

JOHN
It's coming from right
around…

(waves a hand over the space)

…Here.

They both look miffed.

JOHN
But there's nothing there.

TRACY
But there is.

JOHN
What?

TRACY
Right there would be the
ceiling of the living room.
The living room I'm standing in. The one you've
climbed out of.

John looks to her. To the space. Shakes his head.

JOHN
No. It's gotta be the rafters.

TRACY
It's coming from right here.
You said so.

JOHN
Then I was wrong.

TRACY
You weren't though.

JOHN
Tracy, we're in a theater. The entire room is an auditory hallucination.

TRACY
Someone is walking upstairs.

JOHN
Ummm…there is no upstairs here, honey.

TRACY
But there is.

JOHN
Honey…

TRACY
The bedroom. Act Two.

They hear the creaking again. John leans forward, reaching out for where it's coming from.

TRACY
Careful. Don't break your neck for a family drama.

JOHN
Think Duggan would take a moment of silence?

TRACY
Only if it was written in.

They listen for the creaking.

TRACY
Let's set up the upstairs.

John outright laughs.

JOHN
Honey! You realize it's impossible for someone to be walking—

TRACY
We gotta do it anyway. Let's do it next. Why not?

JOHN
We gotta make sure this one is right first.

TRACY
It is. It's great.

John looks down at the living room, shakes his head yes, agreeing with her.

JOHN
Okay. The upstairs bedroom is next.

John descends the ladder.

When he gets safely to the bottom, Tracy begins removing pieces from the stage. We discover that most of them are on wheels. John goes into the theater seats, to where the sound-man would be stationed, and turns some music on.

They strike the set to a song.

They bring in the pieces of the upstairs bedroom. A bed, fully made. A dresser. A nightstand. The walls and one window, open, with parted drapes. Lamps for the dresser and nightstand. They finish as the song comes to an end.

They step back to the front of the stage, their backs to the audience, eyeing the set they've put together.

JOHN
Gotta switch the lamps. Duggan will scream if the large lamp is on the small table.

Tracy crosses the room and sits on the end of the bed.

She looks up at John, smiling sadly.

TRACY
Looks a bit like a boy's bedroom.

She looks to the open window.

TRACY
And that doesn't help.

JOHN
It's in the script.

TRACY
I know.

(pauses)

But when your son is stolen from your own house, from his own bedroom, when you're inside the house…a family drama in a house is probably not the best show to work on.

JOHN
Let's strike it.

TRACY
No. It's okay.

JOHN
But it looks good.

TRACY
But that's not why you want to strike it.

JOHN
Tracy, come on. You're not the only one riding this roller coaster.

TRACY
Come sit with me? On the roller coaster?

John crosses the room and joins her on the bed.

Tracy lays her head on his shoulder. They sit in silence for a minute.

JOHN
Jesus, remember how he—

TRACY
Holland. Just…say his name, homey.

JOHN
Holland. Remember how Holland kept moving about his room, non-stop?

TRACY
Non-stop.

JOHN
It got to the point where I was worried about him.

TRACY
Worried he was gonna shit his pants and it'd run down his leg.

They laugh until they are only remembering again.

TRACY
He loved being on set.

JOHN
A stagehand in the making.

TRACY
Yep. I used to ask him, 'What makes a cellar a cellar?'

(sitting up more, getting excited)

He helped you roll a fuckin carriage out once!

JOHN
Oh my God. I didn't even know he was doing that.

TRACY
You wouldn't have let him!

JOHN
I wouldn't have let him. He was half the size of the fuckin wheels.

(pauses)

And Duggan got pissed at us because he said it was lawsuit waiting to happen.

They sit with their memories a beat.

TRACY
Can you imagine caring about anything like a lawsuit ever again?

JOHN
I haven't cared about a lot of silly shit in about six years.

A loud CRASH sound causes both to stand up quickly. John actually goes to look out the window.

TRACY
Something fell over.

JOHN
That's two things now.

They exit stage-left and return a minute later.

JOHN
I have no idea.

Tracy gets down on her hands and knees and puts her ear to the stage.

JOHN
What are you doing?

TRACY
It sounded like it came from below us.

JOHN
Couldn't have.

TRACY
Okay, but it did.

A second distant crashing, this one farther away, has both looking at the floor.

John gets on his hands and knees beside her.

TRACY
Is there a trapdoor on this stage?

JOHN
No.

A third sound makes the first two impossible to deny.

JOHN
A haunted theater.

TRACY
A haunted house.

John shakes his head. Tracy stands up.

TRACY
It's coming from the kitchen. We gotta strike this set. Set up the kitchen.

John shakes his head.

JOHN
No. No! No fucking way.

TRACY
It's coming from the kitchen.

JOHN
The kitchen, Tracy?

TRACY
Come on.

John sighs agreement.

Tracy exits stage left. John walks out into the crowd again, to where the sound-man would be. Turns music on.

They strike the set as fluidly as they put it together. When the stage is empty, they dance together, romantically.

Then they're rolling in the kitchen sink, the countertop, cupboards, a window, a table and chairs. John carries out a box of props; a knife holder, salt and pepper shakers, pans.

Tracy stands before an open cupboard. She's looking over her should at John.

JOHN
What is it?

Tracy pulls a piece of a plate from the cupboard.

TRACY
The dishes are broken.

JOHN
Okay. They fell over. Are there extras?

Tracy only stares at him.

TRACY
John. The dishes are broken. What does broken dishes mean to you?

JOHN
I'm not doing this. No fuckin way.

TRACY
(defiantly, strong)
Then I'll do it.

She steps from the cupboard with a broken dish in hand

TRACY
We were breaking dishes the night Holland was taken.

JOHN
Stop it.

TRACY
We were being funny. You started it. You threw one across the kitchen. Then I

did it, too. We broke three, four plates as it stormed outside and someone snuck into our fucking kid's bed-room and took him.

JOHN
Stop it right now!

Tracy shakes her head no.

TRACY
Yell all you want. But what the fuck is going on here?

John turns from her, faces the phony stove.

Tracy opens other cupboards, checking the dishes and glasses.

TRACY
John. I heard him.

JOHN
What are you talking about?

TRACY
Earlier, when I was alone on stage. I heard him call for me.

John shakes his head no.

JOHN
It's too much, Tracy. This, whatever this is, this ends now.

He makes to roll the kitchen island offstage.

But a distant voice stops him.

Daddy!

John looks to Tracy, like she's somehow responsible for it.

JOHN
Tracy, what's going on?

TRACY
(looking up)
Holland?

John looks up. He looks to the audience.

JOHN
He's in the theater, Tracy.
He's here!

John runs from the kitchen.

JOHN (O.S.)
HOLLAND!

He runs through the theater seats, calling his son's name as Tracy searches the cupboards, the refrigerator, the stove.

They meet again at center stage.

JOHN
I heard him. I heard him, too.

TRACY
I know you did.

Without looking at one another, they reach out and hold hands.

TRACY
Is there a storm in the sound base?

John looks to the crowd, to where the soundman would be.

JOHN

Gotta be.

Tracy nods. John steps past the window, gets down from the stage, and goes to where the sound-man would be.

He searches through a sound bank. The theater is filled with the sound of a moving train and its whistle, a crowded restaurant, the sounds of a street, the sound of the woods, and, finally…

…A storm.

John looks to Tracy.

TRACY

(calling to him from the stage)

Less thunder, more rain.

John searches through different types of storms. Some are gentle, others are not.

He pauses on one in particular, deep distant thunder, rain that sounds cold. He looks to Tracy. She's already nodding.

TRACY

That's it. For sure.

(pauses)

I know what we need to do.

JOHN

Tracy, I don't think—

TRACY

There were a number of sounds. Not just the storm.

(pauses)

The TV was on. We'd broken the dishes. We were talking.

John begins nodding to what she's saying.

JOHN

Okay.

TRACY

We need to do that again.

JOHN

Okay.

John steps to her but she begins rolling items out.

TRACY

We both heard him offstage because that's where he was. To us. Offstage.

This seems to resonate with John.

TRACY

So we need to go back in the living room. We'll hear him again from there.

John nods without argument.

THEATER GOES BLACK.

When the lights come on again, both have their backs to the audience, assessing the living room.

TRACY

No.

JOHN

No.

They move together, moving the couch from the left to center stage. They move many items; lamps and a credenza, a mirror, a coat rack, the door.

John exits stage-left and adjusts the lights.

TRACY
(calling to him)
That's good!

The sounds of the storm continue.

When John returns, he does so with a TV.

TRACY
Yes. Plug it in.

John gets behind the TV, then exits stage-right and returns with an extension cord. He plugs the TV in.

Static fills the screen.

TRACY
Okay. We'd just put Holland to bed.

A creaking above causes them both to look up to the "ceiling" of the living room.

JOHN
But he didn't go to sleep yet.

Tracy shakes her head no. Thunder rolls.

TRACY
Right. He was playing, running back and forth.

The creaking continues.

TRACY
And…and…we were…having a drink! Sit down!

She points to the couch. John quickly goes to it and sits on the edge.

TRACY
Watch the TV!

John angles himself to face the static.

Tracy leaves the set, stage-left, and returns with a prop bottle of wine and prop glasses, too.

TRACY
Here. Drink.

She pours invisible wine into the glass, then hands the glass to John.

John drinks.

Creaking above. Thunder outside.

TRACY
You were there, yes, and I was…

She moves to the easy chair, then comes back to the couch.

JOHN
You were on the floor, your back to the couch.

They share a look that says, We remember all this because what happened to us was too terrible to forget.

TRACY
You're right.

She gets to the floor and backs up to the couch, wine glass in hand.

JOHN
Your back was touching my legs, too.

She inches closer to his legs.

JOHN
We watched a movie. Autumn Snow. Part of it.

TRACY
Autumn Snow. I can't see a clip of it without crying.

JOHN
Same here.

TRACY
We said how bad it was. We drank a glass each. Then…

(thinking)

…A second glass.

JOHN
Yeah, because by the time we went into the kitchen we were toasted.

TRACY
Had to be. We broke dishes on purpose.

They go quiet a second. But not for long.

JOHN
Give me a second glass.

Tracy pours him a second glass of wine, does the same for herself.

They drink.

JOHN
So now…now we're drunk. We're feeling it. Are you sure we didn't have a third glass?

Tracy's eyes get wide.

TRACY
John, we did a shot.

She's up fast, exiting stage-left. John watches the static, looks up to the "ceiling." Tracy returns with a prop bottle of booze.

She hurries back to her place on the floor, her back to the couch and John's legs.

TRACY
We were watching this bad movie and drinking wine and you…you! You said let's do a shot every time this movie gets worse.

John nods.

JOHN
Pour the shots.

She does. They raise their glasses to shoot 'em.

JOHN
Cheers.

TRACY
'To Holland watching better movies than we do.'

They both look surprised. They've remembered the exact cheer.

They drink their shots.

TRACY
Then we got up and…

JOHN
…Went into the kitchen…

TRACY
…To get something to eat…

JOHN
…Cause we were drunk-hungry…

TRACY
…And so…

Creaking from above. They both look up.

Thunder rolls. The static plays.

JOHN
I'm listening for him. Are—

TRACY
But if we hear him again, then what? What do we do?

John eases himself off the couch.

JOHN
We're gonna go upstairs before he's taken this time.

John paces in front of the couch. The he yells as loud as he can. Screaming for the pain of having lost Holland. Tracy stands and goes to him, hugs him.

The TV goes from static to a movie. The way they're standing, Tracy can see it. She steps from John, toward the TV.

TRACY
John…

But John is pacing, at the foot of the stage now.

TRACY
John!

John turns to look at her. She's sitting on the floor with her back to the couch again, wine glass in hand.

She's pointing at the TV, tears in her eyes.

JOHN
Tracy…

TRACY
John…it's the movie.

Confused, John looks to the TV.

JOHN
Oh my God.

Tracy nods. She pats the couch.

TRACY
Get your wine glass, John. Autumn Snow is on.

It is. On the TV, two men dressed in period piece attire confer in a garden.

JOHN
Tracy…I'm a little scared.

TRACY
That's okay, homey. So am I.

John looks up as thunder seems to shake the set.

He takes his place on the couch, sips his glass of wine.

TRACY
Jesus, John. I remember every line of this.

JOHN
So do I

TRACY
(piecing it together)
We were watching this movie.

JOHN
We had drinks in our hands.

TRACY
You…

Tracy gets to her knees, turns to face him.

TRACY
You used the bathroom.

John nods.

Tracy stands up.

TRACY
You gotta use the bathroom.

JOHN
There isn't one.

But Tracy's already rolling the easy chair to the left end of the stage.

TRACY
There, that's the toilet.

John nods.

JOHN
Okay.

TRACY
Okay, use the bathroom.

John gets up and sits in the easy chair.

Tracy walks back to the couch, gets on her knees with her back to it.

TRACY
And I watched the movie while you pissed…

(pauses)

Except…no. I didn't just watch the movie.

(pauses)

I went into the kitchen, first, alone, to look for food. But I…

She looks to the TV.

TRACY
I called out to you how bad the movie was.

(pauses for re-enactment)

John! This movie is junk!

JOHN
(from the toilet)
It's terrible!

Tracy gets up and rolls the door offstage, rolls the kitchen island back in. Rolls the cupboards in, too.

She pulls plates from the cupboard.

John enters.

TRACY
Honey, wanna do another shot?

John nods. They are re-enacting the exact conversation.

Thunder rolls.

Tracy pours two shots with the prop whiskey bottle.

They drink them fast. John grabs a plate.

JOHN
Wanna see something cool, Trace?

TRACY
Of course.

JOHN
It's a trick.

TRACY
Really?

(tearing up)

Amazing.

JOHN
Watch me…

(tearing up, too)

…Break this dish in half.

John throws it. The dish cracks against the stage.

Tracy grabs a plate.

TRACY
Oh? It's that kind of night?

She throws her plate, too.

Tracy cries harder. John lifts another plate to throw but they hear another creak above. They look up.

Then Tracy seems to have a revelation.

TRACY
Okay, wait. So we know it happened sometime between now and when we stopped watching the movie.

JOHN
(afraid)
How do we know it didn't already happen?

Tracy points up.

TRACY
Cause we heard the floor creaking seconds ago.

JOHN
That could have been the person who took him.

Tracy shakes her head no.

TRACY
I know Holland's creaks. That wasn't the other person. Not yet.

They go silent and look to the "ceiling."

JOHN
We need to strike this set. We need to set up the bedroom. Now.

TRACY
Wait. Wait.

John waits, but it doesn't look easy for him.

TRACY
Whoever took Holland didn't come in through the window.

JOHN
Come on. Let's do this. The bedroom~

Tracy shakes her head. Her face is torn between a smile and grueling realization.

TRACY
He may have gone out the window…but he didn't come in that way.

(pauses, redirects what she's saying)
I've never said that before.

JOHN
Said what?

TRACY
That I know Holland's creaks. But it's true, John. I do. I always have.

JOHN
I believe you. So…

Tracy steps out from behind the island, goes to John, takes him by the hands. She leads him to the foot of the staircase.

TRACY
I need you to remember now.

JOHN
That's all I'm doing. Remembering.

TRACY
After we broke the dishes… we went back to the movie. We gave it one more shot.

JOHN
(impatient)
Yes.

TRACY
And I was sitting like we were, my back to your legs.

JOHN
Yes. Come on.

TRACY
And I looked over my shoulder.

JOHN
Tracy, I can't remember—

TRACY
Yes. Yes you can. I looked over my shoulder, to the stairs. You looked, too.

John tries to remember.

TRACY
You said…'Does Holland wanna watch this bad movie, too?' That's what you said. John. Remember.

JOHN
I remember that. Yeah. Okay.

TRACY
It wasn't Holland on the stairs.

John looks to the phony stairs.

JOHN
You're telling me someone walked right up those steps? With us sitting right here?

TRACY
Yes. It wasn't Holland who made that noise. I know that now. It was someone else.

They hear a creaking. This one different than the one they've been hearing.

Without speaking, John runs to the bottom of the stairs. Tracy is steps behind him.

TRACY
Dress the bedroom. He's on his way up there now. Dress the bedroom!

They move fast, rolling the couch out of the room, pushing the bed all the way in.

The creaking continues. Heavy feet on old wooden steps. Thunder rolls.

They move the stairs, the lamps, the TV, and replace them with the desk, the dresser, the window, and, finally, the bedroom door.

The creaking continues.

JOHN
Tracy! The bed! Move the bed closer to the wall.

But Tracy's already doing it.

TRACY
There.

They pause, eyeing what they've done.

John looks to the bed. Squints at the pillows that are partly covered in shadow.

Thunder rolls.

TRACY
Okay. The living room, the movie, the dishes—

JOHN
The stairs, the bedroom, Holland.

TRACY
And so now…now…

Tracy looks to the bedroom door.

TRACY
…Now the person who took Holland should walk through that door. Right…

(pauses)

…now.

Silence.

Then…

The bedroom door opens.

The Director Duggan (40s, long overcoat) enters the set.

DUGGAN

(surprised)

What are you two doing? The first act is the living room.

Both stare at him, eyes wide, frozen.

DUGGAN

Either of you feel like explaining this?

JOHN

Duggan…

DUGGAN

Did you not read the program?

Tracy steps forward.

TRACY

Where'd you take him, Duggan?

Duggan looks from John to Tracy and back again.

DUGGAN

What…what are you talking about?

But something in his voice suggests he might know what they're talking about.

TRACY

You couldn't stand him on set. You couldn't stand him at all.

Duggan looks to the bed, to the open window, seems to take notice for the first time the storm coming through the speakers.

DUGGAN

What do you mean, Tracy?

John inches closer.

JOHN
You took Holland, Duggan.
What'd you do with him?

Duggan shakes his head.

DUGGAN
Have you two lost your
minds?

Tracy picks a piece of the broken dish off the stage as John inches closer to Duggan.

Then, from the shadows on the pillows on the bed…

HOLLAND
Mommy?

Tracy almost drops the piece of broken plate. John turns fast. But it's Duggan who actually rushes to the bed, looming tall over the boy under the blankets

DUGGAN
How?

John grabs Duggan, pinning his arms behind his back.

TRACY
Holland, look away.

Tracy slashes Duggan's throat with the broken plate.

Blood erupts.

John let's him fall limp to the floor.

Then…

HOLLAND
Can I look now?

Tracy and John rush to him. John gets to him first and lifts him from the bed.

The relief is palpable throughout the theater. Indescribable.

JOHN
Oh my God. Holland. Oh my God.

Tracy touches his face, his arms, his hands.

TRACY
Holland…

She looks to Duggan on the floor, looks to the bedroom door.

JOHN
We have to go. We have to take Holland and go.

TRACY
Wait.

JOHN
Tracy…

Tracy steps back into the bedroom, looks to Duggan.

TRACY
We have to strike this set.

JOHN
We have to go!

TRACY
We have to hide him.

JOHN
Where? There's nowhere…

But he seems to get what she means. He sets Holland down carefully on the floor. He kneels in front of him.

JOHN
Listen, buddy.

Tracy is already rolling items out of the bedroom.

JOHN
Mom and Dad need to dress a cellar.

Tracy rolls the bed offstage.

HOLLAND
Can I help?

Tracy comes to him, kneels, as John gets up and begins wheeling the dresser out.

TRACY
Yes. You can help. Tell us… tell Mom and Dad…what makes a cellar…a cellar?

Thunder rolls as Holland answers her, as Tracy stands up and leads Holland to the already half-vanished set of the bedroom.

THE END

Guest of Honor Interview

By Cecilia Dockins

CD: Your debut novel *Bird Box* was nominated for a 2014 Bram Stoker Award®. Since then, you've been nominated a total of four times. How does it feel to be a Guest of Honor this year? I mean, you're in great company with horror legends such as Kathe Koja and Robert McCammon.

JM: Just about everything that's happened since *Bird Box* was picked up by HarperCollins has had a layer of surreality to it. And then again, why not this book? Why not me? Why not you? If I'm going to espouse the ceiling-less capabilities of men and women (and I do) then it's up to me not to fall for the dreaded imposter syndrome. But I gotta say…it gets a little harder when Robert McCammon and Kathe Koja are on board. These two are giants, you know that, we all know that, and for great reason. I just read *Mine* recently and I'm thinking, "Shit man, okay, you up for this?" And Kathe is about as "high" as horror can go. Just brilliant, true artists who, like you and me, chose horror, either at some defined point or as a tracking for their entire careers, in which to tell their stories and we're all insanely richer for it. So, to say I'm honored almost feels silly. Do I feel some sense of having "arrived" for "sharing a stage" with them? Maybe. And why not? I would advise anybody else to feel that way and so maybe I should feel the same. But make no mistake, I will be observing all other guests of honor with eyes of awe, the whole convention long.

CD: What a terrific response and quite a humble one, too. You've mentioned in other interviews writing from a "free" place. How do you get in the "free" mindset? Is there any advice you would like to give artists struggling with their inner critics?

JM: I guess you could say I'm lucky that way. I made an actual decision when I started out to lock "creativity" in a safe room in my head. I'd heard enough stories of people beating themselves up to the point where they wouldn't even try to the stories they wanted to tell. That scared me deeply. Still does. I've understood from the start that it's gonna take an almost militant optimism to get all these books and stories and songs on paper. Because one of craziest parts about writing a book is maintaining the enthusiasm for the original idea. Meaning: it'll probably take you months to write the thing and somehow you gotta stay excited for that whole season or more. But when you really think about it...what's not to be excited about? Even if you write yourself into a corner, or discover you don't like what you're doing, all these things are still under the umbrella of writing in the first place... and what else would you rather be doing? What else comes with no self-doubt, no self-examination? And if everything, literally everything, we do involves riding an emotional roller coaster...why not choose writing? So, whenever I see trouble coming, I remind myself that I'd rather be doing what I'm doing, even struggling with what I'm doing, than just about anything else short of falling in love with Allison all over again. And if you don't feel that way, then maybe you're not a writer. And that's okay! I don't mean that in a mean way. I mean, people do what they love. If you love it, and you must, you'll do it. One other thing: don't wait for inspiration. Inspiration, to me, is a monster who stands outside your room, always on the verge of coming in but only so often actually doing it. The *inverse monster:* it horrifies you by not showing up. If you're working regular, day to day, eventually you won't be able to tell the difference between the days you were "inspired" and the ones you weren't.

You know, sometimes it's difficult for me to articulate these sentiments in the same way that it'd be hard for a kid to explain why he or she likes the summer. But I appreciate the chance. Thanks for the question.

CD: *Bird Box* is an unrelenting ride through a post-apocalyptic hellscape. My thoughts wandered back to Malorie long after I'd finished the last page. But out of all your novels, I have a particular fondness for your Weird Western, *Unbury Carol.* The concept of premature burial is so frightening. If you suffered the same condition as Carol Evers and was buried alive, excluding all communication devices (cellphone, bells, flares, etc.), what one object would you choose to keep you company in the endless dark?

JM: What a question. First off, thank you for the good words about *Unbury Carol.* Means the world. And so, what object, what object...

I think I'd ask for the hand of someone who had also been buried alive. Yes, I'd ask for the severed hand of someone who had to go through it as well. That way I could hold that person's hand and while my fate would not look good, I'd be able to tell myself to quit complaining, that this had happened to others before, and to try everything I could to make it a noble end. I'd also consider a bomb. Explode out of the grave? Probably not the safest route.

CD: Cemetery Dance Publications will be releasing your newest novel *On This, the Day of the Pig* Halloween 2018. What can you tell us about the book?

JM: *On This, the Day of the Pig* is a story about an animal who has taken a quantum leap, whose intelligence far surpasses his penmates. Thing is, his mind surpasses ours, too, only he doesn't entirely understand that yet. What he does understand is that he can control the farmer, the farmer's family, and, eventually, the entire town, as they come to the pigpen, one by one, with a mind to slaughter this pig who is rumored to have psychic abilities. Imagine a pig with a mind like a spider's web, and the townsfolk who get stuck in it. I cannot wait for this one to come out. It's my family's favorite of mine. They ask me about it all the time, when's it coming out? What's the cover like? I'll include the cover here for you. Done by a friend in town named Slasher Dave. I think the book has a lot of good energy, the right kind, as I had the time of my life writing it, not caring if it got out of my control, intentionally letting it fall to pieces, pick itself up again. My father's friend read Pig alone in a cabin in northern Michigan. She seems mad at me for it.

CD: In your opinion, what are three elements every "good" horror story must have?

JM: Hard one for me to answer because I'm out here pining for elements I've never seen before. I realize that sounds either 1) impossible or 2) a lofty thing to say. But the truth is, for me, the scariest movies and novels I've read are the ones where I'm asking myself *who made this?* It's as if the fear of the unknown can stretch beyond the screen or the page and actually occupy the space of the creator him or herself. *The unknown artist.* Or maniac! Perhaps maniac. I think that's why a lot of first-time filmmakers make the scariest movies. Cause we don't recognize their style. But if I was pressed to come up with an element that I love to see in a novel, it's the fear the author feels, him or herself. I want the author to be scared of what they're writing. Blah blah someone who is "in control" of the journey. I get the willies when I sense the author was as scared hearing the story (in their imagination first, I suppose) as I am reading it on the page.

CD: What are you working on now?

JM: Working on a new book, a couple feature scripts, a couple smaller scripts. I'm considering making a serialized audio cast of an eleven-hundred-page book I just wrapped. I don't see, right now, when it could come out, and so why not release it in its own odd way? My book *Inspection* comes out in April on Del Rey. This one is special to me, means a great deal, and I just can't wait to hear what people think. I'm also working on a story for Ellen Datlow, something that (if I can pull this off) will be an honor of a lifetime for me.

Cecilia Dockins, a native Tennessean, grew up fishing in the creeks and rivers deep in the backwoods of her hometown. She earned her B.A. in English from Middle Tennessee State University in 2010 and is a graduate of the Odyssey Writing Workshop.

She has passed instruments in surgical suites and slung drinks in bars. Currently, she reads for *Pseudopod* as an associate editor. When not writing, she spends her free time digging through decaying boxes at local bookstores or the occasional barn for the forgotten, the lost, and the bizarre.

congratulates
our 2018
Lifetime
Achievement
Award
winner

GRAHAM
MASTERTON

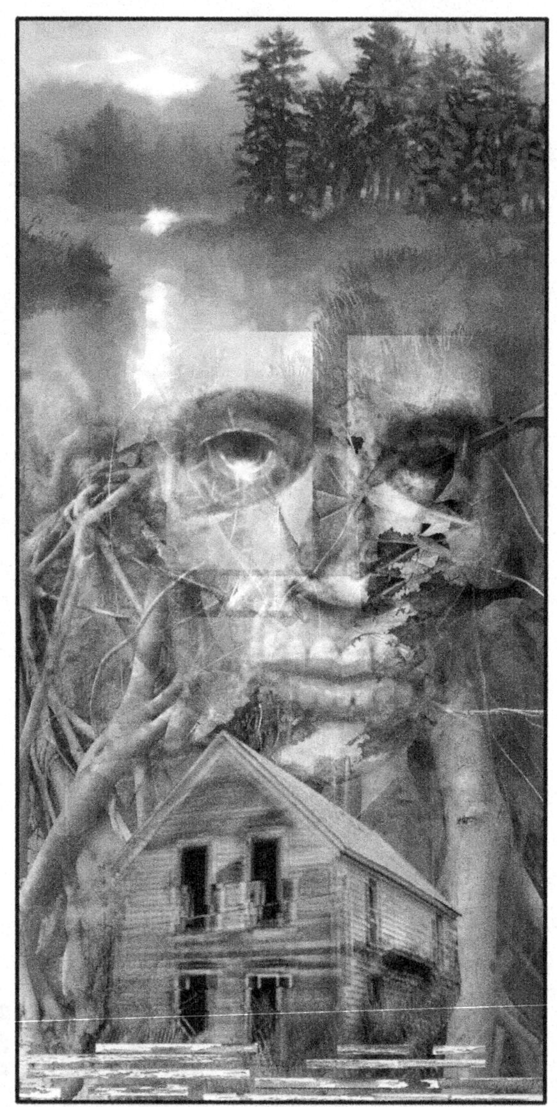

Robert McCammon

Guest of Honor

In the 1980s, as horror exploded in popularity and books featuring glowing eyes and demonic children crammed supermarket paperback racks, critics and fans alike often talked about the genre's three primary practitioners: Stephen King, Peter Straub, and Robert McCammon. A one-time journalist who grew up in the south during the era of civil rights activism, McCammon produced a string of popular novels beginning with *Baal* in 1978; he explored ancient cults next with *Bethany's Sin* (1980), vampires with *They Thirst* (1981), the legacy of Poe's most famous family with *Usher's Passing* (1984), a post-apocalyptic world in *Swan Song*, and werewolves in *The Wolf's Hour* (1989). He took horror seriously enough that in 1985 he co-founded (with Joe and Karen Lansdale) the Horror Writers of America (later the Horror Writers Association), and he was one of the first recipients of the organization's Bram Stoker Award® (he won b
th the first short fiction award for his story "The Deep End" and the first novel trophy for *Swan Song;* later, he edited HWA's first anthology, *Under the Fang*. In 1991, he released what many consider his best book—the coming-of-age tale *A Boy's Life*. He is a recipient of HWA's Lifetime Achievement Award, and his forthcoming releases include *The Listener* and *He'll Come Knocking at Your Door*.

Death Of A Hunter

A Story by Robert McCammon

(Reprinted from *The Hunter From the Woods,* published by Subterranean Press in 2011)

When he found the gray wolf dead with its throat cut and its eyes gouged out, Michael Gallatin knew they had come for him.

He sat in a brown leather chair in the front room of his house, which had once been a church and was to him still a holy place of solitude and reflection. The structure was made of dark red stones chinked together with white mortar. It had a narrow tower topped with a white spire and a walkway around it. Up in the tower were panes of stained glass colored crimson and dark blue.

Darkness was gathering outside, across the dense Welsh forest that shielded Michael Gallatin's home from the rest of the world. It was the eleventh day of July in the year 1958. He was listening to Ralph Vaughan Williams' The Lark Ascending on his record player. He knew that when the music was over and full darkness had fallen, he would get up from this chair in which he'd sat so many times, listening to music or reading before a polite fire, and he would go out to meet them.

Because they had come for him. And he doubted if he would ever return to this house the same as he'd left it, if he returned at all.

They were professionals. They were killers of the highest order. How many there would be, awaiting him out in the night-black forest, he didn't know. But they had executed one of his wolves—one of his companions—and he knew that if he did not go out to meet them tonight another wolf would die in his place. They wouldn't stop until all his companions were dead, murdered by the fast blade and then mutilated by some brutal Oriental instrument, and he could not—would not—allow that to happen.

So he sat in the company of the music, waiting for the dark.

He wore black shoes with soft soles, gray trousers and a dark blue cotton shirt.

The air was warm outside, unseasonably warm even for the middle of summer in Wales. The hunter's moon would be shaped like a scythe tonight, perfect for cutting down old things that no longer had much use in this world.

He was a hard-used forty-eight years old. His thick hair had turned fully gray on the sides, with a small thatch of gray at the front. His face was still ruggedly handsome and his eyes were still luminously green, yet he knew how slow he'd become. He knew the onset of age. He knew what had been and what was to be, if he lived through this night. He was not the man he used to be, nor for that matter the wolf.

He thought of getting up and pouring himself a glass of Talisker, his favorite brand of Scotch whisky from the isle of Skye, but he decided against that. It had the salt taste of the sea in it, which he so enjoyed. One drink would be a pleasure, but one drink might give the killers a further advantage. No, if he lived through this night he would drink a toast to his miraculous survival at the dawn. But he doubted very seriously if he would ever taste Talisker again.

His left shoulder had been bothering him today. The shoulder he'd broken in the crash of a Westland Lysander aircraft in the North African desert in 1941. It was stiff and altogether unyielding to his will. His right leg today was also a traitor; it had been snapped in two places as he was caught in an avalanche on Monte Leone in 1952, when he'd been on the trail of the infamous professor of murder Dr. Shatterhand and his doxy of death Sabrina Neve. He had a headache that came and went, the nagging reminder of many fists, blackjacks and other items intended to knock his brains out. It was a wonder he still had any brains left at all.

He checked his Rolex. On the table next to him was a glass case that held a Breitling wristwatch with a plain brown leather band. He kept the watch working, though he never wore it. The watch was not his to wear.

The music ended, on its soft high lingering note.

He stood up. The darkness outside was almost complete. He took off the Rolex, took off his shoes, took off his socks, took off his trousers and underwear and shirt. He went out the door into the summer night, and drawing a long breath of fragrant pines and green moss he thought he might never come home again.

But he was certain he was going to kill at least one of them tonight. He would not go easy. He would not go without demanding a price be paid.

Opening the soul cage was more difficult than it used to be. The hinges creaked a little. The wolf balked, wanting to stay comfortable. It came when it was beckoned and it answered its call, but it was an older wolf, a slower wolf, and it had become a little bit hesitant of the pain of change.

Because the pain was the one thing that had not diminished. If anything, the pain had increased by many times. It was a hard birth for the wolf now, and a hard rebirth back to Michael Gallatin the man. Older bones for both wolf and man made the change slower, in each direction. The pain was exquisite. The pain that brought the scents, sounds, colors and forms in an explosion upon the senses unknown to ordinary men was almost too much to bear.

Almost...but then there always came the power, and though that had also diminished it was still the alpha and omega of the wolf, and it was still worth the journey from man to beast and back again.

He walked past his dark green Range Rover. He changed, as he stood in front of his church. He changed, in the dark with the yellow scythe of the moon hanging amid the clouds. He changed under a million million stars. Maybe he shuddered in pain and shed a few tears, but he changed.

He had never asked for this. Had never dreamed of it, when as an eight-year-old boy in Russia he'd followed a drifting white kite into a forest just like the one here in Wales he was about to penetrate. He'd never asked for this; it had been thrust upon him, whether he'd wanted it or not.

And now, as he contorted into a green-eyed wolf with more gray hair than black on its flanks and a certain injured stiffness in its stride, he thought how all these many years he had not been a hunter from the woods so much as he'd been a wanderer in the wilderness. It was the fate of all humans to wander in a wilderness, some made for them by others, some made by themselves. And the wilderness could be all of life, from beginning to end. A trackless wilderness that held no reference points nor easy places of rest. It was a place of hard demands and no acceptance of mistakes. It was a place that whittled a man of action down to a sleeper in a brown leather chair on a Sunday afternoon. And it was a place that could be so terribly lonely that the heart broke into a thousand pieces at the merest memory of a woman's name and her touch in the night.

Michael could not go there. Not to that place. So he put his wolfen head down, and his wolfen body propelled itself forward, and though the old aches and agonies whispered through him and wanted to slow him down he loped onward into the woods, nearly soundlessly, his eyes seeking movement in the tangles of trees and folds of vegetation. They were here. They were close. Tonight there would be death.

Death had always been at his shoulder. It had always been leering at him, in the faces of many enemies. As he ran, searching, he thought of his trial by fire on the Caribbean island of Augustin Mireaux, the industrialist who had sold his soul and his nuclear missile plans to the Red Chinese. He thought of his battle against the drug-created assassin known as Chameleon that had begun in Paris, moved to Rio de Janeiro and ended in the Amazon jungle. He thought of his narrow escape with Aurore Bardot from Edward Wintergarden's sinking submarine under the polar ice. He recalled Simon Tollemache's barracuda pool, and the bloody massacre on the golf course at St. Andrews. He remembered Tragg, the killer with hypnotic eyes and two-tone shoes. He could trace in his memory every step through the deadly funhouse of Phaninath Po. All those and more remained in his head, though some he fervently wished he might forget. He wished he might forget about the Ginshi Kazoku—the Family of the Silver Thread—and the murder of the man he'd known as Mallory, but he could not.

This was why he was a hunter tonight. This was why he was ready to die, if he could kill at least one of them.

He loped onward at an easy pace, tasting the air for humans.

These killers were careful. They were using an odor mask, which could be as simple as pine soap or as complex as a homeopathic drug. The Family of the Silver Thread was famous for its creation of exotic pharmaceuticals useful to the criminal underworld, as well as for its international trade in weapons and military secrets. It was said that the Silver Thread was woven through thousands of tapestries in dozens of countries, and trying to remove such a global intertwining of interests based on money and power was impossible and for the most part fatal.

Last year Michael had succeeded in small part, by crippling a faction of the Silver Thread in Hong Kong. One of their weapons warehouses had gone up with an earsplitting bang, a courier with a large suitcase full of money had found himself staring at a set of fangs just before they seized his throat, and the floating mansion of the jet-setting newspaper mogul and Silver Thread leader Anthony Tong had been sunk to the bottom of the bay with Tong's body along as fishfood.

Something jumped in the brush as he approached. A rabbit, running for its life. It didn't get very far before one of the other wolves emerged from the night to pounce on it, tear it to pieces and eat.

Michael went on, slinking close to the earth. There were many other wolves here. Real wolves, not questionable miracles such as himself. They came, stayed as long as they pleased, and then drifted away again. A few ran with him on a regular basis and seemed to see themselves as his 'pack' and he the alpha. Two days ago a new wolf had appeared in an area Michael thought of as the Four Brothers, which was a sloping meadow that held four huge granite boulders. The new wolf, coal black and smelling of maleness, had been lying up on one of the stones basking in the bright sunshine. When it saw him it sat upright, perhaps also recognizing the large black wolf with gray sides as the ruler of this domain. Michael noted that this new male had the rarity of ice-blue eyes, and the commanding way it held itself made him wonder if he wasn't going to have to put up a fight to keep his kingdom.

Getting old was a bitch.

Michael suddenly stopped on his prowl through the woods. He had sensed something: a slow movement, a gliding from one patch of pure dark to another, a tensing of muscle before an action. He wasn't sure what it was, but it was there. An owl hooted distantly and another answered. The noise of the night's insects was a low susurrus.

He waited, all his senses on high alert.

When Valentine Vivian had retired six years ago to his estate in Wessex and begun writing paperback spy novels that no reader on earth could take seriously, a new hale and hearty boy had taken the reins of Special Operations. This one was straight out of Oxford, he wore natty tweeds and a regimental tie of the Royal Green Jackets, and he smoked a meerschaum pipe like a whorehouse chimney burning buggy bedsheets.

This new boy, by the name of Cordwainer, greeted Michael Gallatin one day in his office with the brusque statement I understand you're quite the hero. Only at that early point Cordwainer had understood nothing. After a summoning to Valentine Vivian's estate where the master of suspense interrupted his latest epic to inform Cordwainer of things that Cordwainer needed to know, from that point on Cordwainer had declined to have Michael anywhere near his office and peered around corners to make sure the hero wasn't lurking in the shadow of the potted ficus tree.

Michael began moving again through the Welsh woods. Slowly… slowly…inch by inch. His left shoulder protested this movement, and his right hind leg felt on the verge of a cramp. His eyes ticked back and forth, measuring space and darkness and distance. His nose sniffed, searching the air. His ears were up, twitching.

After the scene in Hong Kong, Mallory had come to visit Michael in Wales. It seemed to Michael that Mallory had always looked like an elderly man, but maybe part of it had been stagecraft because Mallory in his dark blue suit and with his white hair combed and parted looked not much older to him than the day they'd sat drinking Guinness at a North African airstrip sixteen years before. Mallory had to be in his late seventies by now, yet perhaps he had against all odds retained the soul and spirit of a hale and hearty boy.

Valentine Vivian had been the head of Special Operations. Cordwainer What'sHisName was currently the head of Special Operations. But Michael knew that this man sitting in his den, smoking a black briar pipe, was Special Operations, and it was a lifelong position.

The word, Mallory confided, was that the Silver Thread had taken photographs with a long-lensed Leica. That Michael had been trailed by their professionals and the pictures snapped at an unfortunate moment.

Michael had known what he meant. The Family of the Silver Thread had photographic proof of him changing from man to wolf, or back again.

Be very, very careful, Mallory had told him. They may want your skin, or your heart, or your head. Or they may want all of you. So be very, very careful.

But not more than a month later, it was Mallory who had not been careful enough. Missing for more than a week, he was found in the trunk of an abandoned taxi in an East London junkyard with his throat cut and his eyes gouged out. Valentine Vivian hired a small army of bodyguards and went on an author's tour of America, his author's name being Evelyn Tedford, and Cordwainer the new boy bought an attack dog to patrol his recently-acquired electric fence.

Had something moved, or not?

Michael got still. He heard the owl hooting again, and another answering. It came to him that just possibly they were not owls after all.

The night hung on the edge of violence.

There was this hero thing, Michael had often thought in less troubled times. This concept of the man of action. After all this time, he realized Rolfe Gantt had been right. Everyone loved the hero, but the hero walked alone. It was the nature of the hero, to be solitary. To live life on his own terms, and in his own time. To be neither rushed nor to rush toward oblivion, yet oblivion would claim the hero just as it claimed every ordinary man. And love? Ah, that. Love.

What woman was it who could truly love the hero? Oh, they might wish to brush against the heroic flesh, or to have some fling in the heroic bed and make for themselves some memory of a heroic night, but love? No. When the chips were down and the night was cold, it was the ordinary man who won the heart. The man of meat-and-potatoes, the man who stayed fixed in place, the man who saw his destiny and future in a family, the man to whom wife and daughter or son transformed life into a hero's dream.

But such was not to be, for a hunter from the woods.

The death of a hunter loomed large in Michael's mind on this night, as it did on many nights. He was old and he was tired. He was hurting and he was slow. What was ahead for this hunter, who had already given everything? There was only one thing left to give: his life, in exchange for transfiguration from what was to what will be, as the lark ascends into the heavens and the last soft note fades slowly out.

But it was not a soft note he suddenly heard, that made his wolf-bones jump and his green eyes widen.

It was an explosion that cracked across the forest and echoed from every rock in the meadow of Four Brothers.

It was, he realized, the sound of his house being destroyed.

Several explosions followed the first. He saw the leap of fire through the trees and smelled the bitter tang of gunpowder in the concussive wind. They had blown his church to pieces so he might not find sanctuary there. They wanted him out in the open. They wanted him to know fear, because they moved as silently and swiftly as any wolves in the dark.

And then a shadow shifted before him, very near, and the black arrow from the black bow fired by the ninja in black came at him with a serpent's hiss.

Even as he twisted his body to escape, Michael Gallatin knew the arrow would find its mark.

It did. It hit him on the right side. Its soft plastic tip, about the size of a ripe fig, burst open on contact. It splashed and streaked his gray hair with the bright green glow of chemical phosphorescence. He was well and truly marked.

The ninja moved again, in a blur. A gloved hand opened and closed.

A net of some fine and pliable metal caught moonlight as it bloomed in the air. It sailed toward the lycanthrope, expanding as it came. Michael saw the fallen tree to his left and the narrow space between it and the earth. He flung himself into the opening, his claws digging into the ground for traction. The net hit the tree above him, snagged on its stubs of dead branches, and the wolf pulled in his breath to flatten his ribcage and scrabbled under the trunk. Then he quickly turned to face his attacker. With a running start he took a powerful leap, pushed off with his hind legs against the treetrunk and fell upon the ninja.

It was not to be so simple. The ninja retreated. With incredible speed that turned the wolf's leap into a slow-motion exercise, the assassin threw up a roundhouse kick that got Michael in the belly. As the wolf's body twisted again, this time in pain, the ninja got his balance and drove a rock-knuckled fist into the center of the chest. He was gone as Michael crashed into the underbrush.

Michael drew a wounded breath and righted himself. He saw the ninja moving through the foliage on his left. With an instant's pause to calculate distance and speed he took off in pursuit. The ninja was fast and he was nimble, but this was the wolf's world. Michael caught the killer's right ankle between his teeth and crushed it. The ninja suffered in silence, but would not go down; he gave a one-legged leap toward the nearest tree and began to climb it, using what Michael thought must be small metal pitons embedded in his bootsoles. Michael leaped up, caught the man's left ankle and dragged him down. The ninja whirled around and like a cornered animal fought with everything he had: fists to the skull, a knee to the muzzle, stiffened fingers thrusting toward the eyes and the edge of the hand chopping for the throat. They did their deadly dance in silence, as flames crackled from the werewolf's church and red sparks whirled to heaven.

Michael took a blow to the side of the head that made him whuff with pain. He dodged a strike meant to blind him. Then in a split-second calculation his animal instinct determined where the fist would be next and his jaws were there waiting for it. He crunched the fingers and torn human flesh to shreds. Blood sprayed into the air. The ninja gave a quiet noise not unlike a sigh of resignation.

His remaining hand came at Michael with a slim-bladed knife in it and plunged the blade into the wolf's left shoulder.

But Michael had his bloodlust at full charge now and the sharp bite of Japanese steel would not turn him aside. When the ninja withdrew the knife to strike again, the wolf gripped his arm at the elbow and with a ferocious thrash broke the bones and nearly tore the limb from its socket. The knife flew away from dead fingers. Michael seized the throat and ripped it open from ear-to-ear. A glistening black flood washed over his muzzle. Then something gave a small pop on the ground next to him and smoke welled up into his face. His eyes stung. He smelled an odor of bitter almonds. His lungs hitched and his heart was racing. He held his breath, even as the second gas grenade exploded behind him. A second ninja had joined the battle.

Michael let the first one slither to the earth and then he turned and ran. At full speed, or whatever speed he could manage. A third grenade popped to his right, spewing a noxious cloud. He squeezed his eyes shut and ran blindly. Even a half-breath of the stuff was strong enough to nearly knock him senseless. He thought this was how they must have subdued his companion, then slashed the throat and taken the eyes. Maybe the gas had worked its will on Mallory, too. He began to feel his usually innate sense of direction betraying him; where was he, and where was he going? He crashed through a thicket and fell through thorns and down an embankment into a hollow where a pool of water smelled green. He plunged his head into the pool and opened his eyes to wash them out. Then he shook his head to clear it as best he could and lapped up water with a tongue that felt burned.

He stood breathing hard through swollen lungs, his heart pounding. He saw the woods through a drugged mist. When he tried to move, he staggered. Wait, he told himself. He kept breathing, deeply and slowly. Maybe he could get his heartbeat regulated. He listened to the night and for the things that stalked in the night. How many ninjas there were, he had no way of knowing. He was going to have to get out of this hollow before they found him here, dazed and confused. And go where? he asked himself.

There was only one answer.

Go back to what had taken him to Octavius Zloy's trailer in the dead of night. Go back to what had brought him out of the ruined church in the Russian village, when he'd seen Valentine Vivian being carried away by men with guns. Go back to what had made him ask Paul Wesshauser if he could make a torpedo. Go back to facing Rolfe Gantt's pistol and saying he would let no man tell him what to do on the last day of his life. Go back to telling the Gestapo's Ice Man to take his hand off Franziska Luxe's arm.

Go back to being a man, even if he wore a wolf's clothing. Go back to the fight.

Always, always…go back to the fight.

Michael Gallatin climbed up the embankment, pushed through the thorns and the thicket, and he was very much aware that his phosphorescent glow would bring them coming now, at any minute.

He was ready to kill, and he was ready to die. But he would go out as he had lived, and no fear would cripple his cause.

A wind moved through the trees. It stirred the new leaves on the old branches. It was the zenith of summer, and looking up at the scythe of the moon Michael opened his mouth and howled for what life had meant to him. For the joy of it, and yes for the sorrows too. All were important, in the grand scheme of things. He had not chosen this path. It had chosen him. But he thought—he hoped—he had walked it well and with honor, as both wolf and man.

They fell upon him from the dark.

There were two. One whirled a chain around Michael's throat and tightened it so hard the blood thundered in his head. The second had a baton in one hand and a net in the other, and Michael realized they meant not to kill him but to trap him. To take him on a drugged journey and place him before the Family of the Silver Thread, whose scientists would like to know what little boys who became wolves were made of.

Michael turned toward his attackers. With a snarl and show of fangs that would have dropped any ordinary man to his knees, Michael first lunged toward the ninja who chained him. He got a kick to the muzzle from a man who was as quick as a cobra, but Michael was not stopped nor was he slowed. He hit the ninja with all the power he had and slammed the man's back against a tree. Then lifting up on his hind legs and pinning the ninja with his forepaws he tore into the masked face as one would scoop the flesh from an exotic fruit. He saw the wet terror in the man's eyes as fangs tore meat and muscle away from bone, and in a frenzy of killing Michael shivered to his animal core. He enjoyed it.

The chain loosened. Michael pulled it free from the ninja's hand. The thing in front of him had no lower jaw but it was trying to scream. Something stabbed him on the left side. In the next instant he was lifted off his hind legs and thrown to the ground and he smelled the ozone of the electric shock after the searing pain had ripped through him. He struggled up to his knees, his muzzle dripping blood and his eyes full of red fire. He realized he was connected on the right side by a pair of wires to the baton in the remaining ninja's grip.

A finger moved, a spark jumped, and the current delivered agony to Michael Gallatin.

As the shock tortured him, he changed back and forth. From wolf to man and back again, an involuntary reaction to the electricity. He fell again to his side, in wolf form, and tried to get up again but once more the finger moved and the current obeyed and the electrical shock coursed through his body in waves that took him from wolf to man and man to wolf in a matter of seconds. His mind felt blasted; he had no sense of abrupt change, but rather that he had always been both wolf and man at the same time all his life and he had never known it.

He told himself to get up. To keep fighting. He reached for the wires to yank their hooks out of his flesh.

But the next long and terrible shock told him to stay down, and to give up.

He lay as a man, weak and naked and bleeding. His strength was gone. He watched as the ninja came forward to throw the net, and then maybe there would be another gas grenade or a blow to the head and Michael Gallatin knew his freedom would be over.

The death of a hunter, he thought in his suffering and near-delirium. He tried to change back to his more powerful form. He couldn't open the soul cage. Not this time. The wolf was paralyzed by shock, and the door of the soul cage was sealed shut.

The ninja came forward, a graceful evil.

He never reached his destination.

For in the next instant a coal black wolf sprang at him from the side, and bearing him down to the earth it planted its paws upon his chest and took his throat between its jaws and with an explosion of power nearly ripped the head from the neck. Then it cracked the ninja's breastbone like an eggshell and winnowed its muzzle in and plucked out the still-beating heart. It turned its head to show Michael Gallatin the prize, and Michael saw that the black wolf's eyes were ice-blue.

The wolf ate the ninja's heart.

It licked the last of the blood from around its mouth.

Then it stood up on its hind legs, and with a shiver of anticipation it began to change.

As the black hair disappeared into white flesh, as the bones remade themselves and the spine drew its tail inward, as the ears became human and the face began to compose itself, the man walked toward Michael. He stood about two inches over six feet and he had a narrow-waisted body with wide strong shoulders. He moved with confidence, and Michael thought there was some arrogance in there as well. Fully revealed, the man was maybe in his mid-thirties, with thick black hair that tumbled over his forehead. He had a handsome, intelligent face with high cheekbones and the elegant nose of a lost aristocrat. A Russian face, Michael thought. The man's intense blue eyes remained fixed on Michael, even as he knelt down and pulled the hooks out from Michael's phosphorescent-streaked side.

Michael just stared in amazement at this walking miracle. But he realized he recognized the eyes. With a start, he remembered whose they were.

The younger man spoke with a distinctive Russian accent. A warmth came up in his eyes that melted all the ice away.

"My name is Peter," he said.

And he added, "I think you are my father."

Guest of Honor Interview

The One Real Terror I Have

By Kevin J. Wetmore, Jr.

For any horror fan, Robert McCammon (Rick to his friends), needs no introduction. But here is one anyway, as it is useful to remind ourselves exactly how much he has contributed to our field and our organization. In a sixteen year span, from 1978 to 1993, he published a dozen novels, including some of the best horror of the period: *Swan Song, Stinger, The Wolf's Hour, They Thirst, Mine, Boy's Life* and *Gone South*, among others, not to mention a short story collection (*Blue World*) and a number of uncollected stories. He has explored traditional monsters and genre tropes and reinvented them, making them his own. Vampires? Check. Werewolves? Check. Aliens? Check. End of the world? Check. Psychopaths? Check. Scary cults? Check. The man knows horror and how to write it.

After a hiatus from the world of publishing (more on that below), McCammon returned with *Speaks the Nightbird*, a new novel heralding a series of novels set in colonial America, the most recent of which, *Cardinal Black,* seventh in the series, will have been released by the time you read this. He began a second series of novels in 2013 with *I Travel By Night*, featuring Trevor Lawson, Confederate veteran, gentleman adventurer and vampire. The stories concerning Michael Gallatin, the werewolf spy from *The Wolf's Hour* were gathered in 2011 in *The Hunter from the Woods.* Other novels have appeared regularly over the past half-decade: *The Five* (2013), *The Border* (2015) and *The Listener* (2018), all demonstrating his skills as a storyteller and his virtuosity at moving through period and genre, blending them to create compelling and insightful tales.

His work has been recognized with five Stoker Awards (including both Novel and Short Story for *Swan Song* and "The Deep End" in 1987, then novel twice more—for *Mine* (1990) and *Boy's Life* (1991)—and short story for "Eat Me" (1989), with another three nominations. He also received the 2012 Bram Stoker Lifetime Achievement Award and the 2008 Grand Master Award from the World Horror Convention. He also edited *Under the Fang,* the first HWA anthology, in 1991. McCammon's name is synonymous with genre-bending and genre-blending horror. It was my honor to be able to email back and forth with him in conversation, edited below for clarity and flow.

KJW: Hello, Robert. Well, let's start with: where does that storytelling impulse come from and why horror?

RM: I think a writer is born…and of course has to develop, but I think that for whatever reason the desire to both read or hear stories and later to create them is there from birth. I wish I knew a more definite answer to that particular mystery of why a person becomes (and is born with that initial ability to become) a writer, but I don't. The same is true of whatever "type" of story the writer wants to create…another mystery, though I will say for myself that I was always drawn to the supernatural or what used to be termed "the weird". Why? I guess there are psychological reasons, but they're beyond me to explain.

KJW: What should a reader expect from a "Robert McCammon novel"? Is there even such a thing, given how much you bend genre and initially switched from genre to genre in your writing in the eighties and nineties?

RM: I've never thought about what a "Robert McCammon" novel would be defined as. I certainly didn't want to be stuck in any particular genre, but the publishing business being what it is it's going to happen whether you like it or not. That's just the business mindset. But I hope that what comes through mostly in my work is my affection for my characters and the feeling that they're real people…without that, I think any story would fall flat. The reader has to first and foremost care for the people they're reading about.

KJW: Your work in the last century—*Swan Song, Stinger, Mine,* or *Gone South*, for instance—was often set in the then present or the recent past—*The Wolf's Hour* in the 1940s, *Boy's Life* in the 1960s, for example. Your work this century has been at a distance from the present. The Matthew Corbett stories in early colonial America, the Trevor Lawson stories in post-Civil War America, and most recently *The Listener* in the Great Depression are all historical fiction. Why the shift and what are the challenges of writing horror fiction in the more distant past?

RM: It wasn't a conscious shift, it was just that I had story ideas that had to be set in those earlier time periods or they wouldn't work. I enjoy reading history and doing historical research, but you can get bogged down in research and you have to know how much to use and what to discard. That's just something you learn as you go along…and again, a lot of this is just what I would call "gut instinct". I'm the first one to know if something works and it feels real or if it doesn't.

KJW: You edited the first HWA anthology, *Under the Fang*—where did the impetus for that volume come from, how was the experience of editing it and might you ever be tempted to edit another anthology of other writers' work?

RM: I was asked to do that to help what was then the fledgling HWA. And no I definitely would not do that again. It was not fun, simply for the reason that I was placed in the position of "editing" other writers who had much more experience than I did at the time, and I'm not enough of a diplomat and certainly not a good enough editor to ever want to repeat that. So…NO!

KJW: Speaking of short story collections, I am a huge fan of *Blue World* and first encountered your work back in *Twilight Zone*. More recently, *The Hunter from the Woods* collects the Michael Gallatin stories. Since BW you have published several more uncollected stories. You also mentioned in an interview that you were thinking about compiling a collection of Matthew Corbett "shorts"—brief stories about his smaller investigations similar to *Hunter*. Might a McCammon anthology be something we might see anytime soon?

RM: Oh I loved doing *The Hunter from the Woods* because each story was "fast in and fast out." I didn't have to spend a lot of time and mental friction creating my lead character, and it was great fun to chart Michael Gallatin's progression from youth to older age. And yeah I'm thinking about doing a similar thing for Matthew Corbett's investigations that are asides from his conflict with Professor Fell. Actually, Matthew's world is interesting (and the book may well be titled *Matthew's World*) because I've created so many leading characters in those books that I can use any of them in a short story or novella…Hudson Greathouse, Minx Cutter, Katherine Herrald, and more to come, so it really is like the creation of a world with overlapping characters and situations.

KJW: What is your writing process? For example, how do you get from first idea to *The Listener* on the bookstore shelf?

RM: Think about the whole concept, put pressure on the idea to see if it falls apart anywhere, then mark out a few signpost scenes at beginning, middle and end (which may change according to what the characters want to do and how the novel starts to take shape) and then go to work. I'm not a very efficient worker, though. I start out fairly slowly, feeling my way along, and then the last two months I'm pulling all-nighters and grinding myself into a paste.

KJW: Despite your earliest work not being set in the American South, since then you have embraced the region as setting for much of your fiction. Do you consider yourself a Southern writer?1

RM: A Southern writer? Maybe, because I know the landscape and the people pretty well, but I don't like to be constrained by that title.

KJW: Fair enough. What writers do you read to scare yourself?

RM: You know, I'm not scared by anything anymore. And I didn't really become a writer to scare people…I became a writer because I had that desire to tell stories, and I never really thought about fitting into any particular genre or regional title.

KJW: What work of yours do you hear most about or are asked most about by readers and fans?

RM: *Swan Song, Boy's Life* and *Speaks The Nightbird.* I have heard of people being buried with copies of *Boy's Life* in their coffins. Once in a while I get surprised by something, like a lady who's read *The Wolf's Hour* thirty times, or a fan of *Mine* who has read it over and over until the book fell apart. Also once in a while I hear raves about *Gone South* by readers who've just discovered it. All good!

KJW: *Freedom of the Mask* was the sixth of nine proposed Corbett novels. *Cardinal Black* will be out (and devoured by folks like me) by the time this is published. Two left. What might we expect and why only nine? When did you decide on that number and is this a "Repairman Jack" scenario (with a nod of the head and apologies to F. Paul Wilson), where after the last book in the series, prequels and other stories outside the main narrative may occasionally be found?

RM: It was going to be ten with a break in the middle for a book of Matthew short stories and novellas (like the above *Matthew's World*) but I decided it would take too long for it to come out and readers might get upset that they had to wait for long for the next novel, so the number became nine. And the way it worked out, nine is what I need to tell the whole story arc…no less, but certainly no more.

KJW: What are you working on now? What projects appeal to you? What makes you think, "yeah—that's an idea I want to develop"?

RM: I'm finishing up the Matthew Corbett series. Two more books to go, then I want to write a book I've been thinking about for many years. Beyond that, who knows?

KJW: It's 2018 - let's talk politics. In your more recent novels T*he Listener* and *River of Souls*, race in America is a key theme. Both are historical narratives set in, shall we say, less enlightened times, but with characters who have somewhat progressive attitudes towards race. One of the markers of villainy in each novel, in fact, is angry, overt racism. We see that in some of the stories in *The Hunter in the Woods* as well. It seems prescient in these narratives that race in America would begin to dominate the discussion in the second decade of the twenty-first century. Is this a conscious theme emerging in your work? Given that these three narratives represent the eighteenth century and the early twentieth century, do you see racism as an ongoing American horror of sorts?

RM: I think a lot of these issues simply come upon you when you're writing (particularly historical work) without your planning on dealing with them from the start. At least that's true in my case. Really…what more can be said about racism without illustrating an example of it? In *The Listener,* it's just "the truth" as it was in that era, and Curtis has to face it on a day-to-day basis. As a matter of fact, it's just part of his life and he's come to accept it. Within the train terminal it's a matter of ugly words and attitudes…however, once he gets on that dark road and is come upon by the group of angry young white men it becomes a matter of life-and-death. The darkness and isolation of the road has a lot to do with it, as the darkness and isolation hid (and fostered) much of the racism and horrible violence of that era.

Will racism ever be completely overcome? Probably not, because the issue is so complex and multi-layered. In *The Listener* I am illustrating what was the attitude at the time and how someone who could not fight it had to bend before it in order not to break.

KJW: Many reviewers have compared *The Border* to *Swan Song,* and certainly the comparison has merit—in a post end-of-the-world America a small group of folks go on a journey following a seemingly magical youth who promises a kind of deliverance from the horrors. Yet I also see a lot of common ground with *Stinger*—aliens invading, people being taken over and transformed, the Southwest as site of apocalypse, hell—one of the locales in *Stinger* is called Bordertown. So obviously there are returns of a sort to earlier material. Do you think about that while writing, or do you ignore what you've done before? Are there motifs or ideas that you think, "I want to explore that more in the next one," or just happy coincidences because of your own proclivities as a writer?

RM: Actually I never thought of *Swan Song* while I was writing *The Border*. I wanted The Border to be my "battle of the aliens" book, and I considered that the challenge of it was going to be showing how Ethan was taken over by the Peacekeeper in small increments, and how he and the humans around him reacted to that. I wanted to do a book with a lot of slam-bam special effects, and the interesting thing to me was to take Ethan from being basically a busted-up young boy (who should've been dead) and transforming him into a super creature whose only limit of power and knowledge seemed to be that he could not answer the questions about God presented to him because he too (like the humans) was denied that knowledge. So Ethan became my fascination in the book…how to portray that kind of transformation.

I guess it's fun to end things because it's a way to explore your own feelings about what you would think and do in a situation like that. I very likely would be one of the first to curl up and die, so it's interesting to watch the progress of the characters you have made through the "mess" you have thrust them into.

The Border is actually a political piece. One side uses red-beamed weapons and the other uses blue-beamed weapons, and the people are caught between, infected by the poisons that spew out from the fighting. I actually don't care much for either the Republican party nor the Democrat party…the former has a smash and grab philosophy and the latter seems to want to get into and control every facet of American life. Thus the Gorgons destroy everything in sight and the Cyphers walk through walls. So *The Border* is my political statement as well as my "battle of the aliens" book. I once overheard someone talking about politics and saying that the only way to get out of the current mess was to "start over".

Thus the ending of *The Border*…a rewind, if you will, and a re-start.

KJW: As one of the most celebrated HWA members, Guest of Honor at this con, and someone whose body of work is ongoing and growing yet also celebrated for its longevity, what advice do you have for writers just starting out? Your unhappiness with publishers is well known and documented, yet the industry has also changed since your first hiatus. Advice on how to keep going?

RM: Yowch! Kind of a difficult question to reply to, because if you know my history with mainstream (New York) publishers you probably already know that I think the disrespect they show to their talent is an abomination. They look down on the very talent they should be celebrating, but then again they're business people and the great book-loving editors of the past are dead and gone. I have had the distinct displeasure of having to deal with editors who wanted me to make changes in books that I knew—KNEW in my writer's born heart—was wrong, and the changes were going to hurt the book. So I wouldn't make the changes…and when you defy mainstream publishing editors you make enemies for life. I will say that I grew up thinking that New York editors were gods and could only make good and godlike decisions…and was I ever WRONG!!!

Jeez! *Boy's Life* would have been destroyed if I had followed the changes an editor wanted me to make and *Speaks The Nightbird* would have been mindless and stupid pablum. That was probably my worst experience in the business, fighting for *Speaks The Nightbird* at Viking Press and ultimately pulling it out of submission there.

As to advice…wow. The publishing business has gotten harder and harsher. I would say that if you have to write, you have to, and that's it. We may be in a situation now where if a writer's first book is not a huge bestseller and makes huge money he or she might not get another chance, and I hate that because every artist—yes, ARTIST—needs the opportunity to experiment and fail. The artist needs to be able to break the bonds of genre and try something new, something brave, something insane, something that really really may not work but they have to TRY. But…the business being what it is, the bonds of genre are tighter than ever and experimentation is frowned upon…as it was with both *Boy's Life* and *Speaks The Nightbird,* because both of those were way different from what I'd done before. Interesting now, of course, that both those books are still in print and still going strong and I've read reviews of *Boy's Life* referring to it as a "classic". So my belief in myself paid off, but not without making those enemies I mentioned previously.

Well, my advice is…believe in yourself and what you're doing, do the best you can and fight for the life of your work. I will also say, however, that the mountains to be climbed have gotten a lot harder and steeper than the mountains I went up, and I'm very sorry for that.

KJW: Thank you. And now, short-answer lightning round, just for fun, dollar values are double, first thing that comes to your mind, only a few words. In *Meg*, the popcorn film of the moment, a giant shark menaces people in the Pacific. What giant creature would menace you and who would play you in the film version?

RM: Jellyfish. I would be the guy on the beach drinking margaritas and never going near the water and my one line (played by Gregory Peck, and that ages me but what the hell) would be "Look at that big huge jellyfish out there! Hand me another 'rita, would you?"

KJW: What book (not yours) do you wish you had written?

RM: I absolutely love *Jonathan Strange & Mr. Norrell* but I never could have written it. Truth be told I had a hard time getting into the book and had to start over twice but once I really got into it… amazing! No, only the great and excellent Susanna Clarke could have written that. God bless her I hope she writes another…but writing that book in the way she did—with all the copious book-within-a-book footnotes—would have put me in the grave.

KJW What is the scariest monster?

RM: Stupidity. Its cousin in monstrosity is the combination of Arrogance and Insecurity. Very ugly creatures.

KJW: What is the scariest thing about Alabama?

RM: A sixty-six-year-old man who smokes cigars and drinks bourbon on his front porch while watching the world pass in motion. Absolutely terrifying.

KJW: An angel appears before you and says you must now be transformed into a character from one of your own novels. Which character and (briefly) why?

RM: No angel would do that to me. My characters go through too much torment and misery.

KJW: Now that self-publishing is possible and many of the bigger names in horror are releasing e-books that traditional publishers ordinarily wouldn't release, is there any chance we might see *The Village* available to the public?

RM: I doubt it. I've had offers but I realize that after all the build-up of this book people might not like *The Village* or it may be disappointing…and that is the one real terror I have always had…of disappointing people's expectations. So, no.

KJW: And that ends our lighting round. Thanks, and thank you for your time. It's been a pleasure. I look forward to seeing you in Grand Rapids.

RM: Thank you.

1.It should be noted that McCammon was born in Birmingham, Alabama and continues to live there. It is a shaping influence on his work.

Kevin J. Wetmore, Jr. was co-Chair of StokerCon™ 2017 and StokerCon™ 2018, and volunteer coordinator for StokerCon™ 2019. He is a proud member of the Los Angeles HWA chapter and the author of *Post-9/11 Horror in American Cinema* and *Back from the Dead*, as well as dozens of articles and book chapters on horror theatre, horror cinema, and horror culture. He edited *Uncovering Stranger Things.* He is also the author of several dozen short stories published in such venues as *Cemetery Dance, Midian Unmade, The Cackle of Cthulhu*, and *Enter at Your Own Risk: The End is the Beginning.* You can learn more about him and his work at www.SomethingWetmoreThisWayComes.com.

Lynne Hansen

Kaaron Warren

Guest of Honor

Shirley Jackson Award Winner Kaaron Warren published her first short story in 1993 and has had stories in print every year since. She was Guest of Honour at World Fantasy Convention in 2018 and has been shortlisted for the Stoker Award and the World Fantasy Award.

Her stories have appeared in Australia, the US, China, the UK, and elsewhere in Europe, and have been selected for both Ellen Datlow's and Paula Guran's Best of the Year Anthologies. Kaaron has lived in Melbourne, Sydney, Canberra and Fiji. She has published five novels (*Slights, Walking the Tree, Mistification, The Grief Hole* and *Tide of Stone*) and seven short story collections, including the multi-award winning *Through Splintered Walls*. Her most recent short story collection is *A Primer to Kaaron Warren* from Dark Moon Books.

Her novella "Sky" won the Shirley Jackson Award and was shortlisted for the World Fantasy Award. It went on to win all three of the Australian genre awards, while *The Grief Hole* did the same thing in 2017.

Kaaron was a Fellow at the Museum for Australian Democracy, where she researched prime ministers, artists and serial killers. In 2018 she was Established Artist in Residence at Katharine Susannah Prichard House in Western Australia. She's taught workshops in haunted asylums, old morgues and second hand clothing shops and she's mentored several writers through a number of programs.

She will be at New Zealand's Geysercon in 2019. You can find her at kaaronwarren.wordpress.com and Twitter: @KaaronWarren.

The Gate Theory

A Short Story by Kaaron Warren

Jesus fuck, the road is long. You don't think about distance in Canberra, where a drive to Sydney takes three hours, to Melbourne seven, but then there are towns along the way.

Civilization.

Out here there is nothing but the long, red road.

My sister Lillian comes and goes. She's only vaguely interested in Jake, the guy driving; wait till later, when I have at him. Then she'll spark up. Now, she doesn't realise he's actually pretty attractive underneath those dusty clothes.

And he's quiet, which is good.

He met me in Katherine, straight off the Darwin bus, greeting me like an old friend. I wasn't sure yet where he stood on the community itself. I was there to shut it down, "in a peaceful and quiet manner," I'd been told. "No fuss." This was the project that would set me ahead, put me high up on the 'must promote' list. I wanted to get it right.

Would he try to convince me otherwise? I didn't mind him trying but it wouldn't get him anywhere.

Lillian whispered, "Do we like him?" and I laughed, then coughed to cover it up.

I wondered if he could smell her and thought it was me, so I pulled out some ylang ylang hand cream to cover it up.

My sister Lilian has a smell about her now. Roses gone brown on the edges, or a glass of wine left out overnight. It gets stronger when she thinks I'm heading for trouble. She's addicted to trouble. She always was an addict although it looked like I was. She loved my failures, fed off them like a hungry man sucks up spaghetti.

Every time she found me asleep in the gutter, every time she washed my face, every time she scared off another shit boyfriend; that's the stuff that made her feel good.

We were always better when there was a third. Someone we could both focus on. Otherwise it was like two relentless beams of light directed at each other.

If she had a boyfriend, or I did, we'd freak them out with our intensity. If we both had one at the same time it was okay but that somehow rarely happened.

When we were kids it was the same with best friends. We'd become obsessed with them, buying them presents, making them things, always wanting to be with them until they tired of us and walked away.

Addictive personalities, even then.

Growing up I always knew how much better she was. She got the good marks at school, she had all the future.

After she died things changed for me. Did she have to die for that to happen? That's what my biographer will ask.

I changed. I was lucky enough not to have a record, and my parents put me through Uni as a mature-age student, in some ways pretending Lillian never existed, that I had always been the good daughter, not her. That I was 18 and nothing bad ever happened.

* * *

I took a large sip of water.

"So you work in Canberra?" Jake asked. "That must suck."

"I like it, actually. Get to be in the heart of things. In the middle of reality."

He snorted at that. "Not much reality down there. Man-made lakes, pollies, fake people."

I crossed my legs so my skirt hitched mid-thigh. Faced my knees towards him. "The only thing I've ever had to fake is an orgasm. And that wasn't my fault."

He laughed and looked sidelong.

"Eyes on the road," I said. "Don't want to kill anyone."

Lillian snuck her hand into mine. She doesn't like it when I talk about death.

The sex stuff? She loves that.

I don't recommend holding your sister's hand while she dies. It's like opening up a gate, like an electrical gate is opened by the touching of the hand and the ghost gets through.

It's true. Every ghost that hangs around is here because some idiot held their hand and opened the gate.

This is my gate theory.

I watched her life shut down. She seemed to blur, and I thought it was because I was crying and my eyesight wasn't sharp, but then it came into focus and she seemed to hover above herself until she disappeared.

It was hard to get warm after that. Even on a sunny day I felt chilled, as if someone stood over me, blocking the light. I ignored it, pretended she wasn't there, for a long time.

Until.

Until I met Giles. The first man who was sadder than me, had a worse life, who hated himself more. Our seduction was comparing awful behaviour, "I drowned my own dog," was his, and he said, "And I think I'm a father but I'm not sure and don't care, and I drink a bottle of vodka a night and have NO FAMILY to speak of and no friends."

I told him about Lillian, how she'd be alive today if it wasn't for me, a great artist or actress or some kind of famous thing. I said I didn't mean for it to happen and yet it had.

And then we made love. He hadn't done it before, not properly. "I don't deserve this," he kept saying.

"No, you don't," I said, but I didn't deserve happiness either.

He stopped partway through, looked over his shoulder. "How did you manage that? Lick my feet when your mouth is way up here?"

But it was her, my sister, squatting naked on the end of my bed, her tongue lolled out, her flaps swollen and red like tongues as well, all glistening.

Later, he curled into a ball as if I'd beaten him.

"Sad man," Lillian whispered. She was with me, now, and I heard her. "Sad sad sad man."

She's sitting in the back seat, legs spread. She won't stop fiddling with herself.

* * *

"We can have a break here if you like. Well, we better."

It was a small hotel. Flies everywhere. Men on the verandah, leaning over it, staring.

"I can drive for a while," I said.

"Sure. I still need to…"

He wasn't sure if he was supposed to be formal with me. Court shoes, neat skirt, silk blouse. Hair in bun. I looked official.

"This the Government lady?" one of them asked. "Gonna shut the abos down?"

Jake nodded.

"Only trouble is they come into Durram Downs," another man said. "Become our problem, don't they? All right for you, getting them off your backs."

"Beer?" Jake said.

My sister nodded. Floating around the men, sniffing at them. She loves a worker. Loves the rough trade.

"I really don't want a beer. Maybe when we get there."

"Just leave the bastards be," one man said. "They'll be dead before long and no one will have to worry about them."

I wasn't going to argue with an idiot.

We didn't speak much. I concentrated on the road. On keeping to a reasonable speed (although Jake told me no one gave a shit about the limit out here) and avoiding the animals that seemed to be using the highway like we did.

As we approached Durrum Downs I said, "Are they all going to have an opinion for me here?"

"Fraid so. It affects all of us."

"So, what? You think we should leave them alone?"

"Some people think so."

"But they're killing themselves. It's not like they're happy and healthy."

I'd been sent here because there had been "a rash of deaths." A rash of suicides, as if the deaths were a nuisance, an itch, and all that's needed is the application of ointment and the skin will be smooth again.

* * *

There were two hotels in the town and I'd chosen the right one; it had an automatic door and air conditioning. The other one was at the end of town, near the small doctor's office. I hate the smell of anything medical.

Not your fault, people said, but everyone knew it was. I couldn't get myself to the clinic so Lillian showed up and took me, forcing me into the shower, making me wear her kind of clothes.

That's all I wear, these days. Am I stepping in for her? Living the life she should have led?

Maybe.

But it's better than the shit life I was living for myself.

Not your fault that whoever it was (they never did find out) was refused service at the clinic and came out wild, really wild. Banged into us both but I kept my footing. She didn't and into the path of the car.

I never let go her hand.

The hotel room was fine. Small, and decorated in nasty mustard colours, but it was clean, at least. The air conditioner didn't work, but the fan did.

* * *

There are homeless people in Canberra but I rarely see them. They've got their spots; between pillars, in the alleyways, and I don't go there.

Here, though.

We walked out to find food, and we had to step over them. I tripped over one, who grunted, and then my eyes came into focus and I could see them all.

"So many people on the streets," I said as we entered the town's only restaurant. "Chinese and Australian," it was called.

"Them?" Jake said. "Yeah, well. They don't like living in houses."

I watched them through a split in the dirty curtains. Like ghosts; most people looked through them.

We drank beer because it was so hot and the wine list was Red or White. I drank a lot. Thirsty. When I burped, and he laughed, not at me, but affectionately, I knew I'd sleep with him.

I'd probably known from the moment I saw him, actually. Known that I'd do it, but that laugh confirmed that he would.

At the hotel, I did the fumble with the key thing. It wasn't fake; my sister was so excited she grabbed at my fingers, wanting to hurry me up, and it didn't help.

We had a six pack of beer and I had a balcony, so we sat out there, slapping insects, sharing stories. He went into the bathroom. My sister followed him. I heard a shout, so he'd seen her.

"Jeez. It feels as if there's a hole in the wall and someone's staring in," he said.

He shuddered.

"We better turn the lights off, then," I said, and I led him inside.

Jake proved to be slightly more interesting than I thought he would. Bigger dick, for one thing. And while he professed to a warm heart, he didn't mind a bit of pain.

* * *

The ceiling fan provided little relief. It was too hot with two of us in the bed, so he went to his room, kissing me quite lovingly.

"We'll head out early," he said. "Before it gets really hot."

* * *

A short drive the next morning. I'd ducked out first thing and bought him a small gift; just a beer glass, but I thought it was a nice gesture. He looked a bit stunned. He'd get used to it. I tended to give my people lots of gifts.

"Just warning you, the place is a shit hole."

"That's why we're shutting it down," I said. "Makes sense."

"Only problem is they all end up in town where no one wants them."

"Programs will be set up. Extra teachers. That kind of thing. Much better for them."

He didn't answer. Was he thinking of all of those people on the streets? I'd heard a child, crying in the night, but sometimes Lillian cried like that so it didn't bother me.

I had less sympathy that other people because yeah, it's hard to get out of the gutter but it's not impossible.

I did it.

He pulled up at what was once the police station. The cops were the last to go.

The silence was enormous. No wind, no movement. The most incredible stillness. I felt set in resin, or made of glass. I felt as if a single step would crack the whole place open.

"Where is everyone?"

"Only ten of them left. The rest have seen sense and head out. When the grocery store shut, most of them got it."

We walked to a large house up on stilts. It was brightly painted and someone had once cared about the garden because it was laid out neatly with pebble paths and a bird bath.

"They all shifted in here when the shop owner moved out. He was the only one of them who had any money. Shoulda seen what he charged for a beer."

"Did you come out here often?"

"Nah. Helped transport a few of them. Helped move the merchandise."

"Drink it, you mean."

He smiled. "You can talk," he said, and he grabbed me there, on the street, and kissed me hard and deep. I heard my sister roar and if there had been some place not full of flies, I might have.

Later. Save it for later.

We walked up the stairs. The stillness hadn't changed but I could hear a low murmuring.

He put his hand up to knock but I pushed the door open. They didn't own this place, they were squatters. You don't knock on the door for the benefit of squatters.

It was dark inside the house, well-shuttered against the heat. The fans were still, power long since shut down. We passed through the small entrance and into the room where they all sat.

What struck me first was how tired they all looked. I'd seen that weariness; hospital staff in the drug zone, into their 30th hour of a shift. Pure exhaustion and hopelessness.

"G'day," Jake said. "This is Emma Macquarie. She's gonna talk to you about moving."

They all tucked themselves in, pulled away from me.

"You might want to shut up, mate. Not helping," I said, but I winked and showed him the tip of my tongue so he knew I still loved him.

"Who's boss here?"

An elderly woman stood up. She was as tired as the rest of them, but her shoulders were straight and she walked right up to me, standing a metre or two away, looking into my eyes.

"No bosses here. I'm the matriarch, though. The old lady, the grandma."

"You've got good family. Good people. Anywhere you live will be home. We'll make sure you stay together."

Yeah, we'd try. But seriously? Looking at the disparate ages? It probably wouldn't happen. They'd get used to it.

"This is our place. Always has been. You take us from here you cut off our breathing." And she sucked in a couple of hard lungsful of air to demonstrate.

I didn't believe that bullshit.

"All the buildings will fall down and no one will fix them."

"We can fix them," one of the men said quietly. "We fix things fine."

"And we can live outside in that guy," the grandmother said. She pointed out of the window. A giant baobab tree stood there, its limbs reaching out ten metres or so, its trunk almost as wide. It gaped open, looking like a brown vagina. I whispered this to Jake.

"Seriously? Don't you think so?" and that actually shocked him.

We went out into the backyard. There were fewer flies there, but a lot of canvases sitting out in the dust. "Part of the art," one of the men said.

To humour them I stepped inside the tree.

It was beautifully cool, but claustrophobic. There was a young boy resting there, on bright blankets. No pillow.

"He's pretty sick," the grandmother said. "Hot as."

"Where's the doctor?" and I'd fallen into the trap because no doctor came out here.

"We need doctors," they said, but I said, this is why you need to move. You know? It's not a human right to have medical care no matter where you live.

Heat radiated off the boy and I didn't want to go near him.

"Hold his hand," Jake said, "show some compassion. Pretend you care."

For that shit I would fuck him again, later. Fuck him up, leave him so filled with self-loathing he'd never go at me again.

But I held the kids hand. It was dry. Gritty.

"He really does need a hospital," I said. "If you lived close to the city we could facilitate that." It seemed astonishing how much they didn't get it. "We can take him now, if you like. We can fit about five of you in. Get your stuff later."

I counted in my head, thinking two minutes more holding the kid's hand would be enough. But my sister climbed onto the bed and squatted over his chest, looking into his eyes.

"He's about to go," she said. "Hold on tight."

I dropped his hand. Gate Theory. But the fuckwit picked it up. My idiot companion.

That boy was the first ghost in town.

His mother lay beside him in that massive tree trunk, weeping. The grandmother stroked her hair, murmuring beautiful words I could not understand but wish I'd heard myself, at least once.

Jake said, "We should leave them for today. We'll come back for tomorrow."

* * *

I drove myself the next morning, not wanting his influence. There was noise in the back; calling, and wailing, and shouts.

The boy's mother had fashioned a noose, which she tied around the baobab tree. Her son floated close by, nodding, squeezing himself, as if excited, as if anticipating her arrival in his world with great delight.

"He loves you," I said.

I looked at Lillian. Her mouth was a tiny 'ooh', waiting to see what I'd do. This was my choice. A first me for in a long time. Choosing as me. Not as Lillian.

The grandmother said, "What are you doing? You should stop her. She won't listen to us. Get your police friends in."

One of the men laughed. "Yeah so she can die in a cell."

They agreed.

"I'm not going to do anything," I said. "Can you see him? Your boy?"

They all nodded.

"I can see my sister as well," and I told them about her, the comfort she gave me. How happy she was; how the world to her was always happy, and she was never hungry and felt no sadness.

"Would we stay here?" the grandmother asked. "Would we stay here, in this place?" She tapped her chest to mean the land.

"I'm not sure. My sister comes with me everywhere. But our place is here," and I tapped my heart, too. "We have no other place."

She nodded.

That sense of peace and quiet hung over all of us.

"I can leave you to it, or I can stay," I said, knowing I would need to hold the hand of the last of them, at least."

"Please. Stay." The grandma kissed me.

One by one they went, holding hands. My sister did her best to welcome them. No one can shift you now, she said. This is your place.

The last man left alive was packed, ready to go. As if he could take it with him.

"We're done. We're finished," he said. His face was wet with tears, and the backs of his hands, from wiping.

"You'll live forever."

"But no new ones. No growing family. It ends here." He wept.

Some people are never satisfied.

They all slipped out like boiled broad beans slip from their skins.

Jake arrived, with a cop in tow.

"We thought there might be trouble. There often is. But figured you'd call if you were really in trouble. Jeez, it's a ghost town. Where are they?"

"They all left. All squeezed in the back of a ute," I said. "Left everything behind. But it's crap, all of it, anyway. They reckoned they had a place to go."

"They never showed up at Durrum."

"They're sorting themselves. Give them a couple of weeks," I told him. "They don't want to come into town. They're going to find a place deep out there. Where none of us can touch them."

"I didn't take you for a kind one," he said. I think he was genuinely surprised. "What about the kid?"

"He recovered," I said, although Jake had seen all that I had seen.

The ghosts were all hidden around the place; in the rocks, the trees, flattened in the red dirt. The men didn't look at all; as far as they were concerned it was over. They didn't care about evidence, or bodies, or anything.

I wondered if my sister would stay behind, but no. Already she was playing with herself, ready for a night of fun with the two men.

I was tired of it all, though, and keen to get out of there.

* * *

Jake watched me pack my few things. I kept waiting for him to tell me not to go; the longer I waited with the silence, the angrier I got.

He'd try to sleep with ordinary women, try to wipe the memory of me away, but he never would. I knew that but he didn't know it yet.

He got someone else to drive me to Katherine. I left him a note; he'd read it and realise what he'd lost.

Thing was, it was good for all. I did the thing I was sent out to do, and I did it peacefully. Quietly.

And all those people who wanted nothing to do with the real world?

They got their wish, too.

Guest of Honor Interview

By Eric J. Guignard

EJG: Hi Kaaron, and great to have the chance to chat with you again! First, of course, immense congratulations on being named a Guest of Honor for StokerCon™—it's well deserved!

Now, assuming being a StokerCon™ Guest of Honor to be one those items in your "literary bucket list," and coming off the back of being a GOH for World Fantasy Con, AND coming off backs of multiple industry awards that you've been receiving over the past years, what other writing goals do you have left to accomplish? Is there an ultimate ambition, that, should you reach it, you can shout up to the heavens, "I am Kaaron Warren and I have made it!" (Or are you already in that place?!)

KW: Pretty sure I'll never think I've made it! I have a lot of goals. Finishing the next novel, and the next. Finishing the novella, the short story. Never running out of ideas, never losing the drive to write.

I'd love to be published by *The New Yorker* because I've enjoyed their fiction for years.

I'd love to go on a worldwide book tour and talk about myself endlessly, meeting fascinating people, and sampling the local dishes wherever I go. I reckon if that happens, I'll think I've made it!

EJG: I'm certain that is soon to come for you! Who else in the world do you think deserves awards or greater recognition?

KW: Goodness, this is a tricky question! I think almost anybody who is writing well deserves greater recognition. Awards are a thing all their own, depending on many factors to make it to the short list, and I don't think anyone 'deserves' to be on those lists.

I'd like to see genre writers find a stronger place in world literature, be it on the many writers' festivals, widely-read book blogs, all of that. We write some of the most thought-provoking, challenging fiction published and I hate to see it dismissed in some circles.

EJG: I recently published a book examining your work, *Exploring Dark Short Fiction #2: A Primer to Kaaron Warren,* which is meant to be an accessible introduction and study of your short stories. I selected five reprints (plus your original work) that I thought gave a good representation across your style and voices. It was also a chance to promote some of my favorite works of yours, such as "Guarding the Mound," "Death's Door Café," and "Sins of the Ancestors." There are so many others of your tales that I adore, such as "The Hanging People," "Cooling the Crows," and "Air, Water and the Grove"…I could go on!

With all this, how do you balance writing such works so prolifically (and insightfully!) while working a day job, engaging in other interests, AND raising children?

KW: It doesn't always work, to be honest. At various stages of life the writing process has been far harder. At the moment, it helps that my day job is one that doesn't take any creative juice, because I work part time in a second hand shop. It actually refreshes the wells quite a lot, because of the items that come into the shop and all of the interactions I have with people during the day.

Part of it for me was accepting that fact that I wouldn't always have hours to work on a story. Sometimes it might be minutes, and I'd take advantage of those minutes. I'd always be observing, keeping my eye out for details and clues to where a story might go. Reading whenever I could, broadly. It's about being ready to write when you have the time to write.

EJG: I like that. I used to work in outside sales, and there was a common saying by managers they liked to throw around based on the movie, Glengarry Glen Ross: "Always Be Closing." For us writers, I'm going to promote your quote as, "Always Be Observing." A truism!

Anyway, on any given "writing" day, what's your average word count?

KW: I don't ever have a word count. I have allocated tasks, and time set aside, and I achieve what I can in that time. Word count for me isn't as important as the thinking process. There is research, there is plotting, and much more.

EJG: You've released four novels, multiple novellas, five collections, essays, and well over one hundred heart-rending tales of cross-genre work. What do you think is the best way to market a new release, either from your own experience or experiences you've learned from others?

KW: Another tricky question and one I'm not sure I'm qualified to answer. I think for me it is about doing your best work at all times, so that there is anticipation for a new work. Stay true to your voice so that readers know they will find something in your work they won't find elsewhere.

In any marketing, try to be interesting. There's no point in Tweeting out "buy my book." You need an engaging Tweet that might start a conversation. In any interview, be interesting and bold and honest. You want people to read what you have to say and engage with it. Make the most of any opportunity. Say yes to events if you can, and go to other people's events as well to see how they present themselves.

EJG: All great advice, Kaaron. From the plenitude of your works, who is your favorite character that you've created?

KW: As you know I don't create particularly lovable characters. I do nonetheless love them all, though. Each of them sits fully formed in my mind, like friends I knew once, or school mates I've almost forgotten. They'll reemerge every now and then.

That said, I think Stevie, from Slights, is my favorite. She still makes me laugh, and horrifies me, and I still feel weepy when I think of how the book ends.

EJG: And, as befitting to close: Please tell us, your fans, what does the future hold for Kaaron Warren's writing career?

KW: I have one finished novel and one on the go, and I'm thinking about writing the next one inspired by a series of murders in Melbourne in the 1930s.

Cemetery Dance will publish "Bitter" as part of their novella series next year, and a story in Nate Pedersen's Sisterhood anthology is upcoming.

My novella "Love Thee Better" is in Rebellion Publishing's Creature, edited by David Thomas Moore.

A couple of weeks after StokerCon™, I'm GOH at New Zealand's GeyserCon, in Rotorua, which is full of hot mud, geysers, and steam!

EJG: Sounds like great fodder for a post apocalyptic yarn! Thank you so much for your time, Kaaron, and congratulations again on all your recent endeavors.

Eric J. Guignard is a writer and editor of dark and speculative fiction, operating from the shadowy outskirts of Los Angeles, where he also runs the small press, Dark Moon Books. He's won the Bram Stoker Award®, been a finalist for the International Thriller Writers Award, and a multi-nominee of the Pushcart Prize. Outside the glamorous and jet-setting world of indie fiction, he's a technical writer and college professor. Visit Eric at: www.ericjguignard.com, www.darkmoonbooks.com, his blog: ericjguignard.blogspot.com, or Twitter: @ericjguignard.

MWM

Stephanie M. Wytovich

Guest of Honor

Stephanie M. Wytovich is an American poet, novelist, and essayist. Her work has been showcased in numerous anthologies such as *Gutted: Beautiful Horror Stories, Fantastic Tales of Terror, Year's Best Hardcore Horror: Volume 2, The Best Horror of the Year: Volume 8,* as well as many others.

Wytovich is the Poetry Editor for Raw Dog Screaming Press, an adjunct professor at Western Connecticut State University, Southern New Hampshire University, and Point Park University, and a mentor with Crystal Lake Publishing. She is a member of the Science Fiction Poetry Association, an active member of the Horror Writers Association, and a graduate of Seton Hill University's MFA program for Writing Popular Fiction. Her Bram Stoker Award-winning poetry collection, *Brothel,* earned a home with Raw Dog Screaming Press alongside *Hysteria: A Collection of Madness, Mourning Jewelry, An Exorcism of Angels,* and *Sheet Music to My Acoustic Nightmare.* Her debut novel, The Eighth, is published with *Dark Regions Press.*

Follow Wytovich at https://www.stephaniemwytovich.com/ and on twitter @SWytovich.

Poetry

By Stephanie M. Wytovich

Seduced by Monsters

There's a crocodile in my bed
a merman in my shower
and sometimes when I leave my apartment
I feel your hand on my shoulder,
Your breath on my neck,
A story I've read a thousand times,
One that I can't seem to shake,
Can't seem to put to sleep
Because there's a madman in my closet,
A sociopath between my legs
And there's no remedy for the bite on my shoulder,
To the vampire that drains me at night,
To the wolfman who eats my heart
Because I share my home with nightmares
Open my door to fiends,
And I have no one to blame but myself
When the lights out go,
When I start to scream,
When I realize that sometimes,
Yes, sometimes,
Monsters are just monsters,
And nothing more.

(Published in *Sheet Music to My Acoustic Nightmare*,
Raw Dog Screaming Press© 2017)

Your Ghost

You live in my bookshelves,
In the spaces between the walls where my nails raked the plaster,
Where my screams went to hide when it all got to be too much;

There are parts of you under my doormat,
Stuffed between the cushions of the couch that I burned,
Lodged somewhere deep inside my purple backpack,
The one I threw in the river after our last night.

Yes, you live in my mouth,
In the taste of honey and freshly ground mint
On the edge of burnt toast and coffee grinds
From the roasted beans I threw out six months ago

In fact, there are pieces of you still stuck in my throat,
Wedged in the lining of my stomach,
Swimming in my self-induced vomit
From when I tried to purge the memory of your tongue

Yet inside me, you multiply, flourish,
Like infected seedlings pumping poison through my veins
The essence of you bubbling in my blood,
Forever reminding me that you're here to stay,
That you're not leaving any time soon.

(Published in *Sheet Music to My Acoustic Nightmare,*
Raw Dog Screaming Press© 2017)

Versions of My Mutilated Self

My self-portrait is off,
off like the version who smokes in abandoned tunnels
off like the version who slips into the black
off like the version who whispers into palms

pulls magic from the stars
takes curses from the earth
licks afterlife from the graves

My self-portrait is bleeding,
bleeding like the artery I accidently hit
bleeding like the words I used to try to get you to stay
bleeding like the girl who lives in her memories
fears voices long past gone
feels pain inside her walls
sleeps with monsters in her dreams

My self-portrait is bone,
bone like the calcium I have to take to get better
bone like the leg I shattered on the road
bone like the color of my hospital walls
Yelling for you to let me out
Begging for you to come back
Pleading for you to stay away

Because this self-portrait is better,
Better like the bleached floorboards of my home
Better like the missing organs in their chests
Better like the dying flowers on my desk
screaming about absence
crying about pain
laughing about emptiness

the emptiness of it all.

(Published in *Sheet Music to My Acoustic Nightmare*,
Raw Dog Screaming Press © 2017)

Because I'm Stained Red

My bathtub is filled with blood
And I'm not sure how that's possible because I don't have a drain
But the red is bubbling, brooding, beckoning,
And my clothes are falling off, collecting in small piles as I move
From my bedroom to the hallway

And I can't remember a time when my life
Wasn't red, wasn't ripped open and dripping messages,
Screaming at me to stitch it back together again

Because Dad told me it would get easier
When he found me at 19 on our porch covered in bruises
in piss, soaked in fear with my nails in my calves,
But my bathtub is still filled with blood
And I'm still soaking in it

Unable to turn away from the severed hallucinations,
the faulty suicide trips, the gunshot that is my first memory,
always reminding me that loss is what permanently stains me red.

(Published in *Sheet Music to My Acoustic Nightmare*,
Raw Dog Screaming Press © 2017)

Ballet of Knives

She eased the knives out of the drawer and waved them
through the air as if they were multi-colored
ribbons in a dance routine. Her ballet was soft, filled
with monotone twirls and a light passé, and when she scraped the blades
against the walls, she did so in a delicate pirouette, leaving
scratch marks in the paper while the blur of her black
leotard moved before an audience that was no longer there.

This time I'll dance the blood ballet.
This time, I'll nail it.

The knives were her people now, those long, silver sticks of
metal that dove through the air and sliced failure like a practiced
balancoire. She worshipped them, performed for them, and when she
made a mistake—when she tripped or stumbled, fell or went out
of position—she cut a thin, one-inch line into her thigh as a
reminder that perfection isn't an option. It's a necessity.
Especially when dancing in blood.

It Was Hunger

And we were in love in lust and I kissed her, oh did I kiss her, and I wanted her, needed her wrapped her legs around my neck, dove into the wet diamond of her femininity, my hair tracing circles on her milk white thighs as I left crimson kisses on her flesh, it was sublime, it was ecstasy and I was cutting and tearing, biting listening to her scream, and she came in waves of blood and I drank it up like the wine it was, cherry red and sweet as I ate her from the outside in.

(Both published in *Mourning Jewelry,*
Raw Dog Screaming Press © 2013)

Return to Sender

My stomach is a dirge of unopened letters
Lick the wax seal, tear into me with your tongue
I can't remember the last time someone read to me
or the way foreign words sound
tumbling off someone else's lips.

Behind my eye, I hear the scrape of envelopes
All these fingernail clippings stuck in my throat
Do you feel the emptiness of forgotten signatures?
The unanswered proposals lingering on fingertips
stained by stamps and ink?

The weight of it gags me, this staunch repression,
this hidden doorway of truth.

It's been seven years since I've thought of you
The smell of your disease still rotting in my drawer
Tell me: when the sun disappears, will our notes cremate
with our ashes? Will the secrets we wrote, be but quiet
hauntings in our place?

Dear Adelaide, I Want to Eat You

A Short Story by Stephanie M. Wytovich

(For Michelle)

The toilet smelled like shit and cinnamon, and Adelaide threw up twice before she was able to open the letter.

Pull yourself together. It's not like this is the first one.

Fletcher had been sending letters to 395 Caster Street once a week for three months now, and that was after Adelaide had changed her phone number, moved towns and was mindful not to leave a forwarding address with anyone, not even with her parents or her best friend. After what happened last time between the two of them, she thought it might be best to take some time from each other, and when she looked in the mirror late at night—the lighting dimmed from the three blown-out bulbs above her mirror—the scars on her cheeks reminded her that she was making the right decision. Never mind what her heart told her. Right now, she wanted—no, needed—to be alone, to maybe figure some things out and process the feelings in her head, but see, some men—some monsters—don't work that way.

Those types of creatures are always hungry.

And like most predatory beings, they don't stop until they're fed.

Deep breath. In and out. One, two, three…

She wiped a line of orange spittle off her mouth, her hands shaking from anticipation, the aftertaste of yesterday's Thai food still lingering on her tongue.

She ripped the letter open, already reciting its contents in her head.

Dear Adelaide, I want to eat you.

It didn't say he was sorry, that he regretted scaring her in the parking garage last January and wished he could take it back. No. It said he wanted to eat her, devour her. That he, Fletcher Owen, wanted to consume her.

She read the words twice in her head and then once in a quiet whisper.

The area between her legs grew wet.

The envelope, a soft eggshell white with a red interior and gold trim, fell to the ground like a quiet feather while the letter grew heavy—almost lead-like—in her hands. She tried not to think of the way he touched her, how he had the power to send her body into these uncontrollable fits, but memories of him trailing his fingertips across her navel started to surface as quaint recollections of how her back turned to ice, a lilywhite sheet of gooseflesh, perked and rigid, nestled into the film strip that played behind her eyes.

The first time he licked her neck, her teeth went numb.

Dear Adelaide, I want to eat you.

She set the letter on end table, the one filled with nineteen books she hadn't read yet, but swore she'd get to this year, but probably wouldn't, and collapsed into her lima bean-colored chair. The cushion tried to swallow her from the ass up, but she had to admit that the suffocating hug it wrapped her in helped to stifle the slur of feelings that churned in her stomach and heated her loins.

* * *

Adelaide remembered the first time she saw Fletcher.

She was twenty-nine years old and attending a showing of Salome, a somewhat grotesque, yet beautiful opera by Richard Strauss that detailed the fatal attraction Salome harbored towards the uninterested prophet Jochanaan. Unaware that the performance was only one act, Adelaide found herself sitting at the bar with a half-full glass of Chardonnay, curious as to how the story would continue when the protagonist was just murdered after kissing the lips of the freshly decapitated Jochanaan. Deep in contemplation, Fletcher's voice startled her.

"Do you think Salome deserved to die?"

Jostled from her thoughts, Adelaide struggled to find her voice. "Oh, um, well, I don't know. It seemed rather harsh to me, if I'm to be perfectly honest." She crossed her legs and played with the ring she wore on her pinky finger. "I mean, sure, it's a little extreme, but it's just a kiss."

"Just a kiss, eh?" said Fletcher. "I think I like how your mind works. What's your name?" "Bold of a man to ask without introducing himself first," she said.

Fletcher smiled a charming grin, and for a moment, Adelaide felt herself smile back. "It's Fletcher. Fletcher Owen. I work here with the Cultural Trust and I, too, think it's quite extreme to be murdered for something as harmless as a kiss."

Adelaide felt herself blush and was suddenly glad she had decided to wear her black, short-sleeved Vera Wang dress. Usually she hated it because it wasn't comfortable and she was self-conscious about showing her cleavage, but she wanted to look special tonight since she was treating herself to a night out despite the stack of financial statements on her desk that she still needed to format. "Well, it's nice to meet you, Mr. Owen."

"Fletcher," he corrected her, his one hand held up in pause.

"Okay then. Fletcher it is," she said. "My name is Adelaide by the way. Adelaide Swanson."

Fletcher lifted her hand and brought it to his lips. "What a beautiful name. Well, let me assure you, the pleasure is all mine, Ms. Swanson."

Adelaide sipped what was left of her wine, the musky scent of Fletcher's cologne in a cloud around her. He was tall—maybe 6'1" or 6'2"—and impeccably dressed. His black shoes, carefully shined, reflected the glistening gold features of the bar's high ceilings, and his tie rested against a fitted jacket that covered, what she no doubt assumed to be, a chiseled set of pectorals. *There's nothing more attractive than a man who knows how to dress.*

"I'm curious what's going to happen in the next act," said Adelaide, her heart racing in her chest.

Fletcher laughed then. "Tell me. What do you think will happen?

Adelaide hated when people put her on spot like this because she was afraid of sounding stupid. "I'm not sure to be honest. It seemed like a pretty closed story, but maybe something will happen along the lines of Antigone? Maybe there will be a conflict over where to bury the body?"

Again, Fletcher smiled. "That's quite a brain you have there. I'm sure Oscar Wilde would have done well to have you by his side during the original composition. Perhaps you could have been his muse?"

"Oh, I very much doubt that."

"I think you doubt too much, and trust yourself too little," he said. "However, I'm sorry to tell you that the show is quite finished and that the theatre will soon be closing for the night." Adelaide set her glass down as the hot sting of embarrassment began to dress her face. "That was it? But it was so short!"

"Yes. It's only one act, my dear."

"Well then. I guess it's time for me to pay and get out of here before I humiliate myself some more then," said Adelaide. "It was very nice to meet you."

Fletcher leaned in and grabbed her bill off the table. "Or, you could let me pay for this, and join me for a drink next door? I'd like to hear more of this continuation story of yours." Adelaide wasn't used to men making passes at her, and at that point in her life, she'd only slept with a handful of men—and okay, one woman—but there was something about Fletcher that intrigued her, something alluring that whispered it would be okay. Maybe it was that his voice sounded like soft rain, or how his eyes connected with hers, never once—to her knowledge—looking to her breasts.

What's the worst that could happen? At the very least, I'll have a nice conversation and get some free wine. Who knows, maybe I'll even fall in love.

"Sure," she said. "That sounds lovely. I'd like that a lot."

* * *

Adelaide took a shower, the sting of the water hot on her back and neck. She shampooed her hair and scrubbed her arms raw in a forever attempt to remove Fletcher's touch from her body, but afterwards, she still felt violated, disfigured.

A broken doll.

A cracked piece of china.

She wrapped herself in a clean towel that she'd used a lavender softener on with hopes that the gentle fabric would have a calming effect on her skin, but one look in the mirror brought her back to reality, her face a battleground of scars.

Her hand traced the bite marks on her right cheek, a sumptuous collection of indents and pits that outfitted her appearance in dresses of pink flesh newly born and raised in hills of freshly-grown tissue. She had left the bathroom door slightly open—she hated the way the steam collected in the small space—and now found herself staring at the letter on the end table. It provoked her with its inevitable promise, a beautiful threat written in elegant calligraphy.

Dear Adelaide, I want to eat you.

Outside, the spring storm danced on her tin roof in a melodious pitter-patter that attempted to quiet her thoughts. She put a kettle of water on the stove and turned the burner to high. In moments of stress, she drank Earl Grey tea. A ritual she, too, now had Fletcher to thank for.

Adelaide hated Earl Grey tea, but it was the only thing that calmed her down.

"Fuck you, Fletcher. You and this tea choice."

She adjusted her towel, and sat at her computer to wait out the scream. According to her phone, she had 489 unopened emails, and in the spirit of staying distracted from the letter, she figured now was as good a time as any to sort through them.

The first one was from her mother.

The second one was from her brother, the next from her boss.

Her cat, Oliver, a year-old black Bombay, stared at her from across the room, his yellow eyes two menacing orbs that glowed in the dark shadows of the bookcase he'd crawled into. "Stop looking at me like that. It's not like I'm going to respond," she said, unsure of who she was trying to convince.

Oliver let out a screech and darted out the room.

"Nice," she said. "I feel loads better now, thanks."

Sarcasm wore thick on her tongue as she tapped her foot in a nervous fit, an anxious habit she'd recently picked up and mildly found comfort in.

Adelaide had rescued Oliver a little over a week after she'd moved in because while she'd wanted companionship, she wasn't sure quite—no, she was quite absolutely sure—that she didn't want it to be human. Oliver fit the bill perfectly, and his soft black fur calmed the squall in her head when she felt like being social, which as it turns out, was close to never.

In the bedroom, she heard him shriek, but decided to let him cry it out . She didn't have the patience to deal with whatever he'd found himself entangled in this time. Much like her, he needed to learn to get out of his own mistakes.

All right, who else is trying to fight for my attention today?

Adelaide scrolled through her emails, deleting message after message, sales pitch after coupon, before she moved on to her spam folder. A month ago, she'd blocked Fletcher's email address from her Google account, yet there in front of her sat a handful of emails, all with the same headline.

Dear Adelaide, I want to eat you.

"For Christ's sake. Can't you take a fucking hint?"

When he first told her that in person, she'd laughed at the idea of it, never thinking for one second that he was serious, a real wolf in sheep's clothes. Furious, she clicked "select all" and was about to hit "delete forever" when curiosity got the best of her. She opened the emails one by one, but they all said the same thing:

8:00 p.m.
659 Haven Ave.
Wear the dress.

Fear collected in her chest as she swallowed another memory.

Adelaide knew exactly what black dress he was talking about and it sat in the back of her closet, wrinkled, and not-yet-washed, still full of stories from the last, and only time, she'd worn it.

January 15, 2013.

She still had the hospital receipt in her top desk drawer.

* * *

Stephen's Ristorante, January

The bartender handed Fletcher another drink and he walked over to the corner table in a confident swagger that made Adelaide's heart race.

"You look delicious in that dress, by the way. Have I mentioned that already?" he said, careful not to hide the fact that he'd been eye-fucking her non-stop ever since she'd ordered her third martini of the evening.

"I think you might have mentioned it once or twice," she said.

"Well, it's true nevertheless," Fletcher said. "If you'll forgive me for saying."

Adelaide felt her cheeks flush red.

She nervously twirled her hair around her finger.

Fletcher was the type of man that most girls dreamt about but never found. At least not girls like Adelaide. While she was conventionally pretty, there wasn't anything particularly special about her, and her normalcy paled against the 5'10" blonde pistols that frequented the bar scene in stilettos and outfits that challenged the line between evening wear and lingerie. Struggling to break the awkward silence that had fallen between them, Adelaide nervously cleared her throat. "So, you mentioned that you work for the Trust?"

Fletcher nodded as he leaned forward and took her hand in his. "Yes, I have for quite some time, but I'm much more interested in hearing about what you do for a living. Unless, of course, you'd rather not talk shop."

Fearing she'd made a mistake, Adelaide quickly interjected. "No, no. That's fine. I freelance, mostly. Do some auditing and consulting work here and there. Nothing impressive." "Flexibility to do what one wants in life is always attractive." She took another sip of her drink, downing this one much faster than the others. She felt the gin go straight to her head and the room began to spin.

"Well I get to stay in my pajamas most days, so I'm afraid that's the level of attractive we're dealing with here," she said. "I feel like today was the first time I put on actual clothes in maybe two weeks."

Adelaide immediately cursed herself for admitting that, but to her surprise, Fletcher laughed.

"I do fancy myself a woman in flannel," he said. "Tell me you leave your curlers in, too." Slightly embarrassed, she gave a half-smirk that was both flirtatious and snarky, hoping to come across as playful instead of awkward.

"Very funny, but my hair is naturally curly, thank you very much," Adelaide said. "A couple years ago, I would have killed for straight hair, though, but I've since learned to tame it. Well, almost."

She pointed to her subtle waves, hoping they weren't too frizzy from the circle of sweat that traced the outline of her face.

"Tame it?" asked Fletcher, a hint of mischief in his voice. "Why on earth would you want to do that? Why not let it run wild instead?"

With that, he kissed her hand, his lips lingering on her skin a second too long.

Everything grew hot, the intensity of the moment too much for her. She couldn't even remember the last time she'd kissed a man, let alone slept with one, and right now, all she could think about was sleeping with Fletcher.

The sound of tomorrow's hangover pounded hard behind her eyes.

She gulped hard, bit her lip, tried to focus on her breathing, but she couldn't' even remember the last time she'd given a man a blow job, let alone spread her legs. She couldn't do this.

"Oh, um, well it's getting late," she said, unable to control her anxiety. "I should be getting home."

Disappointment wore on his face, but he remained a gentleman, and brushed it off as if he, too, agreed. "Of course. I've kept you out much too late. Please, may I at least call you a cab?"

"Oh no worries," she said. "I drove."

"Then let me at least walk you to your car," he said, pressing for what she imagined to be a moment alone with her disguised as a chivalrous act.

"Yeah, okay," she said. "That's very sweet of you to offer."

Adelaide stood up, adjusted her dress, and grabbed her purse. A little tipsy, she was nervous about the impending kiss, but somehow still excited, and if she was completely honest with herself, a little hungry for it, too.

With his hand on her back, he ushered her out the door, and as the cool air slapped her face, she couldn't help but wonder how he would taste.

***

The kettle hissed and the steam burned her thumb.

Adelaide poured the boiling water into her favorite mug—one that said "#restingbitchface"—and then threw an Earl Grey sachet inside. She thought twice about it, but ended up scooping a spoonful of honey in there, too.

The tea was scalding, but she drank it anyway, her tongue numb as she tried to block out the memory of his mouth, so soft and alluring at first, the shock of it all a nightmare she had yet to wake up from. If she thought about it hard enough, she could still feel the throb coming from her scars, her cheek a hospice of dead, and quickly - dying, cells that sat upfront from their bed of flesh like freshly -electrocuted Frankenstein monsters.

Dear Adelaide, I want to eat you.

Tears cut loose from her eyes as she remembered him pushing a strand of hair behind her ear. He cupped her chin, ran his thumb across her cheek, his eyes never leaving hers. When he leaned in to kiss her, he didn't wait for her to meet him. He took her lips hostage, a playful bite here, a tender lick there. Her body had erupted in winter, her hair, standing on edge from the intensity of his touch.

When he ran his fingers against her stomach, teasing the line of her stockings, she felt her eyes roll back in an almost hypnotic excitement.

Adelaide thought she was falling in love, that she had finally found someone kind, gentle. She wasn't expecting his teeth.

She rubbed her wrists at the memory of him grabbing her, how he threw her against her car, the bulge in his pants pressing against her thigh. She'd asked him to stop, begged him even, but he kept kissing her, down her neck, down her chest.

Adelaide had pushed, but he'd pushed harder, one hand holding hers, the other turning her face away from his. She recalled that there were four black cars in the garage that night, not including the one she was thrown up and sure to be raped against.

Admittedly, she was surprised when he licked her face, his tongue a warm, juicy slug, but the pain from when he bit her, the amount of blood that seeped from beneath her eye, almost put her into shock. Ravenous, he chewed, his face that of a rabid dog.

She never saw him take out the rag, had little memory of him putting it against her nose and mouth.

She blamed herself for breathing, for not having a higher tolerance.

Dear Adelaide, I want to eat you.

When she woke up in the parking garage, she'd grabbed for her phone, quickly called 911. She couldn't remember what she said, maybe she just screamed, but they arrived fast, and the doctors told her after the stitches and the rape kit, that Fletcher—was that even his real name?—hadn't fucked her; no, he'd merely just tried to eat her.

Succeeded to, in fact.

Adelaide sat down at the computer and reread the email, her gaze lingering on his name. She set her cup of tea next to the computer, let her towel drop. She imagined the curve of Fletcher's lips, felt the dip in her face where her skin had sunk and swollen. Even now, after all the months, she recalled his smile immediately when she first woke up in the morning, heard his laugh throughout the day and night in the empty spaces of her apartment. Fletcher Owen both terrified and aroused her, the charm of a poisonous snake, smooth yet venomous.

In the forefront of her mind, she heard Salome sing, her voice every studied soprano's wet dream.

She still thought death seemed too harsh a punishment for her.

It was just a kiss…

She just wanted a taste…

With the memory of his teeth inside her, Adelaide found her hand between her legs, hot, wet, already hating herself for what she was about to do, but couldn't stop.

Dear Adelaide, I want to eat you.

She came hard, knowing he already had.

Guest of Honor Interview

Weighing of the Heart: Stephanie M. Wytovich on Horror, Death, and Writing

By Karen Bovenmyer

Stephanie M. Wytovich is a Bram Stoker Award®-winning American poet, novelist, and essayist. Her work has been showcased in numerous anthologies such as *Gutted: Beautiful Horror Stories, Shadows Over Main Street: An Anthology of Small-Town Lovecraftian Terror, Year's Best Hardcore Horror: Volume 2, The Best Horror of the Year: Volume 8*, as well as many others. She's the Poetry Editor for Raw Dog Screaming Press, an adjunct at Western Connecticut State University and Point Park University, a mentor with Crystal Lake Publishing, a prolific creator and, I am convinced, has powers over space and time.

I had the opportunity to participate in Stephanie's How to Write Killer Dark Poetry session last StokerCon™ using HWA Mary Wollstonecraft Shelley Scholarship funds. I learned a lot about myself and my writing in her session and created the pantoum "Filling a Kettle" that appears in this anthology. I'm thrilled for the opportunity to interview her.

KB: Guest of honor at StokerCon™!!! Woohoo! This is so exciting. How has the horror community influenced your career?

SMW: The horror community has been a vital part to my career, whether we're talking about successes, support, friendship, etc. I honestly feel like I found my tribe, and it's so nice to have the support of your fellow peers and colleagues through every step of the game, whether you're just starting out, in need of mentoring, or you're a seasoned veteran.

I know that when I attended my first World Horror Convention in 2012 in Salt Lake City that I was not only scared, but quite intimidated as well. I was just starting out, had barely found my footing in the genre, hardly knew anyone, and to much surprise, I was met with open arms and I ended up leaving with friends, tons of books, great memories, and the energy to keep working on my novel, and subsequently, my career.

I know I've said it before and I'll say it again: the horror genre has some of the best, most welcoming people in it, and if we keep nurturing that sense of community, I think we're only going to see it grow.

KB: What do you feel defines horror from other genres? Is it the subject matter? A mood? The choices a character makes?

SMW: For me, I've always looked at the horror genre as the genre that's not going to sugarcoat anything for you. It's blunt, to-the-point, and it doesn't care if what it presents is ugly, gross, or a hard pill to swallow. As such, I think a lot of people shy away from it because it's a genre based in truth; it's not going to lie to you about what's waiting for you outside your door…or in your basement… or tucked inside the body of your spouse. It teaches us how to survive, makes us ask the hard questions about faith, morality, and desire, and by doing that, it allows us to evolve, to learn more about ourselves and our wants, needs, and gut reactions.

I'm a big believer in that in order to understand how the world works, how people work, that we need to understand the good and the bad, the beautiful and the grotesque. We need that balance, that dichotomy of light and dark, and horror gives that to us unabashedly.

KB: You mentioned being fascinated with Greek and Egyptian mythology as a child. What stories still resonate with you as an adult?

SMW: Oh yes. I'm completely fascinated with Greek and Egyptian mythology, and for my high school graduation project, I actually mummified a cat. I dissected it in the biology department with my teacher, then went through the drying out and wrapping process, and then fashioned a sarcophagus and canopic jars out of wood with my dad. I even wrote spells and curses on the box in hieroglyphics. As you can probably guess, Egyptian death rituals and their process of grieving continue to intrigue me, my favorite story out of the bunch probably being *The Weighing of the Heart Ceremony*.

And yes, I do have a slab from the Carnegie Natural History Museum of it hanging in my bedroom.

KB: You've shared how vital your writing space is to your creative process. If you're traveling, what helps you cross the threshold into the right mindset for writing?

SMW: My writing space is very intimate and necessary for me to create, and so when I travel, I bring bits of it with me so I can put together a make-shift altar to spend my time in. For instance, I usually bring quartz, my rosary, two sets of prayer beads, my journal, a selection of tea from my kitchen, and some dried flowers.

If I'm in a position where I can't necessarily prepare and gather all of the above before I travel, I tune into my space with a handful of playlists that I've created on my Spotify account to help me pick up where I left off and get in the right mindset.

KB: How does being a teacher and editor intersect with your writer-self? Has teaching or editing influenced how you create? Are those separate "brains"?

SMW: For the most part, I've found that the three overlap almost indefinitely, and I really enjoy the challenges of working in all these fields because, in the end, I think they make me a better writer and reader.

The constant editorial work I'm doing with students or clients helps me learn better ways to teach to different learning styles as well as recognize patterns of misuse in my own work. Discussing literature and literary theory also helps me become a better editor and writer because it allows me to see plot structure, character effects, symbols, and philosophies more clearly, and then as a result, I can help apply that to both my own work and to my client's stories. I don't think any writer can go wrong with constantly reading and talking about books, whether it's in the classroom or on social media, and the only downfall to juggling all of this is that I only have 24 hours in one day and sometimes can't get to everything on my to-do list when I want. Even with that said though, I wouldn't trade anything for the world.

KB: You've shared that *Sheet Music* and *The Eighth* pushed you out of your comfort zone and challenged you. What did you learn about yourself while writing them? What challenges are you looking forward to next?

SMW: *Writing Sheet Music to My Acoustic Nightmare* felt like the denouement to the trauma I've been writing about for the past five years. It taught me that it's okay to get personal with my readers, that being honest is terrifying but rewarding, and that writing continues to be cathartic for me, and so maybe I'm ready to share some stories through memoir or narrative essays rather than just through poems. It also showed me that even though I love horror, that I also like writing with a literary bent, too, and as such, I've been exploring a new facet of my writing in a collection I've tentatively titled *These Handwritten Suicides.* It's something I've been playing with on-and-off for the past year or so, and it's a very slow process, but I'm enjoying the challenge immensely.

The Eighth, however, was a game changer for me because I was able to prove to myself that 1) I could write a novel, and 2) I could create a world big enough to base a fantasy series in. As such, since its release, I've been making a switch to focusing more on writing fiction, and I've been encouraging myself to write and submit to anthologies more while still working on *The Eighth*'s sequel: *Deadly Sin.*

KB: How do you recover from a particularly emotional writing session?

SMW: I tend to write at night, and I'm always writing with a cup of tea in hand, so once I finish, I like to take a long, hot shower, rub some lavender under my eyes, and go right to bed. My dog, Apollo, is usually attached to my hip, so having him to snuggle with helps, too!

KB: I'm very grateful to Stephanie for this interview, and for the many entertaining hours I spent looking up cat mummification. We both hope StokerCon™ attendees have a lovely time at this year's convention. We'll be here, just around the corner, like the sound of something falling slowly down the stairs of an empty house, stepping from the shadows to peel back the sugarcoating, revealing the heart within.

Karen Bovenmyer was HWA's 2016 Mary Wollstonecraft Shelley Scholarship awardee, is the Assistant Editor of *PseudoPod* Horror Podcast Magazine, graduated in 2013 from the University of Southern Maine's MFA in Popular Fiction, and teaches and mentors writers at Iowa State University and Western Technical College.

MVVM

Lifetime Achievement Award

Graham Masterton

This year the Horror Writers Association announces Graham Masterton as Lifetime Achievement Award winner. He will receive the award at StokerCon™ 2019, held at the Amway Grand Plaza Hotel in Grand Rapids, Michigan. Masterton has provided many years of dedicated commitment to the horror community and the writing and publishing industry.

"Members on the selection committee have fond memories of Masterton's books," reported HWA President, Lisa Morton. "Graham Masterton has influenced many horror writers. We are truly thrilled to bestow him with this award." HWA offers the Lifetime Achievement Award once a year and employs a hard-working committee for the selection process. Recipients are chosen through stringent criteria. The rules require a unanimous vote from all committee members.

Graham Masterton is highly recognized for his horror novels, but he has also been a prolific writer of thrillers, disaster novels, and historical epics, as well as one of the world's most influential series of sex instruction books. He became a newspaper reporter at the age of 17 and was appointed editor of *Penthouse* magazine at only 24. His first horror novel *The Manitou* was filmed with Tony Curtis playing the lead, and three of his short horror stories were filmed by Tony Scott for *The Hunger* TV series. More recently, Graham turned his hand to crime novels with *White Bones*, set in Ireland, swiftly becoming a bestseller. This has been followed by five more bestselling crime novels featuring Detective Superintendent Katie Maguire. He has also published a grisly 18th century crime novel, *Scarlet Widow*. Graham's horror novels were introduced to Poland in1989 by his late wife Wiescka and he is now one of that country's most celebrated award-winning authors. A new horror novel *Ghost Virus* will be published in French in 2019. He has established an award for short stories written by inmates in Polish prisons, Nagroda Grahama Mastertona "W Więzieniu Pisane". He is currently working on new horror and crime novels and resides in Surrey, England.

Upon learning of this award, Graham Masterton said, "At the age of 10, I discovered how to give my friends a tingle of fear by writing a short story about a man who was decapitated but walked around singing "Tiptoe Through the Tulips" out of his severed neck. That's how my career in horror began. I am gratified that all these years later my tingling has been recognized by the Horror Writers Association."

Lifetime Achievement Award Interview

By John R. Little

I remember very well the day I picked up my first Graham Masterton novel, *The Manitou,* in 1976. That may seem like forever ago, but it's still fresh in my mind. I immediately knew I had an author I would follow wherever he wanted to take me.

Masterton became a long-term favorite, with books coming each year like clockwork, each as good as the last.

When I had the opportunity to interview him for this 2019 StokerCon™ souvenir book, I just about jumped out of my pants.

The interview was conducted by email, not long before the convention. The above photo is Graham Masterton and (sometimes) co-author Dawn G. Harris.

JL: Did you always want to be a writer? And in particular, a horror writer?

GM: When I was about 10 years old, my parents took me to see *Twenty Thousand Leagues Under the Sea* starring Kirk Douglas as Ned Land the harpooner. I loved the film so much (especially the fight with the giant squid) that I rushed home and wrote my own version in a blank school exercise book. It had similar ingredients—Hans Lee, a harpooner, a submarine, and a giant squid—but I invented my own story. I bound the book in cardboard and drew an illustration for the front cover and sold it to my best friend for a penny. That was my first royalty!

After that I continued to produce these self-published books, some of them featuring Hans Lee but other characters as well. I even produced my own weekly comic *Flash* which I wrote and illustrated. At the age of 12 I discovered Edgar Allan Poe and his *Tales of Mystery and Imagination*, which impressed me deeply, especially *The Pit and the Pendulum* and the blazing dwarf. Nothing like a blazing dwarf to liven up a story, I always say. I wrote dozens of short horror stories which I used to read to my friends during recess at school. Years later I met one of my old friends who had come become a city broker, and he complained that after I had read one of my stories, he hadn't been able to sleep for months. It was about a man who is decapitated but continues to walk around singing *Tiptoe Through the Tulips* out of his severed neck.

I won the school magazine prize for a short story, "Sophonisba," about a man who murders his wife and uses his bones to decorate the outside of his house. Then, at 14, I wrote my first full-length horror novel, *Morbleu*, which was about a major company, financially doomed, run by vampires. Unfortunately for several American corporations, who might have found it helpful, the manuscript is lost!

Sometimes you look back at your life and realise that what you thought was a disaster at the time turned out to be the best thing that ever happened to you. My parents moved to Sussex in the south of England because my stepfather changed his job. Because of that I had to leave my all-boys school and start my sixth-form (pre-college) education at a mixed school, with girls in it. I promptly forgot about Shakespeare and Byron and Keats and turned my attention to Jane and Charmienne and Jill. At the same time, I discovered the Beat writers…Lawrence Ferlinghetti and Gregory Corso and Jack Kerouac, and in 1965, when *The Naked Lunch* was published in Britain, William S. Burroughs. The Beats spoke directly to how I felt, and I loved their explicitness and their daring, and that led me to ignore the classic English writers that I was supposed to be studying nearly as much as the girls. After only two terms at this mixed school, the headmaster expelled me. My father, who was a cantankerous Army Major, almost detonated with anger.

I got a job as a greengrocer selling vegetables and I was actually quite good at it—so much so that at the age of 17 I was offered the job of manager of the shop. But the day before I was due to start, I was told that there was a vacancy for a trainee reporter on the local newspaper *The Crawley Observer*. I applied for the job and they gave it to me, and that was one of the greatest breaks ever. In those days local papers were staffed by retired London reporters who really knew their stuff…how to write a gripping news story, how to write headlines, how to sub-edit, how to cast off type. They also knew how to interview people so that they would tell you everything, and that was critical in my development as a writer.

On my very first day I was sent out to interview a woman whose husband had won a cycling trophy. He wasn't there himself, but she was going to tell me all about it. Not exactly front-page news but the kind of little story that brings local newspapers a loyal readership. I talked to the woman for about twenty minutes about her husband's achievements and wrote them all down in my brand-new notebook. As I was about to leave, though, she said, 'He beats me.' I said, 'What?' And she said, 'Yes…he beats me, and he shouts at me, and if I cook a meal he doesn't like he throws it against the kitchen wall. I've tried to talk to my family and my sister about it but they only say that it was my fault for marrying him.' We went back to the living-room and sat down again and for the next hour she told me everything about her troubled marriage—all the punching and the slapping and the sex life that was almost like repeated rape. I said very little but listened and nodded and asked her occasional questions, and I didn't feel embarrassed about asking her to give me some very intimate details. As I returned to the newspaper office, I felt like Saul on the road to Damascus…as if the clouds had opened and I had been given a great revelation. I realised that—as a sympathetic stranger—I could ask people almost anything about their personal lives, and they would tell me, because they knew that I wasn't going to judge them, and that it wouldn't go any further. That insight became the basis for the whole of my future career as a reporter, as a magazine editor, and as a writer of fiction.

JL: Your first novel, *The Manitou*, was a big success, and it was quickly made into a movie with well-known actors. What was it like for your first novel to be such a success?

GM: It was cool, to use a phrase from the time, especially when the late Bill Girdler picked it up at LA airport and immediately decided to make a movie out of it. At the same time—and I hope this doesn't sound blasé—I had been published with a by-line ever since I was 17. I had a weekly pop-music page in the newspaper, and when I was 21 I wrote a sex book called *Your Erotic Fantasies* under the pseudonym of Edward Thorne, followed by *Girls Who Said Yes*, also by Edward Thorne, and several best-selling sex guide books under my own name. It was certainly gratifying, and it made us enough money to put down a deposit on a house, but I considered it to be my job, and I still do. The evening of the premier was great, though. We watched the movie, chatted with Michael Ansara and Lalo Schifrin who wrote the music, and then went off to the Palm on Santa Monica Boulevard for a steak and sat next to Paul Michael Glaser (Starsky). Then a final celebratory cocktail at Dino's.

JL: You've written in a very diverse number of genres: horror, thrillers, historical sagas, disaster novels, crime novels, humor, and sex instruction books. You've been successful in all these fields. What's compelled you to try these different types of books? If you sit down to write a new book, how do you decide which type of book to tackle?

GM: It's my newspaper training that leads me to write in different genres, although I have to confess that at the beginning of my fiction-writing career I had no idea what a 'genre' was, and didn't particularly care. It was a disadvantage in one way, though, because *The Manitou* and *Salem's Lot* were published around the same time, and while Stephen King went on steadily with more and more horror novels to build up his audience, I started diversifying and after *The Revenge of the Manitou* didn't write another horror novel for two or three years. If I see an interesting story, just like a newspaper reporter I want to develop it and write about all its possibilities. Like *The Sweetman Curve*, for instance, which was based on a news report about politicians trying to influence the US elections by intimidating those members of the community who had the most political sway in any particular community. (In my novel, killing them.) Then I wanted to write massive historical sagas about the oil industry in America (*Rich*) and the building of the transcontinental railroads (*Railroad*.) These books all sold very well. *Maiden Voyage* was high in the NY Times bestseller list, but I should have kept plugging on with the horror. I returned to it eventually with *Tengu,* about a Japanese demon taking revenge for Hiroshima, and *Night Warriors,* about ordinary people being recruited to become extraordinary soldiers and fight evil spirits in other people's dreams.

The sex books came from my years as editor of a British men's magazine *Mayfair*. After four years on the local newspaper I wrote an incredibly arrogant letter to the publisher of *Mayfair* and after an interview in the swimming-pool of the Royal Automobile Club in London they gave me the job. One of my onerous duties was to go to the studios where the centre-spread girls were being photographed and interview them for the stories that would accompany the pictures. This was where the intimate interview technique came into its own, because they would sit there stark naked and tell me all about their boyfriends and their sex lives. Eventually I had the idea of writing a series of articles for the magazine based in their anecdotal accounts of their sexual problems (and pleasures.) This was when I was asked to write the Edward Thorne books.

After three years I had a bit of an argument with the boss of *Mayfair* and was offered the job of editing the UK edition of *Penthouse*. Bob Guccione had just started publishing *Penthouse* in America and so I became a frequent visitor to New York. While I was there I met Howard Kaminsky the publisher of Warner Paperback Library (and the cousin of Mel Kaminsky aka Mel

Brooks). He commissioned me to write an anecdotal sex guide *How A Woman Loves To Be Loved* by 'Angel Smith.' Angel was on the cover in a wet T-shirt and she was gorgeous—so gorgeous that she received tons of lascivious fan-mail. After she was sent a condom ('which I have rolled onto myself, darling Angel, and rolled off again') I decided to write my sex books under my own name. *How To Drive Your Man Wild In Bed* was published by Signet and to date has sold five-and-a-half million copies in various languages—including an extraordinary number in Poland where it was the first non-medical sex book published after the fall of Communism in 1989 and was brought out as *Magia Seksu* (Magic Sex.)

When I was editing *Penthouse* I also made friends with Xaviera Hollander (*The Happy Hooker*) and the late dominatrix Monique von Cleef. They both gave me one or two useful tips to pass on to my readers.

Incidentally, *How To Drive Your Man Wild In Bed* is one of only eight books still banned in the Republic of Ireland, because it suggests right on the last page that a woman who has inadvertently been made pregnant by her lover might consider a termination. Now that a referendum in Ireland has led to the repeal of the abortion law, I have lodged an appeal to have the ban lifted.

I started writing crime novels when my late wife Wiescka and I were living in Cork in the Republic of Ireland in 2000. Horror was going through a difficult time saleswise then, and had been since 1996, so I decided to try a wider audience. Apart from that, Cork is a fascinating city, with its own extraordinary slang and back-to-front Irish logic—'Go and fetch me ten pounds of potatoes, will you, but don't get the big ones because they're too heavy to carry.' I also wanted to write about a woman detective who has been promoted to fulfil the feminist agenda in An Garda Síochána, the Irish police, but finds that she has to fight not only crime but her misogynistic fellow officers. I find it a great challenge writing about female characters, but it helps that all my life all my closest friends have been women, and still are.

JL: For horror readers who may not have read any of your work, where would you suggest they start?

GM: As the King said in *Alice In Wonderland,* 'Begin at the beginning, and then go on till you get to the end: then stop.' (Not that I have yet come to the end...I have just been commissioned to write a haunted house novel.) *The Manitou* is a good start. That will give a reader a flavour of what I do. Then it depends what kind of horror they like best. *The Night Warriors* series is closer to fantasy; The *Devil in Gray* is more of a grisly crime procedural mixed with the history of the Civil War and occult elements; the series about Jim Rook, a remedial English teacher in LA with supernatural sensitivity is lighter and written with a slightly younger audience in mind; *Prey* has echoes of HP Lovecraft with a guest appearance by Lovecraft's gibbering multi-lingual creature Brown Jenkin. My new horror novel *Ghost Virus* has been described as 'utter insanity' and was partly inspired by *The Overcoat* by Nikolai Gogol and partly by my friend Dawn G Harris who is not only an author but runs a charity shop. I have also published five collections of short stories, several of which were adapted by Tony Scott for his *Hunger* TV series, notably *The Secret Shih-Tan* about Chinese gourmet cannibalism. A full bibliography of all my books and short stories can be found on my website www.grahammasterton.co.uk

JL: What is a typical day like for you?

GM: I start with a mug of horseshoe coffee—so-called by the American railroad workers who wanted their coffee so strong that you could float a horseshoe in it. Then I read the *Irish Examiner* online, especially if I am writing a crime novel featuring Detective Superintendent Katie Maguire. If there's anything particularly interesting I will contact my friend Caroline Delaney who is the *Examiner's* assistant news editor. Then I answer any messages that I may have from readers. After that I sit and write for three or four hours. Early in the afternoon I'll take a walk on Epsom Downs which are right at the back of my house and buy a newspaper and then I'll come back and write some more. In the evening I might meet one of our sons who live close by or go out for dinner and a drink with Dawn and talk about writing.

I go on quite a few promotional trips, too, and have several in the diary for this year—especially in France, where *Ghost Virus* is heralding a revival of horror after a longer hiatus than in most other countries. I shall be in Noeux-les-Mines, Epinal and Douai for various fantasy festivals, as well as Mons in Belgium. Those festivals are always highly enjoyable. I have been invited by a Polish reader to go to her wedding in the Tatra Mountains close to the Slovakian border and I will take my friend Kinga. Polish weddings tend to go on all night and sometimes into the next day, or even *days*, with lots of dancing and lashings of wodka. The last Polish wedding I attended was for Marysia, who was the (very pretty) publicity director for my Polish publishers. My wife Wiescka had passed away only a few months earlier and I was finding it difficult to write, since Wiescka used to read and comment on every chapter as I wrote it. Marysia offered to do the same if I sent what I had written to her every day by email. It is thanks to her that I was able to get back into writing horror with *Community* and *Forest Ghost* and subsequent books. We are still in touch.

JL: You have several book series that have multiple (sometimes many) volumes, such as The Manitou series, Katie Maguire, Rook, and others. Do you deliberately imagine a series when you write the first one, or do you publish the first one and then decide you're not done with the characters after all?

GM: I have never started a series with the intention of it being a series. As many other writers will tell you, characters once created take on a life of their own and quite often will almost write your book for you, sometimes in ways that you never expected. Harry Erskine the fake fortune-teller in *The Manitou* is probably the closest character to me, so I suppose it was inevitable that I would write more about him. Readers have contacted me and asked me what he's doing now, and I have to say that I've called him several times but he tells me that he's quite content reading Tarot cards for rich old ladies and is very wary about having another encounter with Native American demons. (I tell fortunes, too, using a deck of cards called the Parlour Sibyl, which dates from the court of Louis XIV. They are eerily accurate…much more than Tarot cards.)

JL: What's the most important thing you've learned about writing after more than 40 years in the business?

GM: Don't write about anything that anybody has ever written about before. Of course there are qualifications to this, because vampires and zombies are still popular, but if you are going to make your mark you need to come from left field. *The Manitou* was successful because almost nobody had written about Native American demonology before. Sitting Bull's grand-daughter took me to The Russian Tea Room in New York and bought me lunch to thank me, as well as giving me a framed portrait of good old Sitting Bull. I wrote one novel about vampires, *Descendant*, but it wasn't the usual bite-the-neck vampires…it was about the *strigoi* as they really feature in Romanian mythology. Also…never ever pay to have your own work published. If it's good enough, you will find a publisher eventually.

JL: You maintain a message board where you chat directly with your readers. Not many writers do that, as they prefer to communicate through Facebook or Twitter. How long have you had the message board, and do you ever see dropping it in favor of more common social media?

GM: I have had the message board for maybe 10 years now. I like it, because it's very personal, but of course I have a Facebook page too and also Facebook pages in Poland and France, and now and then I post some irrational remarks on Twitter. I also have an official Polish website. My connection to Poland is very strong because my maternal great-grandfather was a wine-merchant near Warsaw, and my late wife was Polish. We first visited Poland in 1989 and I go there at least two or three times every year. Three years ago during a promotional visit to Wroclaw I was taken to talk to the inmates of Wolow maximum security prison. Afterwards I suggested to the Warden that I start an annual short story contest for them—the Graham Masterton Written In Prison Award (*Nagroda Grahama Mastertona W Wiezieniu Pisane*), The idea was taken up enthusiastically by the Polish Prison Service and every penal institute in Poland takes part. This year we will be publishing an anthology of the best stories, all of which are extremely moving and inventive.

I also sponsor the *Prix Graham Masterton* for the best horror novels and short stories published every year in French. The prize for that is the statue of a demon with a very large dong (I didn't design it.)

JL: Over the years you've some books under pseudonyms. Was that due to the volume of books you were publishing? Or was it for other reasons?

GM: It was mainly down to the number of books I was writing. Simon & Schuster suggested Thomas Luke for *The Hell Candidate* and *Heirloom* for this reason, although when horror wasn't selling so well I wrote two thrillers under the name of Alan Blackwood, *Kingdom of the Blind* and *Holy Terror* simply to see if I could launch a second career. All of these books have now been re-published under own name, notably *The Hell Candidate* which describes an American President whose election is down to the fact that he is possessed by Satan. I wrote it originally when Ronald Reagan was running, with the help of his older brother Neil, with whom I used to drink in Rancho Santa Fe.

JL: You've published seven books in *The Manitou* series. Do you expect more will be coming at some point?

GM: Possibly. As I say, I'll have to ask Harry.

JL: What's your own personal favorite of your own work?

GM: Probably *Trauma*, which was based on a newspaper story I read about a woman crime scene cleaner in LA. It is more of a novella, and I was originally thinking of publishing it under a female pseudonym, because it deals with Bonnie Winter, a crime scene cleaner who is gradually being mentally worn down by the grisly aspects of her job, as well as a bullying husband and an obnoxious son. A shorter version was published by Cemetery Dance but then it was picked up by Pocket Books and named Best Original Paperback by Mystery Writers of America. But then I always love my latest book the best…I am mad about *Ghost Virus* because it is totally bonkers.

JL: Which authors do you enjoy reading?

GM: I don't read fiction these days because I am critical enough of my own writing, let alone any other authors. I really used to enjoy Nelson Algren and Herman Wouk because of the simplicity of their wording and yet the complexity of their stories. The way that Wouk turned around the sympathy of the reader in *The Caine Mutiny* is amazing. And of course William Burroughs. I first wrote to him when he was living in Tangier and when he came to London we became friends. I commissioned him to write a series of articles The Burroughs Academy for *Mayfair*. We used to talk for hours about how to write so that the reader is unaware of the presence of the author—becoming El Hombre Invisible, he called it. Together we used to deconstruct and rebuild sentences to bring out as much meaning as we could. The result of that was *Rules of Duel*, a 'cut-up' novel set in 1960s London which we put together. It lay in my desk drawer for years before Telos Books had the nerve to publish it.

I enjoy reading Dr Sabina Brennan, who is a neuroscientist at Trinity College, Dublin, and one-time actress in the Irish TV soap opera *Fair City*. I first met her in Cork when she and I were appearing on an afternoon TV show and I asked her if she had ever thought of writing a book. She has now—*100 Days To A Younger Brain*—and we are planning to write one together *Brain Box*, to benefit children with brain injury and mental challenges.

There is one fiction exception: the work of Dawn G. Harris. I guided her through writing her debut novel *Diviner*, about a young woman with a supernatural talent to see people's characters in their faces, and together we wrote a short horror story "Stranglehold," based on her experience as a charity shop manager. Within three weeks, "Stranglehold" had sold in seven countries, including Cemetery Dance in the US, Okolica Strachu in Poland, Sema in France, Lifokos in Greece, Strike in Bulgaria and Darker in Russia.

Dawn and I will be writing more horror stories together and by early 2020 we should have enough for a book. I find it extremely refreshing to write with a clever young woman because of the added insights she gives me into female thinking and because she is just as picky about my writing as I am of hers. Even after all these years, and all these novels, it's good to have somebody who's close enough not to be afraid to say, 'You know something, Graham? That's a load of old rubbish.'

John R. Little is a Canadian writer of dark fantasy and horror. He's been fortunate enough to have been nominated for the Bram Stoker Award® four times, and he's won one time for his novella, *Miranda*. John's most recent novel, *The Murder of Jesus Christ,* is being released to coincide with this year's StokerCon™.

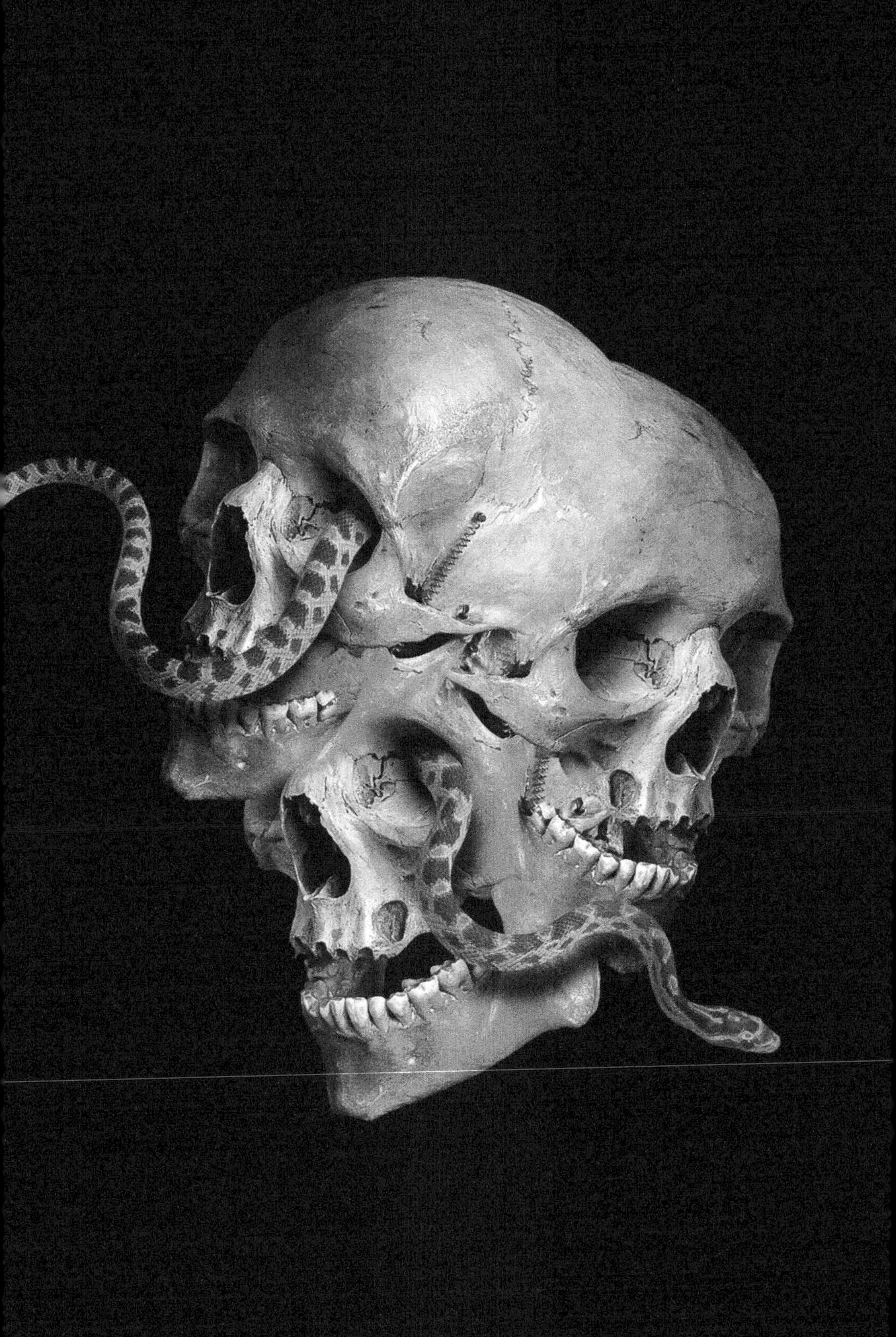

Specialty Press Award

Raw Dog Screaming Press

The Horror Writers Association (HWA) proudly announces Raw Dog Screaming Press as the recipient of the 2018 Specialty Press Award. Each year the HWA recognizes the accomplishments of a noteworthy small press. The Specialty Press Award brings recognition to an outstanding publisher of horror, dark fantasy, and weird fiction.

After editing *The Dream People* literary journal, Jennifer Barnes and John Edward Lawson founded Raw Dog Screaming Press to specialize in "fiction that foams at the mouth" and to offer authors a path around the publishing gatekeepers of the early 2000s. Their five imprints span dark, weird, blue-collar, and literary fiction and nonfiction for adults, children, and young adults.

Raw Dog Screaming Press emphasizes community and cultivates authors' careers. Most of their authors have published multiple titles with them. The press collaborates with authors and team-builds at DogCon events, forging camaraderie among their authors. They take an interest in new writers publishing debut books. The press developed a relationship with Seton Hill University, one of the few colleges offering a Masters in Writing Popular Fiction.

They champion niche categories of books, most notably horror poetry. Working with editor Stephanie M. Wytovich, and publishing stellar poets such as Christina Sng and Michael A. Arnzen, they've made a significant impact on the popularity and visibility of genre poetry. Raw Dog Screaming Press has distinguished itself by working with authors from unexpected quarters, such as internationally renowned musicians Till Lindemann (Rammstein) and Donna Lynch and Steven Archer (Ego Likeness), as well as feature film director S. Craig Zahler (*Bone Tomahawk, Brawl in Cell Block 99, Dragged Across Concrete*). They have also been fortunate to work with many critically acclaimed authors, including Jeff VanderMeer, Lucy A. Snyder, Jeffrey Thomas, James Chambers, and Lance Olsen. The result has been 200 superb books. Many titles have been optioned for film and translations into French, German, Indonesian, Italian, Russian, and Spanish. Raw Dog Screaming Press titles have received Bram Stoker Awards®, the PEN/Hemingway Award, the Sir Julius Vogel Award, and the Wonderland Award.

When not leading workshops at conventions around the country, or at universities like Seton Hill and Rutgers, the Raw Dog Screaming Press team regularly hosts workshops at their Broadkill Writers Resort on Delaware Bay and at their yearly DogCon event. For more about Raw Dog Screaming Press, please visit www.rawdogscreaming.com

2018 Mentor of the Year Award

JG Faherty

The Mentor of the Year Award was established in 2016 to recognize a writer who has offered extraordinary service to the Horror Writers Association's Mentor Program, which pairs newer writers with more established writers. Mentors work with their mentees on developing their craft and their business, in the interest of assisting writers in establishing careers. This year, the Mentor Program Chair has chosen JG Faherty as the 2018 Mentor of the Year.

Upon hearing news of the award, JG said, "It's really an honor to be chosen as Mentor of the Year. I am a firm believer that the Mentorship program is one of the most important benefits of membership we have, and under Brian Hatcher's guidance, it's reached new heights of success. Way, way back in the dark ages (2007 or so), I was a mentee, working on my first novel. I got lucky enough to be paired with then-president Deborah LeBlanc as my mentor. She helped me immensely with my novel and several short stories, and in the process became a friend as well. Without her help, I might never have sold that first book. Because of her, and because of other people in the organization who've taught me that giving back is one of the most important things Active members can do, I signed up as a mentor the moment I earned my Active status. My goal is to help each of my mentees the way Deb helped me, because that's what writers should be doing, helping other writers succeed. And I'm happy to say that along the way, I've made several more friends. What could be better?"

A life-long resident of New York's haunted Hudson Valley, JG Faherty is the author of 6 novels, 9 novellas, and more than 60 short stories, and he's been a finalist for both the Bram Stoker Award® (The Cure, Ghosts of Coronado Bay) and ITW Thriller Award (The Burning Time). He writes adult and YA horror, science fiction, dark fantasy, and paranormal romance, and his works range from quiet, dark suspense to over-the-top comic gruesomeness. After directing the HWA's YA program for two years, he implemented the organization's Library & Literacy Program, which focuses on author-library relations, using horror as a tool to entice more people to read, and supporting library reading and writing programs for young adults. He has also served on the Board of Trustees since 2011. As a child, his favorite playground was a 17th-century cemetery, which many people feel explains a lot. You can follow him at www.twitter.com/jgfaherty, www.facebook.com/jgfaherty, and www.jgfaherty.com.

2018 Silver Hammer Award Winner

Jess Landry

The Horror Writers Association is pleased to announce that Jess Landry has been chosen for the 2018 Silver Hammer Award. The HWA presents the Silver Hammer Award in recognition of extraordinary volunteerism by a member who dedicates valuable time and effort to the organization. The award is determined by HWA's Board of Trustees.

Working as Head Compiler, Jess is a key member of HWA's Bram Stoker Awards® Committee. The Head Compiler is responsible for checking every work that is recommended by a member. She adds links to works for authors/publishers/editors that are on the HWA's Recommended Reading List, often answering hundreds of emails throughout the year regarding works. As a part of the Awards Committee, the Head Compiler is expected to write the Co-Chairs should an issue arise and give input regarding the matter, as well as giving input throughout the year as we continuously strive to improve the system. The Recommendations branch of the binary awards system wouldn't work without her hard work and dedication.

She also works in Membership Outreach, contacting dozens of new authors every year to invite them to join the organization.

Upon being informed of the award, Jess commented, "When I first joined the HWA in 2014, I had no idea what I was getting into or what kind of people I would encounter, but when the opportunity to volunteer arose shortly after I became a member, I jumped at the chance. Since then, I've been lucky enough to lurk behind the scenes with some fantastic folks and have come to appreciate all the hard work that goes into maintaining our close-knit community. It takes everyone working together to make the HWA run as smoothly as it does, so I'm truly honored to have been selected for the 2018 Silver Hammer Award. And it's a good thing all I have to do is type this, because I'm honest-to-Jeebus speechless. Thank you!"

Jess Landry

From the day she was born, Jess Landry has always been attracted to the darker things in life. Her fondest childhood memories included getting nightmares from the *Goosebumps* books, watching *The Hilarious House of Frightenstein*, and reiterating to her parents that there was absolutely nothing wrong with her mental state. Since then, Jess's fiction has appeared in many anthologies, including *Twice-Told: A Collection of Doubles, Monsters of Any Kind, Where Nightmares Come From, Lost Highways: Dark Fictions from the Road,* and *Fantastic Tales of Terror* (which features her Bram Stoker Award® -nominated short story, "Mutter"), among others. You can visit her on the interwebs at jesslandry.com, though your best bet at finding her is on Facebook (facebook.com/jesslandry28), where she often posts cat gifs and references *Jurassic Park* way too much.

2018 Richard Laymon President's Award

Brad C. Hodson

Instituted in 2000, the Richard Laymon President's Award is named in honor of Richard Laymon, who died in 2000 while serving as President of the Horror Writers Association (HWA). As its name implies, it is given by the HWA's sitting President. The Award is presented to a volunteer who has served HWA in an especially exemplary manner and has shown extraordinary dedication to the organization.

HWA President Lisa Morton has chosen Brad Hodson to receive the 2018 Richard Laymon Award. As HWA's Administrator, Brad has served HWA for many years, overseeing both the organization's day-to-day operations and also coordinating much of the yearly StokerCon™ events. As President Lisa Morton noted, "The definition of this award states that it goes to an especially dedicated volunteer, while Brad is our only full-time employee. However, I figure that what Brad puts in every week goes so far beyond the forty hours we pay him for that he's surely our hardest working volunteer as well. HWA owes much of its growth to him, and this recognition is long overdue."

"Joining the HWA has truly been a life-changing experience," Brad said, when informed of the award. "From networking to access to the resources that let me start making professional sales, it's helped my career immensely. But, more so, the Administrator position has been a godsend. The amazing people I now get to interact with on a daily basis have enriched my life in so many ways. And having a day job that revolves around a genre I adore while assisting writers and educating readers has, even at its most stressful, been fulfilling in so many ways. HWA's President for most of my time in the position has been Lisa Morton and I couldn't ask for a better boss. Lisa has always trusted my opinions and empowered me to do what needs to be done while simultaneously offering guidance and resources to do so. I've worked for major companies in the entertainment industry and it's rare to find an environment like I have with the HWA. When I first took over as Administrator, we only had 350 members and almost all of them were in the US and Canada. I've watched that number grow to over 1500 members in 27 countries in a few short years. There's a reason for that growth: the President, Vice President, Board of Trustees, and all of the volunteers are passionate about the Horror Writers Association. And that passion is infectious. I'm happy to have caught the bug and am truly honored to be this year's recipient of the Richard Laymon President's Award."

As an author and screenwriter, Brad C. Hodson is proud to be the Administrator of the Horror Writers Association. A sampling of his various duties includes managing the member database, the renewal system, StokerCon registration, and serving as the communications hub for the org. He works with other organizations, such as the Author's Coalition, to advocate for creators and help keep HWA initiatives such as our scholarship program funded and paying out to recipients. Managing the day-to-day nuts and bolts of what keeps the organization running has given him a special appreciation for the genre, the creators and fans that champion it, and the volunteers who work tirelessly behind the scenes to provide HWA's members with the resources at their disposal.

EDGAR ALLAN POE

Lynne Hansen

While at StokerCon™

By Brian W. Matthews

It's late on Thursday or Friday, you've traveled who knows how many miles to reach the scenic western side of Michigan, and now you're camped out in your room. You're here, you've got your feet up, and now comes the big question—what do you do next? Well, if you're reading this rocking souvenir book, that's a good start. It contains a list of events happening throughout the weekend. Not sure where to start? Just step outside your door and let the mood take you where it will. The road goes ever on and on, a wise old Hobbit once said. Your road through StokerCon™ can be filled with as many experiences as you wish; they're yours for the choosing. Here are some of the high points.

Panels

StokerCon™ provides more panels and lectures than any other offering. Convention attendees can get the skinny on horror topics of all kinds. Ever wonder what it would be like to be part of a beta reading group? What kind of research goes into writing a prequel to *Dracula*? How difficult is it to adapt a massive novel like Stephen King's *The Stand* into a screenplay? Scary books. Scary movies. Scary games. Check the schedule for panel topics and choose the ones that interest you the most. Attend as many as you wish. Whether you are an author, a publisher, or a fan, panels can help you get the most out of your time here.

Horror University

The HWA has a strong history of partnering with and advocating for education. Consistent with that emphasis, StokerCon™ devotes a large segment of its programming to educational classes. Some of the best and brightest of the HWA offer workshops which will explore in deep detail the art of writing and of being a writer. Each workshop lasts two hours and will require some sort of work product by the end. These hands-on, interactive workshops will help elevate your skill as a writer. Each workshop is offered at an additional cost, and you must preregister to attend.

Ann Radcliffe Academic Conference

Now in its third year, the Ann Radcliffe Academic Conference is a growing and increasingly popular part of the Horror Writers Association's Outreach Program. Throughout the day on Thursday and Friday, presenters will offer papers on various aspects of horror—movies, books, comics, music, television, poetry, art, etc. Different from StokerCon™ panels, which delve more into the craft of writing, the Ann Radcliffe Academic Conference hopes to expand the academic scholarship of the horror genre. The Ann Radcliffe Academic Conference requires no additional fee to attend, other than your conference registration.

Dealer Room

Books, movies, wearables, memorabilia, collectibles—we love everything horror. Make sure to visit the Dealer Room in the Ambassador Ballroom East to see what publishers, booksellers, authors, artists and other vendors have to offer the discriminating buyer. Have a favorite author who's attending StokerCon™? Buy a book from one of our dealers and have the author inscribe it over to you. See something that is totally unique and special? Open your wallet and take it home with you. Want to know more about a small press? Stop by their booth. They would love to chat about their work. Take time out of your busy schedule to wander the booths and see what treasures you might find.

Mass Author Signing

Back by popular demand! On Friday, May 10th, at 5 p.m., attendees will gather in and around the Dealers Room for a mass author signing. This is a perfect opportunity to get that favorite novel signed by the author, in addition to wandering the dealer booths to snag that perfect piece of horror memorabilia. As an added attraction, the HWA will hold an Ice Cream Social during the first hour of the signing.

Librarians' Day

The HWA is proud to present a day-long program dedicated to librarians. Becky Spratford, horror reviewer for *Booklist* and author of *The Readers' Advisory Guide to Horror, 2nd Edition*

[ALA Editions, 2012], and Emily Vinci, fiction manager at the Schaumburg Township District Library in Schaumburg, Illinois, have assembled a stellar group of panels for this year's event. Programming will include:

Even Immortals Have Their Beginnings: The Research and Writing of Dracul, presented by Dacre Stoker and J.D. Barker.

Fandom Programs @ Your Library, moderator Emily Vinci leads a panel of ex-perts, including local library workers, authors, and publishers, as they share their secrets to providing programming for fandom communities, regardless of genre and across all age ranges

Introducing Summer Scares, hosts Becky Spratford and Grady Hendrix introduce you to both the titles and some of the authors identified as official 2018 inaugural "Summer Scares Selections."

Podcasting, host and podcaster Scott Edelman leads a panel discussion with authors and library workers who have started their own successful podcasts and YouTube book channels.

Small Publishers, Big Voices, Becky Spratford moderates a panel of some of her favorite small presses whose books you should consider carrying in your libraries. Panelists include Grady Hendrix, Josh Malerman, Will Errikson, Stephanie M. Wytovich, Erik Johnson, and others.

Final Frame Film Competition

Join us Friday night in the Ambassador Ballroom West for the HWA's 4th annual Final Frame Film Competition, a celebration of the darkest and weirdest short horror films submitted from around the world. Select films will be screened and a grand prize winner announced at the film competition's cocktail reception. The Final Frame Award and cash prize will be awarded to one film and filmmaker as decided by our panel of judges—among them, producer and director Josh Boone (*The Fault in Our Stars, X-Men: The New Mutants*) and author and screenwriter John Skipp (*Nightmare on Elm Street 5: The Dream Child*).

Readings

For most of us, reading a story thrills us, but have you ever listened to the author read one to you? Our author readings provide an opportunity for attendees to listen to—and learn from—some of the best readers in the business. The readings run hourly, starting Thursday afternoon and ending Saturday afternoon. Pick several that interest you and go listen. And don't forget the newer reader. Show them some love, too.

Pitch Sessions

Have you ever wanted to pitch a story idea to an editor, publisher, or agent? StokerCon™ 2019 once again offers the popular pitch session event. Each year, over sixty individual pitch sessions are held, giving attendees a rare, face-to-face chance to sell their stories directly to an agent, editor, or publisher. Pitch sessions will be held Saturday, May 11th, from 2 p.m. to 4 p.m., in the Pantlind Ballroom. While advanced registration is required, occasionally we have people who cancel or don't show up, so it never hurts to stop by and check for openings. And don't forget to attend the Pitch Session Panel, held the hour before the pitch sessions start, for important information.

Bram Stoker Awards®

The big event of the weekend is easily the Bram Stoker Awards®. This year, Jonathan Maberry will emcee the awards ceremony for the first time, taking over after a decade-long run by the capable and talented (and occasionally sock-puppet-obsessed) Jeff Strand. But first, if you were fortunate enough to buy tickets to the awards banquet, you will enjoy an hour of food, drink, and friendly conversation. The doors open to the public around 8 p.m. and the Bram Stoker Awards® start. Who will win and who will lose? Who will clock in with the longest acceptance speech and who will bask in their brevity? Just be ready to applaud those who have worked hard to earn their place as a Bram Stoker Award® winner. And when the ceremony is finished, don't forget to head to the Pantlind Ballroom for the afterparty!

Reading Performance Tips

By Linda D. Addison (via Jack Ketchum)

A long time ago in a galaxy right here I started signing up for Open Readings. My technique was to read as fast as possible,don't look up and get off the stage as quickly. I read in monotone with little emphasis on punctuation.

After hearing Eudora Welty and Maya Angelou read I wanted to read my work the way I heard it in my mind, not the rushed, nervous way I had been performing. I made a note of what other writers did that I enjoyed (Jack Ketchum, Veronica Golos, Peter Straub, Tom Monteleone, Gahan Wilson, etc.). I asked people to give me feedback. What completely changed my reading into something wonderful was taking lessons from Jack Ketchum/ Dallas Mayr.

A Summary of What I Learned:

• *Speak louder than you think you should.* Aim for the person at the back of the room.

• *Speak slower than you think.* One: you're familiar with the material; two: you may be nervous; three: listeners need to be able to let images develop from your words.

• *Leave space for reactions.* If there is a place for laughter or other emotional reaction, stop for a breath or two and allow it.

• *Practice, a lot.* Read your work fast, slow, with varying speeds in certain sections. What emotion are you trying to communicate: seduction, fear, laughter, sadness?

• *Tape yourself and listen.* You'd be surprised at how you sound. I learned to like my voice!

• *Practice in front of someone else.* Not for feedback but to get used to reading to another person, practice making eye contact.

• *Try moving around.* When practicing: read sitting, standing, moving around the room; use your hands to emphasize a point. For actual reading, do what you're comfortable with.

• *Props:* it can be interesting to use a prop, for example, I read a story from the POV of a male character in a bar. I borrowed a cigarette and used it (unlit) as I read. I also made my body move in a subtle male way. Props can be hats, stuffed animals, only incorporate what you're comfortable doing.

When Performing:

• Take a deep breath before starting.
• Have something to drink nearby.
• In a sentence or two say something about what inspired each piece before reading; if reading poetry—the audience will welcome a transition from one poem to the next.
• Make eye contact with individuals, pick a person to read to, switching from one side of the room to the other, from the back to the front of the room—work the crowd.
• Always be willing to change the order of the work if you're reading more than one piece (the energy between you and the audience may affect what you want to read next or your mood).
• You can change the words as you read and don't stop if you make a mistake.
• Enjoy yourself, each word, each image, this is your creation!

FRANKENSTEIN

1818

MARY SHELLEY

Ann Radcliffe Academic Conference

"Ann Radcliffe Academic Conference Showcases Horror Studies' Scholarship for Third Year"

By Nicholas Diak & Michele Brittany

Upon becoming academic members of Horror Writers Association, we initially felt a disconnect with fiction writers because we thought that horror writers and academic writers were vastly dissimilar to each other. In finding our community within the association, we wanted to create a conference where we could showcase our horror studies research and writing in a presentation format. The opportunity would also provide a networking opportunity between academic members, and we hoped, would provide a venue to bridge the gap between fiction and non-fiction writers.

The Ann Radcliffe Academic Conference was born at StokerCon™ 2017 aboard the Queen Mary when fourteen presenters convened in the ship's boardroom for one day to present on their respective subjects that included Bram Stoker, Ann Radcliffe, the five senses in writing, horror comics, and many other intriguing topics. On that day, fiction and non-fiction writers learned that each of us shared many traits and practices: we are all seekers of knowledge through hours of research, employ similar tools of writing, anguish over word choice, edit to perfection, and seek outlets to share their "stories" be they fiction or non-fiction. The event solidified "community" amongst a group of individuals, fiction or non-fiction writers, who were passionate (and critical) about horror.

In the second year of the conference, presenters from as far away as Denmark and Australia gathered at the famous Biltmore Hotel in H. P. Lovecraft's home town of Providence, Rhode Island. Spanning two days, there was a wide range of topics that included Koji Suzuki's Ring franchise, writers Richard Laymon and Stephen King, and very young children's picture horror books. There was new ground forged with presentations discussing the significance of word adjectives in Edgar Alan Poe's writings, the significance and contributions of Marjorie Bowen and L. T. C. Rolt, and Australian aboriginal horror. A number of our presenters even served as subject matter experts for panel programming during the larger StokerCon™ event!

Our efforts did not stop with establishing the conference, we also secured a book contract for a horror studies anthology focused on horror literature. A number of presenters from the first two conferences that fit the criteria were invited to be in the anthology. This opportunity gave presenters another venue for sharing their research with others, which was tremendously exciting!

Back for a third year, the conference continues to attract non-fiction and fiction writers, HWA members and non-members, and not surprising, many of the presenters this year are presenting for a second or a third year! As always, the conference programming is free for StokerCon™ attendees. Panel sessions are grouped by common overarching topics, so convention-goers can come for one, some or all of the panels and will receive a variety of perspectives on numerous horror topics. Do stop by, listen to our panelists, and engage in lively Q&A sessions at the conclusion of each panel session!

Please refer to the *StokerCon™ Pocket Guide* or your Sched profile for the programming (panels, panelists, moderators, dates and times of events).

Librarians' Day

Becky Spratford, Coordinator

Back for a third year at StokerCon™ is a special day-long program of panels and presentations for library workers! Librarians, authors and horror fans, Becky Spratford and Emily Vinci are excited to bring you a full day of learning, networking, and fun on May 10th from 9 a.m.–5 p.m. This will be an invaluable continuing education event whether you are a fan of horror, or petrified of it, as we have something for everyone, including presenters from libraries, publishers, and authors from up and comers to household names.

Becky returns as your coordinator for a second year in a row, after first being sucked in when she was feted as a Guest of Honor at StokerCon™ 2017. When she isn't planning Librarians' Day, Becky is what is known in the library biz as a Readers' Advisor. She trains library staff all over the world on how to match books with readers through the local public library, runs the critically acclaimed RA training blog *RA for All* and it's evil twin *RA for All: Horror,* is under contract to provide content for EBSCO's NoveList database, and writes horror reviews for *Booklist.* Becky also writes textbooks for librarians on how to work with horror readers. Her most recent title is *The Reader's Advisory Guide to Horror, Second Edition* [ALA Editions, 2012]. She is also not only a proud Active member of the HWA, but Becky was recently elected Secretary by the membership.

Planning an entire day of programming is no easy task, and this year, Becky invited Emily Vinci, the fiction manager at the Schaumburg Township District Library in Schaumburg, Illinois, to help. Emily's professional interests include promoting the acquisition and appreciation of comics and graphic novels in libraries, as well as creating programming that targets patrons in their 20s and 30s. She presents frequently about pop culture and millennial-targeted programming and co-authored the books *A Year of Programs for Millennials and More* (ALA Editions, 2015) and *50+ Fandom Programs* (ALA Editions, 2017). A lifelong lover of all things pop culture and an avid collector, Emily currently has more than two hundred copies of the Jurassic Park films on VHS and is always looking for more.

Returning by popular demand, panels of authors and librarians will be talking about the appeal of horror, buzzing the latest books, and providing plenty of practical how-to information for library workers. Also back by popular demand is the book swag, free books, and delicious lunch, all included in the price of admission.

But, new this year is an added 15 minutes between each panel. During this time, attendees and panelist will be encouraged to mingle and network in an area dedicated specifically for this purpose. Panelists have all agreed be available throughout the day to answer your specific questions and exchange contact information for further discussion.

Becky and Emily cannot wait to share their passion for horror, genre programming, and great reads for an entire day with our library colleagues. Allow us all to introduce you to the joys of a good scare and provide practical advice about programming, marketing, and collection development for all libraries and all genres along the way.

Please refer to the StokerCon™ pocket guide or your Sched profile for program details and panelists.

Pitch Sessions

By Rena Mason & Brian W. Matthews

Once again, StokerCon™ will offer an opportunity for attendees to pitch their projects directly to publishers, editors, and agents!

What Is a Pitch?

A pitch is a concise, engaging description of your project meant to pique the interest of the person to whom you are pitching your story. Make your pitch short—two or three sentences at most—and be prepared to answer questions.

What Should I Pitch?

Pitch finished projects. Do not pitch ideas. Make sure your work is error-free and ready to submit. However, do not bring the manuscript with you. If someone shows interest in your work, they will ask you to submit it once you return from StokerCon™.

To Whom Should I Pitch?

Chose pitch takers who actually represent your project. If you've written a Young Adult horror novel, make sure the person/people to whom you want to pitch represent/publish YA horror. This is a critical part of the pitch process—do your homework before you decide to whom you wish to pitch. You have one shot with this person. Make sure it counts.

How Do Pitch Sessions Work?

There are a limited number of pitch session for each publisher, editor, or agent assigned on a first-come, first-served basis, in the order the requests are received. When you pre-register for a pitch session, list up to three of your preferred pitch takers. This helps your chances to get at least one of your favored choices.

What to Expect at a StokerCon™ Pitch Session

Pitch Sessions are scheduled for Saturday, May 11th from 3 p.m. to 5 p.m. in the Pantlind Ballroom of the Amway Grand Plaza Hotel.

Prior to the pitch sessions, publishers, editors, and agents taking pitches will appear on a panel to discuss the best ways to pitch your project, what they are looking for in a pitch, and what not to do while pitching. Anyone scheduled to give a pitch is strongly advised to attend this panel. Each pitch lasts ten minutes. You will have five minutes to pitch your project, and an additional five minutes for question-and-answer. At the ten-minute mark, you will be notified that your pitch session is over. At that time, smile, thank the person across from you, and exit the ballroom. We typically have over sixty pitch sessions scheduled, and timing is critical. Any holdup throws the whole schedule off. Also, please report to the Pantlind Ballroom at least fifteen minutes before your scheduled pitch time to guarantee your place.

What If You Don't Get a Pitch Session with Your Top Choice?

Demand is high for pitch sessions. It is possible you may not get your top choices. Don't despair! Most agents and editors attend the full StokerCon™ weekend and are willing to chat with you at other times during the convention—as long as you approach them in a polite, professional manner. Maybe offer to buy them a drink at the bar. But most of all, be considerate, be concise, and don't take up too much of their time.

Horror University: At the Heart of StokerCon™

By James Chambers

No one knew quite what to expect from the first StokerCon™ in 2016.

Rocky Wood, Lisa Morton, Brad C. Hodson, John Palisano, and many others had worked behind the scenes for a long time to lay the foundations for the new convention. Rena Mason bravely agreed to chair the first one, in Las Vegas, leading a hard-working team in coordinating a massive event.

For StokerCon™ 2016, I pitched in as a volunteer and stuffed swag bags, worked registration, and helped attendees find their way around. The latter two tasks proved especially beneficial for meeting people and hearing firsthand what they liked about StokerCon™ (a lot!) and what they didn't (very little!). What impressed me most, though, was the buzz around Horror University.

A new idea, Horror University made its debut that year. A line-up of two-hour, highly focused writing workshops taught by some of the horror genre's most talented and accomplished authors. That first year featured Linda Addison, Michael Arnzen, Patrick Freivald, Jack Ketchum, Jonathan Maberry, John Skipp, Tim Waggoner, and many others as instructors. The topics included writing realistic dialogue, creating original monsters, crafting better plots, poetry writing, making the reader squirm, and much more. It sounded great in concept, but I admit I found myself skeptical about how it would work out in practice.

Convention attendees often find themselves pulled in a dozen different directions. There are panels, readings, author signings, meetings, conversations in the hotel lobby or bar, colleagues and friends to catch up with, books to buy in the dealers' room, sights to see in the city—an endless array of activities to fill the time. Would people carve out two hours for workshops dedicated to writing skills and techniques? How much could a room full of horror writers really learn in two hours? It sounds like a lot of time, but it goes by fast. (The first year I taught a Horror University workshop, my computer's clock froze, and I didn't even realize it until we were almost out of time.)

By day two of the con, my skepticism evaporated.

At the registration desk we answered endless questions about how Horror University would run, what workshops remained open, where they would take place, and what participants could expect. People wanted to confirm their workshop registrations, add new ones, make changes, and many people who hadn't pre-registered wanted to sign up. We answered more questions about Horror University than any other topic. Some of that activity came from smoothing over the inevitable bumps in the road that go with any ambitious new program. Most of it, though, came from excitement and anticipation.

A special energy manifested itself. Once the workshops began and people emerged from them, back into the flow of the convention, Horror University proved itself electrifying. People raved about their experiences. Friends forged in two hours of workshop time continued conversations and compared notes, energized by what they had learned. Workshop attendees caught up with their instructors for informal chats. They talked to other attendees about what they learned and how much it helped them with their writing. The anticipation among those still waiting for the workshops grew throughout the weekend. Some of those who hadn't signed up for any workshops realized they had missed out.

Perhaps the greatest evidence of the serious interest and excitement Horror University generated came when I attended Linda Addison's poetry workshop with a full house, maybe 20 or so students—at 8 a.m. on Sunday morning! A packed room that early on the last day of a con spoke volumes not only about how much people respect and admire Linda, but also about how serious they were about taking every opportunity to learn and improve in their writing.

The Horror University program helped define StokerCon™ and distinguish it from any other genre convention. StokerCon™ offered all the fundamentals of any convention—panels, readings, a dealers' room, pitch sessions, an awards banquet, and plenty of opportunities to mingle and network. But Horror University brought all that into a different and sharper focus. It placed the craft of writing at the heart of the convention. It made writing a priority. It ensured that writers talking about writing became a constant thread of the event. It reminded us that all of the other activities and programming only mattered because of writing, that the wellspring for everything that weekend was the commitment we writers make to sit in front of a blank screen and fill it with words, with story, with life.

Other cons have offered workshops or seminars as part of programming, but Horror University put them in the spotlight. The workshops became a reason to attend the con rather than merely another option for those who did. Horror University stated boldly that StokerCon™ was about writing, about publishing, about learning and advancing in one's career, about professionalism more than any other element of the convention—and people loved it.

This response and my experience in Linda's poetry workshop, reacquainting myself with poetry writing, which I hadn't done for many years, inspired me to try my hand at offering a workshop too. I wound up teaching that workshop, about techniques for writing horror graphic novels, in Long Beach and again in Providence, StokerCon™ 2017 and 2018 respectively. It was another eye-opening experience.

The workshop students came to the session serious-minded and ready to work, interested, committed to focusing on that topic and that topic alone for two solid hours. I realized how much that compressed, two-hour framework really allowed us to accomplish. A lot of information can be conveyed in two hours. It's intense. But the key to pulling it all together lay with the workshop activity. Whether writing short poems based on unexpected prompts, applying new editing techniques to a piece of short fiction, or—in the case of my workshop—scripting pages of graphic novel art with no information about the original story, the act of putting what you've learned into practice cements it in your mind so that you leave having genuinely expanded your writing knowledge and skills.

When I co-chaired StokerCon™ 2018, thousands of details and worries demanded my attention, but Horror University remained a high priority. In the first two StokerCons I saw how it helped define the overall StokerCon™ experience, how it gave writers a tangible reason to travel hundreds or thousands of miles to attend. A writer could expect to work on multiple aspects of their writing, to crack an element of storytelling that troubles them, or even just brush up on the fundamentals or find help with perfecting a specific piece. I made a point of reaching out to all of our past instructors to invite them back for StokerCon™ 2018. Then Lisa Morton, Brad C. Hodson, Angel Leigh McCoy, and I created a submission portal for Horror University proposals so those interested in offering a workshop could pitch new ideas in a consistent format and help the HWA build a database of workshops. And then I contrived to fit as many classes as possible into an already brimming convention schedule.

As anyone who has run a convention can tell you, it's demanding and exhausting. It occupies months of your life before and after, and can really run you down. After StokerCon™ Providence, I definitely needed a break—but one thing I wasn't ready to bid farewell was Horror University. My experience working with the instructors for 2018 was wonderful. They're a professional, helpful, and energetic group, who want to help other writers learn or think about writing in new ways. I loved being part of that, as an instructor, as a coordinator, and a spectator. So during that weekend in Providence, I told Brian W. Matthews that if he wanted me, I'd be happy to coordinate Horror University for 2019. I wanted to keep my hand in helping to make this wonderful, unique aspect of StokerCon™ run smoothly for another year.

Thankfully, Brian accepted, and so here we are, the fourth iteration of Horror University at StokerCon™ 2019. I truly hope that all who take part in the workshops find them informative, enlightening, and enriching, but most of all energizing—that all of this year's workshop students and instructors leave with their writing skills sharpened and their love of writing stoked.

OMNIUM GATHERUM

and bore
her away
from me
Jill

Short Sharp Shocks

By Jonathan Lees Director of Final Frame Programming

Gouge yourself with a needle.

Drag the edge of a page across the soft pad of your finger.

Ram your fist into a wall.

A bit of pain, maybe a touch of blood, and even better a wound.

More often than the written word, and not unlike a minor cut, the short horror film makes its mark and fades away rarely to be seen again.

It's evident in the rich history of scary storytelling that the short story has the ability to provoke, terrify, and unnerve us in a condensed, claustrophobic timeline with a resonance that many long form novels fail to achieve within their scope. The short horror film, like any great nightmare, disappears from existence only to linger in the memories of those that witnessed it. The shelf life of a short is as brief as its running time despite the sometimes arduous efforts it takes to execute them. We, as genre fans, need to keep passing these tales along as we would have for any great campfire creepshow or dusty ghost story of old. The stories only have power if we speak their name multiple times and make them appear to haunt us once again.

The short film mirrors how we converse and how we can approach a narrative to enthrall an audience. Considering our culture's attraction to the hot take, click bait, one hundred and eighty word abominations, episodic binging, and mobile memes, everything is, in essence, a short story and the visual variations have become even more present. So why isn't the short film a more popular form? Why do these movies appear on a festival circuit only to disappear or pop up online to compete for clicks amongst the ghoulish, grinning children broadcasting from their bedrooms? In our age of endless trailers and spoilers, the feature-length horror film may not hold many surprises by the time we finally get to see it in a darkened theater. The short film remains a true surprise and one that grows in power by word of mouth, a forwarded link from a friend, a heated discussion on a comments page.

There is a resonance with a short film that can stick to our bones and tumble around in the black of our brains long after viewing. There isn't a filmmaker alive who hasn't used the format to experiment with their darkest thoughts and learn the process of their craft. We live in a time of interconnectivity of shared fears and nightmares, it only makes sense that these dark visions from every corner of every eye on the planet is passed forth and archived to preserve our nightmares forever.

The movement out of the corner of our eyes.
The breath in between steps on empty evening streets.
The gasp after the rupture of a dark dream.
All these moments are the ones that inform our greatest stories.
The Final Frame Short Horror Film Competition welcomes an annual conversation with our own selected silver screen moments, our own collection of deliberately short, sharp, shocks that we hope never fade away.

MWM

What I Think When I Think Euro Horror

By Daniele Bonfanti

This is not by any means a scholarly article. This is as subjective and biased as they come—see the big I's in the title? This is an impressionistic impromptu. And as I sit I have no idea where it will take us exactly.

The old continent is old. Like really, really old. Each country had millennia to develop unique traditions, through wildly different, non-linear historical scenarios—Romans and Barbarians, Crusades and Dark Ages, Inquisition and Reign of Terror, Age of Sail and World Wars…each giving its own declination to sea monsters, ghosts, witches and witchcraft, creatures of the woods, vampires and demons…an infinite array of mythical creatures and entities to choose among. Each leaving its mark deep in our imagination.

So it would be nonsensical to try and condense all the diversity of European Horror in a short piece, because Euro Horror is, for one thing, varied.

Consider languages, to begin with (as we're talking about writing, in its many forms): about fifty different-speaking countries (*yes, about*, as we don't even have a consensus on that figure—it's complicated), several with more than one official tongue. We don't really know how many are spoken, in total: twenty-four are the official languages of the European Union, plus over sixty "minority and regional" languages with different roots—Latin, Germanic, Slavic…even mysterious pre-Indo-European tongues like Basque. But only about half European countries are part of the Union. In the end, you get an estimate of over two hundred languages. Yes. (…each with its own dialects. And though it may seem surreal, if an Italian guy speaks his dialect, the other guy from beyond the mountain ridge may not understand him. At all. In fact, recently many dialects have been rightly "promoted" to recognized languages—it's a fuzzy line, like poor old Pluto no longer being a planet).

Language strongly identifies cultures, way of thinking, and has of course a huge influence on writing. This veritable Babel can create difficulties and makes it very hard for an author to be known abroad: translations are expensive, limiting market, readership, and earnings. In most countries, professional writers are few, let alone horror writers. Writing in English means telling your tale to the whole world; different story if you write in Finnish or Catalan. Beautiful languages—but so many readers around the globe won't be able to enjoy your work. Anyway, despite these drawbacks, language diversity is a treasure to be protected and cherished, as it safeguards tradition and local identity. Each country, each region, province, city, area has its own distinctive lifestyle, food and cuisine, music, architecture and art, weak points and strong suits, folklore and legends—its own monsters—informing myriad flavors of dark fiction.

So, the last thing I want to do here is generalize. Which leaves me with one possible approach for this: close my eyes, breathe slow and listen, trying a sort of dreamlike alchemic distillation…

…at first it sounds like a symphony too complex to make out, but slowly—and focusing only westward—what I seem to hear is three big orchestras of Euro Horror taking shape, each with peculiar instruments and timbres: I may be wrong, but Mediterranean (if you'll allow me the term here to group Italy, France, and Spain), Germanic, and Scandinavian are vibrating in amalgams of sounds with some common dominants. That's not to say there isn't—for example—a Slavic ensemble. And others. But that's for another time, with more space. And of course, there is the illustrious orchestra of English (meaning UK) horror—but you definitely know English horror already. So, for now let's focus on these three. What am I hearing exactly?

Mediterranean horror feels sensual. Deeply rooted in history and art, it often involves deep research, and builds narratives playing on the elusive border between facts and myth. Style and aesthetics are all-important: how a story is told is as crucial as the story itself—sometimes even more. Often literary, poetic, evocative, descriptive, with a great emphasis on sense of place and meaningful or spectacular locations—both natural and manmade; it can be lovely even while diving into gore.

The Catholic Church is a frequent influence, offering a plethora of cues to the writer and playing a role in shaping stories as it has shaped everyday life for centuries—especially in Italy. Italian horror is also influenced by the golden age of giallo films, and frequently tells sophisticated tales with erotic and mystery elements. French horror has the uncanny fragrance of classic fantastique; it can also be very visceral, managing to always stay refined—and usually ends badly for everybody. Like heads rolling under a guillotine. Spanish horror is more muscular, adventurous, wild and weird, and often colored by a vein of grotesque. Treasures are there to be found, but they can kill you; women, too.

In all Mediterranean horror, the edge between scream and laugh is blurry, macabre humor and comic relief usual elements. Its main engine is passion.

Germanic horror sounds like stark contrasts—like the expressionist black and white of *Nosferatu.* It finds its fuel in the struggle between passion and intellect. It has been like that forever—since Romanticism and before. Philosophy is part of the game, of course, as psychoanalysis, and characters are intelligent, problematic, tormented, complex; authors not afraid to delve deep and face what awaits down there. Not pretty, usually. If the Mediterranean monster is often external, here the shadows lurk more easily inside us.

The Grimms' legacy is a wonderful gateway into the roots, themes and sensibility of Germanic horror: if you haven't read the originals, forget Disney and imagine Snow White's mother, the Queen (no step-mothers to soften the blow here) tortured to death with incandescent dancing shoes. Princesses are raped, children eaten, heads and hands cut off. There's even a guy throwing cow eyeballs to a young maiden as a show of love. The voice of Germanic horror is authoritative. It is generally serious, and can deal with delicate themes, like domestic violence or family problems; it doesn't shy away from larger and current social issues. Narratives are clean and powerful, told with extreme skill and attention to detail. Nothing is left to chance or approximation.

Action doesn't lack and it's well-executed, fast and breathless. And the Teutons pull no punches when it comes to the bloody or graphic parts: extreme in Germanic horror means extreme. There is a good market for hardcore horror as well. In general, horror is pretty popular in Germany and Middle Europe, much more than in Mediterranean-Latin countries, where it keeps being a niche genre—often dismissed as second-class fiction.

If you think Scandinavian horror is dark, cold and harsh like a long, snowy winter with the sun low on the barren horizon, you're not off the mark—but at the same time it can be very weird, surreal and hermetic. A twisted dark humor, that can be downright wacky, often comes into play, maybe to suddenly disappear just as it came—leaving you in a daze—as well as themes like coming of age, loneliness, and lack of communication. Atmosphere and scenery are key, playing in tune with what's going on inside the characters' minds: an icy black field, maybe, but don't forget brightly-colored meadows with no place to hide at all, under a never-setting sun. In a never-ending day without the rest and comfort of night.

It often incorporates mystery elements and a good amount of action and gory scenes. Story comes first, though it is rarely spelled out, and the writing is more often than not straight-forward. Unfortunately, things don't usually end well for Scandinavian characters, and hope isn't anywhere to be found.

Witchcraft and dark deities abound, as Norse mythology and folklore offer a bottomless well of distinct entities to draw from as monsters, and they certainly populate horror stories—but men and women are worst monsters in many Scandinavian stories, with monsters themselves even becoming endangered species.

And here I am, with my eyes open again and the music fading. Maybe, someday, I'll manage to make out the single instruments better—or perhaps I'll be able to recognize an even more general pattern, pull out a single drop from my alembic: the core of Euro Horror. That day, I'll need a book to talk about that drop. For now, I can say that what I brought back from this quick trip is a strong sensation of *complexity*. That's what I'll content myself with answering the next time somebody asks me, "Hey, how's European Horror?"

Complex, I'll say.

Daniele Bonfanti is an Italian born, Spanish resident science fiction and horror novelist, comics creator, and translator—works by Clive Barker, Ramsey Campbell, Richard Laymon, Poppy Z. Brite, Stephen King and many others. He recently co-edited with Alessandro Manzetti the anthology *Monsters of Any Kind.* His fiction received two Honorable Mentions in Datlow's *The Best Horror of the Year.* He's an active member of the HWA.
www.danielebonfanti.com

A Writer's Life

A Trans Woman Tries to Navigate the Prospect of Becoming a Horror Writer (or Not)

By Larissa Glasser

I can only speak from personal experience, and what it was like to be here. I was drawn to the horror genre as a way of processing my fear, depression, and curiosity. Well, also we had Video Advice down the street, and with those due dates, you had to watch "The Evil Dead" very promptly.

I think many of us could have gravitated to horror because it may help us empathize with each other—fear is a part of being human, our species.

And authors and artists get it. Just read that immersive opening passage to Clive Barker's "Dread" from *The Books of Blood*, and/or pretty much anything by Jack Ketchum and you might see what I'm proposing—

Social Justice through creativity and campfire stories.

In addition to becoming a full-on horror and metal nerd by age 15, I shouldered another element of my existence that I knew of vaguely, but had no idea how to reveal it without inviting certain disaster. I'm queer, and unlike some of us, I'm also trans. I was assigned male at birth, but I am a woman. Why else would I have transitioned? Trans women walk *away* from being unhappy, so trans women are women.

Being trans is something that happens randomly, seemingly to anyone, as being born left-handed or having green eyes rather than blue. It's like the rain of frogs in "Magnolia"—it's just something that happens.

However, the global perception of trans people has a long way to go, because post-colonial western society has been conditioned so very many of us to only understand a binary system in gender and sexuality: male or female, straight or queer, rich or poor.

Many refuse to admit to the fact this way of thought is antiquated as those who believe the earth is flat or that babies come out of cabbage leaves. In fact, there are ambiguities in life that directly contradict the flat-earthers—the characteristics of horror fit nicely into that perpetual uncertainty, a literature of ideas, and finding new ways to disturb, frighten, and engage people.

I don't feel qualified to give a 101 on topic of being born trans (I recommend Julia Serrano's *Whipping Girl* as a seminal text). I humbly paraphrase an excellent distinction I've heard: sexuality is about who you go to bed *with,* and gender is about who you go to bed *as*.

I didn't address trans issues in my writing until quite recently, when

I attended a summer workshop with other trans women and (C)AMAB[i] nonbinary writers in Brooklyn. Many of us bonded over our common experience of transitioning, our fear and relief of finding not only ourselves but better opportunities in a mogul-consolidated publishing landscape that tokenizes trans women, or would only let us share our narratives through memoir[ii].

See, it wasn't as if I *needed* express permission to address trans issues in my own fiction, but I feared tokenization and pigeonholing (*she's just a gimmick, because PC culture*). That said, the encouragement of the workshop and meeting others like me certainly helped. The next year, trans authors emerged all the way to an awards ceremony in New York.

So then, trans authors write *from* the dark. All of humanity knows that place. And many of us enjoy going back there.

When I crafted my story "The Mouse" I wanted to address so-called "bathroom bills" that were being introduced nationwide in response to increased trans visibility. I managed to channel and purge a lot of sadness into that narrative, while also trying to take a flamethrower to the anti-trans sentiment growing nationwide as we started to become more visible in society's bright lights.

I wanted to try my hand at writing a *love story* with "Ritual of Gorgons," which found its way into *Tragedy Queens: Stories Inspired by Lana Del Rey and Sylvia Plath* (Clash Books). Another common misconception about trans people is that we are out to trick or deceive non-trans people in the dating scene. "Ritual" is the story of two trans women, both high-profile children of celebrities, who fall in love and exact supernatural revenge upon the paparazzi who stalk them and endanger their privacy.

I then combined a few ideas I'd had marinating into my first novella, *F4* (Eraserhead Press). More irreverent and hardcore than those previous two stories, I still pitch the book as a trans porn version of "Die Hard" and "Event Horizon" on a cruise ship that is surgically grafted into a giant monster's body. I combined my struggle with internalized transphobia and sexual yearning into the main character, Carol Stratham.

Carol is an unwilling celebrity, once she witnesses and reports a murder. She then becomes the target of an internet hate campaign, her life goes through upheaval, and she flees to work on the cruise ship at the invitation of her sister, Roz. Embittered by her loss, Carol is ultimately

i Coercively assigned male at birth

ii Memoir, although perfectly fine as a means of conveying trans narratives, had by the 21st century become a voyeuristic means for non-trans people to wonder at us and obsess over our bodies, rather than our minds.

called to duty (sort of) when disaster strikes and she must save the other passengers from a malevolent supernatural force that has taken their ship.

The monster also plays a major role in the development of her character, but no spoilers. Suffice it to say that I wrote *F4* as a paean to the bad 1980s, hyper-masculinized action movies I had devoured as a young boy, wondering what the heck was going on with her internal contradictions.

I also had "Cloverfield," an innocently modernized, classic-invulnerable kaiju to latch onto. I also love Mech and tall military fiction. Queer trans geek girl reporting for duty.

Literature has the potential to address social issues, and I'm thankful to have realized this close to when I had decided to try and become more serious about writing, creativity, time management, and creativity matrices.

I have a long AF road, but suffice it to say that I hope more trans people will assert their rights through their voices, careers, and activism. Becoming more part of the cultural landscape is something that helped mainstream the gay rights movement gain more acceptance through AIDS Awareness and equal marriage (albeit at the expense/delay of trans rights advancement with that procession). The world itself knows how to ramp scary very quickly, and chaos wrecks from many origins, but the transcription of nightmares makes for great therapy.

Be an ally, seek work of diversity, let it inform some angles in your own creative urge, and let's have valued lives together.

An earlier version of this piece appeared as a guest post on Stephanie M. Wytovich's blog: stephaniewytovich.blogspot.com/2018/02/on-being-trans-woman-in-horror-genre.html

Larissa Glasser is a librarian, genre writer, and queer trans woman living in New England. Her short fiction has appeared in *Transcendent 3: The Year's Best Transgender Themed Speculative Fiction* (Lethe Press), *Wicked Haunted* (New England Horror Writers), and *Tragedy Queens: stories inspired by Lana Del Rey and Sylvia Plath* (Clash Books). Her debut novella *F4* is available from Eraserhead Press as part of its 2018 New Bizarro Author Series. Larissa is a Member at Large of Broad Universe, and an associate member of Horror Writers Association. She is on Twitter @larissaeglasser.

Jill
2013

About Poetry

By Linda D. Addison

Poetry is my first voice, so when you turn the page, *there will be poems!* Verse is another way to tell a story, to set a mood, to inspire, to question; no matter the length or form. Horror has been defined as an emotion and poetry invokes emotions.

The public often think monsters are involved with horror writing, but the monster isn't always a mis-shaped/supernatural devil hiding in shadows. Sometimes the demon is Self, like *Monster, Me* by Stephanie M. Wytovich, or an abominable killer reimagined (ex. *Dyer Died in Silence* by Andrea "Vocab" Sanderson, and *Holmes vs. The Ripper, Part I* by Sara Tantlinger).

Of course, existing concepts/history can inspire observations of known characters/events, like Mary Shelley's *Baby* by Trisha J. Wooldridge, *Little Red in Haiku* by Christina Sng, *Pseudopod* by Karen Bovenmyer, and *Black Ray* by Alessandro Manzetti & Marge Simon.

With poetry, it's not always horror in the strictest sense that moves us, but some shadowy song bringing focus to fragile life and desire (ex. *Basement* by Michelle Scalise, *Polydactyly* by Tanesha Nicole Tyler, *Love Like Starlight* by Angela Yuriko Smith, and *The Milk of Human Depravity* by Wrath James White).

I love words, always have and verse is a way to weave haunting music from day-night dreams of Being, like *Lycanthrope* by Michael R. Collings, *I Bought the Farm* by John Reinhart, *The Tongue We Dream In* by Sheree Renée Thomas, and *Art from The Heart* by Jill Bauman.

My hope is that you will find a poem here that touches your dreams/fears/desire and inspires you to read more by these diviners of past/present/future.

Poetry Showcase

Monster, Me

And other selected poems by Stephanie M. Wytovich

Inside of me, there's a sickness. A darkness that breeds and snuffs out the good, filling me with screams and cobwebs and an emptiness that infects everything that was once alive. It's a slow death and I feel everything: every touch, every kiss, every parting. Sometimes I even think my heart
stops beating; it just quiets and goes kind of still, barely working until it's not. I know it's her, and I know she holds me
tighter than any lover I've ever known, and I hate her—but oh do I love her—and no matter how hard I try to fight, how
desperately I try not to give in, she's always there, waiting, ready, and willing to take me as I am. Broken. Tired. Weak. She
loves and accepts the tragedy of my being and she understands the cuts and the bruises, the stitches
and the scars.

I call her monster and she moves within me, finding her comfort spot where she nestles down deep until her arms are mine, until my legs are hers. I see through two pairs of eyes, and breathe with four lungs, and the disease
that breeds in my stomach is not a cancer of the flesh, but a mutation of the heart. She's
the cure to my epidemic, my anti-suicide machine, and together we/I walk through this life, holding hands and hearts,
whispering secrets and drinking down poisons, mixing black magic remedies and sucking down sage, and together we/I live, somehow we/I survive. My monster, me. The Jekyll to my Hyde.

(Originally published in *An Exorcism of Angels* © 2015)

Nine years, Nine Months

The dead women told me I would never know the feeling
of a full womb, that I was hollow, dried up, and barren,
a useless husk, a mockery of a woman. But they don't know
that I've grown to love that emptiness inside of me as if it were
my own. That I've nourished it, sheltered it, protected it, and
now it moves against my flesh, kicking out and screaming at night,
laughing at them as it grows, for our bond is much stronger
than that of a mother and child for misery takes nine years to
grow, and nine months to birth.

(Originally published in *Mourning Jewelry* © 2013)

Vicious Girls

Creatures,
creatures are what they are—
violent Eves, rotten apples,
victimized damsels, Salem witches;
they bit the snake that fed them
drank his poison,
pulled out his fangs
and now they bleed,
they bleed once a month for his death,
the death of the devil who cursed their wombs
for they are vicious,
they are venomous
they are women,
and they will wait,
patient and persistent,
ever-enduring
and damned
and they will sing,
sing in covens, sing in brothels,
sing for men,
sing for whores
and their words will kill
they will damn
they will puncture
for they sing with lips,
lips not of mouth but of sex
sex that weakens, that confuses,
that traps
and once they have you
have you between their legs,
they will kill you,
they will eat you,
and they will love you
the only way
that they know how

(Originally published in *Brothel*© 2016)

Black Ray

By Alessandro Manzetti & Marge Simon

Prinzenregentplatz 27, Monaco
April 30, 1945

Lee takes off her dirty boots
filled with Dachau's mud
and gets in the Hitler's bathtub
blending her polarized skin,
the golden powder of a surrealist muse
and a necklace of sea sponges,
with that still virgin water,
which seems to be waiting for an angel
after serving so long a cold demon
without gills, blood and sperm
enduring the awful perfume,
—like snake oil—
of its former owner.

Lee's breast, turned into a living reef,
half submerged in that reddish foam,
is surrounded by eddies of memories
—and by the tongues of the dead
she saw in the concentration camp—
headed to her mind, so quickly.
Hundreds of photo shoots,
human fences, charred voices
and a patchwork of forgotten faces
floating in the river, near there
like a flexible armor encrusted with eyes.

Then a familiar face appear,
it's him, Man Ray, the rider of the absurd
—he looks good wearing that tinfoil hat—
He shows her a wedding dress,
white, sewn with fishing nets,
and then a army uniform, black,
with golden teeth instead of buttons.

"You choose, princess," he whispers
before vanishing like bath salts,
blue, melting around her thighs,
in that bathtub of the monster,
the same as any other.

She remembers the wounds
after a bath with him and leaving
him dripping wet on his own.
She dreams of painting him
black on black.

She stands to towel dry,
feeling dirty all over again,
marked with dark sludge,
like those faces at Dachau
that won't wash away.

(Originally published in *War* © 2018)

Basement

By Michelle Scalise

Our innocence's still buried there
just listen to us breathe.
Press your ear to the basement door
like an inquisitive child,
watch the handle chipped in paint
shudder from the other side,
imploring you to free us.

One glance downstairs and I swore I'd never return.
A man without a face vowed
it was just an old heater
that took up half the dirt floor
ascending to the ceiling like a god
only Nazi's would have prayed to.
Its oven door, rusted from years and heat
swayed back and forth on a broken hinge,
a fetus strapped to a swing.

He laughed and I heard hell,
spied bones inside the slab.
His voice retained the charm of a jackal,
"There's nothing evil 'bout the place."
But he had no answer for seared shadows
Walking down the uneven stairs
to receive us to their fate.

(Originally published in *Dark Voices* anthology © 2018)

Polydactyly

By Tanesha Nicole Tyler

I was predestined to be seen as a monster.
When I came from my mother's womb,
the hospital room bore witness to a
newborn with 12 fingers and 11 toes.

They call this Polydactyly.

When I Googled "polydactyly"
The browser asked
"Did you mean pterodactyl?"
By that, I'm sure I was predestined to extinction.
My screams fossilized and called history,
as if my history could be recorded so easily.

I never see people like me in the history books.
Authors think as long as they mention
the man with a dream and how this country
eventually realized that slavery was
kind of really fucked up,
It's enough to satisfy the hunger in our starving bellies.

Some representation is better than none.
At least, that's what I've always been told.
I learned that when something is broken,
It is to be disposed of instead of trying to fix it.

In fourth grade I jumped out of a swing,
landed wrong, dislocated my right pinky toe.
When I awoke from surgery, the doctor
explained to me that it was too
complicated to reconstruct the bones
so they ultimately decided to take it off.

Now that I only have 9 toes,
I guess that still makes me a monster.
A monster that feels things.
You see, my nerve endings are all intact,
essentially it's like the toe is still there.

A phantom limb that still feels pain.
Being this Black feels like a phantom limb.
Invisible to everyone else but me.

This isn't supposed to be a poem
about what Black feels like.

Isn't supposed to be me telling you
that I am more afraid of my sister
wanting to go to college in
Baltimore because of the color of her skin,
and not because she's in a wheelchair
and has no family that far East to look out for her.

This shouldn't be me telling
you that when I watched
a 7 minute video of a white cop dragging
a young Black girl across the grass
by her hair, I couldn't help but feel her pain.
As I watched him kneeling for
2 minutes on her back,
it was my airway that started to close.

This fictive kinship is what Black feels like.

This was never supposed to be a
poem about what Black feels like though.

This was just supposed to be me telling you
about how I had a toe that the doctors
took off because it was abnormal to them.
And this story is probably not normal to you.

Normal is funny you see,
in the Black community extra digits are normal.
Functional even.
To cut them off is to say one can do without.
Which is to say not necessary.
Which is to say there are parts of me
not worth keeping.

(Originally published in *Sycorax's Daughters* © 2017)

I BOUGHT THE FARM

By John Reinhart

For sale: quaint organic vegetable and livestock farm on 100+ acres, fully staffed with established CSA, all farm assets included, includes water rights, large farmhouse, good condition, profitable, affordable

The shepherd was a wonder
and I only lost sheep
when he was away
every full moon.

I never saw the man who milked the cows
before dawn and after sundown
and the boy who tended them in the field
was hard to find and had an Irish accent.

The chickens were tended by a man
named Urgh who was ghastly pale—
Hungarian, I think—
and lumbered uncomfortably.

Helga ran the CSA and mixed the compost
in a giant black cauldron that
bubbled furiously and smelled
like dead rats combined with teenage socks.

There was no accounting for the
accountant, though the numbers
always looked good—
I paid him in gold.

No one ever explained why
the farmhouse was a Gothic castle
and the eerie clouds never wandered far,
but it all seemed too good to be true
until…

(Originally published in *Star*Line 38.2*, Spring 2015)

Love Like Starlight

By Angela Yuriko Smith

Darkness cheers
and hides perfection.
No curve, smooth and smiling
hides under this basket.
Hushing answers.
Conjuring peace.

The raven night
veils your lids
healing, gentle and cool
washing dreams in watercolor
shades of shadow and
hues of galaxy.

The hot morning berates
with beams to pin us
like stiff specimens—
butterflies on cardboard—
soft feathers smearing
midnight blue
against rough brown.

The dragon day
casts us away
unforgiving, harsh and hot
burning our dreams
into ashen minutes
that fall into schedules.

Our love becomes starlight
in the morning, invisible
in the glam and yammer
exchange of hours
that chase us
from ask to task.

Pseudopod

And other selected poems by Karen Bovenmyer

After Lovecraft's *Dunwich Horror*

The skin was thickly covered with coarse black fur,
and from the abdomen a score of long
greenish-grey tentacles with red
sucking mouths protruded limply

And from the abdomen a score of long
cries reverberated in the air, shivering with
sucking mouths protruding limply
kissing empty air with flinching passion

Cries reverberated in the air, shivering with
love, yearning for touch
kissing empty air with passion flinching
Reaching like me, unanswered

Love, yearning for touch
My hand lifted
Reaching, unanswered, like me
until we touched, stroking gently

My hand lifted
Tentacle coiling, uncoiling
and we answered, stroking gently
each skin thickly covered with coarse black fur

(Originally published in *Apex Magazine,* June 2015)

Filling a Kettle

A pantoum after *Ali Baba and the Forty Thieves*

Filling a kettle, she took the oil to the kitchen and
brought it to a boil over the hearth. Then taking the
kettle back to the courtyard, she poured boiling oil
into each jar, scalding the hidden thieves to death.

She had brought it to a boil over the hearth. Then taking
lessons from her grandmothers, she poured carefully
into each jar, scalding the hidden thieves to death
and felt not guilt nor shame but a strange curiosity

An eye for an eye from her grandmothers, she poured
Hot death onto trapped men, a lingering way to die
And felt not guilt nor shame but a curiosity strange
Screams burning barren somewhere deep inside

Hot death onto trapped men, a lingering way to die
Filling a kettle, she took the oil to the kitchen
And barren screaming somewhere deep inside
The kettle back to the courtyard, pouring boiling oil

What Dolls Eat

Our cat, Puddles, never missed breakfast, until today. When I told my daughter, she said the dolls, which she tucked in their beds each night, were also missing. Puddles loved to play with them—carrying them by the hair, leaving a porcelain hand poking from under the couch or a tiny spikey shoe at the top of the steps. At last, we found them in the 1/12-scale gazebo, sipping plastic red wine. My daughter had forgotten she did not put them away, but that did not explain their sticky hands and faces or the shine in their open, painted eyes.

(Originally published in *The Were Traveler* © 2015)

LYCANTHROPE

(For Robert McCammon's *Wolf's Hour*)
And other selected poems by Michael R. Collings

Lycanthrope: 'werewolf'; from Latin lycanthropos, from Greek lukanthrōpos, 'wolf,' (from *wjkwo) +anthropos, 'man.'

While I may fraternize with sprites
And other creatures, banals and trites,
I doubt that it's within my power
To give the Wolf his proper hour.

It's easy enough to limn his claws,
His massive teeth and massive jaws;
More difficult—and here I cower—
To give the Wolf his proper hour.

There is a certain innocence
That horror stories can't dispense
About the wolf in his clotted bower
To give the Wolf his proper hour.

It's not his fault…say what you might;
Not through his choice, but by a bite
The beast emerges in full flower
To give the Wolf his proper hour.

The mind withdraws, the body looms,
And in his secret midnight glooms
He feels thought fade and blood-lust lour
To give the Wolf his proper hour.

But with the dawn, he knows the pain
Of human sorrow once again,
And, frighted, waits for moonrise dour
To give the Wolf his proper hour.

In mannish form he must decide
Which future fate he will abide:
To slay his traitor-body now, or
To give the Wolf his proper hour.

There's dread…revulsion—but there's more:
   Pathos beneath the blood and gore.
And that is why it's beyond my power
   To give the Wolf his proper hour.

(Originally published in *Words Words Words* © 2018)

Ommatophorous

Ommatophorous: New Latin, from Greek ommat-, ómma 'eye' + o + phorous (New Latin -phorus, from Greek -phoros 'bearing.' (Pronounced 'om-uh-tof-er-uh s.')Stygian: from Latin, stygius, from Greek stygios, from Styg-, Styx 'Styx,' from Stux, from stugnos 'hateful, gloomy.'

It slips through mist and Stygian night…
The silent creeper slithers;
It comes with death and chilling blight—
At its caustic touch, grass withers.

Its tentacles are smoothly sleek,
No suckers grasp rash prey
To wrench them to the pulsing beak
And tuck them fast away.

Where a visage should appear…
Nothing but age-creased skin:
No eyes nor nose nor jutting ears—
Just a maw to take food in.

Still it never loses track
Of victims, goal, or path;
It never misses its midnight snack
Or suffers hungry wrath.

And yet it navigates so well…
It must be SONARous—
A valid guess…but truth to tell,
It's ommatopherous.

(Originally published in *Words Words Words 2—The Darker Side* © 2019)

The Tongue We Dream In

And other selected poems by Sheree Renée Thomas

Our first language was wet
mournful questions rang
like falling stars
in red clay throats

No milk teeth to help
form words, our eyes
made syllables, cries strung out
on ropes of tears, thoughts
dangled on twisted threads
of hope

Our first language was touch
balled fists of unlined fingers
grasping for fire, tendrils of light
blazed in eyes, molten with liquid fear
skin pricked and pierced with
stories to be told, lives to unfold
through the dark tunnel of years

Our first language was song
a bell hangs in our hearts
rings with every bloody drumbeat
songs to reduce souls to ashes
and songs to sing them anew

Our first language
was wet touch singing
ourselves across the darkness
into life, in our dreams we sing
in the first tongue, the language
before birth

Diary of a She-Creature, or the Little Death

Grief settles on her brain like ash
pain knotted in a twist of spine
she rests on the skin of memory
a beast for the waning light
she circles dark rings of ruin
runs through the listening night
lungs strain for crisp moon air
the flight that ignites
knees, limbs, flesh
in the morning she is all teeth and gold
she digs into the wet soil of sleep
digs, dreams still filled with hunger

Church of the Saint of Dead End Streets

Save us from ruin, the great bell wails
each of us has something to sacrifice
something to survive

(All originally published in *Sleeping Under the Tree of Life* © 2016)

The Milk of Human Depravity

And Other Selected Poems by Wrath James White

Holding the wolf to your tit
it suckles
snuggles in your warmth
your scent
of lavender and sex

You stroke and caress
its downy fur
it growls and chews
your gumdrop nipples
drinks from the milk
of human depravity
as you feed the feral beast
within you

It will grow hungrier
it will need meat
flesh
blood
it will learn
how violent we humans can be
and it will long
for the wild
we civilized monsters
deprived it of

And it will long
for the savage instinctive
unconditional love
we civilized monsters
are incapable of

Untitled #2

Enthralled by your flesh
In love with you utterly
your body, mind, and spirit
and if you died tomorrow
I would eat your corpse

Sympathy for Frankenstein

Watching as it rots
as everything lovely dies
I do understand
wanting to revive the dead
cheat oblivion
reanimate lost passions
expired and mourned
All I want is what I had
And I held heaven once
I would raise a graveyard for it
to hold it again
kiss life back into its carcass
in lightning and fury
I share his dark obsession
My sympathies for Frankenstein

(Originally published in *If You Died Tomorrow I Would Eat Your Corpse* © 2018)

Art From the Heart

By Jill Bauman

Visions swirl engulfing him
as he swallows their vapors.
Remnants suspend in air
as a fleeting memory.

Intertwining images
fade, then reappear.
Sparks ignite, scatter,
like random heavenly stars.

A balloon, soars aloft,
floats through the atmosphere.
Bubble bursting, dissipates,
gone forever from consciousness.

Blank white surface challenges him,
a stark reminder,
waiting for space to be filled
with illusive dreams.

Splashes of vibrant colors
interrupt tranquility,
patterns erupt like lava
flowing down the mountainside.

Squinting, peering, he steps back,
his eyes penetrate his soul,
images transformed,
created from the heart.

Outstretched hands beckon,
from the canvas, enticing him to enter
the tree-lined trail to faraway mountain peaks
that peer through the mist.

His transformed world envisioned,
he steps into his creation.
Sitting at the swollen roots of a worn ancient tree,
melding with paint and canvas enduring, forever.

Holmes vs. the Ripper, Part 1

By Sara Tantlinger

November 1888,
cold metallic tang of blood
billows up in the atmosphere
hovering, haunting
crimson pollution in Victorian streets.

Slightly after the witching hour
a woman cries, "murder!"
Violence is nothing new here,
neighbors turn away, shut their ears
slicing off sound as he slices off
a woman's breasts.

Around 10:45am,
a landlord goes to collect rent
Mary Kelly's is overdue,
she doesn't open the door
blood smears the broken window.

Mary Kelly is nothing more
than a gumbo-stewed organ soup
scarlet flesh pile, skinned down,
inhumanly carved up on the bed
a massacre of mutilation.

There will come a debate after this,
was she truly the Ripper's last?
Are the following Whitechapel murders
his or someone else's?

At this stillborn, chilled moment
Jack remains the most brutal
servant of the Devil.

At this stillborn, chilled moment
H.H. Holmes hears
backward whispers slithering
into his small ears

You can do better
You can do better

(Originally published in *The Devil's Dreamland: Poetry Inspired by H.H. Holmes* © 2018)

Mary Shelley's Baby

By Trisha J. Wooldridge

A dream was gifted.
  A malformed monster child pulled back the curtain
  watery yellow-white eyes stared
  looking for love in his father's
  terror-filled eyes
    and found none.

So she took the abomination to her breast
and let it suckle milk and blood
  and made an album of its life.

Electric mortal mystery
  and anatomy lessons from corpses
made short work of Inimmaculate Conception.

Psychology and analysis
  were the creature's
  bedtime tales.

Though her water broke
  and carved many rivers,
too many navigators
  forgot
    the sea
  that birthed their roads.

So she sits in the dark,
  still rocking her monster.

(Originally published in *Nothing's Sacred Volume 4* © 2018)

DYER DIED IN SILENCE

By Andrea "Vocab" Sanderson

She went from a shutter to silence
Eyes glazed over with the void of stillness.
As if illness suffocated the sight right out of her sockets.
A pocket of air emptied out of her wrinkled throat
One last hallowed gasp before she passed
and the cloak of death covered over her frigid soul.
Sheol opened its' gluttonous grasp to swallow her whole.
Boney hands reaching around the rope noose
that choked her esophagus and
asphyxiated her malevolent being.
She felt the slow collapse of her lungs.
Life was expunged from her sturdy tyrannical body.
She swayed oddly in the gallows like a broken wind chime.
She wavered awkwardly like a kite string entangled amongst tree twigs.
She died with her heart darkened scorched by wickedness.
Her soul was as pitch, as the bottomless abyss.
Fittingly, Amelia Dyer died, in the same manner in which she had
murderously slain hundreds of innocent infants,
stricken with unfortunate circumstances.
She died unwillingly, yielding only to the restriction of air.
She died suspended in midair.
Even in her death, no one is truly aware of how many children she
carelessly killed for profit and gain.
Only the Thames River will stream confessions of her infamous name.
Its' waters quivering from the deserted bodies she buried there,
Countless babies forever enslaved in this liquid grave.
Many going unclaimed and some were never recovered.
Their grief stricken mothers went howling, like La Llorona, to the grave
tortured with uncertainty. Amelia took no pity.
Legions of greedy spawns feasted through her intentions.
Amelia killed as many as six children in one day.
Her stern thin lipped scowl will haunt the annals of history.
No darkness can hold a candle to her flame of vile infamy.
Cruelty was personified through her sick twisted mind. She filled 5 books
with her confessions line for line. 'Baby farming' and murders were her
crimes. She died on June 10, 1896,
Hanging from the scaffold, she shuttered into silence.

(Originally published in *Sycorax's Daughters* © 2017)

Little Red in Haiku

By Christina Sng

flash of red
through the woods
alarums

old goat
tougher than expected
long lunch

sweetness
of maraschino cherries
baby smells

roleplaying
another species
something new

calmness
tenderizes the meat
grandma not grandma

clear anomalies
the sharpness of teeth
and claws

the speed
of younglings
chest arrow

her sobs
as he fades to black
grandma bones uncovered

(Originally published in *Star*Line 40.4* © 2017)

How Can Joining HWA Help You?

Whether you're an aspiring writer working toward your all-important first pro-level sale or a seasoned novelist with a dozen books to your credit, HWA can help further your career through networking, mentoring, information trading, and promotional resources. If you're a producer, publisher, editor, or agent, you'll find our networking resources invaluable for finding dedicated, productive writers to add to your stable. If you're a librarian or bookseller, you'll have an inside track on talented writers, hot new books, and likely award winners. And if you're a fan, you'll have access to the writers you love and will get to be an important part of the oldest and largest organization dedicated to horror.

©2018

Nonfiction

"In Search of Marjorie Bowen: A Work in Progress"

By John C. Tibbetts

There it was, a little poem, handwritten, on a scrap of paper:

My life was not set in pleasant places
In the jostle of the hundreds I always stood
alone.
I saw the devil look through many laughing faces
And often felt his likeness rising in my own.[i]

I had already spent two days at the Yale Library examining the papers of British author Marjorie Bowen (1885-1952). The unpublished poem bore no attribution. It was tucked away in a folder that also contained pages and pages of handwritten notes, letters, publisher's contracts, and photographs. Everywhere, the handwriting was virtually illegible and the images unnamed. When were they written? Under what circumstances? Why were they never published? Those lines leaped off the page and waggled their dark, beckoning, fingers at me.

Also, among the scattered archival papers was a handwritten card to Bowen by Sir Arthur Conan Doyle, dated 3 July 1916. Responding to his reading of one of Bowen's *conte cruels* in *Shadows of Yesterday,* he wrote: "May I say how really splendid I think your new book…I don't like women's work as a rule, on account of a certain lack of substance, but here the detail, the atmosphere and the dramatic effect are all equally good." Questions abound: Did the two writers ever meet? Did they at least correspond? Surely, their shared pleasures in historical novels and grim short stories revealed some sort of affinity and demanded a contact of some kind? This could be of great significance. But Doyle authority Jon Lellenberg, who has agreed to investigate the matter, so far has come up with nothing that is more than speculation.

My search into the mysteries of the life and work of this most estimable of British writers, whose more than 150 published works included some of the finest novels, stories, and biographies of the last century, is inspired and rebuked.

To write nonfiction is to stub your toe on reality.

I am presently under contract from McFarland Press to submit a critical and biographical study bearing the title, *The Furies of*

Marjorie Bowen. I could never have anticipated what I was getting in to when I first considered tackling the subject. How could I know that several volumes I already had in my library, bearing authors named "Joseph Shearing" and "George Preedy," were actually by Marjorie Bowen? How could I know that "Marjorie Bowen" wasn't her real name, either? (That has turned out be Margaret Gabrielle Vere Campbell?) Like the grin of Lewis Carroll's Cheshire Cat, the name "Marjorie Bowen" floats out there, itself a fiction, somehow insubstantial, faintly mocking, always beckoning…

Despite the presence of two autobiographical memoirs and a bare handful of essays by her admirers,[ii] we're not quite sure just what manner of person she was: (1. Why is she so obscure today after enjoying a measure of celebrity in her lifetime; (2. How did she transmute a lonely, neglected, and untutored childhood into a protean body of work that displays considerable historical grounding (she was an authority on William of Orange) and cultural erudition—from references to the Roman Lucretius, to the Jacobean playwright John Webster and the French painter Watteau; (3. Who did she know, what did she read, how did she write; (4. And how in the world did she find the time to write while enduring two troubled marriages, two world wars, and the responsibility as the sole breadwinner for her family? Most intriguing: How did she survive and excel in a male-dominated literary community? To this last I must confess that I can find little information regarding any associations she may have had with her female contemporaries, notably Rebecca West (a single letter from West exists), Virginia Woolf (whom she cites in a letter), and Vernon Lee and Daphne du Maurier (about whom she says nothing whatever). Much further research is warranted.

She herself described something of her attitudes and methods toward historical research in her Introduction to a volume of stories called *Shadows of Yesterday*:

> If one could look back—beyond the dust, beyond the years to the time when all these dead things were fresh—when the originals of those portraits moved and worked and laughed, when beer was really brewed in those jugs and tea drunk from those cups, when those cards were dashed on to the playing table, when that sword graced some gallant's thigh, that paste necklace some woman's

> neck…If one could look back to those times, might not one find curious stories, sad stories, and gay stories attached to these old worthless objects?—as staring at ashes one may recall the flames.[v]

Yes, we, too, consider all of these things. But it requires as much speculation as verifiable facts to turn them into a history that is authentic and true. But even the facts, as G.K. Chesterton once observed, can lead us in the wrong directions.

Let me turn to Bowen again. In her remarkable story, "Ann Mellor's Lover," which, as is the case with so many of her stories, describes the process of fleshing out a tiny clue into an entire history. The narrator has no idea at first what he is getting in to when he stumbles across a piece of paper bearing a penciled portrait of a woman. His search is as much intuitive as it is factual. The narrator's words could be those of Bowen herself:

> My peculiar affinity with the past has always been rather overwhelming—a kind of haunting preoccupation, wholly pleasant but teasing, like something you can't place or explain or reason about…It's a great diversion to me, a great interest, and sometimes a queer sort of pain, too.

From that first moment he sets eyes on that paper, he confesses, "I knew that it was a clue that I was bound to follow through the labyrinth of the past. The feeling was that I knew all about it—the whole story, but could not for the moment remember it." But soon the crude drawing assumed in his mind "a warm-coloured human face; she lived before my inner eye, a complete creature," yet one that was a "dark, troubled creature about whom I felt such excitement."[iv] It is *empathy* as much as dogged investigation that leads to some kind of truth, provisional at best, as it turns out in the story.

And so it has been with all of my own nonfiction writing. Heretofore, I have enjoyed subjects who, in addition to my enthusiasm for their works, conveniently provided me a mountain of facts and viewpoints. In my *Peter Weir: Interviews* I traveled to Sydney, Australia, where I had access to the man himself, interviewed his cinematographer, and investigated the resources of the Australian Film Institute and Archives. Likewise, in my *The Gothic Worlds of Peter Straub* I logged many hours with one of the most amiable and compelling gentlemen on the planet, enjoyed the support of his wife and many of his contemporaries, and had access to his newly installed papers in the Fales Archives at New York University. Even in my studies of artists no longer living, when, obviously, first-hand encounters were no longer possible (at least this side of the Veil)—*Dvorak in America, Schumann: A Chorus of Voices*, and *Douglas Fairbanks and the American Century*—I pursued opportunities to interview other historians and commentators. Indeed, as a professional journalist as well as an academic, I find that most times the line between wears thin.

Alas, Miss Bowen is no longer available. And she seems in her lifetime to have submitted to the intrusions of few interviewers.

No, Marjorie Bowen demands that I read her works, a most agreeable injunction. Yet, even here, there are roadblocks. Aside from a dozen titles or so, the majority of her books are long out of print, and I have had to scan numerous book sellers' lists, examine the World Catalogue, and apply to Interlibrary Loan through my home base at the University of Kansas. Some titles yet remain Out There, lost in some literary purgatory, like so many of her characters. Yet, we persevere. The DNA in the literary bones of her stories might help fill in the chasms of the unknown. In that respect, I subscribe to the words of cultural historian, Walter Benjamin. I put them in italics:

> *"The traces of the Storyteller cling to the story the way the handprints of the potter cling to the clay vessel."*[v]

I believe wholeheartedly in that. Despite what textual critics, among others, may say, I am convinced that writers may run, but they cannot hide. The problem here is that Bowen was so damned *prolific*, witness her many pseudonyms. I confess that I have managed so far to consume only representative titles from her vast output—a dozen of the weird and historical novels (especially the pagan *The Haunted Vintage* and the 17th-century witchcraft chronicle, *Circle in the Water*); a handful of her essays (she was an authority on William of Orange and wrote passionately in favor of ethical responsibility and against religious cults); and more than a hundred of her short stories (to be without the lyric "Serenata," the autobiographical "Expiation," and the bizarre gothic "The Sign-Painter and the Crystal Fishes" is to be without three of the handful of finest weird tales this side of Arthur Machen.[vi] To be clinical about it, I try to trace from the accumulated data the patterns and consistencies—to connect the dots, as it were. But there's seemingly no end to it. Every time I locate and read yet another novel, one more story collection, an additional hard-to-find essay, I think—*how could I have done without this?* It's a lament as much as a discovery. We subscribe to the words of the Pulitzer-Prize winning bookman, Michael Dirda, who says the scholar's "malady" lies in its "perfidiousness": "Its sufferers can never fully finish their research. Always, like the elusive blue flower of the German romantics, there beckons yet one more important text to peruse, just a few more documents to consult…[and] the sense that somewhere the key work awaits, that single reference that will turn the lock and open a new era."[vii]

Amen.

Alas, the imperative to *read everything*—try as I might—must inevitably be frustrated. I need more lifetimes than Bowen herself enjoyed, to fully encompass her works.

The work continues. In addition to my work at the Yale Library, I have published two essays, spoken at last year's Ann Radcliffe Conference, and initiated a correspondence with the Bowen Estate in Cornwall, England. My enthusiasm and fascination with the woman and her work, begun so long ago with the chance discovery of her short story, "The Bishop of Hell," continues unabated. Her very elusiveness is both a veil and an enticement. Although her position in the literary community of her day, is unchallenged, her status today is at issue. Consummate Professional? Literary artist? Hack writer for hire? To her contemporaries Marjorie Bowen the respectable novelist seems to have come across primarily as an admirable exemplar of the dedicated mother and artist. Yet, to those of us privileged today to know her celebrated gothic horror stories, we also see a woman limned in flames. Neither the Angel in the House nor the Madwoman in the Attic—but both. As G.K. Chesterton once observed of Charlotte Bronte—in words I apply here to Bowen—"She was at best like that warmer and more domestic thing, *a house on fire* [my italics].[viii]

In sum, I think this declaration by Mme. Lesarge to her twin sister, in one of her finest stories, "The Last Bouquet," brings us closest to her identity as an artist and a woman:

> "I daresay you think that I am completely degraded, but pray don't waste any such pity on me. I am successful—I

always have been successful. I am, in a way, triumphant over everything, over the usual conventions, the traditions that bind women, over the usual stupid emotions that cause them to waste their hearts and lives; over all the pettifogging duties and obligations that wear away a woman like you."[ix]

John C. Tibbetts is an Associate Professor in the Department of Film and Media Studies at the University of Kansas, where he teaches courses in film history, media studies, and theory and aesthetics. As an educator and broadcaster, he has worked as a news reporter for CBS Television and National Public Radio; produced classical music programming for Kansas Public Radio; written (and illustrated) 26 books, more than 250 articles, and several short stories. His most recent books are *Performing Music History* (Palgrave Macmillan, 2018), *The Gothic Worlds of Peter Straub* (McFarland, 2016), *Peter Weir: Interviews* (Mississippi, 2014), *The Gothic Imagination* (2011), and *Composers in the Movies: Studies in Musical Biography* (Yale University Press, 2005). John has researched, written, produced, and narrated two radio series, the 15-hour *The World of Robert Schumann* (currently being broadcast worldwide on the WFMT Radio Network), and the 17-hour *Piano Portraits* (broadcast on Kansas Public Radio). He was awarded in 2008 the Kansas Governor's Arts in Education Award, presented by Governor Kathleen Sebelius. Currently in preparation is *The Furies of Marjorie Bowen*, a critical study of the celebrated British Gothic author.

---

[i] Unpublished poem by Marjorie Bowen, the Bowen Papers, Beinecke Libarary, Yale, Box 25, Folder 182.

[ii] I am indebted to critic Michael Dirda, Jon Lellenberg, and T.E.D. Klein for their patience with my many questions; and in particular to Jessica Amanda Salmonson, for sharing information with me via email correspondence about her research on Bowen. She edited Twilight and Other Supernatural Romances (Ashcroft, BC: Ash-Tree Press, 1998).

[iii] Marjorie Bowen, "Introduction," in Bowen, Shadows of Yesterday: Stories from an Old Catalogue (London: Smith Elder & Co., 1926) , 5.

[iv] Marjorie Bowen, "Ann Mellor's Lover," in Twilight, 91-93.

[v] Walter Benjamin, "The Storyteller," in Illuminations (New York: Schocken Books, 1968), 91-92.

[vi] Respectively, from the story collections *Bagatelle, Dark Ann,* and *Curious Happenings.*

[vii] Michael Dirda, Readings: Essays and Literary Entertainments (Bloomington and Indianapolis: Indiana University Press, 2000), 117.

[viii] G.K. Chesterton, The Victorian Age in Literature (London: Williams & Norgate, 1913), 114-115.

[ix] Marjorie Bowen, "The Last Bouquet," in Bowen, The Last Bouquet: Some Twilight Tales (London: John Lane the Bodley Head, 1933), 11.

Short Story Collections

By Thersa Matsuura

It was always my assumption that short story collections were things only the hallowed writers who have already 'made it' were allowed to do, authors who had sold hundreds of stories, a half dozen novels, and had an award or two under their belts. No-names like me didn't get their stories bundled up to be sold to the masses.

At least that's what I thought.

I'm the author of two story collections—"A Robe of Feathers and Other Stories" and "The Carp-Faced Boy and Other Tales". The latter was nominated for a Bram Stoker Award® (2017) alongside the likes of Joe Hill and Josh Malerman. That right there is a dream come true for me.

But how did I do it?

First, and this is the preacher preaching to the choir here, I know—but I read a lot of short story collections, everything I could get my hands on, both in and out of the genre. I've always loved reading collections and wanted to know how they were put together, what worked and what didn't. I noticed some were more chaotic, good stories but no overall symmetry to the book, while others had an underlying connectedness, rhythm, dare I say beauty to them.

Next, I began writing and submitting, writing and submitting. I believed (rightly so) that the more stories you have published the more attractive you'll be to a potential publisher. During this process I found my voice, found the heart of what drives my writing, and found that there were certain pieces that while different had a weird sort of affinity to one another. They seemed to naturally fit together, and it wasn't simply that they were all of the same genre either.

It was here that I convinced myself that I was doing something that hadn't been done yet. I don't think it matters whether I was right or not. What matters is it gave me a boost of confidence and really ramped up my enthusiasm for writing tales that could potentially be collected into a single book.

Part of my confidence was that I felt I was introducing the reader to something they might not know anything about. Yes, we all know a lot about Japanese horror and *yokai* and folklore, but I decided to dig deeper and discover the things that weren't portrayed in anime or manga. Then, on top of that, I thought why not invent my own world where these beasties of yore still existed, and superstition held more weight. Again, it's not like this hasn't been done before. But I had so much fun inventing this world, giving it its own special rules, and then naming my own special genre: mythical realism.

I think the point is not to try and create a new genre, but to give yourself some guidelines for your future collection. Yes, every story should be able to stand on its own and shine, but as a whole they should all come together to bring more to the reader, more meaning and depth and possibly secrets.

Thinking about the threads that can tie a collection together is fun, too. Instead of just genre—we are all writers of dark fiction—you can link your stories in other ways.

You can have the tales all occur in a unique time or interesting place. But why not do more? How about combine the two and have a group of stories all set in the same strange place but jumping back and forth through time?

Another interesting way to connect your stories is through characters. Have your characters make appearances in other stories, switching the protagonist and antagonist from tale to tale. Have a very vibrant protagonist make a cameo in a different story. You could also change up points of view and have a single event witnessed by different people until the event itself becomes so skewed we the reader must figure out whom to trust and whom to not. It will be a different book for every person who reads it. An object, a color, or a phrase could be present in each story as well. All used but differently so. Like I said, dreaming up this rules can be a lot of fun. The ideas are limited only by our creativity.

We all have our own very unique voice, but also our own unique way of telling a story. Telling individual stories is one level but writing with an eye to gathering those tales and having them as a whole tell us a bigger story is something I think distinctive to a short story collection. You can be much more looser and mysterious than when you're writing chapters in a book.

I suggest you read and write and submit, all the while considering how every piece you finish might fit into a bigger whole. Don't be afraid to tear down and rebuild a story. With every tale we tell we grow as writers, so too does our story telling abilities.

Also, don't wait until you've finished to start jotting down notes to use when you are finally ready to query publishers or agents. Use the constraints of your imagined future collection to fuel your creativity. Don't be afraid to do something different or whacky. There is plenty of mundaneness out there and you are not it.

Thersa Matsuura is a long-term expat who has lived half her life in Japan. She is the author of two short story collections: *A Robe of Feathers and Other Stories* (Counterpoint LLC, 2009) and *The Carp-Faced Boy and Other Tales* (Independent Legions Press, 2017). The latter collection was a finalist for The Bram Stoker Award®(2017).

Thersa is also a graduate of Clarion West (2015) and a recipient of Horror Writer's Association's Mary Wollstonecraft Shelley Scholarship (2015). She has a monthly podcast (Uncanny Japan) that focuses on the obscure and weird from Japanese culture.

What Is The Horror Writers Association?

The Horror Writers Association (HWA) is a nonprofit organization of writers and publishing professionals around the world, dedicated to promoting dark literature and the interests of those who write it. HWA was formed in the late 1980's with the help of many of the field's greats, including Dean Koontz, Robert McCammon, and Joe Lansdale. Today—with over 1250 members in countries such as Australia, Belgium, Brazil, Canada, Costa Rica, Denmark, Germany, Honduras, India, Ireland, Israel, Italy, Japan, Netherlands, New Zealand, Nicaragua, Russia, Spain, South Africa, Sweden, Taiwan, Thailand, Trinidad, United Kingdom and the United States—it is the oldest and most respected professional organization for the much-loved writers who have brought you the most enjoyable sleepless nights of your life.

One of HWA's missions is to encourage public interest in and foster an appreciation of good Horror and Dark Fantasy literature. To that end, we offer the public areas of this web site, we sponsor or take part in occasional public readings and lectures, we publish a blog and produce other materials for booksellers and librarians, we facilitate readings and signings by horror writers, and we maintain an official presence at the major fan-based horror and fantasy conventions, such as the World Fantasy Convention and the World Horror Convention.

HWA is also dedicated to recognizing and promoting diversity in the horror genre, and practices a strict anti-harassment policy at all of its events.

As part of our core mission, we sponsor the annual Bram Stoker Awards® for superior achievement in horror literature. Named in honor of the author of the seminal horror novel Dracula, the Bram Stoker Awards® are presented for superior writing in eleven categories including traditional fiction of various lengths, poetry, screenwriting, graphic novels, young adult, and non-fiction. In addition, HWA presents an annual Lifetime Achievement Award to a living person who has made significant contributions to the writing of Horror and Dark Fantasy over the course of a lifetime.

Jill
2005

Anthologies

A Bouquet of Flowers

By Michael Bailey

You've written a flash piece, a short story, a novelette, perhaps ventured into novella-length territory; maybe your manuscript took a day, a week, a month, maybe longer to compose. Hopefully you've stashed it away somewhere to marinate, passed it on to beta-readers, re-written sections, thrown away the first page [or first few because most stories often don't know where to start], or you have at least gone through a few drafts before calling it *done*. Is it ready? Probably not. Try again. Is it ready now, this masterpiece? Good. Let's call it done and sell the thing.

"But *where*?" you might ask, always on the search for decent per-word pay rates. An anthology is a good place to start, if any are seeking submissions. Wherever you plan to place it, however, keep in mind that there are certain rules to follow if you ever want your work to appear in print. For the sake of simplification, let's focus on the anthology.

The anthologists, they are [not] gods; they are [not] gatekeepers.

Before going further, the difference between *collections* and *anthologies* must be defined, as well the origination of the word 'anthology.' There is often confusion between the two. Collections contain multiple works by a single writer—bound red roses, for example, all from the same source. Anthologies contain single works [of all types] by multiple writers—bound flowers of various color from a multitude of sources. It's that simple.

An anthology is defined as "a published collection of poems or other pieces of writing." The word 'anthology' is derived from the Greek *Anthos* [meaning *flower*] and—*logia* [meaning *collection*], or *anthologia*, a word denoting a collection of the "flowers" of verse. So, an anthology was originally defined as "small choice poems or epigrams, by various authors." A *bouquet* of the written word, in other words.

And the anthologists, the modern bouquet-makers, they are people, and they are on your side whether you believe it or not. They can become friends—people you want on your side [if treated properly], as much as they can become enemies—people you will never side with [if treated poorly]. They are creators [gods], like you, albeit with much wider scopes in that they are responsible for creating larger stories out of many smaller stories. Anthologists are readers, first and foremost. Most read more *un*published work than published, and *very* few are writers themselves. Anthologists are editors, some recommending minor adjustments while others requiring more extensive editing, depending on the *want* of the piece, and its current condition. And they are compilers [gatekeepers], in that by creating anthologies they must first filter through hundreds if not thousands of stories before making final selections on a select few.

Why would anthologists [or their publishers, or *anyone,* for that matter] ever want to spend money on what you've created? Are you worth it? How beautiful is your flower?

Some math: An anthology receives a thousand short stories, with only twenty to be included. This means you have a 2% chance of making the cull if what you've created is good enough [it better be], and adhere to guidelines. Factor in that most pro-rate anthologies are often half-filled with stories from *invited* writers, and your chance of inclusion drops to 1%. Factor in that sometimes anthologists first fill 75% of a book before ever offering a "call for submissions," and that number drops to roughly half of a percent. Your odds, they are small.

This thing you've created. What is it? It's *flash* if under a thousand words, *a short story* if between that and seventy-five hundred, *novelette* if between that and seventeen thousand five hundred or so, and *novella* if between that and forty to forty-five thousand, which gets you into short *novel* territory. Novellas, they mostly have their own market now, albeit small, and the market for short novels is almost nonexistent. If what you've written—your darling, perfect manuscript—has dipped into novel-length, then anthologists no longer concern you. In fact, if your story is anywhere over five thousand words, it's going to be a tough sell to an editor for an anthology unless longer works are specifically sought.

Is your manuscript close to short story length? Six thousand is close, right? Seven thousand? Eight? Guidelines in short fiction markets most likely call for five thousand words or fewer, but editors don't mind a little padding, right? Yes. Yes, they mind. Guidelines are established for a reason, and unless unrealistic [most likely non-professional, *a la* "calls for submission"], if you don't adhere to a few simple rules [word count caps, content, formatting, *et cetera.*], your story will go unread, in most cases, attachment unopened. Your story will be trash. Like fancy fonts? Like single-spacing? Like overwriting [not necessarily word-count but by what you might consider purple prose]? Like foregoing the marinating / self-editing / beta-reading stage[s]? Like bending guidelines? If so, you will soon become familiar with the term "instant rejection." If an anthologist is specifically seeking short fiction in the five thousand range, and your story is a thousand to three higher than that, or longer, either start cutting, start cutting deep, or don't send your story at all. If it's *close*, get out the red pen; start highlighting, pounding Delete and / or Backspace until your fingers blister; most stories in the six and seven and eight thousand range work better as five, anyway. Cut until it hurts, and then cut more. Bleed your pages until all that's left is what's absolutely necessary. And *never* pad your story for the sake of word count.

Some math: The average anthology runs 100,000 words, give or take. Twenty short stories, each five thousand words, adds up to 100,000 words. And some invited writers [more often than not]—with more selling-factor behind their names—tend to run long and sometimes *get* to run long. If the anthologist doesn't cap payment on a specific word count [the "name" writers thus having more opportunity for income, or even offered *higher* per-word rates because of sell-ability], this in turn eats into the overall budget of the project. For the sake of word counts, this means there is indeed a reason for that hard guideline of five thousand words for the uninvited. It also means your odds of making it into the book *increases* if your word count *decreases*. Why? Editors often seek shorter fiction to make up for "name" writers taking their privileged space. The point? Stick to five thousand words as your own personal goal to benefit most from professional payment, but consider submitting shorter works to increase your chance of publication.

A simple rule to follow: Until you learn the art of self-editing, you will never sell a story to a pro-rate market. Master self-editing, and you will soon find yourself *only* selling to pro-rate markets. Another simple rule: Unless you are specifically writing for markets seeking novelette- or novella-length works, don't ever send a story of such length to a *short* fiction market.

It all comes down to money.

Some math: The average anthology runs 100,000 words, give or take. A pro-rate anthology offers six cents per word [or should, at a minimum]. This means the budget for the work to be included [the words only, the meat] is typically $6,000, give or take, not to mention editor payment, artwork, cover design, publishing costs, marketing, and all those other essentials required to *sell* the book. This means the average anthology budget could *start* anywhere between $8,000 to $10,000, often higher, which in turn means eventually selling enough copies to recoup that cost. The book, if it is to be "professional," therefore, must include only the best, which is why the hard work of the anthologist often goes unnoticed.

Is your story "the best" [not just in *your* mind]? Is your story original? Is your story good enough to survive the great culling of the anthologist? It better be the best fucking thing ever written. In a great bouquet [think the anthologies of Ellen Datlow, Stephen Jones, John Joseph Adams, Paula Guran, Thomas F. Monteleone, and many others], which brilliant burst of life is *yours* on display, or is your contribution lost in a bland display no one will ever remember?

But your story, it's *done*, you've cut your darlings, you've bled the page, so to speak, and you've cut every word not absolutely necessary like the Jack Ketchums of the world. Now what? What's your story worth [to you, to the anthologist]? What should you [expect to] be paid? The answer should always be "professional rate," but that is not always the case in today's market, although it should at least be your first *choice* when deciding where to submit.

Aim high, always. Start at the top, pay-wise. Avoid anything other than "professional" if you can. Six cents per word or bust! For science fiction and fantasy, this can be as high as eight to ten cents per word, sometimes twelve, so, if it fits, why not start there? Avoid "token" rate. Avoid "exposure." Avoid "contributor copy only." Avoid "royalty only." Avoid "flat fee."

Why are you writing? For fun? For exposure? For charity? What is your self-worth as an "author," as a writer?

Let's say your story is the best damn thing ever written. Let's say an anthologist likes your stuff. Let's say he or she has offered to buy your story, or your non-fiction article, or whatever, perhaps after a few minor tweaks, perhaps after some light editing, perhaps after some *heavy* editing. Good. Let's say that whatever it is works for the intended project, and an anthologist has offered you a contract. Good. Do you sign it? Your first instinct is to scroll through, looking for payment information, your mind screaming *Yes! Let's sign this thing!* and your heart racing, and you're all smiles because, out of the small percentage of those not culled, you and your work have managed to squeeze in amidst names you [hopefully] recognize and names you [hopefully] don't.

But the contract…what should you expect? Your goal, as a writer, is not to get screwed, always. It's *your* work, after all, your name attached to the story, or whatever it may be. Despite the *other* names in the anthology, your name is now most important. What are you willing to sign away? Instead of relying on your first instincts of signing your name and dating the contract and announcing your fame to the world, there are important things to consider. Just as you are required to self-edit your work, you should be willing [as is your right] to edit contract details if they are seemingly *un*professional. Yes, you can do that.

Look specifically at the terms. Are you willing to part with your baby for a year, two years, three years, or [never] indefinitely? Are you willing to part with *audio* rights? Are you willing to part with *media* rights? Why would a publisher even need those? Are there plans for such things? Ask. If not, why are they there? And why should a publisher have the right to keep your work in print for the proposed terms? How long will the book be in print? Does the contract allow for inclusion in "best of" anthologies or perhaps a personal collection? If not, it *should*. Does the contract allow for split royalty if the book "makes it big" and starts raking in the cash? If not, only the publisher benefits. Read the contractual terms carefully. Redline what you don't like. Add what's not there. If you are a professional writer, and you are working with a professional anthologist, this shouldn't be a problem.

This thing you've written, this flower, whatever it may be, if it's good enough, and *you're* good enough, the "anthologists," the bouquet-makers, they will always be on your side, and soon you will find yourself not seeking "calls for submission," but waiting for invites into future bouquets.

Michael Bailey is a freelance writer, editor and book designer, and the recipient of over two dozen literary accolades, such as the Bram Stoker Award® and Benjamin Franklin Award. His novels include *Palindrome Hannah*, *Phoenix Rose*, and *Psychotropic Dragon*, and he has published two short story and poetry collections, *Scales and Petals*, and *Inkblots and Blood Spots*. Edited anthologies include *Pellucid Lunacy, Qualia Nous, The Library of the Dead, You Human, Adam's Ladder, Prisms*, and four volumes of *Chiral Mad*. His most recent publications are three standalone novelettes: *SAD Face, Darkroom*, and *Our Children, Our Teachers*.

A Writer's Life

Dangerous Dames

By Amy Grech

I started writing seriously in high school after reading several of Stephen King's novels; I got hooked on Horror at the tender age of twelve, when an aunt gave me a copy of *Cujo*. I've been reading Stephen King's books ever since. Growing up during the 1980s, I noticed there weren't very many women writing scary stories. Inspired, I set out to change that. Why should men have all the fun, writing frightfully good fiction? After all, women are highly attuned to emotions—clearly capable of delivering subtle scares, as well as visceral visions that linger long after the reader turns the final page.

Horror is such a primal emotion. Humans have always endured dread—it's enmeshed in our subconscious—the very essence of our being. Countless stories have been told about what scares us; an innumerable amount await.

When I first submitted my stories for publication, I encountered lots of rejection. Uncertain if this was because I was a woman, or due to the fact I was new to the genre, I eschewed self-doubt and quickly progressed from form rejection letters to the inclusion of personal comments, which proved quite useful. *Fears unfounded.* As the submission process evolved from via snail mail—don't forget to include a SASE—to email, and ultimately Submittable, I grew bolder, grateful for Editors' comments and fresh perspective, which enabled me to grow as a writer and submit my work to another market, where it was usually accepted.

After several stories found homes in various magazines, I challenged myself to send stories to anthologies and have been published in several. Such an honor when Editor Billie Sue Mosiman invited me to submit a story to *Fright Mare*, an all-female author anthology published in 2016, that featured stories by: Nina Kiriki Hoffman, Elizabeth Massie, Kathryn Ptacek, Loren Rhoads, Lucy Taylor, just to name a few. Twenty authors in all. It's a fantastic compilation that demonstrates women can write frightfully-good fiction!

As a female Horror author, several male authors have asked how I manage to write men so well. They're curious about my process for capturing different nuances and mannerisms. My answer is shockingly simple: I write from experience—the men in my life, past and present provide ample inspiration for my characters. Over the years, I've based male characters in my novellas and stories on co-workers, ex-boyfriends, or family. No man that crosses my path is safe from scrutiny.

Whether it's his piercing blue eyes, the scuff of his beard when he kisses me, or the quiet desperation of a homeless man camped out on the sidewalk in front of his cardboard condo, rattling—*clink, clink, clink*—a dark, blue paper cup full of grimy change and crumpled dollar bills that says, *it's our pleasure to serve you* in wavy, white letters that rise like steam, I'm always focused on minute details. A casual passerby that interests me starts out as a character sketch in a little, red notebook I carry with me everywhere, and if he's interesting enough, I'll flesh him out and work him into my latest novella or story.

I've been a published Horror author for over twenty years, and while I've had my fair share of successes, there have been a few daunting experiences, too. I despise the misconception that only men can write effective Horror. During the mid-1990s, when I started to attend conventions I was one of a handful female Horror authors there, part of a vast minority. We women banded together, seeking collective camaraderie.

When I first started out, I felt a bit intimidated by all of the male Horror authors gathered together. I had a male Horror author come up to me and ask, "Who are you here with? Where's your boyfriend?" I would muster up some courage and say, "I'm here promoting my work. Come check out my reading at 3:00 p.m." And some of those guys would show up and admit afterward that I'd managed to scare them.

I received an invitation to attend I-CON, a convention that was held at SUNY Stony Brook in 1998, via an actual letter in the mail—this was before social media's heyday, though, I did have a website back then—as an author guest and returned several times, it was here that I met the incomparable Linda Addison, one of the rare female Horror authors there, and we became fast friends, appearing on several panels together! This was also where I garnered my first handful of loyal fans, who purchased my books and inquired on what I was working on. Such an exhilarating feeling, to be sought after!

From there, I appeared at several other conventions: Chiller Theatre in New Jersey, where I met lots of male Horror authors, like Jack Ketchum and F. Paul Wilson, who were very approachable and interested in learning more about my work. At World

Horror Con in Atlanta, Georgia way back in 1999, I met Ed Lee, who was also extremely welcoming.

The Horror genre is a bit of a boy's club, no doubt about it. The odds are stacked against female authors, but creative, ambitious women will *always* find a way to run with the boys. Besides me, there are over a dozen successful Horror authors come to mind: Meghan Arcuri, Linda D. Addison, Fran Friel, April Grey, Sephera Giron, Nancy Kilpatrick, K.H. Koehler, Sarah Langan, Lisa Mannetti, Elizabeth Massie, Lisa Morton, Joyce Carol Oates, Kelli Owen, Kathryn Ptacek, Gina Ranalli, Lucy A. Snyder, and Lucy Taylor. I've gotten to know several of these lovely ladies at various conventions. I've noticed that we have several personality traits in common: We're all extremely ambitious and self-assured—we're not afraid to speak our minds—we're also very outgoing and savvy.

At last year's StokerCon™, in historic Providence, Rhode Island, I had the pleasure of speaking on a panel comprised solely of female Horror authors. In addition to myself, panelists included Meghan Arcuri, Mary Ann Back, April Grey, and Elizabeth Massie. We packed the room and had a lively discussion about the trials and tribulations of not only how we survive in the male-dominated Horror genre, but how we manage to thrive! Our legions are growing—we know no bounds…

Amy Grech has sold over 100 stories to various anthologies and magazines including: *A New York State of Fright, Apex Magazine, Beat to a Pulp: Hardboiled, Dead Harvest, Deadman's Tome Campfire Tales Book Two, Expiration Date, Fright Mare, Hell's Harvest, Needle Magazine, Psycho Holiday Real American Horror, Tales from The Lake Vol. 3, Thriller Magazine,* and many others. New Pulp Press published her book of noir stories, *Rage and Redemption in Alphabet City.*

She is an Active Member of the Horror Writers Association and the International Thriller Writers who lives in Brooklyn. Visit her website: www.crimsonscreams.com. Follow Amy on Twitter: twitter.com/amy_grech.

Who Can Join HWA?

HWA's Active (voting) members are all published professional writers of horror. But you needn't be an established professional writer to join HWA. Your demonstrated intention to become a professional writer is all that's required to join HWA at the Affiliate level, because we know the first professional-level sale is often the hardest. To demonstrate your intention, all you need is one minimally paid publication in any of several categories. (This might be something as unassuming as a 500-word story for which you've received $25 or more.) Non-writing professionals with an interest in the field (such as illustrators, librarians, booksellers, producers, agents, editors, and teachers) can join at the Associate level without any publications. Check our Membership Rules to see which level you qualify for.

HWA also offers a Supporting Membership for non-professionals who would like to share and explore their interest in horror. Supporting members receive HWA's monthly newsletter and our internet mailers, have the opportunity recommend works for the Bram Stoker Awards® and the opportunity to be involved with HWA's chapters, Mentor Program, and access to some of their favorite horror writers via a private message board.

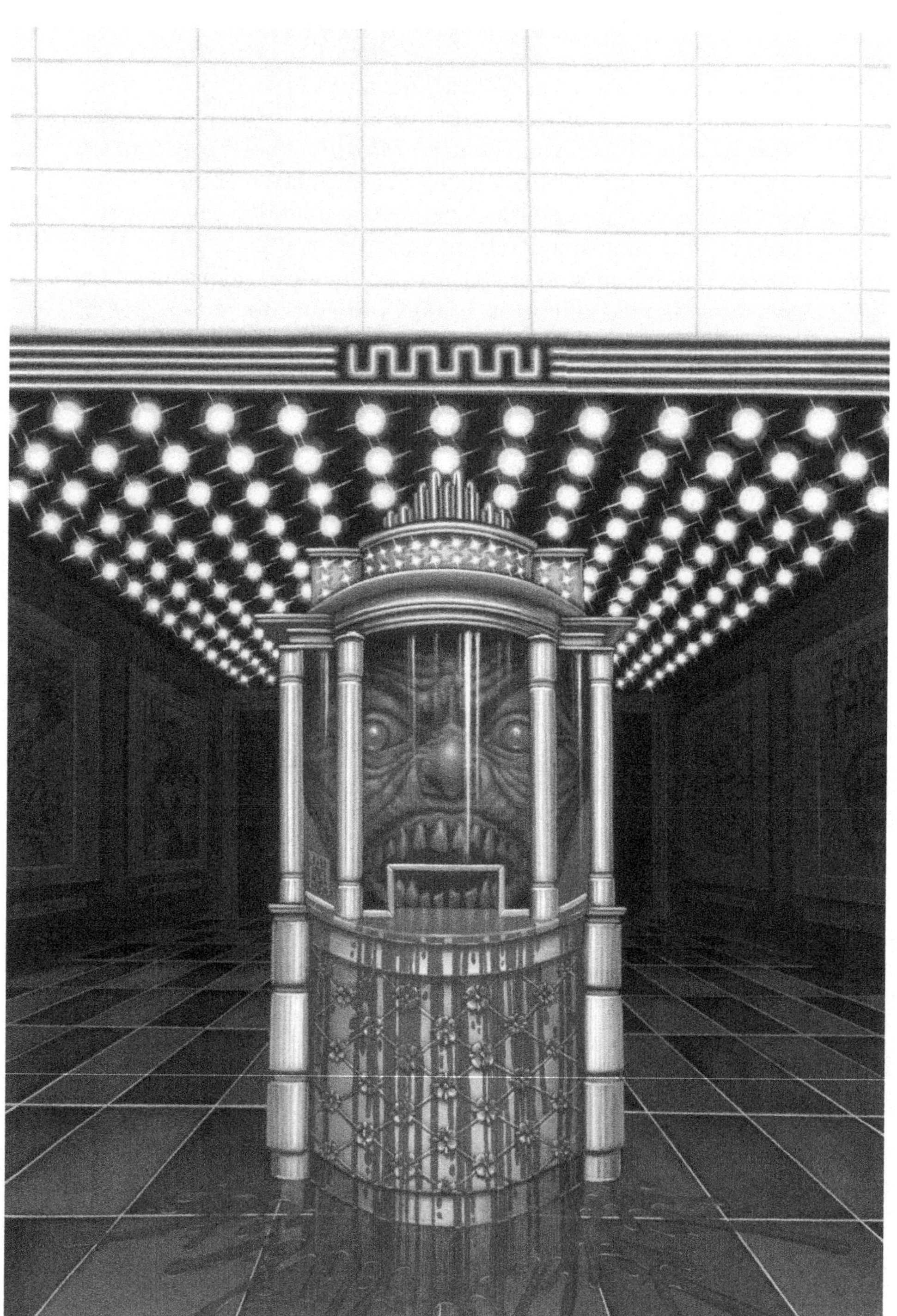

Screenplays

State of the Script

By John Palisano

Big changes have come to how films and television shows are being watched. With the proliferation of online streaming services like Netflix, Hulu, Amazon Prime and Shudder, viewers have more options than at any time previous. With a few clicks, we can stream HD films and television shows, and many of them produced just for these services without the traditional studio system.

Along with having so much instantly available on demand, we've seen a huge rise in popularity of entire seasons of television series being released at the same time. Viewers binge entire seasons, watching one episode after the other with barely a breath.

The success of *Stranger Things* and *Black Mirror* amplified this trend.

What about the screenplays? They, too, are being written differently. Many traditionally trained screenwriters are having to learn how to create series Bibles, a system long employed by television showrunners. In an interview for the second season of *Stranger Things* creators the Duffer brothers mentioned they were not constrained by a television format of seven minute intervals to make way for commercials. Episodes didn't need to be a perfect hour. They could run longer or shorter, and better serve the natural narrative.

In this regard, streaming series more aptly mirrors novel structure. Which is truly how watching a season over a weekend feels. *Game of Thrones* has mastered the art of covering a novel over a season, and we are soon to see a similar adaptation of Anne Rice's beloved Vampire Mythos. This spring also has seen the release on Netflix of Josh Malerman's *Bird Box* an adaptation of his novel. Even classic novels are seeing newfound attention. Shirley Jackson's *The Legend of Hill House* is now a series on Netflix, as well. No longer are adaptations forced to make hard choices in cuts to accommodate the shorter running times of the multiplex.

Traditional film still thrives! What has changed are the faces writing the genre films of today. The horror genre has always embraced those previously outcast. There's no better recent example than Jordan Peele's brilliant *Get Out* last year. The screenplay took home the Bram Stoker Award® and went on to take home the Academy Award's Oscar. *Get Out* was also nominated for Best Picture. Mr. Peele will soon be hosting his journey into none other than *The Twilight Zone.*

Horror films continue to do exceedingly well at the box office, with many sticking to the decades old plan of limited budget, and high-tension storytelling which has done well, audiences can't seem to get enough. The recent adaptation of Stephen King's IT was one of the top grossing films of the year and introduced a new generation to the world of Castle Rock. Horror cinema also continues its long-standing tradition of being a direct or indirect commentary on the state of the world. In the 1960s, *Night of the Living Dead* addressed deep-seated nuclear scares. In today's world, we have films such as *The Purge* telling stories about our divided political climate. *American Horror Story* has always told stories about what's happening now, or has tied things into current events.

Not long ago, launching a career in screenwriting often meant pitching your script to a studio and hoping the project would be part of the less than one percent making it through production. Now there are many more venues and avenues for screenwriters and filmmakers to option scripts, make films, and secure their distribution.

Shows such as *The Walking Dead* have spawned years-long series on television. Horror is big business on television and cable. One can only look to the ratings and diverse new offerings. *Riverdale* imagines the Archie universe in a dark and mysterious fashion. *Midnight, Texas* brings Charlaine Harris's book series to life. *Gotham. The Terror. Santa Clarita Diet, Castle Rock, Ash VS. Evil Dead, Hap and Leonard, iZombie, Z. Nation, Castlevania, Stan Against Evil, Lore, Preacher.*

There seems to be an endless supply of horror television being developed and produced. Audiences of many backgrounds can't seem to get enough.

But how does a screenwriter break in? What is the new path toward being a produced screenwriter? Although most of the studios are now concentrated on larger intellectual properties—Hasbro has a bungalow on the Universal Lot now!—the streaming services have become the independent film studios of today. Without the need to carry a project costing hundreds of millions of dollars, they're able to more easily greenlight smaller projects. They've also got distribution built right in.

Say you don't have an 'in' with either a studio development

executive or a streaming content provider? Many filmmakers have been making their own films and uploading them to YouTube. Professional quality is within most people's hands: their cell phones. With HD and even 4K video easily available on the cheap, and editing software available for next to nothing, it's down to the story. It's down to talent. The technology is there. The talent rises. YouTube and other streaming services are giving a platform to these new auteurs. Some are going on to get deals with larger, more traditional venues. Some are gaining ground on the festival circuit. Some are even making a living off of the streaming revenue alone. Filmmaking is now within reach. Francis Ford Coppola stated in the 80s that with computers, some kid would one day be able to make a movie on a computer in their bedroom and it'd win an Academy Award.

He was right. We're there.

What are you waiting for? Get out there and tell your story—the one only you can tell.

John Palisano is a writer whose nonfiction and fiction has appeared in many genre and literary magazines. He won the Bram Stoker Award® in short fiction in 2016. He's also written articles for websites such as *Shmoop University* and *Backstreets Magazine.*

Say 'hi' at: www.johnpalisano.com and www.amazon.com/author/johnpalisano and www.facebook.com/johnpalisano and www.twitter.com/johnpalisano

Film

By Steven Van Patten

Certain things I let people know out of the gate, others not so much. For example, I may tell people that I saw *The Exorcist* while I was still in grade school, but it's not often that I talk about how I feasted on the TV versions of nearly every Hammer Studios film before I was ten. And for fear of it getting back to my mother, even though I am way too old to be worried about being grounded, I don't usually discuss how I played hooky to go see the original *Friday the 13th* AND the ultra-traumatizing *Galaxy of Terror*. And if you're unfamiliar with *this* GoT, trust me, I shouldn't have been there.

As a teenager, I learned to keep my taste for such things to myself. Because, while scary movies didn't always scare me, I was terrified at the thought of not losing my virginity for being into such things. I don't miss those days, not being able to be honest about who I was for worry of not fitting a certain mold. Glad that's over.

Left in that long ago teenager's place is a much more emotionally secure man with an unabashed and widely acknowledged love of horror films. And while my television crew co-workers often come to me with questions like, "Hey, SVP! You see that *Hereditary* movie yet?" and jokes like "Yo, Prince of Darkness, what're you doing for lunch?" with my HWA brethren, the conversations are easier and less mocking. Which is why most of the members of the New York chapter probably already know that along with all of the sneaking around and late nights begging to stay up to watch *Kolchak the Nightstalker*, there were two very specific incidents involving horror cinema that left me indelibly marked and forever changed.

One involved the film *Scream, Blacula, Scream*. Like it's 1972 predecessor, it involves the great Prince Mamawaulde, who travels to Transylvania to seek help ending the slave trade by talking to a certain ancient nobleman. After a brief altercation with Dracula, the African prince became Blacula, the African replacement for the Prince of Darkness. And while the two movies don't hold the visual and technological weight it takes to please the eyes of the average 2018 movie goer there is one scene that speaks to me right down to my core.

In the scene, Blacula, having successfully fed, is now walking the streets of Los Angeles when he is approached by a prostitute. Barely comprehending or caring that he's being propositioned, the vampire ignores her and pressed on. The rejection earns him the wrath of two pimps, who appear from nowhere and begin to threaten him. After an exchange of unpleasantries, Blacula ends up killing the pimps, but not before he chastises them with a line that I've never been able to unhear:

"You've made a slave of your sister and you're still slaves, imitating your slave masters!"

While there had been a underlying condemnation of the African slave trade woven in the narrative of the films, no other line within the franchise served up a more specifically aimed critique of how the black community may sometimes be working against its best interests. Hearing it changed my life, as it slowly dawned on me that a vampire could have other concerns outside of killing people and finding brides. Unlike Christopher Lee's stoic, stern and single-minded Dracula, William Marshal's dark prince spoke to some things that I didn't realize I needed until I'd seen it. Representation was certainly one of those things. The desire that at least some of my heroes, or anti-heroes or even the super charismatic villains that I secretly love look like me. And like Mr. Marshal's interpretation of a master vampire, I wanted those characters to manifest in a non-stereotypical, non-minstrel show way. As much as I disliked the pimps that approached Blacula, I enjoyed their demise at the hands of an austere and dignified black vampire. Because for me, the vampire didn't so much kill the men as he did kill the stereotypes they represented.

Years later, these feelings would serve as part of the fuel that prompted me to write the *Brookwater's Curse* series. In my own mind, my main character, Christian Brookwater, is a tribute and an extension to what Blacula could have been.

While *Scream, Blacula, Scream* provided inspiration, the other movie I'm going to mention became a source of profound disappointment. I know that the idea that the movie I'm about to name meeting the disapproval of anyone will be preposterous notion to many die-hard classic horror fans, but in this matter, my particular perspective is the key.

Long before I learned to mask my nerdiness with a veneer of cool and a mostly black wardrobe, I was bookish twelve-year-old whose heavy reading schedule was only interrupted by the occasional after school appointment with some bully. Much to the amazement of my English teacher, one of the books I was engrossed with at the time was *The Shining*. As anyone who is likely to read this essay knows, the story centers around a man who takes on a job as caretaker of an empty, isolated hotel resort only to succumb to madness brought on by a mix of supernatural elements and cabin fever. He then attempts to murder his wife and son.

As many know, in the novel version of the story, the crazy man's family are rescued thanks to the son's ability to telepathically summon a kind old soul the family met just before they took over the hotel. That character's name was Dick Halloran, an older black man.

Now, it's important to note that I didn't always sneak off to see my horror movies. Sometimes the faint facial hair that I sprouted very early in life served me well at the ticket booth. But other times, as with *Jaws*, I was able to convince my mother to take me. Such was the case with *The Shining*, as a trip to the movies was presented as a way to celebrate my birthday.

This was a post- *Salem's Lot* TV mini-series world, so I couldn't help but be enthused about seeing another of Stephen King's visions come to life. I think that's how my Aunt Patsy ended up being invited. Which was fine, because given what I thought was going to happen, I figured we would all enjoy it.

Unfortunately, I was still a child. And I don't possess a time machine. Otherwise, the cynical, TV show stage manager with over two decades of show business experience that I am now might have made the trip back to 1980 to warn myself. I might have pointed out that as heroically as Dick Halloran is written in the novel, the fact that sweet, endearing Scatman Crothers (and not a Richard Roundtree or Fred Williamson) had been given the role might be an indication that this was not going to end well.

Dick survived the rescue in the book, but was hit with an axe in the chest in the movie. I trust I didn't need to provide a spoiler alert. I'm sure this was a minor detail to many people, including director, Stanley Kubrick. But to my mother and my aunt, neither of them having read the book, this was a big problem.

I'm not going to go into what they had to say about having to endure the sight of watching Scatman Crothers die in such a brutal and seemingly useless way. Just keep in mind that at the time, these are two middle-aged black women. They were New York residents, but they're originally from Alabama. That means they were in Alabama during the fifties and sixties. Do I really need to say more? Let's just say it was a very awkward trip home.

As an adult and a horror movie buff, I have come to respect the film for what it is and through research have come to understand the rivalry between director Kubrick and King. But it didn't lessen the effects on me. In fact, from that night on, my desire to create my own stories has been overwhelming. Allowing myself some self-reflection, my joining the rank and file horror literature scene was has been my way of making up for countless times I have witnessed the already marginalized be shoved even further back and celebrating the times that they've broken through.

Be the change you want to see in the world. Yes, that's an incredibly cliché note to end on, but in the case of my particular journey, it is also very pertinent.

Steven Van Patten is a celebrated writer and Brooklyn native. He has penned five novels; *The Brookwater's Curse* trilogy is about an 1860s Georgia plantation slave who becomes a vampire. *Killer Genius: She Kills Because She Cares*, and the sequel, *Killer Genius 2: Attack of The Gym Rats* features a hyper-intelligent black woman who becomes a socially conscious serial killer. Most recently he's released a collection of short horror stories with co-author Marc. L. Abbott titled, *Hell at the Way Station.*

SVP's short horror fiction appears in horror anthologies like *Hell's Kitties, Hell's Hearts, The Shadow Over Deathlehem* and *A New York State of Fright.*

SVP can be found on Facebook by searching his name and under @svpthinks on Twitter and Instagram.

When he's not writing scary stories, he can be found stage managing television shows and live events like *The VMA Red Carpet Preshow* and filling in at ABC's *The View* most Fridays.

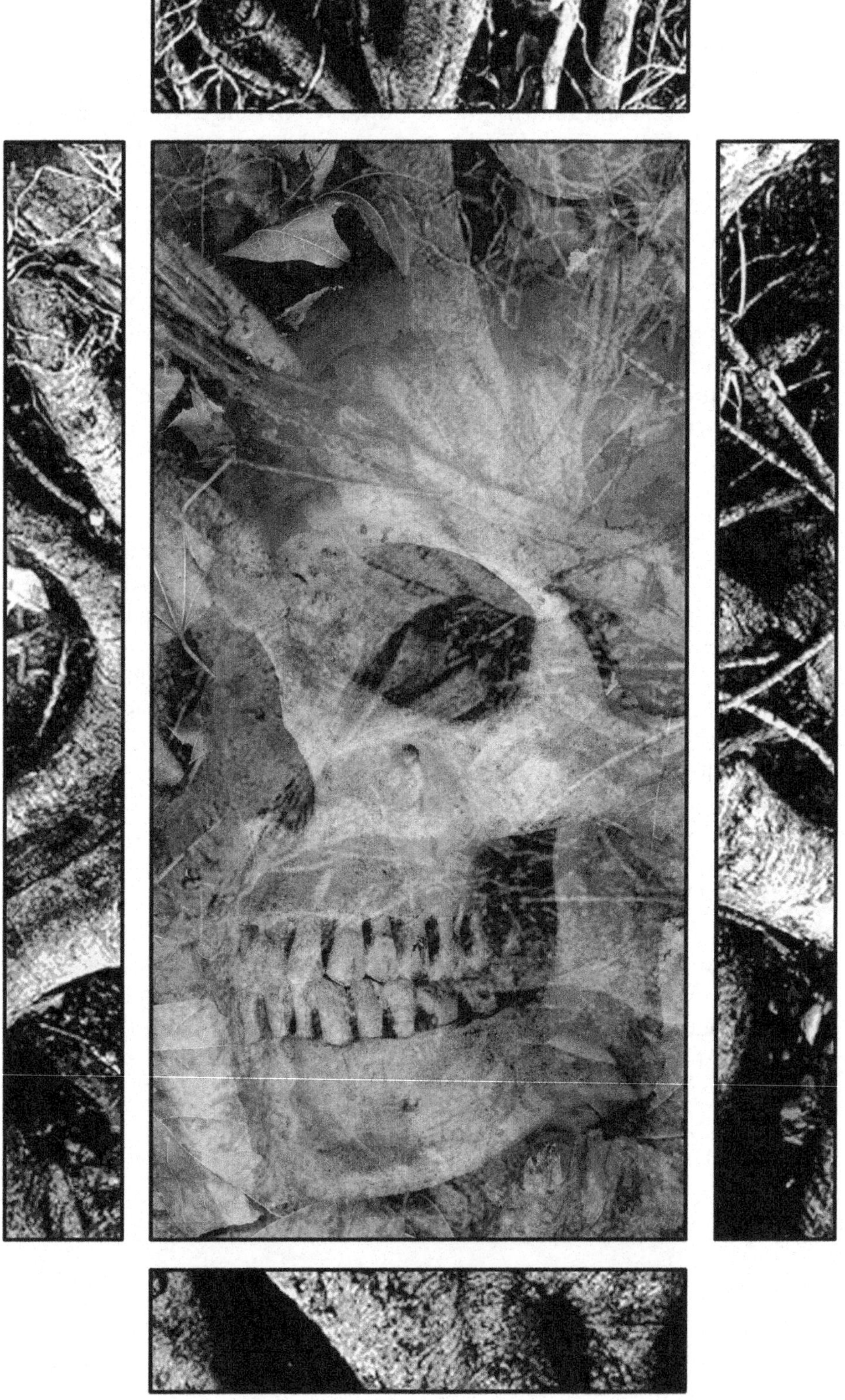

A Writer's Life

What was *That?!*

By LH Moore

You do not have to believe in ghosts, just in the possibility, and during my six years as a ghost hunter I had the chance to find out about that possibility for myself. Whenever I would share this, even those who were on the fence about their existence had a story for me. Over the years, I have collected them from family, co-workers, friends, friends of friends—anyone who had opened up to me about their experiences. My file is somewhat thick now. As writers, we often use personal experiences to inform our work and spur the imaginations of our readers and I am no different. In addition to the stories that I have heard from others, I can use my own.

Every city or town should have a paranormal investigation group or expert(s). I spent much of my time as a ghost hunter with a great group that did investigations in D.C., Maryland and Virginia. We were often contacted by historical societies, historic sites and museums to come out and look into what was going on there. This was just before the proliferation of ghost hunting shows with their infrared cameras and other expensive (at the time) gadgets.

The very nature of ghosts is how common they seem to be. Over and over again, residents of homes or staff at sites with unusual things going on would tell us "We just wanted to know that we're not crazy…" I knew from experience that they were not. Sometimes just our presence helped to bring them a peace of mind. I've seen and felt and been through some things myself. Like hearing quick, light footsteps going down the hallway in the middle of the night during a private residence investigation or the spirit who, when we listened to a playback, clearly told us "NO" when we asked if we were welcome there.

During an investigation at a Civil War field hospital, we were being shadowed by a radio show. One of their hosts, a tall, athletic guy filled with bravado, asked us what he could do. We all looked at each other and immediately said "Rookie duty." Our group had a method we used to break new members of their fear, usually done at a haunted former warehouse in Old Town Alexandria, Virginia. We told him to sit at the top of the stairs to the basement in the dark and just listen to see if he heard anything down there. All of us had done it ourselves at some point, so we wanted to see what would happen. We left him for fifteen minutes and continued our investigation. Before the fifteen minutes were even done, he came rushing up to us, trembling and shaken. When we asked him what happened, he said he could hear a little girl crying.

There were no children on site…at all.

There were some real hacks and craptacular crackpots out there, trust me, but that's with anything. I think that with ghosts and ghost hunting, the very subject matter itself is so up for debate that it's like a field day on both sides sometimes. Of course, some would say the same thing about me for even venturing to say that 'Yeah, this s—t is for real.' All I know is what I've experienced first-hand. It's all that I can go by.

I once stayed at the John Brown House in Maryland, near Harper's Ferry. Everyone on site was downstairs excitedly talking when we heard heavy footsteps, like someone in boots, walking above our heads. Everyone went silent, slowly looking upwards in unison. As the floorboards were wide planks with spaces that we could see through, we could also see that there was no one upstairs.

I am African American and so was a teammate, two of the very few ghost hunters of color in the country. Over our monitors we could hear the neighbors patrolling the perimeter and saying that they were going to "get us." I realized that I was more afraid of humans than of ghosts and was given a choice that night: stay outside in a tent in the cold with the threat of the neighbors or be able to lock myself inside the haunted house.

I chose the house.

My job in the group was as its historian and chief debunker. Many times, the history would not match up to the stories at all, making it easy to rule out. Other times? They were verified or created more questions for us. And then there was Ireland.

Our group went to Ireland, investigating and staying at castles and visiting historic sites such as the Neolithic cairns and tombs at Loughcrew. The castles lived up to their reputations, including Leap, a historian's dream. At one castle, a group of us went for a walk to the nearby lake. It was eerily quiet as we walked through the woods. "Oh no," Barry, our Irish guide said as he steered us around a fairy ring, its white mushrooms creating its familiar shape. "Do not step through that!" There were no birds singing. No animals were stirring. Only silence and the sounds of the lake lapping against its shore and the whistle of the wind. If there was ever a place that could make you believe in legends, Ireland was it.

In the castles themselves, a housekeeper quit while we were there after seeing "something" and our teammates heard voices and saw a woman's ghost in an office. One castle particularly stood out: Ross Castle in Co. Meath. A 16th c. tower stack with a great house attached, I ended up copying its guest book, which was filled with accounts through the years. We decided to investigate the top room of the tower, rumored to be haunted by a pooka—a shapeshifting entity. As we sat there in the complete darkness, the bathroom lit up with a blue light and then the room itself would become even darker. I could see shadows moving among us and just outside the doorway. A clairvoyant teammate told us what was coming in and out, including one entity that was crawling, pulling itself along the floor. They also said that there was an older grandmother figure there who was keeping the spirits away from me. I have never run during an investigation, but I broke one of our own rules and literally fled down the spiral staircase afterwards. Remember how those legends could be real? That night I wasn't willing to find out.

Many ghost groups don't last very long for the usual reasons such as time, egos, apathy, member attrition, boredom, burnout—and ours was no different, as we folded in 2007. It was a privilege to have had those experiences. After all, how many times do you get to have free rein at historic houses and sites? I use my experiences and those of others in my work, which tends to have elements of the supernatural or paranormal in them. For all that I know about ghosts, there is still so much to learn and maybe someday we'll have all of the answers. Until then, I will continue to share what I know with you through my fiction.

And who knows? Maybe someday you'll experience something yourself for real too.

LH Moore's historical speculative fiction has been published in all three *Dark Dreams* anthologies of Black horror writers; the Bram Stoker Award® Finalist anthology *Sycorax's Daughters; the Black Magic Women* and *Chiral Mad 4* anthologies, Apex and *FIYAH* Magazine, and an upcoming story in *Fireside Magazine*. Moore also had a poem published in *Apex Magazine* and contributed articles to the *African American National Biography* (Harvard/Oxford U. Press). A DC native exiled in Maryland, Moore is a historian with a MA in historic preservation and loves classical guitar, graphic novels, and video games.

Interviewing

Voices Rising From The Darkness: How To Conduct A Frightfully Good Interview

By Gordon B. White

The proliferation of small presses, online venues, and social media has led to a democratization of voices that only years ago would be have been impossible. With all of these new platforms and newly visible artists, many readers are eager to interview their favorite creators and share their enthusiasm with like-minded audiences. Because I have been fortunate enough to conduct dozens of interviews over the years, I am pleased to offer some considerations for conducting frightfully good interviews that will stand out in a crowded field.

The Chosen One(s): Selecting the Venue, Subject, and Agenda

The first questions you must answer are inextricably tied together: *Where will the interview run?*, *Who are you going to interview?*, and *What is your agenda?*

When considering where the interview will run, bear in mind the freedoms and limitations associated with each particular venue. For example, personal blogs can run any content their owners wish, but the views they get and their attractiveness to prospective interviewees varies dramatically. At the other end of the spectrum, featured interviews in established journals or at live events can add clout to an interview request, but may require formal pitches or have certain editorial constraints. Moreover, seriously consider what each venue's audience will want to see.

Tied up in the above consideration is your choice of whom to interview. Although your subject's name recognition or status may be a factor, it should never be your sole consideration. Fake enthusiasm is easy to spot and off-putting, so always choose interview subjects that genuinely interest you. Also think of potential subjects beyond just your current favorite creators—which artists are doing innovative work, conveying important messages, or have undergone significant struggles? Consider what your audience will appreciate learning and which voices you can amplify.

Finally, set your agenda. Why are you doing this and, by extension, what are the subject and the audience getting in return? Your agenda helps determine the "who" and "where" above, but this "why" will also guide all other considerations. For example, if you are introducing a new author, deep dives into background and influences will be more appropriate than if your subject is already widely known. If your interviewee is promoting a new project, then that should be the focus. While you can always go further afield, defining your agenda will focus your preparation and questions.

Sharpening the Ax: Preparation

Although the final product will be a combined effort between interviewer and interviewee, the foundation for a strong interview is laid before the first question is even asked. The key to successful preparation is to *choose a style* and then *do the research,* bearing in mind that *the interview only captures the present moment* in the subject's life and career.

An interview's style will be influenced by its logistics as much as its agenda. The familiar question-answer interviews conducted via email are common because they allow for thoughtful responses at the subject's convenience and can be read at the audience's leisure. Other interviews may develop a more conversational flow through live discussions or when time allows for multiple rounds of written back and forth. Regardless of the logistics, though, always consider the relative space distributed between questions and answers. I prefer to approach written interviews as a collaborative essay where lengthier questions put forth an observation and ask the subject to respond. Other interviewers prefer shorter, open-ended questions that allow the subject to expound in broader directions. There's no right or wrong way, but deciding on a style early on will shape the overall interview.

After the "who," "where," "why," and "how" are set comes the fun part—deciding on "what" to ask. For this, there's just no shortcut to doing your homework; don't just read your subject's works, but their also media packets, blog posts, other interviews, and as much else as you'll need to fulfill your agenda. There's an old lawyer's adage that there are two kinds of questions: those you want to learn the answer to, and those you already know the answer to but want to get on record. This is where you figure out which of each you'll ask. Besides, a well-demonstrated interest in your interviewee proves that you are serious and inspires reciprocal effort.

In doing this groundwork, however, consider that your interview is a snapshot of your subject at this moment in time. To the extent that you want to discuss the past, it should primarily be in relation to the subject's present circumstances. Those who cannot remember the past are condemned to repeat it through lackluster questions and stale answers.

Doing the Deed: Tips and Techniques

You've chosen the time and place, collected your sacrifice...err, interview subject, and now you're ready for the interview. First and foremost, don't be afraid to *have a personality*. Beyond that, keep the interview engaging for the interviewee and audience alike by *minimizing unnecessary background information, breaking the subject out of their headspace,* and *varying the questions.*

What differentiates an interview from a press release or blog post is the interplay between the interviewer's and interviewee's personalities. An interviewer's greatest strengths are curiosity and authority. You demonstrate curiosity by standing in for an audience that is eager to know more, and you demonstrate authority by asking intelligent questions. If your interest in the subject is genuine and you've done your homework, the interview will pop with energy and confidence.

One perpetual consideration is how much background information is necessary in general and for specific questions. If your agenda is to introduce an author, then it's fairly simple (more is better!). Otherwise, remember that your interview only needs enough context to remain accessible after it is published. Trust that the audience can do additional research if necessary, so long as you provide the basics.

While some obvious default questions are part of any interview, you owe it to all involved to delve deeper and break your subject's skull wide open (metaphorically). Creators can become accustomed to living in their own heads and this mindset tends to be exacerbated when answering rote questions. Shake this up by asking about hidden influences, other media, contemporaries they admire, or other external topics. Helping the subject shift their thinking can also inspire more thoughtful answers to even standard questions.

Just as an author modulates their prose to engage readers, an interviewer varies their questions. Initially, the interview's format may provide certain constraints; for example, multipart questions usually work better in writing, where the subject and audience can take their time and refer back. While those same elaborate questions may get muddled in a live discussion, conversations can instead encourage fluid back and forth developments. Regardless of format, however, it is essential to vary the lengths of questions and anticipated answers. Expansive answers can be wonderful, but also build in moments of respite with a few quick ones. Similarly, vary the themes and topics to avoid monotony and fatigue. Above all, consider the interview's flow as a whole, including an introductory beginning, development in the middle, and a satisfying end.

Finally, don't be afraid or embarrassed to follow up. Was an answer unclear? Did one response spark another question? Did you think of something just as you hit "Send"? Just follow up. You and your subject are collaborators on this interview, and you both want to give the audience the best possible product.

Rest in Peace: Final Considerations

Once the interview is done (and proofed and edited—don't skip the grunt work), it's still not quite ready to publish. As a responsible interviewer and member of the literary community, there are two final considerations: *Is this fair to the subject?* and *Is it socially responsible to publish this?*

Sometimes an interview may read differently after sitting for a while, so, before publishing, ask: Would the subject want this to be published as it is? If some answers are unclear or could be misinterpreted, develop those further. If circumstances have changed or if the subject has second thoughts, accommodate those. If there is a flat out error in the interview, address it or edit it. Our past and future interviewees trust us not to purposefully hold them up for scorn or ridicule, so every decision you make should be proof of your commitment.

Finally, you must also decide if publishing the interview is socially responsible. Regardless of your initial intent, does the finished interview promote or normalize harmful views? As the half of the interviewer-interviewee team who decides whether it runs, you bear the responsibility for giving the other half this platform. Make sure that you are happy putting the final product into the world and that it helps build the literary community that you want to belong to. If not, kill it.

And with that, I leave you to it. There are an almost infinite number of ways to get involved with interviewing, but by taking your job seriously and acting with integrity, you can separate yourself from the pack. Good luck!

Gordon B. White has lived in North Carolina, New York, and the Pacific Northwest. He has contributed dozens of reviews and interviews to various genre fiction outlets including *Lightspeed, Nightmare*, and *Hellnotes.* He is also a 2017 graduate of the Clarion West Writing Workshop, and his fiction has appeared in venues such as *Daily Science Fiction, A Breath from the Sky: Unusual Stories of Possession, Nightscript Vol. 2*, and the Bram Stoker Award® winning anthology *Borderlands 6*. You can find him online at www.gordonbwhite.com or on Twitter at @GordonBWhite.

Short Stories

My Process for Writing Short Stories

By Tony Tremblay

When I sit down to write a short tale, I often have nothing more than a single image in my mind, and I use it to open the story. It could be something I caught out of the corner of my eye such as an old man fishing off a bridge, a hole in the ground, or a Korean woman passing through a doorway. On my drive to work, I often find myself daydreaming. An image of a man caught in a snowstorm, a king surveying his soldiers, or a middle-aged waitress pouring coffee could float into my head. No matter the origin, I turn those images around in my mind, examining them, and more importantly, visualizing their surroundings. Not because I'm trying to construct a backstory, nor am I attempting to understand what makes a character tick. Instead, this exercise points me in the direction of atmosphere.

I believe atmosphere is the bait that lures a reader in. I take those singular images and frame them in an environment that brings an initial scene to life. I'll write a paragraph or two focusing solely on descriptions of an area; the weather, the lighting, odors, vegetation, furniture and other details that shore up a feeling of menace or normality. Once I am satisfied with the ambiance of my opening, I move on to the characterization.

At this point, I usually have no idea on what the plot will be, so I let the character steer me in that direction. Take the above example of a waitress. In broad terms, I'll decide if she's an innocent pawn in the story who will have an unfortunate encounter or a sociopath concealing evil intent. With that decision made, I'll insert action or personality traits into the atmospheric paragraphs already written. Once I'm satisfied the opening is going to draw the reader in, I begin to work on the plot.

Whether I have an idea of where I want to go with the story or I'm clueless, I simply start typing. I'll follow my lead character around the area I imagine they're in—work, home, or out on the town. I observe them, looking for quirks that can be exploited. I note their encounters with others no matter how insignificant they might seem. It doesn't take me long for to get a handle on the characters. I'll imagine their vulnerabilities, their strengths, and their fears. Once I understand these attributes, their conflict comes easy.

Twists suggest themselves, and I become giddy at the possibilities. Sparked, my imagination ignites, and I surf the flames. That's when the weird stuff pours out of me. This is my favorite part of the process, and I'll ride this burst of creativity all the way to the end of the story.

In most of my short work, the ending in some way must tie back to the beginning. I do this to give the story extra depth, a sense of completeness, and hopefully an 'a-ha' moment for the reader. Once the story is completed, the hard part starts.

I'll question myself, asking if I made it too easy for the reader to figure out where the story was headed. Is the tale compelling enough or will the readers mind wander at any point? Can dialog replace any internal narrative? Did the tale pack the emotional wallop I was going for? If all those questions have suitable answers, I send it out to my writers group or an editor. In case you are wondering, yes, I said an editor. I want to make sure the story is the best it can be before I send it out.

The downside to all of this is the rewriting—and I do a lot of rewriting. A short story can take me months to finish. When it comes to short work, I'm never in a rush to finish it. Once the piece is done, I go looking for a market. It may mean sitting on it for a while, sometimes years, but when I'm satisfied with it, I want to be sure it goes to a good home. I seldom submit to themed anthologies as I have an aversion to restrictive plotting, in other words, I don't like to be told what to write. If I do submit to an anthology, it is usually on an invitation basis, I am familiar with the publisher, and you can sum up the theme in one, possibly two words.

You might think that after I push that send button the process would be over. It's not. I second-guess myself. I reread it, over and over. Nine times out of ten, I see something that I think I could've done better. Then comes the hardest part of all—the waiting.

Tony Tremblay is the writer of numerous short stories that have been published in various horror anthologies, horror magazines, and webzines. He has a published a collection of these stories called *The Seeds of Nightmares*, as well as a horror novel entitled *The Moore House*. A new collection of his stories is due in early 2019. Tremblay has also worked as a reviewer of horror fiction for *Cemetery Dance* Magazine and *Horror World*. The author lives in New Hampshire.

WAYNE MILLER 2017

Research

Researching for Horror Fiction or Eureka! I found it!

By Lisa Mannetti

Believe it or not, one of the reasons I first came to writing horror as an adult has to do with research—or even more specifically, the ideas and connections arising from this misunderstood stepsister that can (in a real or very significant way) springboard a new story and even spark a novel at any stage.

Now that I have your attention, let me backtrack slightly and say it really helped that back in the Dark Ages when I was in grad school at Fordham that not only were two of my highly respected professors very interested in the current horror scene and its writers (especially Stephen King and Peter Straub), but one of them asked me about my Ph.D. work and my future plans. When I mentioned I figured I'd teach undergrads and write during summers, he told me the world would be a poorer place if I didn't quit the program and write instead, adding that at the tenured level I was intending to pursue and the program I was in—18th and 19th century English Lit—along with the concomitant fact that "the publish or perish" mode was in full swing, would prove to be the death knell of serious fiction writing for me. So I listened to his advice and withdrew from the program midway.

Flash forward a few years (the internet was also still in the Dark Ages, and I knew this because I was an adjunct instructor at two different colleges and when I assigned a topic—say, Jane Austen's *Emma* and its attendant satire of mores and manners—I'd get 30 to 50 papers that were miraculously not only nearly identical in structure and ideation, but tended to use the same wording throughout). The same problems with the Internet's lack of broad, specific and correct information was still true when I switched from teaching to being editor of two local magazines in the Hudson Valley. And there I was trying to write a novel and discovering that I couldn't find anywhere on the Internet what I then needed as crucial background for my work…hmmm.

Well, if there was one thing grad school taught me, it was how to use a card catalogue. And local librarians proved themselves extremely adept at procuring books from all over the county about every aspect of Romany culture and the result was my Bram Stoker

Award® winning first novel, *The Gentling Box.* And no, I never visited either Hungary or Romania at the time, but I got hold of maps and Fodor Guides to assist me and they worked. But here's the part you need to take away: I'm lucky enough now to be able to purchase books that are only in print that I may need for research, but you can take advantage of the "old system" and ask your librarian to ferret out books (for free) from the connected libraries and they can make all the difference.

Okay, this is sounding pretty academic and while you may need to understand certain principles or scientific facts to write your story, novella or novel, there are plenty of other ways to carry out research. The main thing you actually need to know about research is that you only need enough facts to create verisimilitude—that is, to immerse your reader in the world you're creating so that he or she has willingly suspended disbelief and is engaged in your story and invested in *your* characters. We'll be coming back to this idea of verisimilitude and giving the reader just enough to "buy in," because research—for some writers—carries the stench of a dumping ground. But there are ways to avoid it and common sense will carry you through. Trust me on that one.

Nowadays of course, the Internet can be a major source of researching and getting your facts right. There will be images, videos, articles, free books and much more. But how do you follow the thread(s) as you research? When do you have enough? And even more importantly, how can research help you create more terrifying and realistic fiction? The triumvirate of verisimilitude, following leads in research and using it to create horror are related—in fact, they're all prongs of the same sharpened trident. Here's an example of what I mean: in films, we're very used to viewing what's called both B roll and establishing shots—background—as well as constructed sets. In *Manhattan,* Woody Allen uses iconic images of the city to set up where we are and voiceover at the same time to establish character and plot. In the movie, *Everest* there's plenty of B roll of Kathmandu, base camp and Nepalese airports, but when the critical actions occur, no one actually thinks the main characters are fighting for their lives on the 8000 plus meter high Hillary step or at the South Summit. Verisimilitude (in other words images and facts gleaned from research) allows the viewer (or reader) to forget he or she is not seeing every street corner in Manhattan and definitely not watching climbers die up high on Everest. Research, in other words, sets the stage while story and character carry you through and like in film, you want just enough to limn the semblance of your created world.

The easiest way to know how much is enough occurs spontaneously when you gauge the interest level you yourself have in the facts you uncover. If it scintillates you, chances are it will interest the reader, too. As with all writing, the passion you bring to the subject will be key. Say the theme of the antho you're submitting to is The Apocalypse (as it was for me). The first thing I did was Google variants of "Ways the world might end." And there were plenty. I skimmed through the scenarios until I decided the thing that interested me the most was volcanoes. Next I created a folder (and subfolders) in favorites for Internet links on the topic, so I could access what I discovered and visited over the several month-long course of my research. I read articles and watched a lot of videos on everything from Pompeii to Yellowstone to a particularly nasty eruption in 1818 to Krakatoa in 1883.

Meanwhile, one of my own passions over the past twenty or so years happens to be armchair mountaineering. Ever since Jon Krakauer came out with his brilliant work, *Into Thin Air,* I've read every book I can get my hands on and watched every film on the subject of climbing because the very idea—the vertiginous heights, the constant danger, the intense cold, the mental and physical exhaustion, the threat of disfigurement and death—scares the hell out of me. The idea of being mowed down and buried alive under tons of molten lava like the stricken in Pompeii doesn't exactly leave me tranquil either, so when I thought about volcanoes the idea crossed my mind what if climbers were facing the worst because of a storm and then it became the absolute worst it could be because a volcano erupted while they were already trapped in an ice cave? Putting together facts (how far a volcano interferes with and decimates life) and using common sense helped me zero in on Yellowstone combined with folks trapped on North America's highest and most dangerous mountain, Denali. Not only did the Internet help me, it provided a way for my poor trapped climbers to use their own cell phones and access information about past and recent terrors that volcanoes inflict on the people and the planet both short and long term. I chose the facts that jumped out and interested me to use as the anxieties the characters discovered and shared with one another and it worked to the extent that the story, "Apocalypse Then," was the 2018 Bram Stoker Award® winning entry for short fiction.

Passions come to us in different ways. Sometimes they're long standing (hobbies, subjects, avocations), like mine with armchair mountaineering. But sometimes, they develop spontaneously from things we watch, read, occur to us or around us, or learn about. They allow the *what if* to bubble up and surface. Some of the things that affected me deeply (in films and life events) and which I've used to both create new works and trigger pieces I'm stuck in have included radiation poisoning, starvation, witchcraft, the Tarot, cemeteries, Lizzie Borden, conjoined twins, Houdini—well, you get the idea. And some of those things—like the radiation poisoning that occurred to the dial painters after WW 1—clicked as a book idea after idly watching a video called *The Poisoner's Handbook* one rainy Sunday afternoon. Research passion—like ideas—can come from anywhere and no source is too humble if it ignites the power of your imagination. And, as you write, keep researching—if nothing else, it will keep you in the mindset and mood of that particular piece. Even if you don't use the precise information you uncover, consider ancillary research like films as a benefit to the work and a deepening of both your general knowledge of a subject and your own interest in it.

After all, that spark is the reason that you write. The excitement you feel is what motivates you to set it on paper and what carries through to the reader and results in a successful piece of fiction.

Research ideas you love and your work will be all the richer and so, by virtue of your passionate new interest—will you—even if, like me, there isn't enough money in the world to get you within 500 feet of a freezing, snow-laden, avalanche-prone killer of a mountain.

Lisa Mannetti has won the Bram Stoker Award® twice; she has also been nominated five additional times in both the short and long fiction categories. Her story, "Everybody Wins," was made into a short film (*Bye Bye Sally*) and her novella, "Dissolution," will soon be a feature-length film, directed by Paul Leyden. Her novella about Houdini, *The Box Jumper*, was not only nominated for a Bram Stoker Award® and the prestigious Shirley Jackson Award, it won the "Novella of the Year" award from *This is Horror* in the UK. Forthcoming works include several short stories, and two dark novels. Lisa lives in New York in the 100-year-old house she originally grew up in with two wily twin cats named Harry and Theo Houdini. Visit her author website: www.lismannetti.com. Visit her virtual haunted house: www.thechanceryhouse.com. Watch Bye Bye Sally, starring Malin Ackerman on YouTube

The HWA Mentor Program

We feel strongly that one of the best ways we can contribute to the health of the horror genre is by helping to educate beginning writers in the ins-and-outs of both the craft and the business of writing. Yet writing courses are expensive, never last long enough, and rarely deal with the practicalities of establishing a career in writing. For that reason, we've created the HWA Mentor Program. Participating professional horror writers are paired with Affiliate and Supporting members who wish to learn a little or a lot about everything from the craft of writing to the pitfalls of contract negotiations.

Comics

The Smaller Panels within the Larger Story

By R. J. Joseph

The two Saturdays a month that fell after paydays were magically intoxicating. Mama, Daddy, my two siblings, and I all strolled merrily through the neighborhood of duplexes and single family homes, underneath decades old oak trees, up to the bookstore on Main Street. This image may be misleading, as we weren't in a small town, nor were we an average, happy family on a jaunt. Our neighborhood was right in the middle of the large, sprawling metropolis of Houston, Texas, in a ghetto unimaginatively named Third Ward. And we rarely did things that included all five of us, but the adventures to the bookstore turned us into the closest replica of a "normal" family that we ever were.

That reading was so important in our dysfunctional, urban, black household was a panel in our larger story towards "normalcy". We took our visits to the bookstore seriously. The ringing of the bell as we entered always felt like an old friend extending a warm welcome. Inside the shelves and shelves of paper, we all lost ourselves. Mama found refuge in the romance magazine section. My sister and brother ran around touching everything they could reach. I wandered from aisle to aisle, wondering if I could ever read as many books and magazines as I saw, while keeping an eye on my father. I knew I would always find something I liked, but I had to wait until he made his choices, first.

The backstory panel showed that my father liked the same scary and weird stories I did. I had inherited that love of all things horrific from him. There was no way I could get away with trying to talk my parents into buying everything I wanted to read. We just didn't have that kind of money. But there was no need to try and get everything. All I had to do was choose something different from what my father did and then I had double the reading material. He liked comics, in general, and sometimes he selected super hero fare. That was okay and I read them after he discarded them. On those weeks, I had to settle for one magazine or book of my own. But each time he chose an issue of *Eerie Magazine* or *Creepy Magazine,* my heart leapt up in my chest and I thought I'd pass out. As soon as he finished and forgot about those treasures, I was allowed to enjoy them.

The vibrant creepy comics kept me immersed in colorful tales presented one panel at a time. I knew I could always instantly look at the next panel to see what would happen next but I never did. I waited, expectantly, until I had breathed in each panel in its entirety, memorizing the positions of the characters and the text in the dialogue bubbles. I relished in the anticipation of consciously waiting to move beyond each picture and moment in time to the next, only to suspend myself in the next frame. Over and over again I did the same thing, until I had devoured the entire magazine.

I started writing horror fiction in a panel format, with these masterpieces in mind. Rising tension, slow, creeping anticipation, frightful climaxes frozen in time, and breathlessly falling resolutions all marked my own storytelling. I worked to mimic the comics in short stories and saw each step as a frame while I worked through the creative process. I had studied this technique endlessly and when I tried to stray from it, my work didn't have the same power as when I constructed it with this building block framework. Brilliant graphics of my storylines played out in my mind until I achieved the right amount of suspension—the same eager anticipation displayed on the pages of my beloved comics.

I learned how to take a larger storyline and break it down into manageable scenes that had to be self-contained within the larger whole. Even when I wanted to rush to the ending, I understood how to savor writing each component of the story—each "panel"—so that readers could appreciate the build-up and attention to detail. With each story I write, I still work to achieve the most engrossing tale I can manage so my readers are as intrigued as I was those years of reading comic books. Block by block, I build my colorful worlds, aiming to accomplish tiny worlds within the whole world.

I don't always get it right. Sometimes the panels are disjointed and the stories stumble around trying to find their way into being. Other times, I have to break the chipped images down and reconstruct them, painfully figuring out how—or if—they work together. I'm then reminded that some of my own panels are ragged, worn, and dull in some places. They were born of a love of horror shared with my father, but broken down by the dysfunction of our whole story. These fractures are where the panels come back to life, like the jagged scene breaks where one reality bumps another inside of *Creepy Magazine* or the rough edges of the lettering on the covers of *Eerie Magazine.*

I would have loved to have had teachers throughout school who embraced comic books as viable reading sources and writing tutorials, but I never did. Adult after adult, outside of my home, often downplayed the art of comic books, relegating them to the isolated fields of "non-serious" work. In my own classroom, I welcome comics as responsible teachers of writing and informants of the world around us, and I'm just glad my students are reading. I encourage them to practice reporting on their surroundings and our society, panel by panel. I encourage them to write their own stories, one panel at a time, sometimes with jagged letters, always with reverence towards the building blocks of effective writing.

I have first-hand knowledge of the artistry and value that can come from the various panels that make up the larger story of "normalcy".

R. J. Joseph is a Texas based writer and professor who must exorcise the demons of her imagination so they don't haunt her being. A life-long horror fan and writer of many things, she has finally discovered the joys of writing creatively and academically about two important aspects of her life: horror and black femininity.

When R. J. isn't writing, teaching, or reading voraciously, she can usually be found wrangling one or six of various sprouts and sproutlings from her blended family of 11… which also includes one husband and two furry babies.

Y.A. Novels

Why do You Write Horror Novels for Teenagers?

By Kim Liggett

I get asked this question a lot.

The answer is, I don't.

I write horror novels *about* teenagers, because let's face it, there's nothing more horrifying than high school (unless you are that rare unicorn who thinks high school was the best time of your life, and if that's the case, all I can say is…*gross*).

The teen years are ripe for horror. It's the first time you get a real sense of your own power. Maybe it scares you. Maybe you don't like what you see. You push the limits of self-control, your control over others. Maybe you win. Maybe you lose. You might feel like a stranger in your own body. As your sexuality bubbles to the surface, there are boundaries to be drawn, boundaries that might be broken. The constant pressure to fit in, do something to get noticed, be popular, get by unscathed, feels like you're walking an endless tightwire. High school is a place where you can get a horrible nickname just for wearing the wrong outfit or feel like your future is obliterated because you got a B on your history paper, where everything feels monumental. Do or die. You are living in a vacuum of hormones, angst, hopes, fears, dreams and despair. And no matter what happens, you get the added bonus of having to face the same people every day in the lunch room for the rest of your high school career, unless you're lucky enough that your family gets relocated to Siberia. But even then, you can't escape puberty, growing up, the hard lessons that must be learned.

The stakes are high before you've even introduced the first drop of blood into a story.

But YA isn't just for teens. Approximately fifty-five percent of YA readership are adults, which comes as no surprise to me.

In my former career as a backup vocalist, I spent years on the road, swapping stories with bus drivers, roadies, groupies, the talent. In the wee hours, between Tulsa and wherever, whispered from bunk to bunk, were tales of first love, first heartbreak, regret, something we did that we could never take back. Our deepest truths, our deepest hurts, inevitably led us back to those formative years. Beneath the glitz and the fanfare, those are the moments that stuck with me the most.

I think that's why I'm drawn to YA.

In my writing, I like to boil things down. Boil down plot, boil down sentences.

When you boil down a life, it's that short, intense period of time where everything seems to stem, where we began to form our adult selves, negotiate who we wanted to be.

It's the heart of the matter. The root cause. The crux.

And that's where I want to dwell.

At sixteen, **Kim Liggett** left her rural Midwestern town for New York City to pursue a career in music. Along with lending her voice to hundreds of studio recordings, she was a backup singer for some of the biggest rock bands in the 80's. Kim spends her free time studying the tarot and scouring Manhattan for vials of rare perfume and the perfect egg white cocktail. She is the author of *Blood and Salt, Heart of Ash*, Penguin Putnam, *The Last Harvest, The Unfortunates,* Tor Teen, and *The Grace Year*, St. Martin's.

Writing the First Novel

By Tom Deady

I attended my first StokerCon™ in 2016, the year the event was held in Las Vegas. My first novel, *Haven,* was under contract but not yet released. I went to StokerCon™ partly to learn as much as I could from the best writers in the industry, and partly to root for John McIlveen and his debut novel, *Hannahwhere.* Every year, the Horror Writers Association recognizes one author at its annual awards celebration for Superior Achievement in a First Novel. Past winners of this important award include some of the most recognizable names in the horror genre; Bentley Little, Brian Keene, Weston Ochse, Jonathan Maberry, and Joe Hill.

Nicole Cushing's *Mr. Suicide* beat *Hannahwhere,* but something else happened that night. I was feeling completely out of place, a stranger in a room brimming with incredible talent. They announced the winner of the Long Fiction award, Mercedes M. Yardley, for "Little Dead Red," and I watched her accept the award. She returned to her table, which happened to be just a couple away from my own, and sat down holding the Stoker award. She looked at it with an expression that I am at a loss to describe. Wonder? Pride? Joy? Perhaps some feeling that no one word can capture. But I've never forgotten that look. I realized two things at that moment; just how prestigious, how *meaningful* the Stoker Award really is, and how badly I wanted one. Never in my wildest dreams did I think I'd win one just a year later.

I began my acknowledgements for my *Haven* with the following:

> *Writing a book is hard. For a lot of the time, it's lonely hours spent squeezing words out of an exhausted brain, long after everyone else is asleep. It's agonizing self-doubt and crippling fear of failure. Finally, it's time to show the world what you've done...and it's terrifying. I dedicated* Haven *to my daughters because, in a way, this book is like their sibling. I started writing it when they were small children, and finished it when they were both in college. There were years when the book went untouched, overshadowed by life, but* Haven *was always there. Waiting. Whispering in my ear. Growing.*

I look at these words now, just over two years later, and I think it may be one of the most honest paragraphs I've ever written. Because writing any book *is* hard, but writing your *first* book may be the hardest. But like anything else in life, the more difficult the task, the sweeter the reward.

During the process of completing a novel, every writer loses a few battles with the words, the plot, with him or herself. Finally typing "The End" on the last page of a manuscript, however, is declaring victory in the war. Sure, there are other battles ahead; revisions, query letters, rejections, but there are few things that compare to typing those two little words. Those two words pay the debt for every sleepless night, every moment of anguish, every time you thought you couldn't do it.

I finally typed those words on the last page of Haven in 2012. After getting dozens of rejections from agents, in 2014 I signed a contract with Cemetery Dance to publish a limited-edition hardcover and eBook. In December of 2016 I received my author copies, and my dream had come true. But it wasn't over. I attended my second StokerCon™ in Long Beach, CA in 2017. My wife and two daughters were with me at the awards ceremony when my name was called as the winner for Superior Achievement in a First Novel.

The experience still feels like a dream. It is a night I will never forget. I've since had a second novel published, as well as three novellas and several short stories. Whenever people ask which book of mine they should read, I usually answer Haven. Not because it won the award but simply because there is something special about your first novel. You overcome so much during those long, lonely nights of writing. So much doubt, never knowing that you'll finish, not really believing that your writing is good enough. Your first novel may not end up being the best thing you've ever written, but I think it will always hold a special place in your heart. For those of you working on your first novel, don't give up. It's hard and it's lonely and it's frustrating, but all that fades away when you type those two words.

Tom Deady is the Bram Stoker Award® winning author of *Haven* (Cemetery Dance, 2016), *Eternal Darkness* (Bloodshot Books, 2017), *Weekend Getaway* (Grinning Skull Press, 2017), and *Backwater* (Omnium Gatherum, 2018). Deady also has a non-fiction publishing credit with *Rue Morgue Magazine*, and several short stories published. He holds a Master's Degree in English and teaches Creative Writing at Southern New Hampshire University. He is an Active member of the Horror Writers Association and a member of the New England Horror Writers.

Writing a Series

The Agony and the Ecstasy, aka, A Tale of Two Methods for Writing a Series

By Nancy Kilpatrick

Building your own fictional world is fun, but it also requires forethought. No writer wants to be on the other end of a reader's annoyance as in one of those Star Trek or Buffy questions that huffily starts "How come you didn't…" or "That's not what you said in book…"

I have contributed to worlds not of my own imagining: two novels in the Jason X series; one collab in the White Wolf vampire domain. Such realms come with pre-existing rules and often a series bible. At the very least there's usually a knowledgeable editor to keep the writer adhering to the desired territory.

I've also written two original series: *Power of the Blood* (4 novels), and *Thrones of Blood* (6 novels). Creating a world endows a writer with god-like powers of control. That's the Ecstasy! The Agony! comes because the writer alone is responsible for every single thing that goes wrong in the series.

The first series I wrote didn't begin as a series. Decades ago, I was a young writer with a stand-alone vampire novel set in the then future, 2006. I didn't have a plan, just an idea, and a love of the characters and story line. At that time vampires were becoming hot (again) press-wise. I had a great belief that *Bloodlover* would be published. Ecstasy! Thirty-five publishers told me not-by-them. *Agony!*

I felt somewhat discouraged, not enough to quit writing, but I did switch to short fiction for a while until another novel idea wormed its way into my brain and I was forced to write it or undergo a lobotomy.

Child of the Night was my next effort. From it was born yet another novel, *Near Death*. Much to my amazement, one followed the other. I hadn't intended that! But I liked the characters appearing in each other's stories. *Ecstasy!*

I won't go into the details of my adventures in publishing, but here's the overview: Pocket Books wanted *Near Death*. Why? Because *Near Death* is set in NYC. The editor felt Americans could more easily relate to their own country than to a book set in France (*Child of the Night*). Pre-Global Village mentality. Like most young writers eager to see print in a difficult business, I went with the publishing flow. *Mostly Ecstasy!*

My wonderful editor assured me that they would publish *Child of the Night* next. Not chronological, but I figured they knew what they were doing over at Simon & Schuster. *More Ecstasy!*

My wonderful editor quit her job the month *Near Death* came out. The new editor told me that Pocket Books had suddenly placed a moratorium on buying horror novels. *Agony!*

At Robinson Publishing, the editor of the imprint Raven Books wanted to publish *Child of the Night.* The plan included reprinting *Near Death.* If I could write a third book and *Bloodlover* could be the fourth book, each title would come out separately and then as two together in two omnibus editions. *Wild Ecstasy!*

That editor left Raven before *Child of the Night* came out, but was kind enough to insist he be permitted to edit my novel and see it through to publication. *Controlled Agony!*

I now had *Near Death* and *Child of the Night* in print. *Bloodlover* languished.

The editor/owner of a new house, Pumpkin Books, approached me and wanted to reprint *Near Death* and *Child of the Night.* Could I get the rights back and write another book quickly to continue the series? Series? Suddenly, I realized I was writing one. I agreed and produced *Reborn. Ecstasy!*

Unknown to me until after all three books came out, that publisher was involved in a law suit which culminated in the house going out of business, and the owner/editor moving to parts unknown. *Serious Agony!*

A small publisher wanted to know if I had a novel available. Baskerville Books published *Bloodlover.* By then, we were in the 2000s. *Bloodlover* became a flashback novel, re-set in the 1960s, an era where some of the futuristic elements—now commonplace—were at their inception. *Mild Ecstasy!*

The rights to all four novels reverted, I pitched the series to a mid-size house, Mosaic Press, which published them in English and sold foreign rights to several countries. The books were finally out as a set for the first time. *Ecstasy!*

Crossroad Press published the series as ebooks, and sold one of the novels as an audio book. *Serious Ecstasy!*

The biggest drawback I faced with writing four novels in the same world over decades and not realizing for a long time that I was writing a series was connecting all the dots, because I hadn't planned this continuum.

Writing an unplanned series is not ideal. I had no outline, no overview plan. I was winging it each step of the way. There were lots of messy bits that had to be fixed, an overarching plot to create, connections made and smoothed out. Even though by some dark magic the four books became *of a piece*, I do not recommend this method.

My new series, *Thrones of Blood*, is an entirely different entity. I wrote this series assuming it wouldn't be published. I mentioned it from time to time on Facebook as *The Unpublishables*. The manuscripts crossed half a dozen genres and a lot of politically incorrect territory. I was just having fun.

About twelve or so winters ago, I wrote Vol. 1 in one month. Then I began thinking about how *The Unpublishables* could be a fun series to write. I outlined the basic ideas for seven novels all at the same time. I worked on each book depending on how I felt that day, but kept to the idea of folding the stories together, and especially to maintaining the connection with and advancement in each novel of the two overarching series plots. I revised Vol. 1 and cut most of the genres to keep the story more coherent and focused. It and the then novels-in-progress clocked in at about 100,000 words each, + or -. I amalgamated Vols. 6 & 7 and by then had a good grasp of the six-book series. I showed the first book to a couple of writer friends, who deemed it publishable.

As well as the plot of each novel, much thought went into the big picture—the two overarching series plots. This project took more than a decade because I was determined that it make sense, and I wanted to avoid the problems I'd had with the first series being written piecemeal. Each story would, of course, sometimes veer off in an unanticipated direction, as novels will. But, as long as the plot still worked—neither predictable nor out-of-the-blue—, it was good to go. But the two overarching plots were equally important. Both built in each novel and that big picture had to lead to a satisfying conclusion.

If you are so inclined, feel free to pick up Vols. 1, 2, 3 and 4 in print or ebook (5 and 6 coming soon) and see how structuring an overview can build.

This series will conclude by 2020 with Vol. 6. Okay, you've heard that before. Writers have been known to become so enamored with their stories and characters that they just can't let go. I hope to not be that kind of literary smother-mother. Besides, I have other books to write, and maybe other series.

I was lucky with *Power of the Blood*. Working in the dark can be exhilarating, but it's also fraught with many near heartstopping stress storms. I'm grateful that somehow I managed to navigate the rough waters without drowning. But I much prefer the safety of a secure vessel holding it all together: the series outline. That gets me where I want to go without having to plug seemingly endless leaks along the way.

Some suggestions: If you think you're writing a series, ask yourself:

• Why does this story require more than one novel to be told?

• How can one book lead to the next seamlessly without too much 'filler' to remind reader of what they read in the previous book(s)? (Tons of filler—aka exposition—is rarely pretty.)

• Is there a big plot overarching the series, and if not, why not?

• If there is, how are you going to dole out the bits needed in each novel to move that over-plot along without giving the conclusion away?

You likely need to do research, some or extensive. It's a good idea to research all the books you're envisioning in the series at once, that way you'll be less likely to crash into this-won't-work-now-because walls.

The best thing you can do for your series is to know where you're going by identifying the connecting links between the novels that keep that big picture vibrant. Minimize the *Agony!* Maximum the *Ecstasy!* Your readers will be glad you did! Wouldn't you rather end up with accolades than damnation!

Award-winning author **Nancy Kilpatrick** has published 22 novels, over 220 short stories, 6 collections of her stories and has edited 15 anthologies of other people's stories. She's also published one non-fiction book. Friend her on Facebook and Twitter! Website: nancykilpatrick.com

FLAME TREE PRESS

FICTION WITHOUT FRONTIERS

My Art Path

By Jill Bauman

I am an artist. For as long as I can remember, I always wanted to be an artist.

There wasn't any plan or goal. All I knew is that I wanted to live in that space.

I didn't go to an art school, but completed my education as an art education major and taught art for some years. Despite a divorce, which left me to raise my two daughters on my own, I took a chance in the late 1970's, and dared to follow my dream, to journey on the road to the great art unknown.

I lived in Queens, New York, with easy access to New York City, so I scouted out galleries. The most common response I got was, "you paint like an illustrator." I could only shake my head and say to myself, "what the hell does that mean?"

The artworks I created were expressions of how I saw the world, whatever that was? Although I haunted museums and was fascinated with the works of other artists, I knew I had to be me, not them. When I met Walter Velez, I began to understand why galleries saw me as an illustrator. I became Walter's agent and he became my mentor. His rule was, "I will teach you technique, but you aren't to show your work for two years." At the time, it seemed like an eternity. My choices were to go back to teaching or live my dream. Again, it was Walter's wisdom that was the tipping point—he said, "I never want to go through life saying 'I should have.'" That was it! I committed myself to learning all I could from Walter, and life drawing class at the Art Students League in New York City.

Two years later, Walter announced one day, "OK, you can show your art now." The first time I saw an art director, I got a job. Crazy, huh?

Soon I discovered Science Fiction conventions. My first convention was Lunacon in 1979 in New Jersey. At that convention, I was introduced to Charlie Grant. He introduced me to other writers, Alan Ryan, F. Paul Wilson, and many others. I knew I had found my place. Charlie promised that one day, my art would be on the cover of one of his books. At the time, I thought he was just being kind. Two years later, Charlie called to let me know that he had spoken to the editor of Berkley books about my art. I was given my first cover assignment for Charlie's novel, *A Quiet Night of Fear*. Whatever it was Charlie saw, I am forever grateful to him.

I continued to get assignments from Berkley Books including a collection of short stories by Charlie Grant titled, *A Glow of Candles.* That assignment was followed by *The Attack of the Giant Baby* by Kit Reed and it rolled on from there. I continued to work on my skills and soon found a place in publishing.

I became more active in the convention circuit. Charlie Grant called me to let me know about a fabulous small convention on the campus of Roger Williams College in Rhode Island called Necon. The next year, 1982, I attended the convention and have continued until today. That first Necon, some of the guests were, Stephen King, Peter Straub, David Morrell, John Coyne, Whitley Strieber and many more. It was a very casual event. The attendees all got to know on another well. Over the years, many of the writers who attended recommended me to their publishers for their covers. Now, I was considered an artist of "horror art." It was a time, as Grady Hendrix clearly has documented in his fabulous book, *Paperbacks from Hell*, of dolls, creatures, killer plants, clowns, haunted houses, etcetera dominating cover art. I fit right in.

In 1988, The World Horror Association held a convention to gather writers of horror, along with editors, and publishers, and to present the Bram Stoker Awards® for works published in 1987.

In 1990, I received another call from Charlie Grant, this time telling me that a new convention had been organized. It would be the World Horror Convention. It was to be held in Nashville, Tennessee for the first two years. He also invited me to be the first Artist Guest of Honor for that first convention. The Tennessee organizers, Beth Gwinn, Maureen Doris, Joann Parsons, and their staff put together an amazing event. The writer Guest of Honor was Chelsea Quinn Yarbro, the Grand Master Robert Bloch. This convention for writers, artists, publishers, editors, and fans incorporated the Bram Stoker Award®event as well. The two events were held together for many years until they became two separate entities, but for a while came together every two years.

The categories for the Stoker Award have expanded, attendance of the event has grown. The award itself, designed by Steven Kirk, is a haunted house. When the door is open, a brass engraved plaque is displayed with the authors name & title of the work. This is a much coveted trophy.

Looking back, I now see that I wasn't just involved in creating of art; the business of art was a key factor as well. Learning how to sell my talent was essential. It wasn't a conscious thing on my part;

I had a need at the time to learn all I could to get assignments. That meant getting out and getting involved. It meant taking time out from drawing and painting. It meant arranging a way to have people sometimes pick up my two daughters from school. Oh, did I mention, I was a single mom with two young girls? It meant setting up appointments in New York City with publishers, editors, and art directors. It also meant that, to fulfill my obligation to Walter Valez, I found him work too. It meant dividing myself.

Conventions were extremely essential. To attend them meant juggling all these same things: taking care that the children were looked after in my absence, and that Walter was kept busy. I had to earn enough to take care of home, while also spending money on hotels, food, fees, travel. I had to pack art, get to the conventions, set up an art shows, take part in panel discussions, and be alert and awake enough to become involved socially. Okay, I was much younger then.

Over the years I have meet so many incredible, creative people. Several of these friends are "life time" friends. They have become the family I have chosen. I've learned how to experiment with new ideas and techniques. I am following the path, the art path, in every way I can, for there is so much more I want to do.

Jill Bauman has been a freelance illustrator/designer for 38 years. In that time she's produced hundreds of covers for horror, mystery, fantasy, science fiction, and bestselling books for major publishers and small press.

Jill has illustrated works by such authors: Harlan Ellison, Stephen King, Peter Straub, Lilian Jackson Braun, Charles L. Grant, Richard Laymon, Jack Williamson, Hugh B. Cave, Fritz Leiber, Michael Resnick, J. G. Ballard, Steward O'Nan and Justin Cronin and many more.

She has been nominated for the World Fantasy Award five times and nominated for the Chesley Award several times. Her art has been exhibited at the Delaware Art Museum, the Moore College of Art, NY Art Students League, the NY Illustrators Society and the Science Fiction Museum of Seattle.

Canvassing the Spirit

By Jill Bauman

Pure white untouched surface
a void waiting to be filled
as the texture of woven fabric
crossing in angles sends
glints bouncing in random patterns.

Fingers gently stroke the canvas
as shadows dance playfully
in a fluid, silent motion.
The brush hearing an imaginary song
twirls on its head in the paint.

Strokes of brilliant color
break the emptiness with stark reality.
Sparks of inspiration capture
spirits, giving them life,
painting the air, not the substance.

The intangible comes alive as
medium transforms into form.
The gaze transfixed ahead
as an image glares back,
each challenging the other to blink.

©WALTER VELEZ 1982

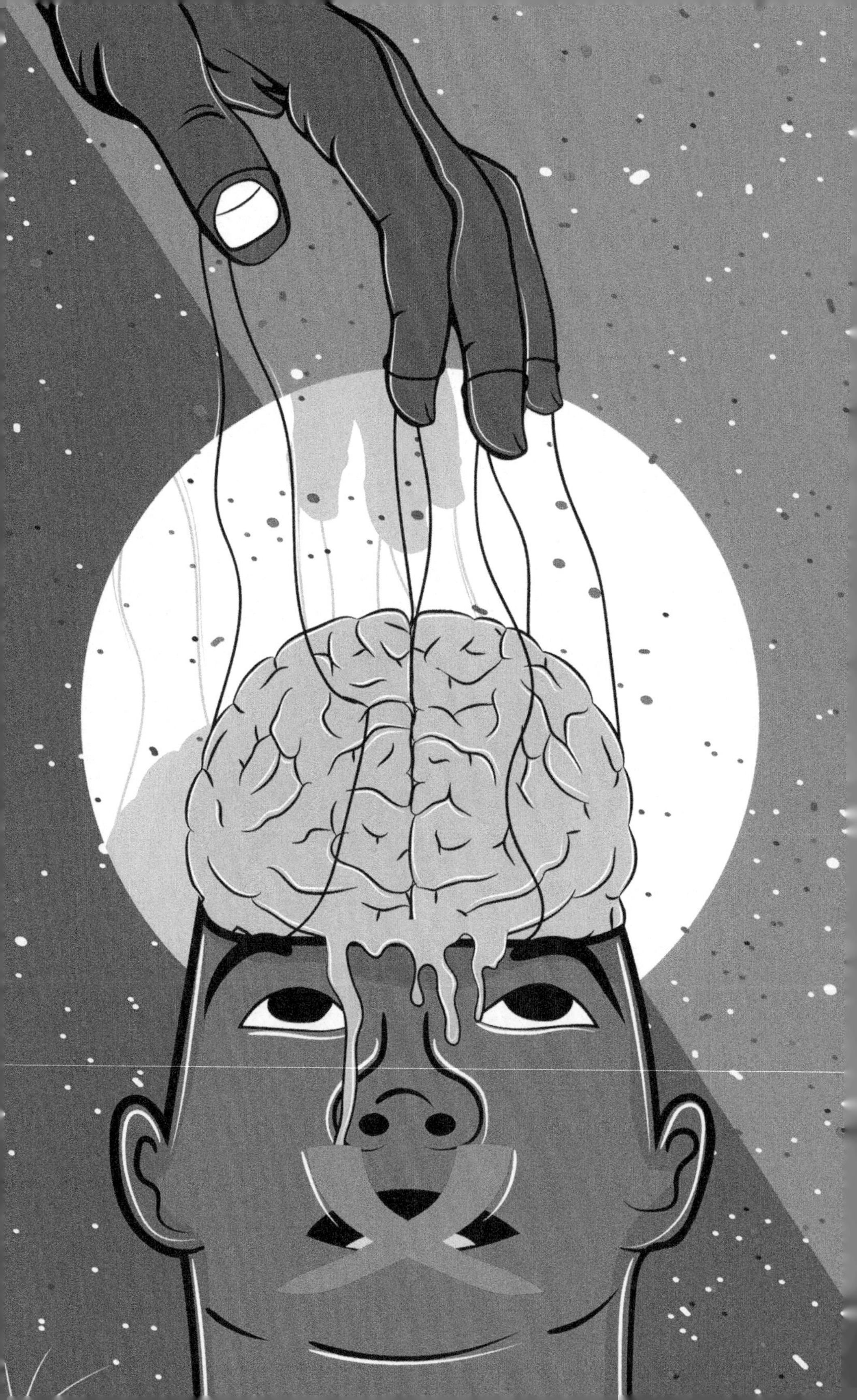

MWM

Lynne Hansen

Bram Stoker Awards®

Congratulations to the 2019 Bram Stoker Award® Nominees

Superior Achievement in a Novel

Katsu, Alma – *The Hunger* (G.P. Putnam's Sons)
Maberry, Jonathan – *Glimpse* (St. Martin's Press)
Malerman, Josh – *Unbury Carol* (Del Rey)
Stoker, Dacre and Barker, J.D. – *Dracul* (G.P. Putnam's Sons)
Tremblay, Paul – *The Cabin at the End of the World* (William Morrow)

Superior Achievement in a First Novel

Fine, Julia – *What Should Be Wild* (Harper)
Grau, T.E – *I Am the River* (Lethe Press)
Kiste, Gwendolyn – *The Rust Maidens* (Trepidatio Publishing)
Stage, Zoje – *Baby Teeth* (St. Martin's Press)
Tremblay, Tony – *The Moore House* (Twisted Publishing)

Superior Achievement in a Young Adult Novel

Ireland, Justina – *Dread Nation* (Balzer + Bray)
Legrand, Claire – *Sawkill Girls* (Katherine Tegen Books)
Maberry, Jonathan – *Broken Lands* (Simon & Schuster)
Snyman, Monique – *The Night Weaver* (Gigi Publishing)
White, Kiersten – *The Dark Descent of Elizabeth Frankenstein* (Delacorte Press)

Superior Achievement in a Graphic Novel

Ahmed, Saladin – *Abbott* (BOOM! Studios)
Azzarello, Brian – *Moonshine Vol. 2: Misery Train* (Image Comics)
Bunn, Cullen – *Bone Parish* (BOOM! Studios)
LaValle, Victor – *Victor LaValle's Destroyer* (BOOM! Studios)
Liu, Marjorie – *Monstress Volume 3: Haven* (Image Comics)

Superior Achievement in Long Fiction

Bailey, Michael – *Our Children, Our Teachers* (Written Backwards)
Hill, Joe – *You Are Released* (Flight or Fright: 17 Turbulent Tales) (Scribner)
Malik, Usman T. – *Dead Lovers on Each Blade, Hung* (Nightmare Magazine Issue #74)
Mason, Rena – *The Devil's Throat* (Hellhole: An Anthology of Subterranean Terror) (Adrenaline Press)
Smith, Angela Yuriko – *Bitter Suites* (CreateSpace)

Superior Achievement in Short Fiction

Landry, Jess – "Mutter" (Fantastic Tales of Terror) (Crystal Lake Publishing)

Murray, Lee – "Dead End Town"(Cthulhu Deep Down Under Volume 2) (IFWG Publishing International)

Neugebauer, Annie – "Glove Box" (The Dark City Crime & Mystery Magazine Volume 3, Issue 4-July 2018)

Taff, John F.D. – "A Winter's Tale" (Little Black Spots) (Grey Matter Press)

Ward, Kyla Lee – "And in Her Eyes the City Drowned" (Weirdbook #39) (Wildside Press)

Superior Achievement in a Fiction Collection

Files, Gemma – *Spectral Evidence* (Trepidatio Publishing)

Guignard, Eric J. – *That Which Grows Wild* (Cemetery Dance Publications)

Iglesias, Gabino – *Coyote Songs* (Broken River Books)

Snyder, Lucy A. – *Garden of Eldritch Delights* (Raw Dog Screaming Press)

Waggoner, Tim – *Dark and Distant Voices: A Story Collection* (Nightscape Press)

Superior Achievement in a Screenplay

Aster, Ari – *Hereditary* (PalmStar Media)

Averill, Meredith – *The Haunting of Hill House: The Bent-Neck Lady,* Episode 01:05 (Amblin Television, FlanaganFilm, Paramount Television)

Garland, Alex – *Annihilation* (DNA Films, Paramount Pictures, Scott Rudin Productions, Skydance Media)

Heisserer, Eric – *Bird Box* (Bluegrass Films, Chris Morgan Productions, Universal Pictures)

Woods, Bryan, Beck, Scott, and Krasinski, John – *A Quiet Place* (Platinum Dunes, Sunday Night)

Superior Achievement in an Anthology

Chambers, James, Grey, April, and Masterson, Robert – A *New York State of Fright: Horror Stories from the Empire State* (Hippocampus Press)

Datlow, Ellen – *The Devil and the Deep: Horror Stories of the Sea* (Night Shade Books)

Guignard, Eric J. – *A World of Horror* (Dark Moon Books)

Murray, Lee – *Hellhole: An Anthology of Subterranean Terror* (Adrenaline Press)

Ward, D. Alexander – *Lost Highways: Dark Fictions from the Road* (Crystal Lake Publishing)

Superior Achievement in Non-Fiction

Connolly, John – Horror Express (PS Publishing)

Gambin, Lee – The Howling: Studies in the Horror Film (Centipede Press)

Ingham, Howard David – We Don't Go Back: A Watcher's Guide to Folk Horror (Room 207 Press)

Mynhardt, Joe and Johnson, Eugene – It's Alive: Bringing Your Nightmares to Life (Crystal Lake Publishing)

Wetmore Jr., Kevin J. – Uncovering Stranger Things: Essays on Eighties Nostalgia, Cynicism and Innocence in the Series (McFarland)

Superior Achievement in a Poetry Collection

Boston, Bruce – Artifacts (Independent Legions Publishing)

Cowen, David E. – Bleeding Saffron (Weasel Press)

Lynch, Donna – Witches (Raw Dog Screaming Press)

Simon, Marge and Manzetti, Alessandro – War (Crystal Lake Publishing)

Tantlinger, Sara – The Devil's Dreamland (Strangehouse Books)

The Gravity of the Bram Stoker Awards®

By Rena Mason

Not the physical weight of the actual award, which is a whopping four pounds by the way, but the serious nature of the award and what it represents. Of course, that kind of gravity means something different to everyone, which is why this topic will get written in just about every StokerCon™ program book and always read fresh to both returning and new attendees.

In the latter part of the 80s, when I was "coughs" still in high school, some of you may have been there and been a part of it, and some of you weren't yet a twinkle in your parents' eyes, a group of well-known horror authors came together and established an organization to represent the genre—now known as the Horror Writers Association—HWA. These great minds of that fabulous decade, also agreed that annual awards should be given out for superior achievement in literary categories representing the genre. Since 1988, some of horror's most esteemed and legendary authors have received Bram Stoker Awards®.

It's not just that these horror greats created the awards, making it an instant honor for the recipients to receive them, but it's as though they were handing them out personally. Even if they don't physically do this, it carries the same weight when the winner's name is called, and the bright lights shine in their eyes, and they're given the award to hold while they try to remember to thank everyone in their life who has helped them make it up there onto the stage. I can only speak for myself, but it resonated with me in this way as a past winner. As well, many of those horror greats have also won the Bram Stoker Award®, putting winners then and now alongside their literary genre heroes. But this isn't a history lesson or a brush-up on the awards for trivia buffs. (Check out the new awards website, or past and recent episodes of the TV game show *Jeopardy* for several mentions over the years regarding the Horror Writers Association and the Bram Stoker Awards® for those.) These are solely the opinions of a past Finalist and recipient of two Bram Stoker Awards® for Long Fiction, First Novel, as well as a tie for Short Fiction, and the 2014 Silver Hammer Award for volunteer efforts with the organization.

Everyone has a story about how they got here—where they are now—there, that place they'd strived to get to. And again, here and there are different for everyone, from nailing that first sentence, completing a story at any length, having a work published, or getting that two, three, four, five, six or even seven-figure book and movie deal. No matter the route to our outcomes, our creative work involves putting ourselves and our work out there. We're all different in how we do this, too, and everyone's advice varies. But truly, the best encouragement anyone has ever given me, is not to worry about anything else, and to just write.

As exhausted or exhilarated as we may be after working on a project, we seek to share it and not for accolades, not for awards, money, or even for our own well-being in many cases. We do it because what we've written needs to breathe on its own, live, go out into the world and be read. I've never heard anyone say, "I wrote this story to win…" anything, ever, and that even includes writing contests. But most of the writers I know tend to avoid those, or go in with something they've already written. Anyway, I digress. None of us goes into the process of writing a work to win an award, but if we hear we could be close, it's only natural to get a twinge of excitement.

Every year when the Preliminary Ballot comes out it becomes the hot topic of many social media conversations, good and bad. This reignites when the Final Ballot is announced. Some voice their disappointment, some discount the awards altogether, some express pleasure with the results, and some point out an increase in diversity among the authors and titles, while others do not. Regardless of their views on the results, they give life to the awards.

Many don't get to peek behind the scenes during the awards process, which consists of two branches: Recommendations by HWA members, and review and deliberations by the category Juries through Submissions. Volunteering on the awards committee, I've experienced communications firsthand with large publishing and entertainment corporations out there that have awards departments staffed specifically to reach out to credible artistic communities and organizations. They contact the Awards Committee responsible for the Bram Stoker Awards®, willing to assist in any way to promote their authors and screenwriters, and that's pretty damn cool. I can tell you firsthand that among them are world-wide, household names of writers, directors, producers and those I can't list but can say with the utmost confidence that most of you consider iconic legends. They also want their work to be reviewed and considered for the Bram Stoker Award®. It's important to them, which makes it important to me, because they are the ones who introduced me to, and taught me to love and appreciate the horror genre.

After the acceptance speeches, after the cheering and clapping have died down, the photo shoot is finished, and comrades and strangers congratulate winners as they walk back to their hotel rooms to safeguard their haunted house prizes, they most likely set the award down on a table or dresser in the room, open the little door, read their name inside and the title of the work they won for. Then they may pick up that statue again, look over all the fine details and craftsmanship that went into making it, and as they hold it, can't help but think that yes, this has some weight to it indeed.

Rena Mason is the Bram Stoker Award® winning author of *The Evolutionist* and *East End Girls,* as well as a 2014 Stage 32 / The Search for New Blood Screenwriting Contest Finalist. She writes horror science fiction, historical fiction/alternate history, speculative fiction, mysteries, and thrillers. Her writing career began over a decade ago by mashing up those genres in stories.

She is a member of the Horror Writers Association, Mystery Writers of America, International Thriller Writers, and The International Screenwriters' Association.

An R.N., avid scuba diver and world traveler, she currently resides in Reno, Nevada. For more information, visit her website: www.renamason.ink.

What Being a Member Means to Me

By Nancy Holder

I've been a member (off and on) of HWA since its founding as the Horror and Occult Writers League (H.O.W.L.) back in the days of the Gutenberg Necronomicon. What HWA means to me is community—from sharing market information for *Chicken Soup for the Unsouled Flesh Eater* and editing each other's zombie flash fiction to hanging out in Los Angeles and San Diego with folks who have seen the Spanish-language *Dracula* and understand why you (okay, I) *need* to spend fifty dollars on skull socks in the StokerCon™ dealers room if such treasures are to be found there—and to fully share my disappointment if they are not.

And StokerCon™ itself is more than a horror convention—it's a family reunion, where those of us who usually correspond on the interwebs can connect and talk shop, eat and drink too much, watch amazing movies, and play tabletop games. I was so shy the first few conventions I attended that I used to sit in the lobby or hotel coffee shop with a horror novel or anthology in the hope that someone would say hi or comment on what I was reading. It worked—so many people loved Arthur Machen—who knew?!—and now some of those early acquaintances have become my closest friends.

I have belonged to a lot of writing groups in my lifetime, but HWA is the only one I have consistently remained in. There's something about "horror people" that separates us from not just other writers but other people-people. I think it might have something to do with the reaction many of us get when we tell someone that we are horror writers (the usual response to my revelation is, "But you're so nice!") We are a little more subversive, transgressive—counting down to the winter holidays by watching *Black Christmas* and *Krampus* instead of *Home Alone* (which sounds promising if you only go by the title, no?) We are not only the lovers of the dark, the weird, the terrifying, the gory and the gross, but the discerning connoisseurs of same, discussing whether there is any redeeming social value to torture porn with the learned precision of Torah scholars debating how many days to celebrate Rosh Hashanah. We can recite chapter and verse of our horror canon ("Once upon a midnight dreary…") and we get why Halloween is the very best of all the secular holidays.

And when we get together, whether it be online or in person, this zest for all things dark and scary and freaky gets amplified and we *know* we are with our people. It's true that we want to be published, to have careers—we are the Horror *Writers* Association, after all—but at our core, we want to mix and mingle with other people who get this passion without any layers of explanation ("Actually, you actually do like horror. Many of the early works of literature were ghost stories, and look at Percy Bysshe Shelley's work, and telling ghost stories is a British tradition…yada yada yada"). We don't have to explain and we don't have to minimize how absolutely much we loved *The Haunting of Hill House* on Netflix even though it had nothing to do with the book. We can cut to the chase. We can shorthand. And we can do it together.

And that's what being a member means to me—it means being a family member. Of the biggest, weirdest, and best family there is.

Nancy Holder is a New York Times bestselling author (the *Wicked* saga, written with Debbie Viguié) and 5-time Bram Stoker Award® winner. She currently serves on the Board of Trustees and stepped in as interim Vice President after the death of much-beloved Rocky Wood. She has written tie-in material for *Buffy the Vampire Slayer* and other TV shows and movies, including the novelization of *Crimson Peak*. She is the writer on the Mary Shelley Presents comic book series from Kymera Press and a faculty member for the Stonecoast MFA in Creative Writing program, offered through the University of Southern Maine. She is a disciple of Mary Shelley and an ardent Sherlockian.

HWA Scholarships

2018 marked the fourth year recipients were selected for the Poetry Scholarship, HWA and Mary Wollstonecraft Shelley Scholarships. Fiction Scholarship Committee: Carina Bissett, J.G. Faherty and Marge Simon. Poetry Scholarship Committee: Karen Bovenmyer, David E. Cowen, and Marge Simon. Committee Members Statements

J.G. Faherty: It was an honor once again to be part of the selection committees for the HWA Scholarship Award and the Mary Shelley Award. As always, it was a difficult pleasure to read all the of entries. A pleasure because so many of them were outstanding in terms of quality and imagination, and difficult because in the end you can only select one person for each award. I wish we had unlimited funds so that we could help each deserving person move forward in their writing careers. But I can only console myself with the knowledge that past recipients have gone on to be published in some amazing markets, and that the others can—and should—apply again next year.

Karen Bovenmyer: I agree with everything Greg Faherty stated, couldn't say it any better! I very much enjoyed writing encouraging letters to our non-winning finalists to explain why their work has merit and encourage them to continue to apply for scholarships. A competition like this opens many possibilities for us to see new work, encourage new horror writers, and spread the good name of our organization as one that helps authors develop. This is also great publicity for what horror is and isn't. The Horror Writer's Association has made a huge difference in my career and I think it's important to publicize how loving and supportive horror authors are.

David E. Cowen: This year was the second time I was given the privilege of being a judge for the HWA Poetry Scholarship. I concur with what others have said but obviously have my own observations, especially from the submissions we received this year we were almost in the position of having to choose the "least worst" candidate. That seems to be the result of a couple of things. First, more people than before simply didn't read the rules. They gave us prose samples, didn't submit a full application and/or just submitted a poem. Second, many didn't actually express a desire to pursue dark poetry as part of their career path. Tighter rules and explanations may help. A submission system that will only accept the application if all the documents required are submitted, if feasible, could help. We are currently addressing these problems and all should be rectified by next year's selection period. Luckily this year we wound up with 2-3 real applicants that allowed us to pick the best, not the "least bad".

Carina Bissett: As a former winner of the HWA Scholarship, I know how much an opportunity like this can change a writer's life. I enjoyed the diversity and sheer passion exhibited in many of the scholarship applications, and found it a difficult task to choose when it came down to the final selections. I think it's an act of bravery to apply for an opportunity like this, and I would encourage all of the participants who didn't make it through the final cut to sharpen their prose, polish their applications, and resubmit when the window opens up again. Persistence is one of the key traits to being a successful writer, and HWA offers a safe place for writers of all capabilities to hone their skills. Submitting materials and accepting rejections is part of a writer's life. HWA offers a multitude of opportunities for writers to practice their craft, and I would encourage participation in the many forums offered. The organization has changed my life, so I know from personal experience that it can help others too.

Carina's Fiction Scholarship Committee Suggestions

One of the key components to being a successful writer is the dedication to craft development. The Mary Wollstonecraft Shelley and HWA scholarships are committed to forwarding continuing education for writers at all levels. Foundational creative writing classes can often be found included in course offerings at local community colleges and universities; however, it can be tricky to find classes with a specific focus on genre fiction. There are a few pioneering institutions that offer low-residency MFA program such as Seton Hill University and Stonecoast at the University of Southern Maine. Western State Colorado University also offers a low-residency MFA in Genre Fiction. However, not everyone is ready to make the time and financial commitment to an MFA program, nor do all writers have access to brick-and-mortar institutions of higher learning. Luckily, there are several other options available. Clarion, Clarion West, Odyssey, and Viable Paradise all offer highly-competitive, intensive workshop experiences. In addition to the six-week intensives, Clarion West offers one-day workshops in Seattle, and Odyssey offers online workshops.

Writers seeking online classes in a non-competitive workshop environment have even more to choose from. For example, LitReactor offers a wide variety of speculative fiction workshops with such working writers as Gemma Files, J. S. Breukelaar, and Nick Mamatas; the Rambo Academy for Wayward Writers (headed by SFWA President Cat Rambo) includes seminars lead by such well-known writers as Seanan McGuire, Fran Wilde, and Ann Leckie; the University of Richard (run by the novelist, short story writer, and editor Richard Thomas) offers in-depth, four-month live workshops in Contemporary Dark Fiction and Advanced Creative Writing; and the Storied Imaginarium includes focused, small group online generative workshops focusing on such topics as Monstrous Women and Intersections: Science Fiction, Fairy Tales and Myth. Regardless of the route you choose, continuing your education and working to improve your craft will open new opportunities and help you to build community. What could be better than that?

Links:

- Clarion clarion.ucsd.edu
- Clarion West www.clarionwest.org
- LitReactor litreactor.com/classes/upcoming
- Odyssey www.odysseyworkshop.org
- Rambo Academy for Wayward Writers www.kittywumpus.net/blog/academy
- Seton Hill University www.setonhill.edu/academics/graduate-programs/writing-popular-fictionmfa
- Stonecoast usm.maine.edu/stonecoastmfa
- www.western.edu/academics/school-graduate-studies/graduate-program-creative-writing-lowresidency-mfa-and-ma
- Storied Imaginarium thestoriedimaginarium.com
- University of Richard whatdoesnotkillme.com/2017/02/16/advancedcreativewritingworkshop
- Borderlands Press Writers Bootcamp www.borderlandspress.com/writers-boot-camp

Poetry Scholarship Committee Suggestions

If you're not a member, we suggest joining the HWA. You will find a wealth of resources for improving your craft. For example, go through the HWA newsletter archives of the Dark Poet's columns *(Blood and Spades)* which addresses all forms of dark poetry, with examples from established dark poets such as Mike Arnzen, Bruce Boston, Ann Schwader, Wendy Rathbone, Jeannine Hall Gailey, James S. Dorr, Michael Collings, F.J. Bergmann, Elissa Malcohn, and more.

Other resources to consider:

- The SFPA (Science Fiction Poetry Association) is run by volunteers, and is worth joining for more information about writing genre poetry (sf/f/h) as well as reading some of the best contemporary poetry, dark or light. Members are provided with quarterly issues (PDF or hard copy) with articles and poetry by members. (www.sfpoetry.com)
- "How Writers Write Poetry" online from The University of Iowa. Viable Paradise (viableparadise.com)
- Poets & Writers Magazine subscription.

Courses in writing poetry (may be part of a writing course) will be evaluated for: openness to genre poetry explicitly mentioned in the (college teacher's) syllabus -published genre author/poet instructing the course title in the college catalog directly mentioning genre-related topics. Statements from Previous Scholarship Recipients

Michael Tugendhat: (Dark Poetry Scholarship, 2015): I was awarded the Dark Poetry Scholarship, but used the funds for a mentorship with an editor at Henry Holt on my novel. Poetry and fiction are understandably different beasts with different needs, but by engaging on one project for a six-month period with an expert from the industry, I was able to see how both forms can benefit from the other. I am now infusing deeper narratives into my poetry, and can thank the HWA for being an organization that believes in their members.

Erinn Kemper: (Mary Wollstonecraft Shelley Scholarship, 2015): I was honored to be the first recipient of the HWA's Shelley Scholarship. The scholarship gave me an opportunity to participate in online classes and focus on developing my craft. I live in a slightly remote part of Costa Rica, where sloths and monkeys and toucans frolic in the trees, but there's not a big writing community, so it was amazing to be able to connect with other writers and writing instructors virtually. I'm grateful to the HWA for their support and encouragement. Cheers!

John Reinhart: (Dark Poetry Scholarship, 2016): My scholarship allowed me to take my first poetry class in 20 years, helped connect me to other writers at StokerCon™, and bit me hard enough that I may never see the sun again, preferring to read and write in the dark. In the two years following the scholarship, I have published six poetry collections. I am eternally grateful to the HWA for this springboard to another plane.

Carina Bissett: (HWA Scholarship, 2016): After graduating from the Creative Writing MFA program at Stonecoast, my work has been nominated for several awards. Currently, I teach an online workshop at The Storied Imaginarium. My short fiction and poetry has been published in multiple journals and anthologies including *Hath No Fury, Gorgon: Stories of Emergence, Mythic Delirium, NonBinary Review,* and the *HWA Poetry Showcase Vol.V*.

Karen Bovenmyer: (Mary W. Shelley Scholarship, 2016): Personally, I learned a lot from taking "How Writers Write Poetry" online from The University of Iowa and also Stephanie M. Wytovich's poetry class at StokerCon™. Going to StokerCon™ was very special and helped me understand how I fit through building relationships with other authors in this field.

Ashley Dioses: (Dark Poetry Scholarship, 2017): As a formalist poet, I am always trying to improve upon my skills and find new forms to try out. This scholarship has led me to an amazing book that, in particular, allowed me to learn a few new forms. I have an obsession with Scandinavian history and folklore, among other interests, and have learned, for the first time, that they had their own ancient poetry forms that could be taught and that were new to my knowledge. I was already planning on writing a poetry collection that would contain a lot of Scandinavian inspired pieces and now I have the knowledge to write them in the old ways that their poetry was written.

John C. Mannone: (HWA Scholarship, October 2017): Since being selected, I have been enjoying the prestige while promoting speculative poems and stories, especially dark ones. I've been sharpening by literary skills with some of the scholarship funds (and some of my own). I have earmarked some of the funds for certain magazine subscriptions and online courses: (1) Attended the February Mildred Haun Conference (Morristown, TN). I'll cultivate what learned about ghost legends. Paranormal aspects occur in my historical novella, Fragments, which continues to near completion (No cost to HWA); (2) Attended the April 2018 Tennessee Mountain Writers Conference (Oak Ridge, TN) where I won first place in writing for young people with a poem Little Wishing Star. And though not dark, it is a speculative piece concerning a Chippewa legend. It was recently accepted and is forthcoming in Red Coyote. (Conference/Workshop Fee $220); (3) Attended the August 2018 Learning Events: A Poetry Workshop with Bill Brown. This yielded a watershed of poems. (Workshop fee $85); (4) As president of the Chattanooga Writers' Guild, I continue to ensure that speculative poetry and prose maintains a voice in our literary community. (My dues over two years is $80).

Volunteering

Slaying it Forward: Why Volunteer for StokerCon™ and HWA?

By Kevin J. Wetmore, Jr.

StokerCon™ 2019 Volunteer Coordinator

Are you enjoying the Con? Are you enjoying this book? Are you enjoying the HWA? You have volunteers to thank for it. I have served as co-chair for the last two StokerCons and am coordinating the volunteers for this one and have found service to the organization to be not only invaluable to my own growth as a writer but also a way to pay back an organization that supports me and my work and has done so much to help me develop, network and grow.

I can list all the reasons why I volunteer, but I thought it might be just as valuable (if not more so) to speak with some individuals who have been recognized for their volunteer work with HWA's Silver Hammer Award, created in 1996 and given "to an HWA volunteer who has done a truly massive amount of work for the organization, often unsung and behind the scenes," taking the form of a silver hammer to honor those who make the time and effort to build HWA's "house."

I asked Rena Mason (2014 recipient) why members should volunteer. Her answer: "Any business is only as good as its employees. In our case, this non-profit organization is only as good as its volunteers and employees. Compared to other writing organizations, I believe the HWA offers quite a bit of information and assistance for its minimal, annual membership fee across the Horror genre spectrum, including writing tips, promotional opportunities, and the ease of networking with others in the community. The organization's leadership listens, and it's always evolving and improving with input from its members, which is one of the most important reasons why I continue to volunteer."

Angel Leigh McCoy (2010 recipient) observed, "Writing is a solitary endeavor. Volunteering for a writers' organization is the very best way to take the edge off the loneliness and to find some support that you mightn't otherwise have." She cites a number of benefits to giving time to the organization: "long term friendships, knowing that I'm doing good as part of a team that supports my fellow writers in all stages of their careers, learning new skills and honing the old ones as I overcome hurdles that come up as technology changes, providing a service needed by members, meeting so many people I'd never have met otherwise, not only so I can brag that I've emailed with my idols, but also that they know me (Never underestimate the power of name recognition.)" Word.

"One of the first things I wanted to do upon joining the HWA was to volunteer," said Kenneth W. Cain (2017 recipient), "in part, because of those before me who set the example of giving back to the community, but also because it felt like the right thing to do." Cain concurs with Mason and McCoy that service to the organization was a great way not only to get to know the organization and its inner workings better, but also a way to meet people and have them know who you are.

For James Chambers (2016 recipient), volunteering was a way back into the horror community after having stepped away from it for a while. He also saw volunteering to run a Con as a means to serving not just the organization, but the individuals who make it up: "A lot of folks contribute to the success of any convention. Many of them go unsung. I wanted to lend a hand and contribute to these events. Once I started, I found it a rewarding and fun way to connect with a lot of folks and help shape the event. If you can pitch in and keep something running smoothly, that goes a long way toward creating a great experience for a lot of folks."

Which is not to say there are not drawbacks to volunteering. Let's be honest. All four Silver Hammer winners agreed that time spent working for HWA is time not spent writing, or at your day job, or with your family. (Although, as McCoy states, "It's important, though, to make room in your life for your people, your tribe. The HWA is my tribe." So you're spending time with your horror family, or, as my five-year old calls them, "The Halloween People.") Chambers also notes that volunteering "means taking on responsibility for activities and events. It brings headaches when things don't go according to plan or there are conflicts to resolve." Mason also concurs: there can be pushback when you put yourself out there. "Some people will find any reason they can to dislike you or find fault with the organization." And yes, that can be frustrating after one has spent hundreds of hours working on behalf of that organization without remuneration. Yet, I would argue, even that becomes a call to volunteer. If you don't like how a con is run, or how the organization is operating, become a more active part—help make a better con experience for yourself and others.

As for me, I, too appreciated what the HWA does and have

met and befriended people whom I have known previously only through their work, which I loved and admired. While I had done a few small things for my local HWA chapter (#HWALA—Los Angeles Wooo!), after the first StokerCon™ I approached the leadership and said I wanted to volunteer, as I had some experience in organizing conferences and conventions. I expected to be asked to do something minor, and instead was invited by Lisa Morton and Kate Jonez (the chair) if I wanted to co-chair the whole thing. I was and am profoundly grateful to be thought competent enough to take on that much responsibility. Yes, it was a lot of work (Kate did so much more than I, though, and her example inspired me); yes it was stressful (but I got to tour the Queen Mary with George R.R. Martin); yes, it was an exercise in on-going crisis management (but it was also an exercise in finding solutions that made others' conference experience better). It was also incredibly worthwhile, and seeing the positive Con experience for so many people made me sign up for another year of more of the same. Yes, the rewards are cool, meeting horror gods is cool, but for me the best part was feeling like I had done things that lifted others in their work. The folks who came to panels, readings, and Horror University sessions (yay Horror U! Go, Fighting Shoggoths! What? That's the HU mascot, right?) left the Con I helped organize as better writers. The benefits I got from volunteering also benefited everyone. How cool is that? And that applies across the organization. The folks who toil on Stoker Juries, or on committees, or helping to run the local chapters often find themselves doing a great deal of work, frequently thankless, but do so knowing that their work makes HWA and writing horror better for all of us. I volunteer because we all get something out of what I do.

Volunteering benefits you, benefits the organization and benefits the individuals that make up the organization. That's triple your time donation, so to speak. Volunteering doesn't need to be constant, but everyone has skills and experiences that can help all of us have a better organization, a better con experience, a better life. McCoy confesses, "I didn't always [volunteer], but as I've gotten older, two things have happened. My skills have developed to the level where I feel like I have something solid to offer, and I have come to understand the power of giving back. Second, there are so many people I cherish in my life now, who wouldn't have been there if I hadn't volunteered for the HWA. So many people I never would have met, or who would have remained con acquaintances instead of becoming friends. I am so grateful for each and every one of them (you guys know who you are)." Me too. See you at StokerCon™ 2020. I'll be volunteering. Will you?

Kevin Wetmore was co-Chair of StokerCon™ 2017 and StokerCon™ 2018, and volunteer coordinator for StokerCon™ 2019. He is a proud member of the Los Angeles HWA chapter and the author of *Post-9/11Horror in American Cinema* and *Back from the Dead*, as well as dozens of articles and book chapters on horror theatre, horror cinema, and horror culture. He edited *Uncovering Stranger Things*. He is also the author of several dozen short stories published in such venues as *Cemetery Dance, Midian Unmade, The Cackle of Cthulhu*, and *Enter at Your Own Risk: The End is the Beginning*. You can learn more about him and his work at www.SomethingWetmoreThisWayComes.com.

Afterword

By Lisa Morton

President, Horror Writer's Association

Like, I suspect, many writers, I grew up as a somewhat sickly only child. If anything was going around, be it as small as a cold or as major as mononucleosis, I got it. I entertained myself with made-up stories, many involving forces bent on destruction. I grew up believing that I wasn't destined to survive past my youth, so I made up stories as fast as I could. Now, with six decades behind me, I still experience surprise (and, fortunately, pleasure) at having far outlived my childhood sense of early doom (and I still make up lots of stories).

Six decades means I've seen a lot of history. Although I don't remember the day that John F. Kennedy was assassinated, I recall the murder of his brother Bobby, and the state of shock it plunged my elementary school into. I remember my grandparents driving out from Indiana to California to join us in July, 1969, so we could all huddle together around the television and watch Neil Armstrong take one small step that was also a giant leap. In 1989, I was a model-maker working on James Cameron's *The Abyss* when a friend who was an editor on the film waved me into his editing bay one afternoon and showed me the first footage of a computer-generated special effect, and I knew instantly that movies had just changed forever. I remember being stunned in April, 1992, when a jury acquitted four police officers of the beating of Rodney King, and then watching my hometown (Los Angeles) burn. And of course, like most Americans, I remember getting an early morning call on 9/11/2001, when my mother told me to turn on the television because we were under attack.

Now, looking back at those events, I don't believe that any of them were as important to the future as where we stand right now. Without a single specific, catastrophic event, we have reached what may be the most critical juncture in the long tale of our species. Every day I look at the news, and I can't help but feel that we've followed a path halfway up a mountain only to find that the trail ends there. Our choices are to turn back, pull out our climbing gear and start inching our way up the sheer rock face overhead, or tie ourselves together and leap off the side en masse.

I take great comfort in knowing that most of us are already

strapping on our climbing gear and getting out our ropes. We write horror so we approach our ascent with trepidation, but we look forward to the happy ending at the top.

In a fine recent article at Aeon.com ("Our Age of Horror"), M. M. Owen talked about why so many believe we're experiencing a "Golden Age of Horror": "Horror can thrive today because ours is a strange and febrile cultural moment." We face new and greater threats every day, whether it's the global warming we were warned about twenty years ago, the risk of increasingly virulent diseases while many of us go without access to medical care, or the backlash we experience when we tell our truths. We may feel as if we're just barely clinging to that sheer granite cliff with bare, bloodied fingertips.

There is good news, though: we're not in this alone. We're all part of a community centered around a form of storytelling that stands ready for this febrile cultural moment. At the heart of that community is an organization—the Horror Writers Association—that has been working toward the future for more than thirty years. We've invited new writers into the fold with support and camaraderie; we've looked for ways to help established writers promote new works; we've supported the creation of new readers with literacy and library programs; and we've welcomed new voices by recognizing and celebrating diversity.

We know that moving forward into the future isn't always easy; we'll sometimes make mistakes, slip a few inches back down that rock wall. There'll be those who will spread the wrong kind of fear and shout that we need to head back down the mountain, to what they see as safety…and instead we'll invite them to join us. The future that HWA is working for is one where horror's choir is made up of voices from across the full spectrum, where those who were once on the outside are now embraced from within, where all authors receive fair and equal consideration on the basis of how well they tell our stories and reveal our darker, occasionally transcendent truths.

Let's climb together.

About the Editor

Linda D. Addison grew up in Philadelphia and received a Bachelor of Science in Mathematics from Carnegie-Mellon University. She is the award-winning author of four collections, including How To Recognize A Demon Has Become Your Friend, and the first African-American recipient of the HWA Bram Stoker Award®. In 2018 she received the HWA Lifetime Achievement Award.

She has published over 300 poems, stories and articles. Her work has appeared in numerous publications, including Essence magazine, Asimov's Science Fiction Magazine, and in many anthologies, including: Dark Voices (Lycan Valley Press), Cosmic Underground (Cedar Grove Publishing), The Beauty of Death (Independent Legions Publishing), Scary Out There (Simon Schuster) and Into Painfreak (Necro Publications). She co-edited the Bram Stoker finalist Sycorax's Daughters, an anthology of horror fiction & poetry by African-American women (publisher Cedar Grove Publishing) with Kinitra Brooks and Susana Morris.

Addison is the only author with fiction in three landmark anthologies that celebrate African-Americans speculative writers: the award-winning Dark Matter: A Century of Speculative Fiction (Warner Aspect), Dark Dreams I and II (Kensington), and Dark Thirst (Pocket Book).

Her work has made frequent appearances over the years on the honorable mention list for Year's Best Horror and Year's Best Science-Fiction. She is a founding member of the writer's group Circles in the Hair (CITH), and a member of HWA, SFWA and SFPA. Her site: www.lindaaddisonpoet.com.

About the Cover Artist

M. Wayne Miller is a well-known name in the field of horror illustration, and is equally adept with science fiction, fantasy, and young adult themes. Welcoming the opportunities of each genre and, frequently, combining them all, he has carved a place among the best in the industry, and continues his quest to learn and grow as an artist and illustrator. His list of clients includes, but is in no way limited to, Dark Renaissance Books, Thunderstorm Books, Modiphius Entertainment, Chaosium, TOR, Pinnacle Entertainment Group, and Necro Publications.

Artwork Credits

Jill Bauman

Pg. 14 "How to Recognize a Demon Has Become Your Friend" © 2011 Jill Bauman; for Linda D. Addison, Necon eBooks.

Pg 226. "Poe 1" © 2008 Jill Bauman; for numbered edition of Poe by Stuart O'Nan, Cemetery Dance Publications.

Pg. 238 "The Passion of Frankenstein" © 2018 Jill Bauman; for Marvin Kaye from Wildside Press.

Pg. 276 "A Garden of Blackred Roses" © 2005 Jill Bauman; for Charles L. Grant from Dark Forces, Lonely Road Books.

Pg. 286 "Nightshow" © 1985 Jill Bauman; from *Nightshow* by Richard Laymon, Tor Books.

Pg. 323 "Deathbird" © 1990 Jill Bauman; from *Deathbird Stories* by Harlan Ellison, Easton Press.

Pg.332 "Spree" © 1998 Jill Bauman; from *Spree* by Lucy Taylor, Cemetery Dance Publications.

Stefano Cardoselli

Pg. 316 "The Slicer" by Stefano Cardoselli, first appeared in *Naraka* by Alessandro Manzetti, Independent Legions Publishing.

Greg Chapman

Pg.72 "Bird Box" © 2018 Greg Chapman.

Pg. 205 "Skull Books" © 2018 Greg Chapman.

Pg. 214 "Frankenstein 1818" © 2018 Greg Chapman.

Alan M. Clark

Pg. 264 "Dry Persistence" © 2018 Alan M. Clark. Interior illustration for *The Assassin's Coin* by John Linwood Grant - IFD Publishing.

Pg. 58 "Oubliette" © 2016 Alan M. Clark. Unpublished.

Pg. 18 "The Goatman" © 2000 Alan M. Clark. Interior illustration for *The Bottoms* by Joe Lansdale - Subterranean Press.

Lynne Hansen

Pg. 144 "The Haunted Forest Tour" © 2017 by Lynne Hansen. First appeared on *The Haunted Forest Tour* by James A. Moore and Jeff Strand.

Pg. 206 "Skull City Grand Rapids" © 2019 by Lynne Hansen.

Pg. 333 "Medusa Triumphant" © 2019 by Lynne Hansen.

M. W. Miller

Pg. 159 "Scratching From the Outer Darkness" © 2018 M. W. Miller.
Pg. 181 "Angler in Darkness" © 2018 M. W. Miller.
Pg. 230 "Mind Flayer" © 2018 M. W. Miller.
Pg. 304 "A Necessary End" © 2018 M. W. Miller.
Pg. 331 "Medusa" © 2018 M. W. Miller.

Jeed "Vejeees" Muhammad

Pg 195 "3skulls" © 2018 Majeed "Vejeees" Muhammad.
Pg. 330"kontrol" © 2018 Majeed "Vejeees" Muhammad.

Rick Sardinha

Pgs. 120, 294, 310 Artwork by Rick Sardinha for *Strange Seed* by T.M. Wright © 2006 Twisted Publishing.

Walter Velez

Pg. 329 "Shatterday" © 1975 Walter Velez. Cover art for Shatterday by Harlan Ellison–Houghton Mifflin Harcourt.

StokerCon™ Committee

Chair: Brian W. Matthews
Deputy Chair: Lisa Morton
Administrator: Brad Hodson
Programming Coordinator: Brian W. Matthews
Dealer Room Coordinator: Brian W. Matthews
Artist: Greg Chapman & M. Wayne Miller
Librarian Coordinator: Becky Spratford
Film Frame Coordinator: Jonathan Lees
Ann Radcliffe Academic Conference Coordinators: Michele Brittany and Nicholas Diak
Horror University Coordinator: James Chambers
Volunteer Coordinator: Kevin Wetmore, Jr.
Communications Director: John Dennehy
Publicity Coordinator: John Palisano
Webmaster: Rick Pickman
Social Media Coordinator: Meghan Arcuri-Moran
A/V Tech Coordinator: Jacques Mersereau
Pitch Sessions Coordinator: Rena Mason
Reading Coordinator: Lee Murray
Guest Liaison: Rena Mason
Bram Stoker Awards® Banquet Coordinator: Lisa Morton
Sponsorship Coordinator: Meghan Arcuri-Moran
Souvenir Book Editor: Linda D. Addison

In April 2020 StokerCon™ comes to the UK for the first time, but will continue to incorporate such popular StokerCon programming as Horror University, the Final Frame Short Film Competition, the Ann Radcliffe Academic Conference, and the presentation of the iconic Bram Stoker Awards®. HWA's President Lisa Morton noted, "HWA is committed to celebrating horror around the world, so I'm especially pleased that our fifth annual StokerCon will be held in the U.K., where we have such a committed, strong chapter." Over four days StokerCon UK will be welcoming an array of some of the world's best dark fiction authors, publishers and speakers for a packed weekend of panels, readings, workshops, book launches and much more. Taking place in Scarborough, just down the coast from Whitby – the town that provided so much of the inspiration for Stoker's iconic *Dracula* – this is an event not to be missed for writers and readers of horror fiction!

A.K. Benedict

Mistress of Ceremonies is A.K. Benedict, author of *The Beauty of Murder* and *The Evidence of Ghosts* (Orion Books). More exciting Guests to be announced soon.

StokerCon 2020 runs from Thursday 16th-19th April 2020, and will be taking place at the historic Grand and Royal hotels in Scarborough. Memberships for StokerCon UK are £100, or £90 if you're a member of the Horror Writers Association, and special hotel rates for convention attendees will be available soon. For more information, visit https:// stokercon-uk.com/ and to purchase your membership, visit https://stokercon-uk.com/join.htm

StokerCon 2020 - Scarborough, 16 - 19 April at the historic Royal & Grand Hotels.
https://stokercon-uk.com

Made in the USA
Columbia, SC
27 April 2019